"I remember you," the paramedic told Brenna as he helped her into the wheelchair.

"Knife wound, end of September."

Brenna looked up into his face. Again she felt the blade as it socked into her abdomen, the damp pavement against her body, the slicing pain beneath her ribs. She smelled the brine of the bay in the air, until she was devoured by the memory, fear coursing through her. . . . *Breathing is hard now. She puts her hand to her pain and feels her shirt—wet, sticking to her. She brings the hand up to her face and sees blood—so much of it, it looks black. The cell phone. She reaches for it, touches it . . . Call 911.*

Brenna's cell phone vibrated in her hand— Just once. A text—and it brought her back to the present. She gasped, the pain fading, the face of the paramedic coming back into focus.

She glanced down at the text from Maya: WHEW!!!! All caps. Four exclamation points. Maybe life wasn't completely brutal and random and unfair. Maybe some things did happen for good reason. How could she *not* feel this way when, in just three months, her life had been saved twice?

Maybe some girls get into blue cars and live.

By Alison Gaylin

ALISON GAYLIN

into the dark

A NOVEL OF SUSPENSE

HARPER

An Imprint of HarperCollinsPublishers

HARPER

An Imprint of HarperCollins*Publishers*
10 East 53rd Street
New York, New York 10022-5299

Copyright © 2013 by Alison Gaylin
ISBN 978-0-06-187825-1

First Harper mass market printing: February 2013
First Harper special printing: October 2012

For Mike and Marissa

Acknowledgments

Many thanks to my great agent, Deborah Schneider, as well as everyone at HarperCollins—most especially the brilliant Lyssa Keusch, Amanda Bergeron, and Lauren Cook. I'd also like to express my gratitude to the always helpful police/high-tech expert Josh Moulin and automotive genius John Voelcker, as well as dear friends and sharp readers James Conrad, Chas Cerulli, Paul Leone, Anthony Marcello, Abigail Thomas (and the rest of the writing group, whom I miss very much, darn it), Jamie and Doug Barthell—and the many others who have helped me and put up with my meshugas. I'd also like to thank Marilyn and Sheldon Gaylin (at whose lovely home much of this book was written); my terrific mom, Beverly Sloane; and as seen in the dedication, my husband, Mike; and daughter, Marissa, without whom none of my books would ever be written.

into the dark

Prologue

"You are a handsome man," RJ said. "Women are drawn to you."

He was sitting in his parked van in front of the studio—*the studio*—and talking to his reflection in the rearview. Truth be told, RJ felt like kind of a jackass complimenting his own looks like this—especially since he'd never been what anybody would consider lady bait. But RJ believed in the power of positive affirmation, no joke. Since the mid-eighties, he'd been reading Louise Hay. In fact, he still owned his original copy of *You Can Heal Your Life*, and sure, Louise had let him down a whole bunch of times since then, but who was he to doubt her now, when all the good energy he'd sent into the universe was finally coming home to roost?

Just this morning after he'd packed up his equipment and printed out the note for his mother, RJ had stood in front of the full-length mirror affixed to the inside of his closet door. He'd taken in his new clothes—the black T-shirt, the slightly worn brown leather jacket, the baggy jeans and the Los Angeles Dodgers cap he'd found online, the bright blue Nikes he'd bought last night from Foot Locker. He'd looked himself up and down and compared it all with the picture he'd printed out from X17 and taped by the mirror for inspiration: Spielberg, wearing the exact same outfit. He'd eyed the bag next to the door and tried not to wince at what was inside: a Canon EOS 5D Mark II he'd maxed out his credit card and then some to buy (the "then some" part being the most troubling . . .) But as Louise might have told him herself, *In order to do the best work, you need the best tools.*

RJ had put all his doubts and fears aside and breathed in healing light and then, only then, had he allowed himself to say it out loud—the most important positive affirmation of his forty-five years on this planet: *"I am a director."*

God, RJ felt great right now. A beautiful camera in his car and a beautiful actress waiting for him, inside the studio—*the studio*. This was what he wanted. This was all he'd ever wanted. Once this thing hit—and it would hit hard, he knew it—RJ would be famous, rich. He would pay back his creditors in no time. Free himself of stress. Focus on his art.

He had more than a dozen fully fleshed-out stories in his head—a thriller about a blind cop with telekinetic powers; a coming-of-age piece set in 1940s London; the heartwarming tale of a failed magician and the rescue dog who saves his life . . . the list went on and on. They'd been slamming around in there for years, these movie stories, begging to be let out—and now, at last, he could give them the attention they deserved. His Breakthrough Project was nearing completion. It was the beginning of the beginning.

RJ threw open the back of his van. He didn't need to unload all his equipment now. He could come back for that with his crew. But he took the Canon with him for two reasons: (1) He wanted it with him when he met everyone, and (2) He was worried that if he left it in the van, the camera would be stolen.

The studio, as it turned out, was in one of the crappier areas of Mount Temple—and that was saying something. RJ was a native New Yorker, and in the course of his life, he'd seen even the sleepiest, slowest towns in Westchester County get fattened and buffed to a fine glow. But somehow Mount Temple had missed out. Neglected by the nineties bubble and abused by the current recession, Mount Temple was the poor relation to Scarsdale and Bronxville and Tarry Ridge, the frumpy uncle who never could catch a break. In a way, the town was like RJ—well, the old RJ, anyway—and so it was fitting that the studio would be located here, near the corner of Columbus and 102nd, an abandoned-looking building between two other abandoned-looking buildings, a tiny auto body shop three doors down practically the only lit-up thing on the street.

"Hey! Hey there, sir!"

RJ turned as he was crossing the street to see a homeless man, sitting in front of a chain-link fence, waving at him. The man looked like an upended dirty laundry basket with a head on top, his face and hair so grimy you couldn't tell what color he was.

"Mr. Steven Spielberg! Love your movies, man."

Had the homeless guy really just said that—or was it a trick of the mind? Regardless, RJ wondered what his film school pals would say if they saw him now—strutting around in his Dodgers cap, Canon EOS 5D Mark II slung over his shoulder like The Man himself . . .

RJ snorted. Even in the privacy of his own mind, that was quite a phrase for him to use—*film school pals*.

After all, he'd flunked out of film school after just three months, and he sure as hell hadn't left any *pals* behind. Bunch of snooty, affected turds, they all were. Trust fund brats who gassed off about French expressionism and Fassbinder and called Spielberg banal—Christ, they didn't even like *Schindler's List*—and looked down on RJ just because he wasn't rich or young or full of noxious gas like they were.

The professors were even worse. And the one guy who pretended to be a friend . . . Shane. Man. More toxic than all the trust fund brats and full-of-shit professors put together.

Truth was, film school sucked. RJ had learned more editing pornos than he would have picked up in twenty years at that place, and that wasn't sour grapes. He knew it for a fact. He thought back to the letter of resignation he'd e-mailed Charlie, his boss at Happy Endings, last night, and hoped it sounded grateful enough. Charlie had to understand, though. RJ was on the verge of a huge breakthrough. Lula Belle, *the* Lula Belle, would soon be in front of his lens—and then, in front of the world. His ship had finally come in.

As he pushed open the door to the studio building, RJ realized he was smiling. "My life is working," he whispered, an affirmation. He believed it.

There was no reception desk in the building that housed the studio—not even a directory. But RJ was too happy to think much about that. With this bare-bones lobby and this crappy address, the studio itself had to be awesome. It was kind of a rule. Once, RJ had gone to a party at an abandoned warehouse on the Lower East Side. One of the porno directors had lived there—nice guy by the name of Byron Ryder—and the lobby was such a craphole, RJ had thought he might catch a disease from it. But then he'd gone up to Ryder's floor-through condo and practically passed out from shock.

It had reminded RJ of that chick's apartment in *Flashdance*—that's how implausibly lush the place was. Giant hot tub made out of real marble. Flat screen that filled an entire wall. High ceilings with nineteenth-century moldings that made your eyes well up, they were so gorgeous. *What you save on building safety*, Ryder had told RJ, *you make up for in personal luxury*.

RJ hit the button on the elevator, and when it opened, he hardly even noticed the piss smell, or the graffiti, or the dried blood on the back wall, probably from a ten-year-old fistfight. RJ's heart pounded. His palms started to sweat. He felt like a kid on his first date. The seventh floor couldn't happen soon enough, yet still he was so nervous. That was beyond the whole starting-his-directing-career thing, too, the nervousness. Within moments, RJ realized, he'd see the face of Lula Belle. He'd look into her eyes. How many men could say that?

The thought made his stomach tighten. How would she look at him—with respect? Gratitude? Disappointment?

RJ pushed the thought out of his mind. Instead, he imagined Spielberg, seeing Kate Capshaw for the first time on the set of *Indiana Jones and the Temple of Doom*. How had she looked at him, this glowing blonde creature—a star in the true sense of the word, a woman who could twinkle and burst into bright light?

RJ had made some dumb decisions in his life, yes. He'd trusted the wrong people, he'd let others down. His learning curve had been slow and dull. But did that matter? No one was perfect—not even Spielberg. Not even Louise Hay. Maybe all those times that RJ had screwed up were like plot points in a movie, each one building on the next and propelling him forward until he got here. Face-to-face with a bona fide star, his Breakthrough Project soon to be completed. All at the same time, all helped by the same events . . . the synchronicity. That alone was proof that everything had been for the best.

"I'll do right by you, Lula Belle," he said to the steel doors as the elevator pulled him up, up, up . . . "I promise."

There must be some mistake. That was RJ's first thought once the elevator doors opened on the seventh floor. His second: *Where the hell is everybody?* The floor looked gutted—clumps of piled-up debris on the cement ground, graffiti creeping all over the walls. RJ knew the building had electricity—how else would he have been able to come up here in the elevator?—but you wouldn't know it from the looks of this floor, the only light struggling in from the narrow windows on the far side of the space.

"Lula Belle?" he called out.

RJ heard muffled voices coming from way down to the right, and so he followed them, his new Nikes scuffing the concrete. He saw a pile of glass shards against a wall, next to something else—something dark and rank he couldn't look at without gagging . . . *This is not a studio. This will never be a studio.*

"Lula Belle?"

"RJ? Is that you?" A woman's voice. The kind that curls up your back and down your legs and into your heart and haunts you forever. *Lula Belle.*

"It's me!" he said, his heart beating harder.

"We're right down here!" the voice said. "Did you pick up the check at the post office?"

He cringed. He hadn't expected it to arrive this early, hadn't even brought the key with him. "I'm sorry. I forgot."

"That's okay, baby."

Baby. He whispered the word, his heart soaring at the sound of it. "You're not mad."

"I could never be mad at you."

Once he got to the open door, which in truth wasn't an open door at all but a *missing* door, RJ took a deep breath. He reached up to smooth his hair but remembered the cap, straightening that instead. He felt the tug of the camera bag at his shoulder and closed his eyes. *My work allows me to express my creativity freely,* he told himself, Louise speaking through him. *I earn good money doing things I love.*

He walked through the doorhole.

The room was crumbling, the walls rashy with mold. But it didn't matter. Nothing mattered but the sight of her, standing in the middle of the room, her robe dropped and pooling at her feet. For a moment, he couldn't breathe.

"My God, you're beautiful."

"Are you ready?" she said, his Lula, his star.

RJ was about to answer, *As ready as I've ever been.*

But then someone else said, "Just a sec." A voice RJ knew, and when he turned around, he saw him, wearing jeans and a black T-shirt that fit him a lot better than RJ's did. He'd managed to grow a thick beard in the years they'd spent apart, and the beard, too, looked better than RJ's.

She brought Shane Smith?

"Hi RJ," Shane said. "It's good to see you."

How strange life was. Last time RJ had seen Shane, that prick had pretended like he didn't even know him— this after ruining his life and his film school career and even getting him thrown into jail. In the past three years, RJ must have played it over and over in his head a million times—what he'd say to Shane Smith if he ever ran into him. And yet now, in the same room together and with a *flood* of water under the bridge—Lula Belle looking on, no less—RJ could only smile back. After all, if it weren't for Shane, RJ's Breakthrough Project never would have happened.

The synchronicity.

Shane got up from the floor and embraced him, and RJ hugged him just as tight. *I'm bringing healing light into my life. Forgiving another person does not make me weak. Everything always works out for the best.* "It's been too long, man," RJ said, only vaguely aware of Lula Belle putting the robe back on . . . and of the nod she exchanged with his old friend.

"Too long," Shane said. "We won't let this happen again."

1

She wants to die.

The memory flew at Brenna Spector like words on a passing billboard—there for just an instant but solid, real. Brenna had been staring at the image on her assistant Trent LaSalle's computer screen—their latest missing person, if you could call what they were looking at a person. She was more a shadow, standing behind a scrim, backlit into anonymity—all limbs and curves and fluffy hair, but no detail, no color. No face. She looked as though she was naked, but you couldn't even be sure of that. But then she tapped her lower lip, the shadow-woman on the screen, she tapped it three times, triggering a memory from less than two months prior . . . *She looks into the girl's eyes with the chill wind biting their faces and icy water everywhere, so cold it burns. Brenna stares at her—poor, pretty mess of a girl. Then at her boyfriend standing behind her, his hand on her shoulder, the fingertips white from the tightness of the clutch. She looks back at the girl's face, at the mascara streaks on her cheeks, looking so awful for the wear—worse than Maya and me put together— and then, into the eyes . . . such fathomless sadness as she meets Brenna's gaze, her boyfriend oblivious, smiling a little.* She doesn't want to be here. None of us do, but this girl . . .

The girl taps her lip three times like a Morse signal. She wants to die.

"She's so freakin' hot," Trent said.

Brenna came back from the memory, fixed her gaze on the screen. "Uh, Trent? She's a *silhouette.*"

"Hey, so are those chicks on truck mud flaps."

Brenna rolled her eyes.

"You'll get it when you see more."

As if on cue, the shadow-woman began stretching her body into a series of suggestive yoga poses—a slow backbend, followed by the sharp V of the downward-facing dog, a seamless shift to standing, after which she reached down, grasped her right ankle, and pulled the leg straight out and then up, until the knee touched the side of her head.

"See?" Trent said.

With shocking ease, she yanked the leg, stolelike, around her shoulder. Her voice was a soft Southern accent, drifting out of the speakers like steam. "I'll bend any way you want me to."

Trent nearly fell off his chair.

"I get it, I get it." Brenna grabbed the mouse and hit pause. "Who is she?"

"Lula Belle." He said it the way a nun might say the name of a saint. "She's an artist."

Brenna looked at her assistant. He was wearing a black muscle tee with a deep V-neck, the Ed Hardy logo emblazoned on the front in glittery red letters. His hair was spiked and gelled to the point where it could probably scrape paint off the side of a bus, and, Brenna now noticed for the first time, he was sporting a new tattoo:

a bright red lipstick print, hovering just above the left pec. Trent's definition of an artist was, to say the least, dubious.

"A *performance* artist," he said, as if he'd been reading her mind. "She's on the Web. You can download her, uh, performances."

"She's a webcam girl."

"No," Trent pointed to the screen. "Lula Belle isn't about porn. I mean, you can get off to her for sure, but . . ."

"But what?"

"Here—I'll show you." Trent moved the cursor, fast-forwarding the screen image. Brenna watched the shadow twist and bend, watched her drop into the splits and pivot, throw her pelvis over her head and somersault backward to standing, watched her pull up a stool and straddle it, legs spread wide as a Fosse dancer, watched her produce an old-fashioned Coke bottle from somewhere off camera, tilt her shadow-head back, touch her shadow-tongue to the tip, and then take the bottle down her throat all the way to the base, all this inside of twenty seconds.

Brenna said, "Well, I guess you could call that an art."

"No. Wait." When Trent hit play, Lula Belle was on the stool, legs crossed, fingers twisting in her hair. "Listen."

" ' . . . and you know that little soft part of your head, Lula Belle? Right next to your eyebrow? That's called your temple. Daddy took his gun, and he put the barrel of it right there at his temple, and he pulled the trigger and his whole head exploded.' That's how my mama told me. I was twelve years old. 'Do you understand, Lula Belle?' she asked me, and my heart felt like someone had taken a torch to it, melted it down to liquid right there in my chest. But I knew I couldn't cry.

I wasn't allowed to cry. Mama didn't . . . she didn't take kindly to tears . . ."

Trent hit pause and turned to Brenna. "You get it?"

"She bares her soul. Shares her secrets."

He nodded.

"And people pay for this."

"Yep."

Brenna shook her head. "Weird."

"Well, the Coke bottle thing helps . . ."

"When did she go missing?"

"Less than three months ago."

"And the client?"

"It was a third party."

"Who was the third party?"

"Another PI. Lula's manager hired him."

"And the PI's name is . . ."

"Brenna?"

"Yes?"

"Can I ask you something?"

"As long as you're not asking me in order to avoid my question."

"Seriously."

"Okay."

Trent cleared his throat. "When I first showed you Lula Belle . . . you . . . remembered something, didn't you?"

"Yeah." Strange how "remembered" could be such a loaded word, but in Brenna's world it was. Since she was eleven years old, she'd suffered from hyperthymestic syndrome, a rare disorder that enabled her to remember every minute of every day of her life, and with all five senses, whether she wanted to or not. It came, a California-based neuroscientist named Dr. Louis Gettis had told her on June 24, 2006, "from the perfect storm of a differently shaped brain and a traumatic experience"—*storm*, as it turned out, a good metaphor, seeing as how the syndrome had descended on Brenna, battering her mind into something so different than it had been before. She had two types of memories now— the murky recollections of her childhood and the vivid, three-dimensional images of everything that had happened from August 22, 1981, to the present.

Brenna could recall, for instance, what she had for breakfast on June 25, 1998, to the point of tasting it (black coffee, a bowl of Special K with skim milk, blueberries that were disappointingly mealy, and two donut holes—one chocolate, one glazed). But her father, who had left her family when she was just seven—he existed in her mind only as strong arms and the smell of Old Spice, a light kiss on the forehead, a story told by one of her mother's friends, years after he'd gone. He wasn't whole in Brenna's head. She couldn't clearly picture his face. Same with her older sister, Clea, who had gotten into a blue car on August 21, 1981, at the age of seventeen and vanished forever. Clea's disappearance had been the traumatic event that had sparked Brenna's perfect storm—yet ironically that event, like Clea herself, was stuck in her fallible pre-syndrome memory, fading every day into hazy fiction.

Brenna had known that would happen—even as a kid on August 21, 1982, the anniversary . . . *Sitting at her bedroom window with her face pressed against the cool of the screen, glancing at the digital clock blinking 5:21 A.M. and chewing grape Bubble Yum to stay awake, her throat dry and stingy from old gum, trying with everything she has to remember the car, the license plate, the voice of the man behind the wheel from a year earlier . . .*

Brenna shut her eyes tight and recited the Pledge of Allegiance in her head—one of the many tricks she'd figured out over the years for willing memories away.

"So?" Trent said.

She opened her eyes, took a breath. "What was your question again?"

"What were you remembering when you looked at Lula Belle?"

"Not much—a gesture," Brenna said. "On October 30, Maya and I were in Niagara Falls on vacation, remember?"

He gave her a look. "I can remember two months ago."

"Well, we were on the *Maid of the Mist*, and there was a girl on the boat who tapped on her lip three times, just like Lula Belle did at the start of the tape."

"What did the girl on the boat look like?"

"Probably in her early twenties. Blonde. Miserable. She was leaving the boat with her boyfriend, and she had mascara running down her face." Brenna looked at him. "She looked like she wanted to die."

Trent's eyes went big.

"I know what you're thinking, but we *all* probably looked that way," Brenna said. "We were getting hailed on. It was freezing and windy and everybody was seasick and Maya called me the worst mother in the world for taking her on that boat in the first place."

"Still," he said. "It could have been Lula Belle you saw. Less than a month after she went missing. On that boat with some jerk-off. Praying to be saved from him . . ."

"Hell of a coincidence."

"Happens all the time."

"Trent, it was just a gesture. Do we have any idea what Lula Belle looks like?"

"No."

"What about this third party? Do they?"

He shook his head. "Her own manager doesn't even know what she looks like. He lives in California. Never met her face-to-face. He maintained her site, made the checks out to cash, sent them to a PO box . . ."

Brenna sighed. "In that case, *I* could be Lula Belle."

"Oh man, that would be so awesome."

Brenna's gaze shot back to the frozen image on the screen. "Do we at least have her full name?"

"Uh . . . no."

"What about her social?"

He shook his head.

"So let me get this straight. All we have on this woman is a fake name, a fake accent, a PO box, and a very obvious skill set."

"You think her accent's fake? Really?"

"Trent."

"Yeah?"

"Why did you think we could accept this case?"

He picked at a fingernail.

"Trent."

"We . . . we only have this one video."

"And?"

"The Web site's been taken down since she disappeared. There's no way of downloading more."

"So?"

"So . . . if we officially accept the case, we can get . . . uh . . ." He cleared his throat. "We can get all the rest of the videos."

"Oh, for godsakes," Brenna said. "You're a *fan*."

"I know, I know . . . I mean, I never heard of her before yesterday, but I can't get her out of my head. I can't stop watching. I don't even care what her face looks like or how old she is . . . It's like Errol said—she gets under your skin and stays there."

"*Errol?*"

"Crap. I didn't mean to say that out loud."

"Errol Ludlow? He's the third party?"

Trent's face went pinkish. He bit his lower lip, and stared at the floor like a shamed kid. "Yes," he said finally. "Errol Ludlow Investigations."

Brenna stared at him. "No."

"He said you were the best around at finding missing persons—that's why he wanted to hire you."

"No, Trent. Absolutely not."

"He wants to let bygones be bygones and—"

"*No!*"

Trent looked close to tears.

Brenna hadn't intended to say it that loudly, but she wasn't going to take it back, either. In the three years that Errol Ludlow had been her boss, he'd put her in serious danger four times. Twice, she'd been rushed to the hospital. Her ex-husband had made her promise to quit and then the one time, three years after Maya was born, Brenna had made the breathtakingly stupid mistake of taking a freelance assignment from him, it had ended her marriage for good. Brenna couldn't let bygones be bygones. Trent should've known that. There were no such things as bygones in Brenna's life—especially when it came to a king-sized bad memory-trigger like Errol Ludlow. "No, Trent," she said again—quieter this time. "I'm sorry you've grown attached to this girl's silhouette, but we can't take this case."

Trent started to say something—until Ludacris's "Money Maker" exploded out of his jeans pocket, interrupting him. His ringtone. He yanked his iPhone out of his pocket and looked at the screen. "My mom."

"Go ahead and take it," Brenna said.

Trent moved from the office space area of Brenna's Twelfth Street apartment, past the kitchen, and into the hallway that led to the living room. Brenna glanced at the shadow on the screen caught frozen, one delicate hand to her forehead—the swooning Southern belle. "Sorry, Lula." Brenna wondered why Errol had accepted a missing person in the first place. From what she knew, he only handled cheating spouses. *Work must be tight.*

She clicked play. Lula Belle arched into a languorous stretch that seemed to involve every muscle in her body and sighed, her voice fragile as air. Brenna watched her, thinking about what Trent had said. *She gets under your skin and stays there . . .* Was Errol a fan, too?

"I miss my daddy," Lula Belle said. "He was the only person in the whole world, could stop me from being scared of anything." She turned to the left and tilted her head up, as if she were noticing a star for the first time. "I used to be afraid of all kinds of stuff, too," she said. "The dark, ghosts, the old lady next door—I was sure she was a witch. Dogs, spiders, snakes . . . even cement mixers, if you can imagine that."

Brenna's eyes widened. She moved closer to the screen.

"I somehow got it in my head that those cement mixers were like . . . I don't know, giant vacuum cleaners or something. I thought they could suck me in through the back, and mix me in with all that heavy wet cement, and I'd never be able to get out, wouldn't be able to breathe."

"Me too," Brenna whispered.

"But my daddy, he made everything better. He got me a nightlight. He protected me from that mean old lady. He told me those dogs and snakes were more scared of me than I was of them, and he was right. But the best thing my daddy did. Whenever we'd be driving and I'd see a cement mixer he'd sing me this song . . ."

No . . . It can't be. . .

"I don't know whether he'd made it up or not, but it went a little like this . . . *Cement mixer/Turn on a dime/ Make my day 'cause it's cement time/Cement mixer, you're my pal/Ain't gonna hurt me or my little gal . . .*"

Brenna's breath caught. She knew the song—knew it well enough to sing along. She knew it like the blue vinyl backseat of the white Mustang her dad had called the Land Shark, knew it like the strong hands on the wheel, the smell of Old Spice, and the voice—the deep, laughing voice she loved, but couldn't hold on to. "*It's okay, pumpkin, it won't hurt you, it's just a bus for building materials.*" Dad. "*Just like the one that takes the big kids to school, only this one is for the stuff they make the playgrounds out of!* Cement mixer/Turn on a dime . . ."

"You know what my Daddy called those cement mixers?" Lula whispered to the camera. "He called 'em school buses. For playground ingredients. Isn't that funny?"

"Man, I'm gonna miss her," said Trent, who was back in the room.

Brenna turned to him, fast. "We're taking the case," she said.

2

Lula Belle didn't have a Facebook page, personal or fan. No YouTube channel, either. According to Trent, there had been a @misslulabelle Twitter feed that had amassed, at one point, more than ten thousand followers—but it was taken down after it was discovered that it wasn't Lula Belle tweeting, but a Bible studies major from Azusa Pacific University with a gift for sexual hyperbole and way too much time on his hands.

Strange that a webcam girl would have so little online presence, but that added to the mystery, didn't it?

It added to something, anyway.

Brenna couldn't get it out of her mind—that cement mixer song, her father's voice, deep but with a smile in it . . . How had this shadow of a missing girl known a made-up song word for word? How had this "performance artist"—with a name, by the way, that sounded like Miss Tallahassee Tractor Pull, 1945—how had she been able to reach into Brenna's head, grab one of the few intact memories she had of her dad, and claim it as her own? So many questions, and Brenna needed answers. She needed them now, and far as she knew, only one person, other than Lula Belle and her manager, might be able to answer them: God help Brenna, it was Errol Ludlow.

She glanced over at Trent. His computer screen was full of Lula Belle—a freeze frame of her sprawled across the chair, deep-throating the Coke bottle. He was sizing up each part of her body in relation to the in-animate objects in order to discern an accurate height, weight, and set of measurements, using a program he'd developed last year after coming across one too many badly taken photographs.

The fact that Trent was cursor-gauging every square inch of his new dream girl without so much as a moan or a "who's your daddy," impressed Brenna to the point of mild shock. She smiled. *Maybe he's growing up.* "Hey, Trent?"

"Yeah?" He didn't take his eyes from the screen.

"Did Errol Ludlow say anything to you about Lula Belle's family?"

"Just that she probably learned the Coke bottle thing from her mom," Trent said. "I think he was being sarcastic."

Brenna sighed. Same old Errol, sensitive as ever.

She Googled Errol Ludlow. The first thing she noticed was a *Daily News* article from five years ago—a profile piece in the Business section called "Errol Ludlow Is Watching You." Brenna had already read it on April 19, 2004 (a Monday), on a Fourteenth Street subway platform waiting for the A train at 9:30 A.M. She scrolled through a few reprints of the piece and a *New York Times* article about "modern-day gumshoes" until she found Errol's Web site, a new one—LudlowInvestigations.com. She called it up, stared at the home page. Her jaw tightened.

Unbelievable.

She printed it out, then tapped his office number into her phone.

The number hadn't changed since the last time Brenna had dialed, yes, *dialed* it at 9 A.M. on October 21, 1998, from the ancient payphone outside the police station in Tarry Ridge, New York, and even now, she had to grit her teeth to keep from feeling the cool plastic of eleven years ago against her ear, from hearing the whir of the rotary dial, such a dated piece of machinery even back then, the scrape of her fingernails against the metal as she called that number, her heart pounding up into her throat, the words spilling out of her mouth as soon as she heard that staccato hello, all too familiar . . .

"Errol, I know it's been a while but I need your help in getting a police file . . ."

"Brenna Spector. My, my. I thought your hubby wouldn't let you talk to me anymore."

"Four score and seven years ago, our forefathers brought forth upon this continent a new nation." Brenna whispered, jolting herself back into the present. It took her a few moments to notice the pause on the other end of the line, and that voice, Errol's voice, enunciating every syllable, just like always. "Con-ceived in lib-er-ty and ded-i-cat-ed to the prop—"

"Errol Ludlow."

"Yes? To what patriot am I speaking?"

She took a breath. "This is Brenna Spector."

"Brenna Spector! What a pleasant surprise."

Brenna stared at the computer printout. *It's not a surprise. You knew I'd call.* "Meet me at the Waverly Diner in half an hour."

"Will do." She could practically hear the smirk.

She hung up without saying good-bye. "Trent, I'll be

back at two." She grabbed her coat, shoved the printout into her bag, and flung it over her shoulder. "If you need me before then, call my cell."

"No worries." He tore himself away from the screen image and looked at her. "Probably won't be here when you get back, though. Got a meeting with Mrs. Shelby at one-thirty."

Brenna nodded. Annette Shelby, an insanely wealthy former client, had contacted her office a week ago. She was paying Trent three hundred dollars an hour to find her beloved Persephone, who had disappeared shortly after their recent move to the city from Great Barrington, Massachusetts.

Persephone was Annette's Persian cat.

An eye roller of a case if there ever was one, but Brenna tried to take it seriously—number one, because it was Trent's first solo job, and *he* took it so seriously, creating three separate computer renderings of the missing pet—one five pounds lighter, one five pounds heavier, one the same weight, though a little worse for the wear—and canvassing every animal shelter in all five boroughs. Number two was the obvious cash incentive, and number three was the fact that, three months ago, Brenna had found Annette's presumed dead husband—and she still felt bad about it. At least the cat probably wanted to come home. "Any news on Persephone?" she asked.

He shook his head. "Tonight I hit the fish market."

"Good thinking."

"Yeah, well, I'm more than just eye candy, B. Spec."

She blinked at him. "What did you just call me?"

"B. Spec," he said. "You know, like J. Lo, only with different letters because, uh . . . your name is not the same as hers."

"Trent."

"What?"

"No more nicknames."

He looked at her. "But . . . where I come from, nick-names are a sign of affection."

"You're a long way from where you come from."

"Staten Island?"

"Figuratively, Trent."

He shook his head, then turned back to Lula Belle. For a few seconds, Brenna watched him, working the measuring tool, staring into the screen until he was once again lost in the world of it.

"Who's your daddy," he whispered.

It wasn't until Brenna was out the door and into the hallway that her thoughts went back to Errol Ludlow, and how, in moments, she'd be seeing him again for the first time in eleven years. What memories would he set off? How was she going to stop them?

Brenna reached into her coat pocket. The previous day, her daughter, Maya, had borrowed the coat, and as expected, the pocket was full of a thirteen-year-old's detritus—gum wrappers, a wadded-up dollar bill, a receipt from Ricky's, a couple of hair ties. *Perfect.* She slipped the hair ties around her left wrist, headed down the hallway, out the door, and down Sixth Avenue.

The cold smacked her in the face, made her eyes water. But Brenna's body was so tense, she barely reacted. *Don't think about him,* Brenna told herself, but still her mind reeled back to October 21, 1998, *the snaking fall chill against the glass of the old-fashioned phone booth outside the Tarry Ridge Police Station, Errol's voice pressing into her ear. That clipped staccato . . . "I can get you the file, but not for free."*

"How much money do you want?" Brenna asks, hoping it's money, hoping it's not anything else. I can give you money. Please ask for money.

"I want you to do one more job for me."

She closes her eyes. *"Errol, I can't. I'm . . . I'm a mother now."*

"One more job. It is an easy one. Guaranteed. Hubby will never find out."

Brenna snapped the hair ties against her wrist. The sting brought her back to the present, to Greenwich and Seventh.

She exhaled. *Works like a charm.*

From across the street, the Waverly Diner sign winked at Brenna. She moved toward it, weaving through a group of slow-moving tourists, past three laughing teenage girls to the crosswalk, narrowly missing a bike messenger as she hit the street. The whole time, Brenna stared straight ahead, touching the hair ties, glad they were there.

"Asshat," Brenna muttered. She was sitting in the Waverly Diner, watching Ludlow through the window. He hadn't noticed her yet, but she'd seen him, waiting at the crosswalk as a cab whizzed by, checking his watch . . . Through the glass and from this distance, he looked exactly the same as the last time she'd seen him. The first time she'd seen him, too, come to think of it. Same graying buzz cut and, as she could see under the flapping trench coat, that same god-awful dark green polyester jacket he'd worn during her job interview on May 21, 1991. Had he gone shopping even once during this millennium?

A young woman tapped Errol on the arm and said something to him. At six-eight, he towered over her and he seemed to take pride in that. He looked at his watch, and said something back. The woman nodded and headed off in another direction. She'd asked him the time, obviously, but from the look on his face you'd think she'd asked him for his autograph. Brenna watched him standing there, smirking to himself like the asshat he was.

God, that smirk. That same, smug smirk . . . Brenna glared at him as he approached the door, hearing Lula Belle again in her head, fingering the computer printout in her bag. *I'm going to wipe that smirk off your face.*

"Will you be eating alone?" Brenna looked up at the waitress—an NYU student-type with bright red hair, a pale cameo face, the delicate features modernized by a lip ring—a good candidate for Errol's Angels, Brenna thought. Streetwise, but with an innocence to the eyes . . .

Ludlow had just pushed open the door and was peering around the room, the top of his head no more than a foot away from the ceiling. His gaze flittered on the waitress and he smiled knowingly. Eleven years since she'd seen him and Brenna could still predict his thoughts.

His gaze shifted to her. "As I live and breathe. Brenna Spector!" Errol shouted the words without moving from his spot, as if this were some private party, thrown especially for him. Errol had always had difficulty observing conventional boundaries. It wasn't entirely his fault, big as he was, but he couldn't enter a room without invading it.

There were about ten other customers in the diner, seven or so in booths, and almost all of them turned and stared at the booming giant in the doorway "You look good! Especially for your age!" he said. "You've got to be *pushing for-ty* these days, am I right?"

Brenna looked at the waitress. "I'm with him."

She chewed on her lip ring and gave Brenna a pitying look.

"Believe me," Brenna said, "I know."

Errol strode up to the table. "You have a delightfully un-con-ven-tion-al look, young lady," he said to the waitress, relishing each syllable, just as always. "You stand out, yet you fit in."

She shrugged. "I model sometimes."

"Modeling is for shallow girls." Errol snorted. "I could make you a private investigator."

"Ummm . . . No thanks."

He pulled out his wallet, slipped out one of his cards, and handed it to the waitress. Brenna noticed the design—it had been new on September 24, 1992. "I'll bet you could get a lot of information out of a man with a bat or two of those pretty eyelashes."

"Information?"

Again with the smirk. "Brenna here worked for me when she was about your age," he said. "Such a naïve little thing back then, wanting to find her runaway sister . . . I taught her everything she knows."

"You know what you want?" the waitress asked Brenna.

What she wanted was to sock Errol in the jaw. "Just coffee."

Errol ordered green tea—his drink of choice for twenty years.

"You never change," Brenna said.

"You would know." He grinned. "That memory of yours . . ." He looked up at the waitress. "I'm sure you have seen Brenna Spector on the news?"

"Stop it, Errol."

"Perfect memory?"

The waitress's face was blank.

"Solved the Iris Neff case?"

"Uh . . ."

"Fabulous interview on *Sunrise Manhattan*. Though the *New York Post* rather unfortunately referred to her as—"

"Stop it, Errol."

"Head-Case Hero. They could have done better, in my opinion. Perfect memory doesn't necessarily make one a head case, but when you're a slave to alliteration, as the *Post* clearly is—"

"I need to check on other tables."

"Suit yourself."

The waitress left with Errol smiling benignly at her rear end.

Once she was no longer in sight, he came back to Brenna. "You really do look good," he said.

"You seem surprised."

"Well, it has been eleven years," he said. "Eleven years can wreak havoc on the female form."

Brenna gave him a sweet smile. "But you've been following me, Errol. You've seen me on *Sunrise Manhattan*, read about me in the papers." She reached into her bag, pulled out the printout. "You know everything about my involvement with the Iris Neff case."

"Yes, and how is Detective Morasco? Page Six spotted you two at some bar . . . which one was it?"

"We've been to more than one bar." Brenna placed the printout of Errol's home page on the table between them and smoothed it out. "And clearly, you read the *Post* more carefully than me."

Errol glanced down at the home page—Errol Ludlow

Investigations in fire engine red against a black background, followed by a list of endorsements. "Oh . . . you've seen this." His face flushed a little.

The first endorsement: *"Errol Ludlow was the best mentor a girl could have—and a truly great man!"—Brenna Spector, HEAD-CASE HERO*

"I never said that, Errol," Brenna said. "I wouldn't say that if you put a gun to my irregularly shaped brain and threatened to pull the trigger."

He cleared his throat. "Whether you said it or not," he said, "it is true. You can't deny that I taught you the bravery and resourcefulness needed to be a private investigator. I didn't baby you. I helped you grow."

"You put me in danger. You put all of us in danger. You sent young girls out there to catch cheating men in the act, unarmed, and you never gave us backup."

He sighed. "Now you sound like that ex-husband of yours."

Brenna shut her eyes tight, a memory slithering into her brain—the ER at St. Vincent's on May 29, 1996, *her left eye throbbed shut, her head all pain, dry, cool sheets beneath her. Jim pushes aside the curtain, baby Maya in his arms, her little mouth moving . . . like she's blowing kisses in her sleep. Brenna tries to smile at him. Her gums hurt. "I guess some guys don't like getting their picture taken." She tastes copper in her mouth. She isn't sure whether it's fresh blood or the memory of it.*

Those eyes, those eyes of Jim's, the hurt in them so big, she has to look away . . . "I can't take this, Brenna. If you work for him anymore . . . one more job . . . we're through."

"Don't be sad. Please don't be sad. I promise. I . . ."

She snapped the hair ties, cleared her throat. "How long has that quote been on your Web site, Errol?"

"I . . . I don't know."

"Since the day of that *Post* headline? October 4. That sound about right?"

He shook his head. "I only put it up about a week ago," he said. "Business wasn't good. I thought it might help."

"And when did Lula Belle's manager call you?"

"The day before yesterday?"

"How long has she been presumed missing?"

"Who?"

She looked at him. "Who do you think?"

"A couple of months. Why all these questions?"

"I need the manager's name and number."

"No can do."

"Excuse me?"

"He prefers to remain anonymous."

"I don't give a damn what he prefers."

"Those are the terms of the contract. And he is paying quite a bit of money to ensure that I observe them." He looked at her. "Between us, he is a very successful Hollywood theatrical agent and does not want his reputation sullied."

Brenna took a breath, so sharp it hurt a little. *Sully this*. "Listen," she said. "I have reason to believe that Lula Belle knows things about me—deeply personal things."

"Really? What things?"

Brenna pressed on. "She's been missing for months, yet this manager of hers calls you up and hires you immediately after you put my name on your Web site."

"I'm sure that's just a coincidence."

"Could be," Brenna said. "But either way, you've got two choices."

He stared at her. "I'm listening."

"You can give me the name and number of that manager. Or I will take this printout, sue you for libel, then hold a press conference and share the many glorious memories I have of the years I spent working for you."

Errol stared at Brenna.

"And as you well know, no one is gonna question my memory."

The waitress returned to their table and set their cups in front of them. "Private investigator, huh?" she said.

But Errol didn't answer. His gaze never left Brenna's face.

"Oookay." The waitress left the table fast.

"If I give you the manager's contact information," Errol said, "can you please not tell him where you got it?"

"My lips are sealed."

Errol sighed heavily. "Give me your phone."

Brenna handed it to him, watched him tap the name and number into her list of contacts.

Her face relaxed into a smile. "You know something, Errol? I take it back. You really have changed."

"I have?"

She nodded. "I don't think I've ever heard you say 'please' before."

3

"Say Gryffindor, sweetums," said Ira, the photographer.

"My name isn't sweetums, it's Chloe," said Chloe Barton, age eight. "And I freakin' hate Harry Potter."

Gary Freeman sighed. *Another day. Another one of these never-ending days.* Gary turned to Chloe's mother. "You know, Ruth," he said, "it's all well and good to have a great commercial look, which believe me, Chloe does—"

"I know, Gary, I know."

"—but the most important quality for a child actor to have—"

"Are you listening to the man, Chloe?"

"—is the ability to take direction."

Chloe glared at him. "You're not a director. You're just a stupid agent."

"That's enough, Chloe," Ruth Barton said. "I'm so sorry, Gary. Chloe didn't get very much sleep last night, and when she doesn't get sleep, she gets cranky."

"*I am not cranky!*"

Gary sighed again—more heavily this time. He released all the air in his body, then inhaled, slowly through his nose. *Out with the stress, in with the positive energy . . .* A couple of weeks ago, he'd taken a breathing class with his wife, Jill. Jill had dragged him to it. *A class in breathing*, he had complained. *What's next—a pissing seminar?*

It's pranayana, *Gar*, she'd replied. *Yogic breathing*, which had done nothing to inspire any confidence in Gary. But to his surprise, he'd found the class helpful. Turned out, he'd been breathing wrong all this time, using only the tops of his lungs. He'd spent his whole life—all fifty years of it—lacking for air. Who knew? *You were right*, Gary had told Jill, just a few days ago. *Remind me never to doubt you or your crazy yoga classes again.*

More air. Who knew? Why couldn't everything in Gary's life be that easy to fix?

For a few seconds, she seeped into his thoughts— The Shadow. Lula Belle. Usually, he made it a point not to think about her, especially by name. But he couldn't help it. She was everywhere and she was nowhere and she was ruining his life.

Lula Belle's subscribers kept writing him, e-mails pouring into his Hotmail address, even though he'd taken down the site a month ago. Every time he dared check LulaBelleadmin@hotmail.com (and granted, that was rare), he would find dozens of them. *Where is Lula Belle? What happened to the site? Did she die? Did you kill her? I want my money back, asshole. Give me my money. It's your fault she's gone and you owe me. I trusted you. I'm going to get you. I'm going to track you down and . . . You don't know me but I know you. I know who you . . . I'm going to get you back . . .*

Sometimes he'd see those e-mails in his dreams. He'd be online, thinking he was alone, and then the words would get bigger and bigger, until they shattered the computer screen and scrolled up and down his bedroom walls and shrieked at him in The Shadow's voice. *Did you kill me, Gary?*

And then, if Gary was lucky, he'd wake up.

Gary closed his eyes. He took another deep breath—a cleansing breath, that's what it was called, as if breathing could make you clean. As his lungs expanded, he felt it at his chest—the cell phone he'd bought, just for the investigation. It was a TracPhone—no GPS, no Internet. No apps like that fruit-throwing game that his daughters loved to play. Just a number he could give to Ludlow. "Only call if it's important," he had said. And so far, nothing . . . He'd kept it hidden at the back of his desk at night and slipped it into his shirt pocket every day, and in five days, the thing hadn't budged. Not once. Ludlow was probably full of crap.

The photography studio smelled like baby powder. It was big and airy, with pale pink walls that Ira claimed cast a flattering light on most people's faces. But there was something about the color—a nursery-sweetness he found hard to take. Ira was one of the best in the business, and so Gary brought almost all his clients here for their head shots. Yet sometimes—now for instance—he felt too dark for Ira's studio, as if his presence might corrupt it, the blackness floating off him, sticking to the baby pink walls with those bright lights humming at him: *For shame, for shame, for shame . . .*

Think it away, Gary told himself. And he did. He always could. You close a door on something in your mind—a person, a memory, a bad dream . . . You close that door and you lock it. You throw away the key. And if you keep it locked, if you make yourself forget there was ever a key to begin with, then eventually all of it will disappear. The door. The memory. The way it makes you feel. The mind is a very powerful muscle.

Ira was trying his best to get good shots of Chloe Barton, but his best didn't seem to be good enough. She was standing on a little platform in the middle of the room with a fan blowing her blonde curls, her doll-like features twisted in a way that brought to mind a *Twilight Zone* episode that Gary used to have nightmares about, back when he was her age. Meanwhile, Ira and his digital camera buzzed around the little girl in nervous circles. "Work it, Miss Thing," he was saying. "Work it like a rock star!"

"I'm not a rock star. I'm an actress," said Chloe, who at eight was just a year older than Gary's youngest, Hannah. "An actress and a model. Rock stars are sleaze buckets. And so are picture takers."

Ira set his camera on the floor. "I can't work with this kid, Gary."

"I'm so sorry," said Chloe's mother, Ruth.

"Sorry for yourself is what you should be, lady."

"You're an ugly man," Chloe told Ira. "And your pants are too tight."

You tell yourself lies for long enough, you start to believe them. Once you believe them in full, once you put your whole heart into it and believe in those lies the way you believe in anything—your country, your family, your God—once you do that, those lies become the truth.

Hadn't she said that herself, in one of her videos?

Maybe Gary didn't want to find Lula Belle. He could get by without the extra money the Web site had been bringing in. He'd tell Jill a client had fired him and so they needed to tighten their belts. She would understand. She would have to.

Powerful as it was, the memory of Lula Belle would fade, the subscribers would forget. And Gary would, too. He would make himself forget. He would close down the Hotmail address, and the subscribers would move on. The Shadow would stay behind her locked door and the door would disappear, and she would, too. He would never hear from her again. It would all be over, but for the dimming memory.

Will it ever dim, Lula Belle? Will I ever get over not knowing you?

"That's it," Ira said. "We're done."

Gary snapped out of it, looked at him. "Do you think any of the pictures are useable?"

"Only if someone is doing a remake of *The Bad Seed*."

Ruth Barton gave Gary a pleading look. "One more chance?"

"Next week we'll reconvene," Gary started to say, but he didn't get to the last word.

"Next week we'll what?" said Ruth.

The phone in Gary's shirt pocket was vibrating.

He held up a hand. "Back in just a few," he said.

"But Gary . . ."

Deep intake of air, slow release, and then he was out the door, in Ira's little courtyard with the colorful tile and the blush-red hibiscus plants and the bubbling fountain in the middle. He moved past the fountain and plucked the phone out of his pocket and looked at the screen . . .

Ludlow.

"Yes?" Gary said.

"I have good news and bad news."

Gary winced. It wasn't just the words themselves that grated—no one ever really has good news when they use that cliché—but the way Ludlow said them, so precise, hanging on to each syllable like it was a goddamn life preserver. Why had he believed this windbag? Gary said, "Yes."

"Which would you like to hear first?"

Jesus. "I don't care. The good news, I guess."

"I've spoken to Brenna Spector."

Gary's eyes widened. "You have?"

"Yep." The P exploded out of Ludlow like cannon fire. Gary practically needed to wipe the spit out of his ear. "And I hired her."

"*What?*"

"You wanted her missing persons expertise—I got it for you. She's on our team."

"But—"

"You don't have to worry about the cost—I'm cutting her in out of my very generous paycheck."

"I'm not concerned about the cost." Gary closed his eyes. "You didn't tell her anything, did you?"

"Nope."

"So," he breathed, "what's the bad news?"

"I had to give her your name and number."

Gary's mouth went dry. "You said you didn't tell her anything."

"Only your name and number," he said. *As if that's nothing, nothing at all . . .*

Gary put the heel of his palm to his forehead and rubbed in slow, soothing circles. "Okay," he said. "Okay. I can deal with this." And he could, he knew. It was what made him such a successful agent and manager, that flexibility. He could roll with the punches, move past Plan A. It was a talent he'd acquired out of necessity. *Don't fall down. Don't freeze. Keep moving out of the room . . .* But that door was locked, the key long gone. And for now, Gary had his job to do. "You're fired, Errol."

"What?"

"Keep the initial payment."

"But . . . that isn't . . . It's not . . ."

"And I will give you the same amount in one month, provided you do not tell anyone else that we have ever met or spoken. Consider it a severance package."

"But . . ."

"Great. It's been a pleasure."

Gary hung up with Ludlow and headed back into Ira's studio. Ruth rushed at him, still apologizing. Gary smiled. "Don't worry about it," he said, Plan B already taking shape in his mind.

Brenna had no intention of calling Gary Freeman—at least not anytime soon. No way was she going to get any truthful information out of a man who'd worked so hard to mask his identity that he didn't even want Errol's subcontractors to know his name. (Hell, the number he'd given Errol himself had been a disposable phone, its minutes bought in advance, virtually untraceable.)

No, Brenna had wanted Gary Freeman's name and number so she could find out who exactly she was dealing with. Who exactly Lula Belle had been dealing with. And once she found that out—very quickly, it turned out, as *Gary Freeman, successful Hollywood theatrical agent*, was all over the Web—she'd be all the more able to understand Lula Belle.

Already, Brenna understood why Freeman had wanted to keep her on the down-low: His life was about as far from that Coke bottle trick as you could possibly get.

An agent specializing in children and an adjunct professor "at several renowned arts schools," according to his website bio, Freeman had been married for twenty years to the same lovely blonde woman, and had three lovely blonde daughters—aged fifteen, twelve, and seven—all of whom seemed to accompany him to any event where he was photographed. Turned out there were many of those. When he wasn't doing paid engagements at high schools and youth centers about navigating the treacherous world of Hollywood "with your values intact," Freeman was participating in walk-athons, auctions, days at the races, and fund-raising dinners for Wise Up—a literacy program for inner city kids founded by his wife, Jill.

Scrolling through Google Images back at her office, Brenna found a picture of the Freeman family, posing with a clown at a Wise Up circus event this past summer. She blew it up so that it filled her screen, and then gazed at Freeman's face—a nice face. *What's a nice guy like you doing pimping out silhouettes?*

He wasn't a classically handsome man. He was stocky and ruddy and slightly shorter than his wife, with a thick hank of graying hair and a nose that looked as if it had been broken one too many times. But there was something about that face—a comfort level in the set of the features, a warmth to the eyes. Brenna imagined he had a wide circle of friends who thought they knew him a lot better than they actually did.

A voice behind Brenna said, "Looks like that dude on the cornflakes commercial." Trent's voice. She recognized it immediately, but she jumped a little anyway. "You scared me."

"I usually have that effect on women. But in a good way."

"There's a good way to scare women?"

Trent started to answer, but Brenna held up a hand.

"The question was rhetorical," she said.

"So who's the cornflakes guy?"

She opened her mouth, then closed it. "Potential client." She minimized the screen. "I thought you were meeting with Annette Shelby."

"Uh . . . that was at one-thirty? There's a little thing at the bottom right side of your screen. It's called a clock. Check it out sometime!"

Brenna glanced at the clock: three-thirty. "Oh no . . ." It was her day to have Maya—the last day before Christmas break, and she had her for the rest of the week. Brenna had been hoping to surprise her, meet her at school, take her out for cupcakes at Molly's, which Maya now liked much better than Magnolia Bakery. But it was too late now. She would be home from school any minute, and Brenna had blown it as usual. She sighed. "Where did the day go?"

Trent shrugged. "Same place it always goes."

And yes, that was exactly where it had gone—the same place. After saying good-bye to Ludlow, Brenna had returned to her office, checked her e-mails, dealt with a large list of potential clients—business had actually picked up *too* much since the Neff case—while trying not to lapse into the past. And that, as ever, had been easier said than done. A woman searching for a long-lost brother, for instance, was named Rachel Fleischer, which had brought to mind Brenna's eighth grade English teacher, Rosemary Fleischer, which had whisked Brenna into third period English, February 11, 1983—the dry heat from the radiator, the smell of chalk dust, and Miss Fleischer detailing the "lethal allure of Desdemona."

An e-mailed photograph—of a boy named Jordan Michaels who'd gone missing in the spring of 2004—was taken in front of the sign for Niagara Falls. And of course that had flung Brenna back, for the second time today, to the *Maid of the Mist* on October 30. *Those biting winds, that hail. . .*

The day had gone where it always went—in and out of wormholes, with Brenna swallowed up by memories, then snapping herself back to reality. Back and forth, back and forth. She turned to Trent. "So how did your meeting with Mrs. Shelby go?"

"Fine." Trent picked at a fingernail.

"You don't look like it went fine."

"It did, but . . ."

"But what?"

He sighed. "Ever get . . . you know . . . emotionally invested in a client?"

She looked at him. "What do you mean?"

"Never mind," Trent said. "So are we officially on with Errol? Did you get the rest of the Lula Belle videos?"

Brenna didn't reply—flashing instead on her last meeting with Annette Shelby. Poor, fragile Annette in her hotel room at the St. Regis on September 30—the room she'd reserved for her and her missing Larry—for the big reunion, the second honeymoon—only to find out, via Brenna, that Larry had wanted to stay missing. Annette, with that sad, searching look in her eyes, Johnnie Walker Black mingling with the scent of expensive perfume.

Annette slips an envelope out of her Prada bag and hands it to Brenna. "Your check," she says. "You'll see I included a little extra for that yummy assistant of yours."

"Yummy? Trent?"

"Come on. Don't play dumb. Those pecs!" Annette *grabs another bottle out of the open minibar, twists off the top, and downs it in one gulp. "God, he's a delicacy."*

Brenna cringed. "Trent?"

He was back at his desk now, Lula Belle on his screen in all her spread-eagle, loose-jawed glory. "Yeah?"

She cleared her throat. "By emotionally invested, you don't mean . . . Uh . . ."

He stared at her.

She tried again. "You and Annette . . . You're not . . . I mean, Annette is a very fragile woman, and after what she went through with Larry, I'd hate to see her get hurt again."

"Why would she get hurt?"

"*Trent*," said Brenna. But then she noticed his bulletin board.

For the six years that he'd been working for her, Trent had covered the board with pictures of himself—on the beach, at clubs, in front of random parked sports cars he'd passed on the way home from those places—always shirtless or close to it, always next to some gorgeous, scantily clad babe with a deer-in-the-headlights look in her eyes. Now, all those pictures were gone. They'd been replaced by photographs of Annette's cat, Persephone. "Mrs. Shelby says it's okay I haven't found her," Trent was saying. "She says we can keep looking—long as it takes. But sometimes I go to bed at night, and I think about her all cold and alone and I can't sleep. Those big sad eyes of hers. They freakin' kill me."

Brenna said, "You're talking about Persephone."

"Who else would I be talking about?"

Brenna smiled. "Nobody."

"Whatever."

"Listen," Brenna said. "It's good that you care about her. It's normal to get involved with your missing person . . . uh, animal . . ." She cleared her throat. "Happens to me all the time."

"Still?"

"You know that it does," she said, Lula Belle's voice in her head again, singing about cement mixers . . .

Outside the door, Brenna could hear footsteps on the stairs. Maya's. At this point, she could recognize them—such heavy steps for a slight girl. She thought about her daughter, the clumsy innocence of that gait, that shy smile and the way she tugged at her hair while she was daydreaming, and she wondered how long these things would last—these faint remnants of childhood.

Of course, Maya wasn't ready to let go, either. Cleaning her room the other day, Brenna had found evidence of this fact on Maya's top bookshelf, behind all her filled sketchpads and the graphic novels and mangas she devoured. *The Very Hungry Caterpillar.* It had been her favorite at age four—the first book she'd learned to read. But on November 19, 2004, when Maya was eight and a half, Brenna had put *The Very Hungry Caterpillar* in a box along with all her other picture books and early readers, and donated it to the library. Five years later, there it was—the same book Brenna had put in that box, its cover riddled with Maya's unmistakable preschool crayon scrawl. *She stole it back*, Brenna had thought, smiling. But she hadn't told Maya that she'd found the book. She never would. *Everyone needs their secrets.*

Maya's key twisted in the front door. Brenna's eyes went to Lula Belle. "Can you minimize that image, please?" she told Trent.

"Sure."

The door opened, just as the phone rang, and Trent answered it.

Maya dropped her backpack on the floor, made for the refrigerator. "Hi Mom. Hi Trent."

She seemed to have grown an inch since this morning—barely thirteen and a half and already she was nearing Brenna's five-nine. "Hi, sweetie. How was your last day of school?"

"Whoa."

Brenna looked up at Maya, saw her staring at Trent's screen. "Trent, for godsakes."

"Aw, bite me, I'm sorry," Trent said into the phone. "No, not you, sir. One sec." He minimized Lula Belle's image and got back to the caller.

Maya said, "Was that like . . . a bottle?"

Brenna cringed. "Never mind that."

"How could anybody *not mind* that?"

Brenna sighed. "It's just a case Trent and I are working on. Nothing you need to be concerned with." She forced a smile, yet still Maya looked very, very concerned. "So, anyway . . . I thought maybe we could go out for sushi—celebrate your first night of Christmas break."

Maya kept staring at Trent's black screen.

"Pizza?" said Brenna. "Greek? Dim sum?"

Finally, she snapped out of it. "Didn't you get my text?"

"Huh? No," Brenna said. "I didn't even hear my phone go off."

"Oh . . . Well, uh . . . I wanted to know if I could stay at Zoe's tonight. Help her decorate her tree."

Brenna looked at her. "Didn't you already decorate your own tree? With your dad and Faith?"

"Yeah, but I'm with you right up until Christmas."

"You make it sound like a prison sentence."

"Mom."

"Well, come on."

"Mom. You're Jewish. You don't have a tree. It's that simple."

"I know. I'm just playing," said Brenna, who sounded anything but playful.

"So . . . you understand, right?"

"Sure." Brenna sighed. "You can spend the night at Zoe's."

Maya peered at her. "You're hurt."

"Give me a little credit. I'm not that much of a wimp," said Brenna, who sounded, to herself, like very much of a wimp.

"Mom."

"Don't *Mom* me. It's okay. We'll have plenty of time together."

"Great! I'll go pack." She grabbed a handful of cheese sticks out of the refrigerator and hurried down the hall, Brenna watching her lanky teenage daughter but seeing the chubby four-year-old from May 8, 2000 . . . *Maya running out the bright yellow door of her classroom at the Sunny Side Pre-School, Maya stumbling into the courtyard, wrinkled white construction paper clasped in her little hands, Maya's pink cheeks and that smile— running toward Brenna, barreling into her stomach, the sun on her messy blonde hair, and Brenna's heart swells at the feel of her, the smell of playground sand in her hair, it fills to bursting.*

"Mommy! I drew this for you!"

"Incoming!" said Trent.

Brenna's phone rang. She glared at him. "Trent. You can't just transfer calls to me without warning."

"Sorry," he said. "But he wouldn't give me his name and he said it was urgent."

Brenna rolled her eyes at him, picked up the phone. "Hello?"

"Brenna Spector?" The voice was kind and resonant—utterly unfamiliar, but with a lilt to it, as if the caller knew her and expected her to recognize him.

"Yes?"

"Is anyone in the room with you?"

She glanced at Trent. "Yes."

"Then please don't respond to anything I am about to tell you."

"Who are you?" Brenna glanced at the caller ID: PRIVATE NUMBER.

"I need to be clear you understand," the voice was saying. "I cannot have you responding, or reacting in any way to any information I am about to give you."

"All right," Brenna said.

"Good," he said. "I am going to give you a number. I need you to write it down—very discreetly. No one is allowed to see the number."

I don't need to write down numbers, Brenna started to say, but he was still talking.

" . . . and call me in exactly five minutes, from a completely private place. This call must be confidential. If I find out that anyone else knows about our conversation, I will never speak to you again."

And I should care about that because . . . "All right."

He gave her the number.

Brenna swallowed hard. She knew it. It was the same number Errol Ludlow had tapped into her phone earlier that day.

"Do you have it written down?" he asked.

"Yes," said Brenna. *Yes, Gary Freeman.*

"You don't need me to repeat any of the numbers."

"No, I don't," she said. "But . . ."

"You know who I am."

"Yes."

He took a deep breath, slowly in, slowly out. And when he spoke again, Brenna felt as though he was with her, in the room, smiling. "I know who you are, too."

4

Gary Freeman was a fan. At least, that's what he told Brenna, once she'd taken her cell phone down the hall to her bedroom and called the number he'd left and assured him, repeatedly, that there was no one within earshot. "Ms. Spector," he said, "I'm one of your biggest fans."

Considering the way he'd been ordering her around for the past two phone calls, it was the last thing Brenna had expected to hear. "You are?"

"Yeah, I admire you so much—the work you've done."

"How do you even know who I am?"

"I heard about the Neff case on one of those shows my wife watches—you know the ones, with all the yentas, sitting around discussing current events and complaining about men?"

Brenna smiled a little. "Yep."

"I was very impressed with what they said about you—how you solved that case, of course, but also how you've dealt with so much family tragedy. You did one interview, I guess? You mentioned a sister?"

Brenna snapped the ties on her wrist. "Yes," she said. "*Sunrise Manhattan*." Big mistake to name the show, because as soon as she said it, she was back into October 5, *the hot TV lights on her face, and Faith sitting across from her, her clear blue eyes glittering in the kliegs as she opens the yearbook, shows her the picture . . . "You miss her don't you? You miss Clea."*

Brenna snapped the hair ties, hard.

Gary was saying, " . . . and I guess you'd call it a disorder? Your memory . . ."

"Works for me."

"I found the book you're in—*Extraordinary Children*. By RF Lieberman. Checked it out of the library."

"My childhood shrink."

He sighed. "I . . . I can't even imagine what your life must be like."

"Most people think it's a gift."

"The yentas did. 'Perfect memory,' one of them said. 'If I had that, I'd never lose my keys again.'" He laughed—but Brenna could hear the tension in it.

"You don't view it as a gift, do you?"

"No. I'm sorry . . . I don't mean to offend."

"I'm not offended. Believe me, if all I remembered was where I put my keys, I'd be a whole lot happier."

"Good," he said. "Good, because I wouldn't want to . . ."

"You didn't."

"Good."

"Is there a lot, Mr. Freeman, that you would like to forget?"

There was a long pause on the other end of the line. "You can call me Gary."

Okay . . . New topic. "You know," Brenna tried, "for a book written in 1990, it's sure been getting a lot of play lately. I'm thinking Dr. Lieberman should give me a percentage of the royalties."

Another laugh, easier this time. "I could work a deal for you."

"I'm sure you could."

Freeman said, "I fired Ludlow."

"You . . . Wait. *What?*"

"That was abrupt, wasn't it?"

"Well . . . yes."

"Sorry. Force of habit. Producers, casting directors. They always want you to cut to the chase."

"You fired Ludlow?"

"I gave him a nice severance payment, but to tell the truth, I don't think missing persons cases are his strength."

"Yes."

"And . . . his voice irritated me."

"I definitely get that," Brenna said. "What I'm confused about is why you hired him in the first place."

"I saw that endorsement from you on his Web site."

Brenna sighed.

"Looking back, I guess that was a pretty dumb reason. But he did tell me that he was still in touch with you. When he said he'd signed you on, I figured, hey, may as well cut out the middle man."

"Why didn't you just hire me in the first place? I've got a Web site, too, you know."

Another long pause, longer than the last. And then finally, "Ms. Spector?"

"Brenna."

"I need to ask you something, Brenna."

"Ask away."

"Are you tape-recording this phone call?"

She frowned. "That's what you wanted to ask me?"

"You realize that by California law, which applies whether or not you are in this state, it is illegal to tape-record another person without his permission. And if you are, in fact, recording this conversation, you are breaking the law."

"I'm not recording you, Gary," said Brenna who never recorded anything—she had no need to.

"All right," he said finally. "I believe you."

You believe me? "Why wouldn't you?"

"I will not permit any of our conversations to be recorded, from here on in."

"Fine," Brenna said. "Agreed. No recording."

"And you are to reveal my identity to no one."

"Not even my assistant?"

"No one. As far as he's concerned, you're still working for Ludlow."

"But—"

"And you are to be the sole point person. Your assistant reports to you and you alone. Are we clear?"

"Yes, Gary. We are clear."

"Good." Gary took a deep breath, in and out. "I know you have a Web site. I looked it up, right after that yenta show. I even wrote down the contact number."

"But you didn't call it."

"No."

"Why?"

Yet another pause. Brenna listened to him breathing again—long, slow, labored breaths—and she wondered who they were intended for, these pauses? Were they due to Gary Freeman's discomfort, or were they intended to make Brenna uncomfortable—because they did. They made her feel as though she was hurting him with her questions—this kind-faced man with his pretty family and his charity events. They made her feel as though all she needed was a bright light and a cigarette and she could break him. And that wasn't what Brenna wanted at all, to break him. All she wanted was to understand. "Why didn't you call me, Gary?"

"Because—" His voice cracked and she flashed on her own father, her blur of a father with his strong hands and his kind voice, Brenna's father at the wheel of his car, sobbing. *My God did that really happen?*

Brenna closed her eyes. "Because what?"

"Because . . . I was ashamed."

It was an affair. Not a physical one, as Gary Freeman had never met Lula Belle—he'd never even seen her face—but an affair nonetheless, Gary had insisted to Brenna over the phone. An affair of the heart, the mind, the wallet.

It had started two years ago—and at a time of weakness, as all affairs do. Money had been tight. Very tight. With more than one hundred and twenty-five thousand dollars in credit card debt staring him in the face, Gary had been on the computer, paying the monthly bills—one thousand dollars for Tessa's modeling course, fifteen hundred and fifty dollars combined for Hannah's and Lucy's piano lessons, and let's not even talk about the looming orthodontist bills for the two older girls (God, why hadn't Gary listened to his mother and gone into dentistry?). Then there were the car lease payments and the mortgages on their Pasadena house and on the second home in Santa Barbara and the yacht they hardly ever used and, of course, there was Jill—his beautiful, serene wife with her spa and salon visits and her yoga classes and all that instruction from those billionaire rabbis at the Kabbalah Center—instruction, of all things, on how to find spirituality in a materialistic world. Gary was staring at those numbers, his hands shaking over the keyboard, his thoughts darkening into bankruptcy, foreclosure, living on the street with nothing to keep his family warm and dry but the philosophy of the Kabbalah . . .

That's when he'd received the e-mail from her.

It wasn't Gary's fault—the debt, that is. After seventeen or eighteen flush years, it had just sort of descended on him, with one client getting fired from a long-standing Disney gig when his voice changed, another bowing out of commercial work when her parents decided she should focus more on school, yet another suddenly un-hirable after getting hospitalized for an eating disorder . . . The list went on. Show business is cyclical, especially when it comes to children, and Gary had swung into a major downturn without preparing himself or his family . . .

Okay, he supposed it was his fault.

Anyway, he received the e-mail from Lula Belle, and he jumped on it. *Make me a star*, it read, *and I'll make you rich*. Sounded like spam, sure, but once he'd viewed the attachment, he was sold. They worked out their deal: He created the Web site, opened a PayPal account, as well as a separate checking account, and then he put his expertise to work—the expertise Lula Belle had told him she valued because *Really, Mr. Freeman*, she had typed, so fragile and helpless. *I don't know where to start.*

All it took was a few strategically placed posts on certain well-traveled message boards, a cryptic Craig's List announcement, subscribers came pouring in. Gary's debt eased. His blood pressure went down. He couldn't have been more grateful. "She was like a guardian angel," he'd said, before realizing how that sounded.

On the second of every month, he'd receive an e-mail

from Lula Belle at the special e-mail address he'd created just to correspond with her. The e-mail would consist of a PO box where he would send a check for sixty percent of the Web site proceeds, made out to cash, as well as four or five attachments, which he would screen before announcing their availability on the site.

This was how it became an affair—Gary viewing those attachments, four or five a month for nearly two years. Gary in the dark of his home office, after his wife and kids had gone to sleep, watching that bare, backlit body, listening to those very private confessions that made his breath hitch in his chest. He could not see her face. He did not know her real name. But never, in Gary Freeman's life, had he ever been with a woman who had made herself this vulnerable before him.

"How do you know her stories were true?" Brenna had asked.

"I knew."

Cement mixer, turn on a dime . . . "Did you know anything about her? Her family?"

"No."

"Then how did you—"

"I just knew."

"Because you—"

"We had a connection."

Between e-mails, Gary would watch Lula Belle's videos again and again until, at some point, she consumed him. Every morning, he'd wake up tingling, her voice slithering through his brain. It was all he could do not to quote her to his family, his clients, all he could do not to speak in her whispery accent, to close his eyes and lose himself in her world, her life, thinking of all those things she'd told the camera, *told him through the camera*. Not the subscribers. Him. The subscribers got sloppy seconds, but he had her first. *He knew her first* . . . "I know," he'd told Brenna. "I sound like a freak."

"You don't."

"I do. See, that's why I thought Ludlow was perfect—he spends his whole life dealing with creepier guys than me. You, on the other hand . . ."

"Don't worry about it."

Lula Belle cleared up Gary's debt. She got him hard. She broke his heart. And then she just left, with no explanation. She'd been gone for two months now—two months without a single e-mail. It was the only thing on his mind—the lack of her—and yet no one knew. Come on, who could he tell? "I'm afraid something may have happened to her," he had said. "I mean . . . God . . . if she ever existed to begin with. Sometimes I feel like I'm going nuts."

"Have you deleted all the e-mails?"

"I have her last one."

"What about the downloads?"

Deep breath, in and out. "I have them all."

Brenna had asked him to forward them to her, along with the last e-mail from Lula Belle, and as many of the PO boxes as he could remember.

"I don't remember any of them. I'm bad with numbers."

Brenna sighed. "Just the locations would be fine. You can probably remember a few locations, right?"

"Of course," he said. "Thank you, Brenna."

"Gary," she had said, finally. "Is there anything else you need to tell me?"

"Pardon?"

Cement mixer, turn on a dime . . . "Is there any other reason you're hiring me—other than my missing persons expertise and yentas saying nice things about me?"

There had been a long pause on the other end of the

line. And then, "What other reason could there possibly be?"

She was off the phone with Gary now, leaving a message for her detective friend Nick Morasco. (Was that how she thought of him now? Her *detective friend*? Man . . .) Already, the secrecy of this case was getting to her. She understood, of course, why Gary Freeman wanted his name kept out of this investigation, but to ask her to lie to those closest to her . . . It made Brenna feel more alone than she usually felt—and that was really saying something. She was mad at herself for letting Maya sleep at her friend's tonight. She didn't want to be all by herself in this quiet apartment, nothing to keep her company but the Lula Belle downloads, the persistent stink of Trent's cologne, and Gary Freeman's voice in her brain . . . *You are to reveal my identity to no one.*

"Wanna come over to my place after work, watch some porn?" Brenna blurted into Morasco's voice mail. She cringed. "It's . . . uh . . . It's not porn actually. It's performance art. And it's for a case. I'll explain when you get here. If you get here. I mean . . . You know . . . if you don't have any other plans." She hung up.

"Smooth," said Trent.

"Shut up."

"No worries. Girls are cute when they sound like idiots."

Brenna rolled her eyes. Without saying a word, she e-mailed the folder of Lula Belle downloads to Trent.

"Hey!" His voice pitched up like a tween girl at a *Twilight* premiere. "You got all of 'em?"

"Now who sounds like an idiot?" Brenna said. "Remember, this is serious work. I want you to try and look at them frame by frame. Pay attention to shadows, the way she moves, any details you might see in the room with her that might give us some clue as to her identity and whereabouts."

"You call that work," said Trent. "I call it what I'll be doing in heaven someday."

"Glad I could make you happy."

"Actually, the props should go to Errol Ludlow," said Trent. "He made good on his word. He isn't such a bad guy, right?"

Brenna winced. "You ready for your trip to the fish market?"

"See for yourself."

Brenna turned. On his desk, he'd spread out a series of poster-sized versions of his cat renderings.

She moved closer. "Wow," she said. "You're an artist."

He really was. The computerized renderings were incredibly detailed, with each version of Persephone—fat, emaciated, bedraggled, glossy and coddled—real enough to break a cat lover's heart. If Trent was unsuccessful in his search, Brenna imagined that Annette might want to frame at least one of these pictures.

"You think I should take all of them?" he said. "I mean, if Persie's been living with all those fish vendors for three months, I should probably just take the fat pic, right? Oh, and I also have another one I just made—with mange . . . What are you smiling at?"

"Persie."

"Yeah, well, some people don't mind if I give them nicknames."

"She's not a person," Brenna said.

He sighed heavily.

"I'd take all the photos, Trent. It's best to keep the bases covered."

"But they're bulky. I don't want to carry them all."

"That's what your man purse is for."

"It's called a messenger bag."

"Sorry." She smiled. "I really hope you get lucky with Persephone."

"Me too." No jokes about getting lucky. Not even his trademark cocked eyebrow. Trent really wanted to find this cat.

Trent slipped the renderings into his man purse. Brenna eyed it as he slung it over his shoulder—pale desert camo, with five big, shiny general's stars across the front and a dog-tag zipper pull. She would've been hard-pressed to find any item of apparel that tried half as hard as that bag did.

"Later!"

After he closed the door behind him, Brenna moved back to her desk and opened the forwarded e-mail—Lula Belle's last. She looked at the date—October 6, 2009. A day after the one televised interview Brenna had done in the wake of the Neff case—on Faith's show, *Sunrise Manhattan. October 6. Tuesday . . . The clock radio is saying her name, waking her up with her own name, only it's a morning deejay voice saying it. Mickey in the Morning—only voice obnoxious enough to get Brenna out of bed, and so she knows she's awake, Mickey on her clock radio . . . Brenna blinks the sand out of her eyes, her the clock glowing 6:58 A.M. and her own name on the radio.* Must have misheard. *"Brenna Spector, that's her name, right?"* How does Mickey in the Morning know my name? Oh God, Faith's show. He knows it from Faith's show. *"The woman who re-members everything—including, uh, the occasional performance malfunction . . . Not like Mickey ever has those . . . heh heh heh . . ."* No, no, no . . . *"Five years later, and she's looking at you, thinking about that time when you . . ."*

She snapped the hair ties on her wrist. *Get out of my head, please, October 6. You are far too embarrassing.*

Brenna focused on the screen, the opened e-mail. At the top, Gary had listed the locations he could remember for the previous PO boxes. There were only three of them, as it turned out: Atlantic City; Portsmouth, Virginia; and Louisville, Kentucky. The Louisville one, the oldest, she'd used for a few months at the start of this year. *Odd*, Brenna thought. Not that Gary would remember only three of the PO boxes—but that they'd be the three most recent. Brenna picked up her phone quickly, called him on the disposable cell.

"Just a sec," Gary Freeman said, by way of answering. Brenna heard shuffling, Gary's muffled voice excusing himself, followed by a door closing. She let her gaze wander past the three addresses Gary had listed, to the last e-mail Lula Belle had sent him. The address she used was sweetpea81@hotmail.com. Cute. And worthless. No factual personal information was required to sign up for a Hotmail account.

"You're alone?" Gary whispered.

"Just for brevity's sake," Brenna said. "I'll always be alone when I call you. You don't need to ask."

He exhaled. "What's up?"

"I'm just curious about these PO box addresses."

"Why?"

"These are really the only ones you remember?"

"I'm sorry, Ms. Spector." He laughed a little. "We don't all have your memory."

"Oh, I know that," she said. "It's just that, in my own experience, everyone's most likely to remember their first time."

"Excuse me?"

"Your first date, your first concert, your first time hearing 'I love you.' The first time you met. People usually remember firsts more than, say, ninths, tenths, and elevenths."

"I still don't understand."

"I'd think you'd remember the first PO box."

"Hmmm . . ." he said. "That's a good point. I guess maybe I blocked it, but let me think . . ." Gary kept talking, but Brenna didn't hear him. She was reading the content of Lula Belle's final e-mail. It was, as Gary had described, just one line. No greeting, no signoff. Just PO box and a location. Brenna stared at it, her jaw going tight.

Gary was saying, "For the life of me, I can't seem to remember—"

"This forwarded e-mail," Brenna interrupted. "This was the last e-mail you received from her. The last PO box she was at?" She wished, more than anything, she could get her voice to stop trembling.

"Yes," Gary said. "Is something wrong?"

"The check you sent there—to that . . . that location. Was it ever cashed?"

"No," he said slowly. "Does the location mean something?"

Brenna cleared her throat. "Probably not to the case," she said. But if he really had read Lieberman's book, then Gary had to know it meant something to *her*. The PO box was in City Island, New York— Brenna's childhood home.

5

In Brenna's dream, her father was crying at a traffic light on City Island Boulevard, head pressed against the wheel. Horns blared all around them and Brenna was staring up at the light, fear racing up her back, through her hair. *"Move it, asshole!"* someone shouted. It sounded as if he were in the car with them—this stranger yelling swearwords at her father, hating her father, her father who was sobbing at the wheel, his back shaking. Brenna wanted to scream. She wanted to tell her dad to close the windows, lock the doors so that person couldn't come in. But she couldn't talk. Why was Dad crying? She'd never seen him cry before. Was it something she'd said? What had she said? How had she gotten here, back in City Island, back in the Land Shark with the sun streaming through the windows and her dad here with her, her dad crying.

She felt a hand over hers. She squeezed it. *Clea*. Clea's hand. Clea's calm voice. *"Daddy, the light is green."*

"Clea!" Brenna gasped herself awake, but still she heard her talking—the same voice, Clea's voice. Clea in the room with her, a young girl talking . . . "and Mama didn't want me to keep a diary, but I told her that Anne Frank kept a diary when she was in hiding . . ."

Not Clea. Lula Belle. On Brenna's computer screen twisted into a backbend, Lula Belle, her long legs spread very wide, her fluffy head thrown back. "Anne Frank named her diary Kitty, and she loved Kitty very much . . ."

Brenna had fallen asleep at her desk, watching the downloads Gary had sent.

" 'You're not in hiding, Lula Belle,' Mama said. But she knew I was. I was hiding from the world, hiding from her."

Brenna had been watching them for hours, in chronological order. She was currently in the middle of month nineteen—there were twenty-three months in all, around a hundred downloads—and as obsessed as Gary and Trent and Errol may have been with the idea of some faceless albeit extremely flexible woman revealing her so-called innermost secrets, Brenna wasn't feeling it.

On the contrary, she'd rather snort bug spray than hear Lula Belle say one more word about herself. Couldn't she talk about anything else? Politics? The weather? Chocolate-chip cookie recipes? Hell, anything would have been a welcome change from this overwrought pseudo-Tennessee Williams monologue Brenna had been slogging through for the past five hours—all of it meaningless, but for the cheesy music of the words.

"I want my Kitty, Mama. Let me have a Kitty of my own . . ."

"I got your Kitty right here," Brenna muttered.

She clicked off the download and gloried, for a few moments, in the hum of the radiator, the street noise beyond, the absence in her New York apartment of sugary Southern accent.

Honestly, Brenna was beginning to think the cement mixer song—like Lula Belle's decision to make City Island the home of her final PO box—was just a bizarre coincidence. Maybe Brenna's father hadn't made up the song after all. Maybe it was just something he'd heard once or twice on the radio, and Lula Belle had heard the same song and created a story to go around it. Because she *was* creating these stories out of thin air, Brenna was certain. The inconsistencies gave her away. In the early downloads, for instance, Lula talked about spending her "whole entire life locked indoors, seeing nothing." But in the later downloads, she waxed on about ocean waves and saltwater air, feeling the sand between her toes as a little girl—and this was just one small example. She loved and missed her father; then she didn't. He had shot himself in the head; then he had simply left home. She took her first lover at fourteen. She was a virgin until she was eighteen and met "the boy on the road"—whom she refused to call by name but prattled on about nearly as much as her sadistic mama. If Gary Freeman honestly believed Lula Belle was baring her true soul to him, then it had to be due to large amounts of blood rushing away from his brain to elsewhere in his anatomy.

Brenna's computer made a beeping sound—an instant message coming in. She felt a slight surge in her pulse, the dimmest spark of the most misguided type of hope.

Jim.

There had been a time, not too long ago, when she and her ex-husband would instant message for hours, every night. She'd loved it.

Brenna hadn't seen Jim in years because she couldn't handle the onslaught of memories that came from looking into his eyes or hearing his voice or feeling the heat he emitted—Jim, *alive and in the room with her.* It was too powerful—and not for the bad memories, either. No, it had always been the good times that made Brenna die a little inside when she recalled them, and that wasn't fair to anyone—not to Jim, or his wife, Faith, or for that matter, Brenna herself.

The instant messaging, on the other hand . . . That was just words on a screen, and it had been different. Jim and Brenna were both bad sleepers and so they'd talk, late into the night, about their jobs, about the news, about Maya. They'd make each other laugh over old inside jokes and give each other advice and send each other links to new songs or movie clips on You-Tube. Nothing too heavy, nothing inappropriate. But every night, for close to a year, until it became something necessary. Weird as it might sound, it had been about as deep and fulfilling a friendship as she'd ever had—until Jim had decided that this time, he was the one who couldn't handle it. Their relationship had become *too* necessary, he explained. And he cut things off. Brenna understood. Of course she did. But at the same time, she could remember it all—every joke and piece of advice and warm recollection and movie clip, every word from Jim that had ever appeared on her screen.

She missed him so much.

Brenna clicked on her online icon. Her breathing slowed. The instant message was from Kate O'Hanlon, her old friend—if you used the word "friend" very loosely. **Got some info on the City Island box**, it read.

Kate worked at the New York Postal Inspector's

Office, and Brenna had e-mailed her asking for her help in finding who the box was registered to, just after speaking with Gary Freeman.

Brenna typed, **And?**

Breakfast. Tomorrow. Artie's.

Brenna sighed. Always the quid pro quo with Kate—and always with a meal included. **Fine**, Brenna typed. **8 A.M.**

7:30.

Brenna grimaced. **Okey dokey!**

She started to go back to the Lula Belle downloads, but that only made her remember that dream again—that strange dream with her father sobbing against the steering wheel. God, Brenna hated seeing men cry. She couldn't stomach it, never could, and never quite understood why . . .

Let's give the downloads a rest.

Brenna went back online. She called up Google, fully intending to do another search on Lula Belle—see if, this time around, it turned up anything other than a marker for her now-defunct Web site, bed and breakfasts, and lost animal postings (turned out Lula Belle was a surprisingly popular name for English bulldogs).

But instead, Brenna clicked on Google Images, her fingers typing in "Jim Rappaport" as if they were powered by something other than Brenna's mind. A dozen pictures popped up, and again with her brain telling her to stop, Brenna was modifying her search, adding "Christmas 1998."

She saw the picture, up in the right corner of the screen—Jim and herself, young and smiling—in front of the tree at the Helmsley Palace, where Jim's paper, the *Trumpet*, had its holiday party that year. The picture was in the *Trumpet*'s archives, and of course, she knew the caption without having to read it—*Senior reporter Jim Rappaport and his wife, Brenna, left their toddler with a sitter to share in the seasonal fun.*

Step away from the computer, Brenna told herself. But she was enlarging the photo and staring into it, into the evening of Saturday, December 19, 1998. She felt the strapless red velvet dress against her skin—bought four days prior at the Dizzy's on Nineteenth and Fifth. And she let herself lapse into the memory, knowing she shouldn't, aching even as she did . . . *The draft in the hotel ballroom chills her back. Goosebumps. Jim's hand on her bare shoulder, and through the speaker system, Brenna hears Etta James singing "White Christmas." Brenna's had two glasses of champagne and nothing to eat and her head swims a little. They're standing right next to the tree—an enormous pine, and Brenna is focusing on a snowflake ornament—white ceramic with sparkles mixed in. It reminds her of something, something from childhood, something comforting and warm she can't quite specify. . .*

"Brenna?" Jim's fingers move across her shoulder blades, and she turns to him. "You okay?"

She gazes into his eyes—brown with gold flecks. She is inches away from him. She can feel his breath . . . "If you're remembering something, tell me, okay? I can help you. I always want to help you . . ."

Brenna's buzzer sounded, and she was back, tears in her eyes, alone. Longing. Why had she done that? Why did she do these things to herself?

Again, the buzzer. "Oh no." Brenna recalled the awkward phone message she'd left five hours ago, word for word. She swatted the tears from her eyes, cleared her throat, went for the buzzer. "Yes?"

"Nicholas Morasco to see Brenna Spector."

A wave of guilt washed through Brenna—*Sorry if I kept you waiting. I was busy crying over someone I don't know anymore.*

She shook it off, pushed the button. "Shouldn't that be Senior Detective Nicholas Morasco?"

"Nah. We're watching porn, I'm off duty."

Brenna smiled, hit the buzzer.

She listened to Morasco's footfalls jogging up the stairs and opened the door before he knocked.

She warmed at the sight of him, standing in the doorjamb with his messed hair and his wire-rimmed glasses, his late-day beard scruff, and his inevitable tweed jacket and jeans combination, all of it working on him for some reason—that rumpled, professorial look. She still couldn't believe he was a cop. "It isn't porn you know," she said. "It's performance art."

"Right . . . I'm definitely gonna need a drink, then."

She grabbed a couple of beers from the refrigerator—a nice Brooklyn IPA that Faith had brought by a week ago—and walked Nick over to the couch. They drank, he talked about his uneventful day at work, and she asked him about the new chief of police in Tarry Ridge—a decent guy, according to Nick (though a second choice, Brenna knew. Nick had turned down the job himself).

Then, she filled him in on everything that had happened over the course of the day—everything, that is, except for her conversation with Gary Freeman. By the time she was through, she was feeling like herself again.

"Errol Ludlow, huh?" said Morasco. "No wonder there's porn involved."

Brenna nodded. She hated lying to him. Of course, this wasn't lying, right? She'd just left out the part about Errol getting fired.

Morasco was staring at her in such a way, though, she had to avert her gaze. He had the type of dark eyes that seemed to see right into your thoughts. Brenna knew that it was largely due to myopia, but still . . .

Brenna got her laptop from her desk, flipped it open on the coffee table, and settled in next to Morasco. "You ready for a little performance art?"

He gave her a half smile. "I'd be lying if I said I didn't wish that was a euphemism."

Brenna felt her face color a little. "Me too," she said, before she noticed how Morasco was looking at the screen—the picture from Jim's Christmas party filling it.

Brenna minimized the picture.

"Pretty dress," he said.

"It's old." She took a very long swallow of her beer, recalling Ludlow, of all people. Ludlow, sitting across from her at the Waverly Diner at 9:45 A.M., watching her with that knowing smirk she wanted to slap off of his face. *Yes, and how is Detective Morasco? Page Six spotted you two at some bar . . . which one was it?*

Ludlow, "knowing" Ludlow, who in reality knew nothing other than what he read in the papers, who had no idea that Brenna and Morasco had kissed only once, on November 9 at 12:45 P.M., in the parking lot of a bar that was never written up in Page Six, and if Ludlow had only seen the look in Morasco's eyes when she pulled away . . . No, that was wrong. Brenna's memory couldn't tell a lie, even a white one. It had been Nick who'd pulled away.

Brenna gritted her teeth. *Don't go there, not now.*

"Lula Belle," Morasco was saying now. "Sounds like a cartoon cow from a milk commercial."

Brenna laughed. "Wait till you see her." She called up the next download and hit play. At the start of it,

Lula Belle was standing, arms and legs akimbo, backlit as ever so that the edges of her hair glowed, halolike.

Morasco frowned at the screen, but within moments, Lula Belle turned to the side and arched her back. Then she slipped into the splits, touching her toes to the crown of her head. "I'm open to you."

"Oh my," he said.

The silhouette rolled onto her back, raised a delicate hand to her brow. "So please, my sweet . . . be open to me."

Morasco moved closer. The screen flickered in his eyes.

"Still thinking about cartoon cows?" said Brenna.

"Uh, no."

She smiled at him. "Didn't think so."

"When I was seven years old," Lula Belle said, "I found a little bird that had fallen out of its nest. I knew Mama wouldn't let me have it, for she believed all animals to be crawling with disease. And so I took a shoe box, and I filled it with warm, soft things—cotton balls, scraps of fabric, even a white cashmere glove my grandma had left behind during her last visit."

"She knows the color of the glove." Morasco took a swallow of his beer. "She has a good memory."

"A good *imagination*," said Brenna. "And just so you know, she says 'Mama' so much you could build a drinking game around it."

He snorted, though his gaze stayed on the screen.

"I put that little bird in that shoe box and hid him in my room under my bed. I found an eyedropper in the medicine cabinet, and I fed him sugar water with such tenderness as to make him trust me." She took a trembling breath. "If Mama were to see me, she'd have been amazed. She thought I was crazy like my daddy. She thought I couldn't take care of nothin' without breakin' it. Mama said that gift for destruction ran through my veins."

"Mama," said Brenna. She raised the glass to her lips, and smiled at Morasco.

He didn't smile back, didn't drink. He set his bottle down on the coffee table and leaned forward, and his expression changed, deepened into something Brenna couldn't quite figure out. It wasn't the rapt, obvious lust with which Trent had watched Lula Belle. Sure, she supposed he could have been turned on and trying to hide it from her, but it seemed to Brenna more of a sadness.

Lula Belle said, "I kept thinking, if I was the reason why that little bird lived . . . then I must have also been the reason why he died. Right?"

Morasco swallowed hard. He closed his eyes.

Brenna clicked off the download. "Powerful stuff, this performance art."

"It is."

"Nick?"

He looked at her.

She knew she had no right to ask, not when she couldn't stand in a parking lot with him for five minutes without lapsing into a memory she couldn't talk about. She knew it wasn't fair, but she put her hand on his, and she asked him anyway. "When you watched that video, what were you thinking?"

Her cell phone beeped out Morse code—the tone she'd chosen for text messages: SOS. "That might be Maya," she said, but the text was from Trent.

At fish market. No sign of Persie. ☹ Hope U R getting luckier on your porn date.

She exhaled. "Trent is looking for a lost cat," she said, her voice trailing off once she caught Morasco's gaze.

"Brenna," he said softly. "It moved."

Brenna blinked. "Excuse me?"

"You asked me what I was thinking about."

"And?"

"During that download. It moved."

"Uh . . ."

"Do you know what I'm saying?"

"I . . . um . . . I think so."

His mouth twitched into a grin. "The *camera*, Brenna."

"Oh . . . Oh, because . . . Wait. *What?*"

"That last bit. When she rolled over onto her side. The angle changed a little—it tilted up."

"You're saying . . ."

"Yes."

"You're saying there was someone else in the room with her. Someone behind the camera."

He looked at her. "There has to be," he said. "Right?"

Brenna moved the cursor back to the middle of the download, muting it before she hit play again.

They watched in silence for several seconds.

"There," Morasco said. "It's at 4:31."

Brenna brought the cursor back, and watched again. And this time, she saw it—a slight change of camera angle; an adjustment. "You are so observant."

"That's why they pay me the big bucks."

A cameraman. Someone in the room. Someone who knows what's behind that shadow—her real name and her age and her height and weight and hair color and maybe even the family she came from . . .

Someone who may have made her disappear.

Morasco was still grinning at her. "So . . ."

"So . . . what?"

"When I said, 'It moved,' what did you think I was talking about?"

Brenna stifled a smile. "Grow up, please."

"I'm not the one with the dirty mind."

"God, it's like I'm talking to Trent."

"I'm just trying to work through your issues."

"Is that a euphemism?"

"You need another beer." He raised an eyebrow at her. "Among other things."

She clicked off the computer and let him get her one, glad for the company and the dumb jokes and the blank screen. And even though she knew that it hadn't been camera movement that Morasco had been thinking about when he gazed at Lula Belle with such sorrow, such ache, she was glad, too, to be able to act as though she didn't.

After Morasco left, Brenna pressed her face against the door, listening to his footfalls until she could no longer hear them. "The camera moved," she whispered. Then she let herself remember that night in O'Donnell's parking lot, start to finish.

"I'm sorry, Nick," she whispered, once she pulled herself out of it. "I'm so sorry."

It wasn't until later, when Brenna was getting ready for bed, that she was struck by yet another memory from her early childhood—soft-focused and murky and close to forgotten: her dad's large hand, cupped around a tiny baby bird, placing him in a shoe box filled with soft cotton. And his voice, warm and gentle. *Put your finger on his chest, pumpkin. You can feel his heartbeat.*

6

"Okay, wait, wait, back up a second," Kate O'Hanlon said around a mouthful of whitefish salad. "What was I wearing?"

Brenna put down her coffee cup. "I already told you what you were wearing."

"Tell me again."

She sighed. *Always the quid pro quo . . .* "Red leotard, black bolero jacket with Michael Jackson–inspired epaulets, denim cheerleader skirt."

"Was the skirt flouncy?"

"Very flouncy."

"What about the shoes?"

"I didn't notice your shoes, Kate."

"How could you not notice my shoes?" Kate took another bite of her bagel, Brenna thinking, *When was the last time you could even* see *your shoes?*

Not very nice, but come on. Kate had gained a significant amount of weight since their last breakfast and information exchange (November 12, 2008. Elephant and Castle. Cinnamon pancakes, bacon, sausage, whole wheat toast and butter)—and she'd easily been three hundred pounds back then.

Not that Brenna cared. It was Kate's body, and she could do what she wanted with it—though Brenna did hope, if this was the way the woman always ate, that Kate was at least on Lipitor. The misleadingly named "fish plate" she was demolishing right now, for instance. The cream cheese portion alone should have come with a complimentary stent.

Thinking about how Kate's arteries must feel made Brenna tired. And that wasn't the only exhausting thing about these breakfasts, invaluable as they were to both Brenna—who'd needed information from the New York Postal Inspector's office on several occasions—and Kate O'Hanlon (née Katie Johnson, reigning queen bitch of City Island Elementary School) for far more personal reasons.

When Brenna had arrived here at Artie's Deli in Battery Park, at 7:30 A.M., Kate had looked up at her from a massive mug of whipped cream–drowned hot chocolate, smiling as if she'd been adrift at sea for months and Brenna was a Carnival Cruise ship. "Tell me what Kurt McKenna said about me at the Eighth Grade Spring Fling," she'd said. Not so much as a *Hello, how has the last year been treating you?* Or even a *Why do you want information about this City Island PO box?* Nothing. Which Brenna was fine with. The less information she had to give the likes of Kate, the better off they both were.

"Sorry I didn't notice the shoes," Brenna said now. "But believe me, Kurt McKenna wasn't looking at them, either."

"Whoa, whoa . . . slow down," Kate said. "Now where was Kurt standing exactly? And what was I doing? What song was playing?"

"'Maneater' by Hall & Oates."

"I loved that song!"

"Figures."

"Very funny." Kate said. "Go on."

"You were dancing with Steve Barkley."

"Who?"

"Steve Barkley. Pierced ear. Spiky hair. Used to beat up Marcus Bladenschweiler every day after school?"

Kate gave her a blank look.

Brenna sighed. "Red Converse high-tops."

"Oh, right! So where was Kurt?"

"Right behind me—at the punchbowl. He was talking to Dave Brinkman while their girlfriends were in the bathroom."

Kate's eyes glinted. "While the cat's away . . ."

"You said it." Brenna stifled a yawn. "So Steve spun you around and I guess your skirt flew up a little and—"

"Could you see anything?"

"I wasn't really paying full attention to your skirt, Kate."

"Okay, okay. So then what happened?"

"Dave says, 'Did you see that? Katie Johnson is so fine.' And then Kurt turns to him and goes, 'I'd torture my grandma's poodle, just for five minutes alone with that ass.'"

Kate smiled, her face warming and coloring—the remembered pleasure of being wanted that badly. "Kurt was going with Sally Kinkaid back then, wasn't he?"

Brenna shook her head. "Mimi Richardson. She was in the bathroom when he said it, and when she came back, he kind of smirked at Dave, like, *Don't say a word*."

"He really smirked?"

"Yep."

"And Mimi didn't notice."

"It was his and Dave's little secret."

She closed her eyes, savoring the moment. "Thank you."

Brenna took a sip of her coffee, waited a few seconds before she asked. "So do you have the PO box info for me?"

"Yep." She took a piece of paper out of her purse, slid it across the table. "Of course I don't need to remind you that you have no idea where you got this name and address."

Brenna nodded, staring at Kate's neat handwriting on the paper—the name: Robin Tannenbaum, followed by an address not in City Island, but in Forest Hills, Queens.

Hello, Lula Belle. . .

Had it really been this easy? All that mystery, all that questioning and obsessing by all those men who knew her only as a shadow, and this was where it led? To a name as prosaic as Robin Tannenbaum? To a suburban New York neighborhood, just forty minutes away from where Brenna was sitting right now? She almost felt bad about taking Gary Freeman's money, considering the small amount of work she'd had to do. Of course, the question still nagged at her . . .

If Lula Belle or Robin or whatever her name was lived in Queens, why did she take a PO box twenty miles away—in the small, water-locked town where Brenna had grown up?

And the name. Robin. Like a broken little bird. . .

Kate said, "I wish I was you sometimes."

Brenna looked at her.

"I mean . . . The other day, I was looking through some old photo albums. I saw this one—I must have been around fifteen. I was in a string bikini at the town pool and I was sitting with this boy. He had this gorgeous strawberry blond hair and he was looking at me like I was the center of the world . . . But for the life of me, I couldn't remember his name."

"There are good memories and bad memories, Kate," Brenna said. "I don't get to choose."

Kate struggled up to her feet, exhaling hard. "Maybe I just wish I was young again."

Brenna heard whispering. It was a couple at the next table, both of them in oversized sweaters and skinny jeans, the Calvin Klein model of a girl staring up at Kate as though she was something that the waitstaff needed to sweep up, as soon as possible.

Back in the eighth grade, Brenna had seen Katie give that same look to so many lesser creatures in their class. But though some might call it karma, Brenna hated people who believed life worked that way—everyone getting what they deserve.

Brenna glared at the girl until she turned away. Then she handed Kate her coat. "Bret Masterson," she said.

"Huh?"

"The strawberry blond. That was his name. He was the lifeguard at the community pool and he was nuts about you."

Kate's face lit up. "Right!" she said. "Thank you."

Brenna followed Kate out the door, thinking about Robin Tannenbaum and what the next step would be, but at the same time, remembering August 23, 1983, at the neighborhood pool, the smell of chlorine and warm concrete and coconut oil, opening the gate, her eyes searching for her friends Carly and Becky . . . *and at the corner of her vision, the diving board where Katie Johnson sits, curled into Bret Masterson, her head resting on his strong shoulder as if it belongs there always. To be her, Brenna thinks.* To be Katie Johnson. Just for one day.

"Do I look okay?" Trent asked Brenna as they cruised up Robin Tannenbaum's tree-lined street in Forest Hills in search of a parking space.

The question—like so many of the strings of words that flew out of Trent's mouth on a daily basis—annoyed Brenna for a number of reasons. For one thing, this was the third time they'd driven past Robin's apartment building, and if he'd been paying half as much attention to available parking spaces as he was to his own reflection in the rearview, they might have been at her door at this very moment. For another, the way Trent looked *never* fit Brenna's definition of okay—and he knew that. Right now, for instance, he was wearing ripped jeans and some kind of sleeveless cowboy shirt that was so tight, it looked as though he'd stolen it off the lead in a fourth grade production of *Oklahoma!*

"You look professional, yet elegant," Brenna said. "Very James Bond."

His eyes brightened. "Really?"

"No. Park the car."

"Come on. I'm serious."

Brenna looked at him. "You do realize that this is a business call," she said. "Not a blind date."

"I'm asking you how I look for business reasons."

"Trent, if you don't stop obsessing over your looks, put your eyes back on the curb, and find a parking space in ten seconds, I'm jumping out of the car."

He turned to her, his expression serious. "Listen. I know why you took me along today."

"My car's in the shop. I needed a ride."

He shook his head. "You took me along for protection. But also . . . more importantly . . ."

"What?"

"Eye candy."

"Oh for godsakes. *Park the freakin' car.*"

"It's okay. I understand, you need me for this. Given the right . . . uh . . . stimulating factor . . . Lula Belle will not hide from us. She will answer our questions, and come along with us willingly. Or *come* along with *me* at least. If you know what I'm sayin'. Get it?"

Brenna took a deep breath, Gary Freeman style. She'd been trying to ease up on the sarcasm with Trent today. It was nice of him to give her a ride here, on a Saturday when he wasn't required to do anything for her. And clearly, he'd had a late night at the fish market. He was only twenty-seven and lack of sleep usually didn't make a difference on his face, but when he'd shown up at Brenna's place this morning, he looked . . . well, thrashed. Like someone had gone at him with a defibrillator for about five or six hours. "I forgot to ask you," she said. "How'd you do last night?"

He grinned.

"At the fish market, Trent. Did you make any progress on Persephone?"

Trent's face fell a little. "No."

"I'm sorry."

"Me too," he said, his eyes going serious. For a few moments, he looked miles away.

"You okay, Trent?"

He blinked a few times. "Awesome."

"You don't look it."

"Thanks."

"I'm not trying to be insulting."

"I know." He smiled. "I'm just spent . . . you know . . . in a good way."

"Ah."

"See, I wound up drowning my troubles at this new club."

"Space."

"No. That closed I think. This place is called Bacon.

And speaking of sizzling deliciousness, I hooked up with the most outstanding piece of—"

"Space, Trent. Parking space."

"Huh?"

"Right there. If you miss it, I will personally torture you to death."

"Okay, okay." Trent pulled over and parallel parked his car—an unassuming 2003 Ford Taurus he'd inherited from his parents that fit in as well in this neighborhood as Trent himself did not. As they both slid out and into the cool air, Brenna said, "I'm glad you had fun last night."

"I don't know if I'd call it *fun*," Trent said. "I mean, that's kinda like calling the Grand Canyon a hole in the ground."

"Okay," Brenna said. "But it's work time now. Can I trust you to stay with me? Pay attention? Be here?"

He stopped walking and turned to her. "Brenna," he said. "I'm always here."

Brenna stared at him—the cowboy shirt unbuttoned to highlight the lipstick tat, the over-muscular, waxed arms, the jeans, artfully ripped mid-thigh—but with a face so honest, it negated the whole effect. She felt a lump in her throat, a sticking guilt, and she was back in her bedroom yesterday, her cell phone pressed to her ear, Gary Freeman's voice knifing through the plastic . . .

"*And you are to reveal my identity to no one.*"

"*Not even my assistant?*"

"*No one. As far as he's concerned, you're still working for Ludlow.*"

"It's like thirty degrees out, you know," Brenna said. "Do you even own a coat?"

"I don't need one. Know why?"

"Because you're so damn hot."

"You know me so well."

"Too well."

As they headed across the street to Robin Tannen-baum's apartment, Brenna held back a little, walking at his side. "You can trust me, too, you know."

"Duh." Trent gave her a sidelong glance, though, and she knew what he must have been thinking. After all, she'd said it as though she were trying to convince herself.

Robin Tannenbaum's apartment was like something out of a fairy tale—or a sci fi horror movie, Brenna wasn't quite sure.

It was a Tudor three-story walkup on a street that happened to be full of them. But it stood out from the others in that it was literally crawling with ivy. Brenna normally liked a little ivy on old buildings—she found it cozy and collegiate—but in this case it just seemed like a symptom of decay, the plant devouring the frail build-ing, pulling it back into the earth. Someone had put a wreath on the front door, a big, clumsy thing, dripping Christmas bells. But it only added to the feeling—the Ivy Monster's bejeweled sidekick.

Of course, that was probably just Brenna's paranoia talking. She was nervous—the same way she was ner-vous about anything or anyone she didn't remember and hadn't had a chance to research. Outside of Lula/ Robin's height and weight—which Trent had gleaned via his computer program—Brenna didn't know any-thing at all about the woman she'd been looking for. What good did it do her that Lula/Robin was most likely five-eight, 125 pounds when she had no idea how she used those proportions in her day-to-day life—not to mention what had made her stop making her videos two months ago, whether she still lived here . . . or whether she was alive at all.

Brenna normally tried to find out a little more about her subjects before confronting them directly. But this was a Saturday during Christmas break, and even if Kate had given her Robin's social—which she hadn't—she wouldn't be able to do much with it, at least until the weekend was through.

But if Brenna was going to be honest with herself, that wasn't why she'd called Trent at home on a Saturday and asked (*told?*) him to drive her here. If it were someone, anyone else, she would have waited. But Brenna had the oddest feeling about Robin Tannenbaum—a craving to see her, to put flesh to the shadow as soon as possible. It was a physical sensation—a pounding in her veins. Brenna couldn't put it into words, though. Not yet. It would hurt too much if she were wrong.

"What a sweet little bird, Daddy. Can we fix him?"

To the right of the front door were three slotted mailboxes, each with a buzzer. She turned to the one marked 2 and when she saw the name on it—TANNENBAUM—her pulse clicked faster.

"I'll take care of him, Daddy. I'll keep him in a shoe box and I'll feed him every day. Brenna can help . . ."

Brenna pushed the thought away, reached for the buzzer.

"Question," Trent said.

"Yeah?"

"If Lula Belle answers the door, what the hell are you going to tell her?"

"The truth."

Trent sighed.

She pressed on the buzzer. Waited.

"Yes?" A woman's voice.

Brenna took a breath. "Ms. Tannenbaum?"

"Yes?"

"She doesn't sound Southern," said Trent.

Brenna gave him a sharp look. "Sssh."

"Who is this, please?" said the voice, which . . . well, Trent was right. No Southern accent to speak of. Not all that sexy, either.

Was it familiar, though, in any way? "My name is Brenna Spector," she said. "I'm a private investigator."

No response.

Brenna closed her eyes. "Ms. Tannenbaum? May I come in?"

Nothing.

Trent said, "I knew the truth was a dumb idea."

Brenna stepped away from the buzzer. "I thought . . . I thought she might want to see me."

Trent frowned at her. "Why?"

"No reason."

But then the front door buzzer was going off and the voice was back, brighter. "I know you," the voice said.

"How would she know you?" Trent whispered, too loudly, as they stood outside the door to Robin Tannenbaum's apartment.

Brenna shrugged, the feeling growing, the wild hope, and for half a second, she allowed herself to think it. *Lula Belle. Robin. Clea.*

Then the door opened.

"Whoa," Trent said.

There stood a tiny, elderly woman in a pink terry cloth robe, carrot orange wig, and thick cat's-eye glasses. She couldn't have been more than four-foot-ten, and she was suffering from severe osteoporosis.

Her humped back gave her a supplicant look, as if she were continuously bowing.

"Ms. Tannenbaum?" Brenna said.

"Yes."

Trent said, "Do you have a daughter?"

"Excuse me?"

"Granddaughter?"

Brenna cleared her throat, held out a hand. "Nice to meet you, Mrs. Tannenbaum. I'm—"

"Brenna Spector, yes. I know you." The old woman smiled, revealing false teeth that were very white and much too big for her mouth. "I've read about you in the papers. You're the Head-Case Hero."

Brenna sighed. "Yes."

"And I'm her studly young ward."

"Excuse me?"

"Trent LaSalle. My associate. Please forgive him, he can't help it."

She gave Brenna a perplexed smile. "Of course. Come in, please."

She ushered Brenna and Trent into the apartment—which felt surprisingly cramped for a floor-through. It was the furniture's fault. Piles of dark wood with polished brass handles and thick, clawed legs . . . it seemed to strain against the delicacy of the pink rug, the needlepoint pillows, the gilded frames on the faded photos . . .

It was the photos that interested Brenna.

"Make yourselves comfortable," Mrs. Tannenbaum said. "I'll get some tea and cookies."

Trent sat down on the couch—a brown leather beast that snapped at the backs of his bare arms. "I'm sorry," he said. "But silhouetted or not, there isn't a version of Aftereffects on the freakin' planet that would make *that lady* look like—"

"Sssh."

"Well, it's true, dude."

"Don't call me dude." Brenna moved over to the window. In front of it stood the enormous credenza, which housed all the photos. "She never answered your question, you know," Brenna said as she peered at the pictures, "about having a daughter."

She heard bustling in behind her, the clinking of plates, Trent saying, "That looks delicious, ma'am."

"Oh, it's just a Bundt cake. Would you like a slice, Ms. Spector?"

"No thank you," said Brenna. But she didn't turn around. She was staring at the photos on the credenza—all of which seemed to be of the same chubby-faced boy. There were several black and white baby pictures, a christening shot, another at seven in a Little League uniform and yet another, nervous-looking in a swimsuit, next to a scowling man that had to be his father—he must have been around ten for that one. There was a teenage photo of the boy, tall and pimpled, with a metallic grin. He was wearing a pale blue tux, holding a corsage box, but he was alone—no date to wear the corsage. It was very faded. Even if you overlooked how outdated the tux and the hairstyle were, you'd have to figure it was at least twenty-five years old.

"That's my son." Mrs. Tannenbaum said it over Brenna's shoulder—though technically, tiny as she was, she was more at her waist.

Brenna turned around. "He looks like a nice person," she said. "Is he your only child, Mrs. Tannenbaum?"

She swallowed hard, her eyes watering. "You'd probably like a more recent picture."

"Excuse me?"

"Oh. I'm sorry . . . I . . . I thought . . ."

"Yes?"

"Well . . . being a private investigator and all," she said, "I was hoping maybe you'd come to tell me where he went. My goodness, some things sound so silly when you say them out loud."

"Where he went?"

She nodded slowly. "He was living here with me for a while but . . ."

"Yes?"

"I haven't seen my Robbie in a long time."

Brenna's eyes widened. "Robbie."

"Yes?"

"Is his full name Robin?"

"Yes."

"*Robin is a dude!*"

"Pardon me, Mr. LaSalle?"

Brenna said, "How long has your son been missing, ma'am?"

"Over two months?" She looked at Brenna, the same way a child would do, waiting to see if she'd answered a teacher correctly. "He comes and goes quite a bit, so I didn't really think much of it at first. He'd been here with me for about a year and a half—he was in California before that. But this is the longest he's gone without calling."

"Two months."

She nodded. "Robbie's a grown man, of course. He can do what he wants. But I do wish he'd pick up a phone."

"How old is he?"

"Forty-five." She looked a little surprised at the sound of it. "Forty-five. My word." She sighed. "Could I go to the police, and report a forty-five-year-old man missing because he didn't call his mother?"

Trent said, "Did he ever mention anything about a Web site?"

Her gaze shifted to the pink rug. "I'm not sure. I know he does some . . . some professional work on his computer."

"Any video work?" said Trent, and Brenna's mind went to Morasco last night, watching Lula Belle, noticing the shift in camera angle.

"He did go to film school. But I . . . wouldn't know about work."

"Did you see equipment in his room at all? Cameras or lights?" Brenna said.

"I didn't go into Robbie's room much."

"Why not?"

In the kitchen, the phone rang. "I'd better get that." She hurried into the other room as if she'd been waiting for the call her whole life. Brenna listened to her muffled voice. "Oh, hello Mr. Pokrovsky. No, no, I'm fine . . ."

Brenna looked at Trent. "What's her deal with him?" she whispered.

"Mr. Pokrovsky?"

Brenna rolled her eyes. "No, Trent. Not Mr. Pokrovsky. Her *son.*"

"Yes, Mr. Pokrovsky, I know them. They're friends of Robbie's . . . No, no of course. Thank you for your concern."

She came back in the room. "Sorry about that. I don't get visitors very often. The neighbors worry."

"Mrs. Tannenbaum," Brenna said. "Why don't you go into Robbie's room?"

She adjusted her bright wig and kept watching the floor. Brenna followed her gaze and found herself staring at Mrs. Tannenbaum's feet—tiny as a child's in fuzzy white slippers, varicose veins wrapped around her weak ankles like the ivy on the side of the house.

"What does Robbie do in there?"

"When my husband was alive," she said, finally, "I found a stack of *Playboys*."

Trent said, "Uh . . ."

"Where did you find them?"

Her gaze lifted until she found Brenna's face. "I found them at the bottom of his closet, under some newspapers—a few dozen of them, including the Marilyn Monroe issue. It was funny to me, because Walter always called those magazines smut, yet here he was with his own secret collection. For weeks, I wondered how I would bring it up with him, until one morning, it came to me. I didn't need to bring it up at all. I could forget I ever saw them. I could let him have his secret. We all have secrets, don't we, Ms. Spector?" She gave her a pleading look.

"Yes," Brenna said. "Of course we do."

"And that one . . ." She exhaled. "Well, it was harmless. More embarrassing than anything else, what with Walter's high moral standards."

Brenna nodded.

"I never let him know I'd seen them." Her eyelashes fluttered behind the glasses. "The day after he died, I threw them out. It was as if they never existed at all."

Trent looked at Brenna. *WTF?* he mouthed.

But Brenna understood. "Mrs. Tannenbaum."

"We don't need to be so formal, do we? You can call me Hildy if you like."

"Robbie has his secrets, too, doesn't he, Hildy?"

Her gazed dropped again. "Yes," she said quietly.

"And do those secrets involve the computer?"

Very slowly, she shook her head.

"I know you might think of this as a betrayal, ma'am. But we're looking for a missing woman. She was on the computer—she made videos and streamed them and sold them to people." Brenna's gaze drilled into hers. "To collect her payments, she used a series of post office boxes. The last one was registered under Robbie's name."

Hildy Tannenbaum's eyes went big. "No. It's some mistake. I don't know what you're talking about."

"You do," Brenna said. "I'm so sorry, but making yourself forget something doesn't make it go away. It's like turning away from an accident. Whether you look at it or not, someone is still getting hurt."

"You're calling me a liar, and I resent that."

"Mrs. Tannenbaum. Hildy. That woman wasn't a stack of *Playboys*. She was connected to many people, and then she disappeared." Brenna took a step closer to her. She stared into her eyes. "She disappeared two months ago—the same time as Robbie."

"Oh my God."

"If you help us, we might be able to find them both."

Hildy removed her cat's-eye glasses. The effort of that small gesture seemed to sap all the remaining energy out of her, and when she put the glasses back on and looked at Brenna, her eyes were bright with pain. "The woman," she said. "The one from the computer."

"Yes?"

"Does she have a Southern accent?"

7

"Focus on your legs," Yasmine, the yoga instructor, said. As always, she began to list all the major leg muscles, describing in her honeyed voice how they were sinking into the earth one at a time—the soleus and the gastrocnemius and the tibialis anterior—each one glowing warm with red chakra energy.

Jill Freeman usually loved this part of her yoga class—shevasana, or corpse pose, it was called, and it was the last pose of the hour. Such a soothing ten minutes: You lie on your back, perfectly still, the lights low, your body and mind cleared of tension, nothing in your world but Yasmine's voice, and those lovely Latin words. Yasmine had been working here for five weeks and she was so intelligent, a med student on leave. The studio was lucky to have her. Sometimes, Jill even fell asleep during Yasmine's shevasana—her voice was that soothing. But today sleep wasn't even a possibility.

Two weeks. Back in grade school, Sister Mary Eunice had said, *With the possible exception of water, anyone should be able to do without anything for two weeks.* Easy to say when you're talking to a bunch of ten-year-old girls who couldn't imagine being deprived of anything more essential than Bonne Bell Lip Smacker or peanut M&M's.

Easy to say, Sister Mary Eunice, when you're a nun.

"Focus on your abdominal muscles—the iliac crest, the umbilicus, the rectus sheath . . . feel them melting into the ground, glowing orange with creativity, joy, sensual pleasure . . ."

Jill wanted to jump out of her skin. *Get it together. Deep breath in, deep breath out* . . . Really, for most couples married twenty years, two weeks without sex wasn't that big a deal. Her friend Cathy, for instance . . . Why, just the other day over coffee at Starbucks, Cathy had mentioned, oh-so-casually, that she and Alex hadn't "done the deed" for three months. Three entire months—and that was fine by Cathy. It was a relief, she'd insisted, considering how demanding Alex used to be before he went on antidepressants. "I can read in bed, now," Cathy had said, as if reading in bed were some wondrous thing. "I don't have to shave my legs every day."

Three weeks ago, Jill might have felt sorry for her. But now . . . Now, she was feeling sorry for herself.

Jill's husband, Gary, had always been great in bed—tender and sweet when you wanted him to be, passionate and forceful when you didn't. In three years of dating and twenty years of marriage, Jill could probably use the fingers on one hand to count the times she wasn't in the mood when Gary was—and it would have been because of the flu, or maybe the last few days of pregnancy. It would have been for real reasons.

"Focus on the muscles that make up the chest—the pectoralis major and minor. Feel them sinking, warming your heart . . ."

When they first got together, Gary's friends would

tease him about how unworthy he was of her. They'd compare the two of them to Billy Joel and Christie Brinkley, speculate that maybe Jill was an actress Gary had hired to make himself look more successful. This because Jill had been a swimsuit model—two inches taller than Gary and nearly ten years younger, while Gary was short, stocky, and rough around the edges, a transplant from the East with dark, knowing eyes. *Dude, what does she see in you,* Gary's best man Chris Curtis had joked during his wedding toast—Chris no great catch himself. *What is your secret?*

But even back then, even as a blushing bride of twenty-two who'd so recently put her Catholic school days behind her, even then Jill had locked eyes with her groom over her glass of champagne and grinned in such a way, the nuns would have slapped her. *If only you knew, Chris Curtis. . .*

But these last two weeks . . . Actually, if she was going to be honest, it had been going on for months. Not the lack of sex—that would've killed her. The distance. Lying in bed together, sitting next to each other in the bleachers for Hannah's soccer game or Tessa's cheerleading or Lucy's gymnastics meet, during silences at the breakfast table or at night on the couch while they were watching TV, Jill would get the odd sense that something was going on inside Gary's brain—something she'd never known about and never would.

What is your secret?

"Focus on your neck—the levator scapulae, the trapezius muscle, which fuses to the deltoid . . ."

Last night, Jill had woken up from a fitful sleep. She'd reached out for Gary and felt nothing. It was four in the morning, and she was alone.

"The muscles in your neck are glowing green with a healing light."

Jill had left the bedroom and moved down the hall, tiptoeing so as not to wake the girls, her feet barely landing on the wood floors. *Midnight snack*, she'd thought. Gary was known to sneak down to the kitchen late at night and, as he put it "relieve the fridge of any leftovers." Jill had crept down the stairs, thinking of what she might say to him when she saw him in the kitchen. She'd scold him, of course, for eating so late. And then she would add something provocative. *I know something you can do that's much better for you.* And he would laugh and grab her and . . .

He wasn't in the kitchen. Jill was about to turn around and go back upstairs, when she'd heard a rustling in his home office and noticed that he was in there, with the door closed. Probably just catching up on work, she'd thought. But still, she had a strange feeling . . . Why was the door closed? Why had he wanted to keep her out? She wasn't the type of woman to put her ear against a door. But still . . .

Still, she could have sworn she'd heard Gary in there, talking.

Jill had gone back to bed, but she hadn't slept. Two hours later, with Gary snoring beside her, she'd gotten up. She'd tiptoed back downstairs and snuck into his office. She'd never been the type of woman to rummage through her husband's desk. She couldn't even imagine being friends with someone who would open her husband's top desk drawer, who would slide her hand in and feel around for evidence of . . . something. But that was what she'd done. That was what she had become.

In the drawer, she'd found a small, disposable phone. And without much thought, she'd flipped it open, clicked on the icon for outgoing calls. She hadn't recognized any of the numbers, but she'd written them down anyway—only three numbers, none of them from this area code.

If he's having an affair, she'd thought, *at least it's long distance. . .*

God, this was all so surreal, Jill thinking this way. *Twenty years going to bed every night with the same man, the man who's held your hand while you've given birth to his three daughters and taught you how to play chess and hugged you so close at both your parents' funerals, the man who puts his head next to yours on the pillow and kisses the back of your neck when he thinks you're asleep, who teases you that no matter how old you get, you'll always be his trophy wife. You think you know that man. You think you know his thoughts.*

"Focus on your skull, and then the beautiful mind it houses. Feel it glow purple with spiritual energy. Feel it," Yasmine said, "feel it." But Jill couldn't feel anything.

After class, Jill said her good-byes quickly. She didn't bother hitting the locker room and showering or even getting changed. She just grabbed her purse, jammed her feet into her plastic flip-flops, and hurried out to her car in her yoga pants and Wise Up T-shirt.

Wise up, indeed.

She slid into her car and stuck the key in the ignition, but instead of turning it, she put her head down on the wheel and cried. Repeatedly, Jill tried to make herself stop, but then more tears would come and she'd be sobbing again, her hair stuck to her face, her nose running, praying no one she knew would walk by.

Talk to Gary, said a voice inside her. *Drive home and ask to speak to him alone. Get him to explain it all—the distant behavior, the disposable phone, what he was doing in his office at four in the morning with the door closed . . . If he's evasive in any way, just show him those numbers you wrote down. He'll have to tell you the truth. And it probably won't be as bad as you think.* It was good advice—the same advice Jill would have given any of her friends.

Jill ran her hand over her wet face. It was hard to believe she'd had that many tears inside her, but at least she wasn't crying anymore. One of the nuns, Jill couldn't remember which one, had told her, "*God is the feeling you get after crying—that sense of comfort and calm.*"

"*You mean, God is* in *the feeling, right, Sister?*"

"*No, dear. God is* that *feeling. He is the calm that gives you strength.*"

Crying had probably been an overreaction—yoga always made Jill emotional. And really, it had been only two weeks . . .

Jill reached into her purse for a Kleenex. But instead, she found herself grabbing her phone, along with the slip of paper on which she'd written down Gary's three outgoing calls. She hadn't planned on calling the numbers—she'd only written them to confront Gary with. But here she was, yet again, surprising herself.

She turned on her phone, and tapped in the first number.

The new girl in Errol Ludlow's employ was just leaving his apartment when his cell phone rang. She was one of those women who looked better walking away than coming toward you. And that was saying something, as her front—all of it—was superlative. Errol smiled, took in the view. "A most delightful visit," he said.

And it had been. He normally didn't allow any of his

employees into his apartment—it was always a mistake to mix business with pleasure—but Diandra was special. Yes, that was what she called herself—Diandra, a diminutive of the Greek Dianthe, meaning "flower of the gods." Errol suspected her real name was probably Madison or Brittany—she was about as Greek as his left butt cheek—but oh, she was indeed a heavenly creature.

"You are a superb private detective," Errol told the back of Diandra. "What you did was truly above and beyond."

She turned, delivering a grin that could melt a man's belt buckle. "Are you talking about the pictures I took at the Hustler Club? Or . . . the way we celebrated my taking them?"

Errol blushed—*blushed*, at his age and experience. Truth be told, he had been talking about the pictures—startlingly clear photographs of some poor, soon-to-be-divorced schmuck by the name of Dr. Marvin Greene with a weakness for double Es and far too many hundred-dollar bills at his disposal. But now that she mentioned it . . . "Well . . . I mean . . . the celebration was . . ."

"Above."

"Yes."

"And beyond."

"God, yes."

"Well let me just tell you, Mr. Ludlow. It is a genuine pleasure to be on your staff." Diandra gazed at him for a few moments, making sure the double entendre landed and stuck.

"Uh . . . thank you?"

She slipped through the front door and closed it behind her. And only then, when Errol could breathe again, did he realize that his cell phone had been trilling for easily thirty seconds. He picked it up. "Ludlow."

"Pardon?"

Errol always made it a point to enunciate. His mother had been hard of hearing, and so since his youth, he'd taken great pains to ensure he was understood by all around him. In other words, no one said, "Pardon" to him, ever. "Lud. Low." He glanced at the screen on his cell phone. California area code. No wonder. They were all high out there. All that smog and creosote.

"I'm sorry," said the woman on the other line. "My name is Jill and I . . . uh . . . I found this number on a disposable phone and . . . well . . . I thought you would be a woman."

"Your husband's disposable phone?"

"Yes."

"What is your husband's name?"

She cleared her throat. "It's Gary. Gary Freeman."

Errol's jaw tensed up. "Gary Freeman?" Wheels turned in his head, scenarios playing out in fast-motion. *Should I tell her the truth? Where would that get me?* "I've never heard of him," Errol said, finally.

"But . . . I . . . I saw several calls to you on the phone . . ."

"You live in Southern California, yes?"

"Yes."

"South Pasadena? I recognize the area code."

"Actually, just Pasadena. Not South."

"Did you ever think your husband might be keeping that phone for a friend? I have several clients in Southern California."

"Clients?"

"I'm a private investigator," Errol said. "My specialty is cheating spouses. You might see how someone wouldn't want a phone with my number on it to be seen by . . . well, I suppose you'd call them loved ones."

"You . . . You're sure . . ."

"You can look me up online, ma'am. Ludlow Investigations. I have my own Web site."

"Yes, but my husband . . ."

"I don't know a Gary Freeman, ma'am." Ludlow hung up.

Moments later, he was looking up Gary Freeman's number in his contacts—the number Freeman had requested, after firing Errol, that he never call again. He took a few moments, figuring out in his head how much his continued silence might be worth. He didn't have much on Gary Freeman, this was true. But he did have Lula Belle's Web address. He had that fascinating download—*such talent!*—and he had the knowledge that Gary Freeman wanted to find Lula Belle, very badly. Errol smiled. He'd been around enough angry wives to know that his keeping quiet about these few factoids could be worth . . . Well, enough to keep Diandra in top-shelf champagne for quite a long while.

He tapped Gary Freeman's number into his phone, his smile broadening. This day just kept getting better and better.

"Why would he ever leave you?" Trent asked Robin Tannenbaum's computer, his hands caressing the keyboard. "You're so beautiful."

Hildy Tannenbaum gave Brenna a worried look.

She shrugged. "He likes machinery."

"I saw this model at the Mac trade show at the Javits, but they wouldn't let me touch it. It feels really good," Trent breathed. "Oh, and hello Miss T–2 line, you comely little wench . . ."

"I don't know whether you realize it," Brenna told Trent, "but you just said all that out loud."

They were in Robin's room—a small, sparsely furnished bedroom with bare walls. Clearly, Robin didn't share his mother's affection for big, complicated furniture—this was more of a dorm room aesthetic— only without the posters, the beer can pyramids, the piles of dirty clothes and stolen orange safety cones. In fact, the only remarkable thing in the entire room was the souped-up Mac Pro, which Trent seemed to be taking an undue amount of pleasure in exploring.

"Any reason why he'd need a high-speed line, Mrs. Tannenbaum?" Brenna said. "Did he do freelance work?"

"Yes," said Hildy. But it was clear she had no desire to elaborate.

Brenna almost felt as though she could turn to Robin, ask him herself. Though Hildy claimed the room had been vacated for two months, it had a look to it as though he would return any minute. The bed was made, yes, but hastily so—the plain beige spread pulled over the pillow but not tucked under it, the shades drawn. A stale, lonely scent hung in the air—sweat, unwashed sheets—and a few Louise Hay self-help books were stacked on the bedside table—a pair of reading glasses and a yellow highlighter perched on top as if he'd just rested them there a few minutes ago. Brenna picked up the top book—*The Power Is Within You*. A recent printing of an old book, dog-eared far from the end, at page 162. Brenna skimmed the highlighted page. *Why would you leave an unfinished book behind?* "Are you sure he actually meant to leave home?"

She nodded. "He taped a note to the refrigerator. Would you like to see it?"

"Sure."

Hildy exited the room. Soon after, Brenna heard groans coming from the computer speakers. She looked up to see a man and three women on screen in a tangle of sweaty gratification, a maid's apron the only item of clothing between the four of them.

"Trent," Brenna said. "Stop looking at Robin Tannenbaum's porn."

"It's not his porn," Trent said. "It's his *job*."

Brenna raised her eyebrows. "He's a porn star?"

"Porn editor. Found this in his Final Cut Pro . . . which sounds kinda dirty if you don't know it's an editing program." He snickered.

"So that's why he's got the high-speed line," Brenna said. "So he can send the edited films to his employer."

"Happy Endings."

"Huh?"

"That's the company he works for—says it at the bottom of all his files." He turned to Brenna. "I've . . . uh . . . heard of them before. They do nice work."

The door pushed open and Hildy walked in.

"Oops," said Trent. He closed the video fast, though something told Brenna that even if he'd kept the clip up there in all its blazing, groaning glory, Hildy would have ignored it. She'd known what her son did for a living, just as she'd known about her husband's *Playboy* stash. Brenna could tell in the way she'd averted her gaze when Brenna had asked her about Robin's involvement with Web sites, when Trent had asked if he worked in film; she could tell in how carefully she'd chosen the words "professional work on his computer." Hildy was going to be tough.

"I have the note." Hildy handed it to Brenna—typewritten and just a few lines long. "He left it for me on October 9."

Mother:

*No need to keep dinner warm. May be gone for
a little while.*

Best, RJT

Brenna looked at Hildy. "Best, RJT?"

"He's never been very demonstrative."

"Really?"

"Not with me," she said, quietly. "Not in the house."

"So you didn't know many of his friends."

"I didn't know any of them." Hildy took a breath.
And for several moments, the only sound in the room
was the soft clack of the keyboard as Trent explored
Robin's computer.

Brenna said, "Tell me about the woman with the
Southern accent."

"I didn't think Robbie actually knew her," she said.
"I walked by his room and I heard this voice and I assumed it must have been a . . . a movie."

Brenna said, "Do you recall what the woman was
saying?"

"I heard, 'Let me go, my love.'"

Brenna closed her eyes, the previous night seeping
back into her mind—she felt her desk chair beneath
her, her eyes blurry with sleep, her mind starting to
fog . . . *Brenna's seventeenth Lula Belle download
plays out, but she's finding it hard to focus. Her eyes
flutter closed for a moment, and then open on the
screen, on Lula Belle on the floor, palms in front of
her, both legs pretzeled behind her shadow of a head.
"I've been with him for three weeks and I don't like
him anymore. He keeps looking at my neck like he*

wants to bite it, and sometimes, I could swear he's got fangs. It's the dust, I know. The dust. It's making me see things."

Brenna squints at the screen. The dust?

" 'Let me go,' I tell him, this man I thought I'd spend the rest of my life with. 'Let me go, my love.' "

Hildy said, "Something about bites on her neck . . ."

"It was a download," Brenna said.

"You're sure?"

"I've seen it."

"Other nights, though," she said slowly. "I mean . . . I couldn't make out what was being said. I tried *not* to hear, to be honest . . . But she sounded so different than the other . . . um . . . female voices on Robbie's computer."

"How so?" Brenna said.

"She sounded as though she were speaking directly to him."

Brenna nodded. "She's like that."

Trent looked at Hildy. "I don't see anyone in his Skype contacts. Of course he could have deleted her."

"I don't know what Skype contacts are."

Trent started to explain, but Brenna wasn't listening, her attention drawn away, as it was, by the pile of books on Robin's bedside table. Underneath the three Louise Hays was a library book. She could tell what it was just from glancing at the spine, but she picked it up anyway. *Extraordinary Children* by RF Lieberman.

She opened it up, glanced at the date. It had been checked out on October 5—the same date Brenna had appeared on Faith's show . . . *The klieg lights shine hot on Brenna's face. She's wearing a long-sleeved black shirt and her hair is down and she sweats at the temples. She craves a drink of water. Faith smiles at her. Her TV makeup is flawless, the warm air between them thick with the sweet smell of it. "You ready, Brenna? We're on in five."*

"Okay."

"I'm gonna start out by talking about your child-hood. That okay with you?" She's got Lieberman's book in her lap. Brenna's stares at it, then looks up, into Faith's sky blue eyes. The lights make them twinkle. "Sure," she says.

"Great."

"Can you tell me something, though?"

"Uh-huh?"

"How's Jim?"

Brenna bit her lip hard. She put the book back. Could be a coincidence, she thought. But if so, it was a strange one. Robin Tannenbaum checks Lieberman's book out of the library the same day Faith shows it to her viewers on *Sunrise Manhattan.* The next day, Lula Belle sends Gary an e-mail, instructing him to send this month's check to a PO box under Robin's name and located in the town where Brenna grew up. Three days later, he leaves a typed note for his mother and is never heard from again. Did Brenna's appearance on *Sunrise Manhattan* trigger Robin's disappearance? Not necessarily. But the fact remained: It happened first.

"You can take the computer," Hildy was saying to Trent. "Do whatever you have to do with it for as long as you have to do it."

"You mean it?"

"I know this will sound strange, but it will be a relief not to have it around."

Brenna looked at her.

"It frightens me," she said. "Robbie spent so much time with it, and he's gone, and I . . . I feel . . ."

"Like the computer took him away?" Brenna said.

"Yes. Like it sucked him in when I wasn't looking, then printed out that note so I wouldn't suspect anything, and . . . Oh, this sounds even stranger when I say it out loud."

Brenna put a hand on her shoulder. "It doesn't. I understand." And she did. She knew what it was like to have someone warm and alive beside her one day, gone the next, the whole house filled with the lack of her—the Rose Royce record on the turntable in her bedroom, the strands of blonde hair in the brush she left behind, the clothes in her closet and the pack of Marlboro Lights stashed under her pillow and the Adam Ant poster on the hot pink wall that she'd painted herself. All of it still there, waiting . . .

Please come home, *Brenna thinks, standing in Clea's old room at 10 P.M., August 29, 1983. She stares up at Adam Ant. He's grinning at her. He's grinning with those mean thin lips like he knows where Clea is, and he could be the man in the blue car. Anybody could be the man in the blue car . . .*

"Robbie didn't take his cell phone," Hildy said. "Honestly, why would someone go away for two months without taking their cell phone?"

Brenna gave her a long look. "Maybe he didn't want to be traced."

"Excuse me?"

"Almost any cell phone can be tracked because of GPS capability," Brenna said. "Even the simplest phone is sending and receiving messages from the nearest tower every few minutes, so the user can be found that way—through triangulation. Right, Trent?"

"But I would never think of doing that," Hildy said. "I can barely use my own cell phone, let alone triangulate my son with towers."

"I'm sure, Hildy," Brenna said.

"So . . . why?"

"Maybe it wasn't you he was worried about."

Hildy's eyes widened.

"Can I have the cell phone, Mrs. Tannenbaum? It would be helpful to look at his contacts."

She nodded. Slowly, she slipped a smart phone out of the pocket of her robe, handed it to Brenna. "It never rings," she said. "I carry it around anyway. Charge it every night. Do you want the charger?"

"Please."

Hildy left the room. Brenna looked at RJ's phone—an iPhone to match the Mac Pro. Brenna wasn't a fan of smart phones. She found them pointless, but she'd used Trent's for a couple of hours on October 19, 2008, when her flip phone died on a stakeout. It was just like this one. She clicked it on, tapped the phone icon. "Weird."

"What?" Trent said.

"Looks like RJ made and received no calls on this thing."

"He probably deleted his call log," he said. "I can recover that."

"You're the best."

"Yeah, I know," he said. "But listen, can you first take a look at this download for me?"

She gave him a look.

"It's G-rated, okay?"

"What is it?"

"Just a picture. It looks . . . personal."

Brenna moved to the computer.

Trent clicked on the picture so that it filled his screen, and when Brenna saw it, her mouth went dry. Her pulse pounded and her head swam and for a moment, she feared she might collapse, right there in Robin Tannenbaum's bedroom, with his sweat smell in the air and his mother entering the room again, his mother standing right behind her, asking, "Do you know those people? Do you, Brenna?"

There is a connection. There has to be, my God, there has to.

Brenna stared at the faded, scanned photo: a blonde girl, around ten, riding a blue bicycle, a much littler girl with curly dark hair balanced on the handlebars. Both were wearing bright, one-piece bathing suits. Both were laughing into the camera . . . *Look at me, Daddy! Look!*

"He loved to take pictures of us," Brenna whispered.

"Who?" Trent said.

"My father."

The picture, circa 1975, was of Brenna and Clea.

8

Somehow, Brenna managed to make it through the next several minutes, Trent doing most of the talking as she tried to quiet the thrumming in her head, the pounding of her heart. *Move through this*, she told herself. *You can fall apart later, but for now stay here. You have to stay here to find Robin Tannenbaum, and now you need to find him. You must find him.*

Hildy Tannenbaum provided them with her son's credit card bills and banking information as well as a few recent pictures of him, then allowed them to open his closet, which was reasonably full—though, Brenna noticed, mostly with summer clothes. At the back of the closet, Brenna found a tripod—but no cameras, cables, lights . . .

Winter clothes, film equipment. He'd left on a film job, most likely on the East Coast.

You could tell so much more about a missing person by what was gone from his room than what remained in it. Brenna had always known this, yet never applied it to her own life. The picture from the computer screen—Brenna and Clea on that bike, Clea's bike—had that ever been in Clea's room? Had she seen her sister looking at it? Placing that very picture in a book and slamming it shut as Brenna walked in . . .

"We'll get the computer back to you as soon as we can," Brenna heard herself say, as Trent finished unhooking the cables and wrapped the monitor in a clean blanket Hildy had given him.

"Take your time," she said. "I have no use for it."

Brenna forced a smile. "That's nice of you," she said. "But all the same, I'd rather not have Trent get too attached to it. He's kind of weird about mechanical things."

"Dude. I'm right here."

"Brenna?"

"Yes, Hildy?"

"That was you and your sister? On the computer?"

"Yes."

"Why would my son have that picture?"

Brenna swallowed hard. "That's the sixty-four-thousand-dollar question," she said. Same thing Morasco had said on October 1, standing across from Brenna in a distraught mother's abandoned kitchen, that musty scent in the air—old furniture, dust— Brenna thinking, *It smells like ghosts. . .*

"Why just sixty-four thousand dollars?" said Trent, which brought her back into the room, nostalgic for three months ago. *A simpler time*, Brenna thought— which made her smile in spite of everything. Breaking into the home of a long-gone grieving mother with a man she was developing a whole bunch of complicated feelings for, yet still it was a hell of a lot simpler than this.

"I remember that TV show," Hildy Tannenbaum said, and Brenna had an urge to call Morasco, to rush to his apartment and show him the picture and cry into his chest like a child. *I don't understand. Please help me understand*. She wouldn't do it, though, she knew. Every time she felt compelled to do something, she had to weigh it against what would happen later—the remembering. But still . . . Still.

I don't understand. Please help me.

"Inspiration," said Trent.

Brenna blinked at him.

He was pointing at a picture that had been taped to the inside of Robin Tannenbaum's closet, next to a full-length mirror—a paparazzi shot of Steven Spielberg, printed out from a computer.

Brenna said, "He wants to be a director?"

Trent shook his head. "He wants to *look* like a director. Like Spielberg. That's why it's next to the mirror. Mrs. Tannenbaum, when you last saw Robin, was he growing a beard?"

She nodded. "It wasn't a full beard yet, but he did stop shaving."

"When?"

"Maybe a few days before he left?"

"Knew it," he said. "Can I take this picture?"

"Of course, but why?"

"I think if I Photoshop elements from it into the recent shots of Robin, we'll get a pretty good likeness of what he looked like when he was last seen."

Hildy stared at him. "My goodness," she said. "I never even noticed that picture."

Trent shrugged. "Only reason why I did is I've got one myself."

Hildy frowned at him. "You have a picture of Steven Spielberg next to your mirror?"

He shook his head. "Vin Diesel," he said. "Not for the shaved head. It's the ink and the bod I want. And you know . . . the fashion sense. Actually, I've got a whole Diesel calendar next to my mirror."

"I have no idea who that is," Hildy said.

Brenna looked at Trent. Any other time, she would've had a field day with this information. At the very least, she would have asked him which exact tattoos he'd copied from Vin and what the ladies thought of the beefcake calendar next to his bedroom mirror. But she didn't have it in her. She didn't have anything in her, except the need to find Robin Tannenbaum—and then Lula Belle—as soon as possible. "Who sent Robin that picture, Trent?"

"A Hotmail address."

"Sweetpea81?"

He nodded, slowly.

How does Lula Belle know so much of my life? Why does she have this picture?

Brenna at ten, shouting for her sister: *"Clee-a! Mom says dinner's ready!"* Brenna opening the door and Clea is putting something into a book. A snapshot. One her dad took. Brenna and Clea on a bike. She's closing the book and she's looking up, she's looking at Brenna and she's shoving the book in a drawer . . . *It's all so foggy. Is this a real memory—or just something I want to remember?* It was impossible to say. Were everyone's childhood recollections this murky—or just Brenna's, made murkier when compared to all the ones that came later?

Does it matter?

Lula Belle had this picture now. Lula Belle knew the cement mixer song. Lula Belle was bound and determined to screw with Brenna's brain until it broke . . . or she was family. Or she was both.

"Are you all right, dear?" Hildy said.

Lula Belle, are you my sister?

"Yo, Brenna?"

Brenna took a breath. "I haven't seen one of my dad's pictures in thirty-two years."

Hildy said, "Why not?"

"He left us." Brenna cleared her throat.

"And your mother was that angry?"

"It wasn't anger . . ." She looked at Hildy and made herself smile. "To Mom, Dad was like that stack of *Playboy*s you found in your husband's closet. You know . . . only without the cute cartoons."

Hildy stared up at her, her eyes buglike behind her glasses, an emotion passing through them. An understanding. "Sweep him under the rug," she said. "Act like he never existed, so he'll never be able to hurt you again."

"Yes."

"Your mother—did she ever speak to you about your father? Tell you stories or . . ."

"No." Brenna's voice trembled. "She never mentioned his name. He must have taken hundreds of photographs of us—she got rid of them all. My mom sculpted and painted—she said she didn't trust cameras. And so all we had was school pictures, and then after Clea went away . . . my mother got rid of most of those. In my mind, Clea is always seventeen because that's the only picture Mom kept of her—her eleventh grade class picture. The one the police used."

Hildy took both of Brenna's hands in hers. Her grip was surprisingly strong, as if to pull her back into the present. It worked. *Stay here.*

"I don't want to be like that," Hildy said. "Robbie's hurt me plenty, but I don't want to make him disappear. He's my boy. I want him back."

"We'll do our best for you," said Brenna. "I promise."

Hildy's eyes started to glisten. A tear slipped down her cheek, and without thinking Brenna took her in her arms and hugged her—her arthritic back hard and curled like a turtle's shell beneath her palms, the orange wig wiry at her chin, all of Hildy so small and brittle, it broke Brenna's heart. "I want to help you," Brenna said. And she did, so very much. She wanted to help them both.

The thing with Trent: He was a douchebag. But beneath that gelled-up, tatted-out, spray-tanned exterior, he was also a friend. And so as prone as he was to say the wrong thing at absolutely the worst possible time, he also knew when to shut up.

After he'd slipped the computer into the trunk of his Ford Taurus and Brenna had gotten into the front seat and buckled up, Robin Tannenbaum's photos and billing information, the contents of his desk, and his phone, too, in a manila envelope in her lap, along with a printout of the picture of Clea and herself, Trent turned to Brenna. "Are you okay?"

She shook her head.

"Do you want to talk about it?"

Brenna shook her head again, and for Trent, that was enough. He turned the ignition and flipped the radio to his favorite station—some Sirius channel that played an awful lot of Justin Timberlake. For most of the ride home, he bobbed his head and tapped his hands against the steering wheel and didn't say a word.

The roads were reasonably clear, though with more cars going into the city than usual on a Saturday—Christmas shoppers. Brenna focused on the cars. Because of her condition, and a knowledge of automobiles she'd perfected after Clea had gotten into a blue one she couldn't identify, Brenna tended to notice cars and keep them in her mind. She read up on them, and could discern most makes, models, and years by sight alone. Brenna took comfort in that as Trent drove— the red 2003–2006 Honda Civic at their side, scooting along behind a beige early 2000s Cabriolet and behind them, the huge, cross-hatched grille of a black Dodge Magnum—had to be a 2005–2008 because those were the only years they made those grilles—intimidating things. They sneered into the rearview.

Year, model, make, color . . . all of it so organized and simple and certain. So easy to identify a car as opposed to a person, who can take off all her clothes but drape herself in shadow, who can lay her soul bare—lay *your* soul bare—but with a phony accent and you don't know who she is, you can't know who she is, until . . .

Lula Belle, are you my sister?

"Bringing Sexy Back" sprang out of Trent's cell phone. Ironically, it was the same song that happened to be playing on the radio. Dueling Timberlakes. "That's a text message," Trent said. "Can you check it for me?"

Brenna picked up his phone, clicked on the text message icon, and looked at the screen. "It's from Annette Shelby. Do you want me to read it to you?"

"I'll read it later." Trent said it in such a way that it made her put the phone down—still she couldn't help but see the text:

I didn't mean to hurt you.

Brenna looked at Trent, the way he stared out the window, his jaw set. She took in the purplish circles under his eyes—the pallor you could see despite the

spray tan—and it hit her that maybe there was something else about Trent's appearance that was different
today. Maybe he didn't look thrashed, so much as lost.
Sad. "You okay?"

He shook his head.

"Do you want to talk about it?"

"Come on, Brenna."

"What?"

"Duh. You've kinda got more important things on
your mind. We're talking possible *family* issues."

"I'd like to hear what happened," she said. "And just
so you know, Maya stopped saying 'duh' in the fifth
grade."

Trent gripped the wheel.

"Listen, I know how much Persephone means to you
and—"

"Don't even say that name to me."

Brenna stared at him. "Why?"

He exhaled hard. "I spent three hours at the fish
market last night. Talked to every freakin' fishmonger
in Lower Manhattan. They really call 'em that, you
know. Fishmongers. Sounds like an insult to me but
whatever."

"No one had seen Annette's cat?"

"No. I showed them all the pictures, normal and
poster-sized. Nada. I had to use a whole can of Axe
spray, just to get the fish smell off me."

"Oy."

"Big fail."

"You did your best. Maybe someone took her in."

"No, you don't understand." Trent was merging into
traffic on FDR Drive. "I called Mrs. Shelby." he said. "I
told her I was sorry, and I didn't mean to let her down,
but I was running out of ideas."

"Was she upset?"

"I thought so." He sighed. "She told me to come over to her place. I thought she was gonna chew me a new one." Trent swerved into the left lane and sped up.

Brenna clutched the arm of the seat. "Hey, take it easy," she said.

But Trent ignored her. "I guess I should have figured it out when I saw all the candles." Trent sped up even more. Brenna was starting to feel nauseous.

"Candles? At Annette's place?"

"I figured she must've blown a fuse. Jeez, suave NYC baller like me—I am so freakin' naïve sometimes. I even asked if she wanted me to look at her box! You wanna know what she said *then*?"

Brenna winced. "Not really."

Trent stared out the window.

"Look. I'm sure she just misses Persephone, and—"

"Persephone died three years ago, Brenna."

Brenna stared at him. "*What?*"

"Natural causes. Before Annette Shelby even moved to New York."

"You're not serious."

He swerved back into the right lane. "She used that cat as a prop. I was a gigolo. Not a player, Brenna. A gigolo. A high-priced, well-kept man ho."

"You're sure that's all she wanted? I mean . . . I understand she's lonely. But she could have just wanted a . . . a friend . . ."

"Candles. Everywhere. And she's wearing this white silk thing . . . It was like a goddamn Mariah Carey video in there."

"Wow."

"She paid me all that money, just to have drinks with her every day and play detective. She didn't hire me for my brains." He sighed heavily. "She just wanted my tight young ass."

Brenna tried a smile. "Normally, you'd be bragging about that."

"I know." Trent turned to Brenna—his eyes were pinkish with hurt. "I guess I don't like being lied to." He lurched back into the left lane, and for several moments, Brenna was in a different car—her mother's white 1978 Buick Skylark. *September 8, 1981, and Brenna's mother is driving to the police station, Brenna in the front seat. She is trying to recall the car —the make, the license plate. Her mother has asked her and she wants to make her happy, wants to find Clea, wants everything to go back to the way it was, wants it so bad . . . But all she can see is blue metal, Clea sliding into it. And that voice, that man's voice. "You look so pretty, Clee-bee."*

"You're going to tell the detective everything you remember."

"Yes, Mom."

Mom's hands grip the steering wheel. Her fingers remind Brenna of white ropes. "I'm not mad at you anymore. I know you were lying to protect your sister, and you thought that was the right thing. But you lied to me for two weeks. Two weeks when we could have found her. I don't want you to lie ever again, Brenna. About anything."

"Yes, Mom." *The vent breathes hot on Brenna's face and neck. Outside, the sky is dead white, like an unfinished painting, like Mom's knuckles on the wheel.*

"Do you understand me?"

"Yes, Mom." Brenna bit her lip and looked at Trent's hands, gripping the wheel. She saw her mother's hands and bit her lip harder.

Trent said, "Did you just call me Mom?"

"What? No. Of course not." Brenna shut her eyes for a few seconds. Recited the Pledge in her head and then, at last, she was back.

"So," Brenna said, "what you told me about going to that club Bacon . . ."

"And getting my pole waxed?"

"That wasn't true, huh? You were really at Annette's."

"Oh no, that was true. I went to Bacon later." Trent stared out the window. "But you know what? When Diandra and I were shaboinkin', I kept seeing Persephone." He sighed heavily. "Seriously, I mean, thanks to Mrs. Shelby, I can't even shoot my load without seeing the face of that damn dead cat." Trent pulled over to the right, got off the FDR at Fourteenth Street.

Brenna looked at him. "Diandra?"

"Yeah, sexy name, right?"

September 30. Brenna's left hand clutches the steering wheel, the cell phone pressed to the side of her head, Trent's voice in her ear, competing with club noise. "What's your name, gorgeous?" Trent is saying now. "Diandra. That is a name that's made to be moaned in ecstasy."

Brenna said, "You knew her before last night."

"Uh, yeah. I met her a couple of days ago, but we didn't hook up until she texted me and told me to meet her at Bacon."

"You didn't meet her a couple of days ago."

"Yes I did."

"You met her at Bedd," Brenna said.

Trent frowned. "I met her in bed?"

"No. Bedd. With two Ds. That was the club's name."

"In Brooklyn? No way. That place is jank. I haven't been there in—"

"Two and a half months. You met her on September

30 at 10:25 P.M. I mean . . . if it's the same Diandra. It's a pretty unusual name."

"What the hell . . ."

"You were on the phone with me, Trent. I was driving to Tarry Ridge and I was having you describe everything you were seeing so I wouldn't slip into . . ." Brenna bit back the memory. "It's no big deal."

"It *is* a big deal, though. You remember stuff about my life that I don't. And you're my boss. You know how freakin' scary that is?" He swerved back into the right lane, knocking Brenna into the door. "Man, I hate tailgaters."

"Why is it scary?"

"Seriously, this black station wagon wants to mount me or something."

"Trent. Why is my memory scary to you?"

He sighed. "If I screw something up, you'll never forget," he said. "I have to be my best with you, always."

Brenna looked at Trent, recalling April 14, 2006, the one time she had met his mother . . . *"He was little Mr. New Jersey Spirit and King of the Saratoga Glitz Pageant, three years in a row. Of course, he was sometimes the only boy in the competition, but that didn't matter to Trenton. He tried so hard. You should have seen his little face light up when he'd hear them clapping for him, it was just adorable. Did you know that he choreographed all his own dance routines? You should have seen the cowboy one!"*

Brenna had never told Trent she knew about his past as a child beauty pageant king—he'd have been mortified, and rightly so. But looking at him now, in his too-tight Western shirt, she saw that little cowboy, so eager to please. *I guess I don't like being lied to.*

"Trent."

"Yeah?"

"I'm going to tell you something, but I need you to keep quiet about it, okay?"

He looked at her. "Okay."

Trent swerved around a slow car—a 2004 Subaru Forester with Michigan plates. "Learn to drive, suckwad!" he yelled. Then, "What do you need me to keep quiet about?"

"We're not working for Errol Ludlow anymore."

"Huh?"

"Ludlow got fired from the case yesterday. We're working directly for Lula Belle's manager."

"Wait. This is weird. Did Errol tell you that?"

Brenna shook her head. "The manager did." She looked at Trent. "I can't tell you his name or his number, and you can't ever talk to him. This case is . . . emotional to him, I guess. Actually, he's incredibly paranoid. It's annoying." She glanced into the rearview, at the car that had been tailgating them. Her gaze stuck. It was the same black Magnum she'd noticed near the start of the ride. She could make out the first two numbers on the license plate: 61. Same numbers. *Maybe he's just going the same way. Maybe it's a coincidence. . .*

"Does Errol know?"

"Know what? Don't drive so fast please, Trent."

"Does he know he was fired?"

"Of course he knows he was fired."

He sped up more, swerved into the left lane.

"Would you *slow down*?"

"Tell me again how I met Diandra."

"I mean it, Trent."

"How did I meet her?"

Brenna sighed heavily. "You met her on September 30 at Bedd. You said she was wearing a pink tube top and that she looked like Jessica Alba from the neck down. She was giving you her digits, but then she got mad because she heard you talking on the phone with me. You tried to explain I was your boss but she walked away and then you told me I was carpet-bombing your game. Now would you please *slow down the freakin' car?*" The crosshatched grille was gone from her rearview. She swung around in her seat. The Magnum was nowhere to be seen. "Damn it."

"What?"

"You lost the Magnum."

"The who?"

"The car behind us," she sighed. "The one trying to mount you."

"He was tailgating us."

"He was *following* us. Since Forest Hills. I wanted to see his plates."

"Crap. I totally suck. I suck so bad. I suck geriatric donkey."

Brenna sighed. "It's best you lost him anyway."

"No. Listen, Brenna. You're probably right about Bedd. You're always right. And she does look like Alba from the neck down. But what I gotta tell you is, as far as I personally remember, I met Diandra a couple of days ago."

"So? She probably doesn't remember Bedd, either."

"I met her two days ago." His jaw tightened. "At Errol Ludlow's."

"*What?*"

"I was leaving Ludlow's office after he pitched the Lula Belle case to me. She was going into the building. Gave me the smush-eye. Know what I'm talking about?"

"No. No, I don't."

"The do-not-pass-go-do-not-collect-two-hundred-dollars-until-you-rip-my-pants-off-and-take-me-right-here-on-the-concrete kinda look."

"You're still being too subtle."

"Yeah, yeah . . . Anyway, she said she knew who I was because of the Neff thing. Seemed to me like she was a groupie. Said she followed me on Twitter and made it sound . . . you know . . . dirty."

"You have a Twitter account? *Why?*"

"That isn't the point."

"I know, but come on. What kind of a person is a groupie for a private investigator?"

"Another private investigator."

"*What?*"

Trent turned to Brenna. "Diandra works for Ludlow."

Her eyes widened. "She's one of Errol's Angels?"

He nodded. "At Bacon, she asked me all about the Lula Belle case, what kinda progress we were making. Said she was a fan of hers. I just thought she was freaky. Into the silhouette, like me. I should have known. A chick that hot always has an ulterior motive."

"Why did you talk to her about the case?"

"Because I thought we were working for Errol, too!" Brenna cringed. "Oh. Right."

"I even told her not to say anything to Errol about us. I didn't want him to think I'm unprofessional."

"I'm sorry, Trent."

"Whatevs." He got off the FDR at Fourteenth Street, headed west toward Brenna's place. "Mrs. Shelby lied to me because she wanted to hook up. Diandra hooked up with me because she was lying . . . After I drop you off, I think I'm just going to go home with this computer and not hook up with anyone for the rest of my . . . Wait. Did I just seriously just say that?"

Brenna felt Trent turning to her, but she couldn't speak. She'd slipped the picture of her and Clea out of the envelope and was staring at it, her eyes starting to blur.

Trent pulled to a stop in front of her building, watched her till she spoke.

"That program you used on Lula Belle," Brenna said, her gaze still glued to the photo. "The one that told you her probable height, weight, and measurements . . ."

"Yeah?"

"Did it give you a probable age, too?"

Trent shook his head. "She's a shadow. I can't even tell you for sure whether the tatas are real."

"Could she be . . ." Brenna cleared her throat. "Do you think it's possible Lula Belle could be in her mid-forties?"

"Well, sure, but . . . Wait." Trent put a hand on Brenna's shoulder. He spoke very quietly. "You think Lula Belle is your sister, Clea?"

She tore herself away from the photo. "Don't you think she is? You said possible family issues."

"I meant your dad."

"Huh?"

"Your dad took the picture. I was thinking maybe she's someone who might know him. You know, today."

Brenna looked at him. "You think my dad kept that picture all these years?"

"He hasn't spoken to you in that long. Never tried to contact you guys . . . Seems like he must have wanted something to remember you by, you know?"

Lula Belle could have gotten the picture from my father. Brenna hadn't even considered that possibility. Instead she had conjured an image of Clea shoving a picture into a book—the same picture she'd seen on Robin Tannenbaum's computer screen.

But even if it had been a real memory, even if Brenna really had walked into her sister's room at that early age and caught a glimpse of Clea hiding a picture, how could she have been able to see it so clearly from that distance?

"I made it up," she whispered.

"What?" said Trent.

For the first time in so long, Brenna was grateful for her disorder, because she saw what she'd be without it: Someone who tried to make facts out of wishes. Someone whose past wasn't the past at all, but a fiction, a propaganda movie she created herself, all in the name of preserving false hope.

How can that be considered "normal"?

"You're probably right," Brenna started to say, but she wasn't able to complete the thought before she saw the crosshatch in the rearview again and 61 on the license plate and then Trent's back doors flew open, two men sliding into the seat behind them.

"Goddamn it, Trent, why did you leave the doors unlocked?" Brenna blurted.

But then a thick arm roped around her neck. Just beneath her chin, she felt the sharp tip of a blade and thought it best, for now, not to say anything more.

9

"What's wrong Daddy?"

Where do I start, thought Gary, who was sitting at the kitchen table, head in his hands, unable to start anywhere—especially not with Hannah, his youngest, who had come in to ask him why the Tooth Fairy had given her only ten dollars last night instead of her usual twenty.

Gary sat up. "Nothing's wrong, honey."

"Is the Tooth Fairy mad at me?"

He looked at Hannah's face and found himself remembering how it felt to hold her when she was born— three weeks early and so much smaller than her two older sisters, an emergency C-section with the most perfect, round little head. *I'll keep you safe*, he had whispered to baby Hannah in a voice only she could hear. Hannah, little fingers plucking at the air, newly opened blue eyes, so big with wonder. *I'll protect you always. . .*

Or had he said that to Tessa?

God, Gary hated it when good memories slipped through his fingers. It was happening more and more lately—the things he wanted to remember moving beyond his grasp while the things he didn't stuck around, screaming in his ears until he beat them into silence. "It was probably an oversight. The Tooth Fairy loves you, Hannah."

She frowned at him. "You look sad."

"I'm just tired, honey." He was trying to "be here now," as they said in Jill's breathing class, but it was so hard to be here with Hannah, to hear her voice rather than that voice in his head—Errol Ludlow's smug, hyper-enunciating voice, spooling through Gary's brain just as clear as it had been over the disposable phone two hours ago—a bad memory, in need of a beating. *I know you asked me not to call. But I have just had the most fas-cin-a-ting con-ver-sa-tion with your wife. . .*

How had Jill found the phone? Why had she called Errol Ludlow instead of talking to Gary about it? Why did Gary's life keep going from bad to worse to worse again still?

Jill thought you were having an affair, but I was able to put her mind at ease. If you would like me to con-tin-ue to do so, however, my silence will cost you.

And what had Gary said? Not *How dare you?* or *I'm calling the police*, or even *Go fuck yourself*. No. What Gary had said was, *How much?*

We can start at $20K a month.

Can I get back to you later?

I'll give you until 5 P.M. EST.

"Hannah, can I ask you something?"

"Sure."

"How would you feel if . . . if we had to cut back a little? On our expenses?"

Hannah's brow wrinkled up. "What does that mean?"

"Well . . . Ballet class, for instance. Would you mind taking a break from it for a while?"

Her lip trembled. "I love ballet class," she said, and he was reminded again at how small she was. *Her troubles should be smaller still. They should be invisible.*

"Don't be upset, pickle. I'm glad you love ballet. You don't have to take a break."

"Then how come you asked?"

"No reason." He snapped on a smile. "Daddy likes saying things that make no sense sometimes."

Hannah giggled. "That's silly."

"I know. I'm a silly old guy."

She giggled some more.

"Listen, pickle, can you go play in the other room? Daddy's got some work he has to do."

"Why are you working in the kitchen?"

He sighed. "You can take my phone with you. Play that Fruit Toss game."

"Yay!"

Thank God for the attention spans of children.

"Phone, please." Hannah held out her hand, and without thinking, Gary went for his shirt pocket—for the disposable phone, the secret phone. His fingertips touched the plastic and his breath caught. He thought of worlds colliding, exploding—which made him remember The Shadow. And for a moment, his dread faded into longing. He missed her backlit body, missed her voice, saying those words that tore him apart. He shouldn't be thinking this way. He shouldn't ever be thinking this way, especially not in the presence of family, but now it was her voice in his head, her words. He couldn't keep her away.

"We could drive away together, my love." That's what he told me, that special boy, the boy on the road.

Gary grabbed his smart phone out of his pants pocket

and gave it to Hannah. His hands were shaking. "I . . . I don't know why you girls love this game so much."

"Fruit Toss is awesome! It makes squishy sounds!"

"We could drive all night," the boy said, *just him and me. "We could beat the murder mile and watch the sunrise in the rearview and love each other. Forever."*

Tears sprang into Gary's eyes.

"Daddy?"

He took Hannah in his arms and hugged her, very tightly, as though he were trying to stop her from floating away. When he let go, his vision was still blurred.

"Now you look sad again," Hannah said.

"I'm not sad," he heard himself say. "I'm angry."

"At who?"

Gary took a breath, like he'd learned in Jill's class. *Deep, cleansing breath.* "The Tooth Fairy."

Hannah nodded, solemn. "I'm sure it was just a oversight."

After Hannah left the room, Gary closed his eyes for a few moments. *I can fix this. I know how to fix this . . .* Before long, it felt like a prayer. *Please, I can fix this, please, please, I know how, just let me figure it out . . .*

He pulled the disposable phone out of his shirt pocket and looked at the outgoing calls—the three of them. Jill had called Ludlow. She'd probably stopped there—or at least at Brenna Spector. Otherwise she'd have phoned Gary by now, asking for a divorce. *I was able to put her mind at ease,* Ludlow had said.

Gary hoped he was right—for now, at least. Gary couldn't afford to send him $20K a month, even for one month. Ballet class or not, that was a simple fact.

From the other room, he could hear Hannah and Lucy fighting—something about Hannah hogging

Dad's phone. Again, Gary thought about worlds colliding. He didn't want to hurt his girls. God, he didn't want them sad. He didn't want to lose them, he couldn't lose them. He wouldn't be able to live. *How did I get to this awful place?* Gary thought. But of course he knew the answer. He'd driven here, all by himself.

We could stay on that road, him and me. That special boy. We could love each other. . .

"Shut up," Gary whispered. "Shut up, shut up . . ." He tapped the third number into his phone.

"Hello?" The voice was barely more mature than Hannah's, so breathy and small, but Gary wouldn't think about that. He couldn't.

"DeeDee."

"Mr. Freeman?"

"Yes," he said. "It's me."

"I couldn't tell from caller ID. You're on that private number again. Don't you have our phone anymore? Did you lose it?"

What the hell does it matter what phone I call you from?

"Hello?"

"I still have our phone," he said, as softly as he could. "It's in a safe place."

"Oh good." She sighed. "I know it sounds silly, but it means so much to me. That phone. Our phone. It's something we share. I see the number on my screen and my heart, my whole heart just . . ."

Gary winced. "DeeDee."

"Yes?"

"I'm in trouble."

"Oh no."

"I'm sorry. I shouldn't be calling you now. Not after all you've done for me already. I shouldn't be burdening you with this stuff." He closed his eyes, a hot weight behind them. DeeDee, his confessor. Baby-voiced DeeDee. "My life is falling apart and I can't stop it."

"Anything," she said.

"You're so young. You've got your whole life to live and I—"

"I'll do anything for you."

"Stop."

"You know I will."

Gary took a breath, absorbed the word: *Anything* . . . "I do know that," Gary said, feeling all the worse for knowing and not stopping her, poor kid. Poor deluded DeeDee, needy DeeDee, pinning so much hope on a man like him. *All she's done for me already* . . . Gary kept trying to forget what she'd done. He kept slamming that door in his mind and turning away, but still it was there, solid and real and shouting at him . . .

He should have cut her loose long ago. He should have hurt her feelings, broken her heart. A better man would have done that.

"How can I help you?" DeeDee said. "Tell me."

Gary breathed deep. He closed his eyes. And with his eyes still closed, he told her. Of course he told her, for there was something new now, something big and broken that needed to be fixed. And being a better man was a luxury neither he nor his family could afford. In a kind, soft voice, he told her about his troubles with Errol Ludlow while hearing Hannah in the other room—Hannah, his baby who should know no pain. Hannah, shouting at her sister, "It isn't fair!"

"Phones please!" said the guy who was holding the gun to Trent's head.

Trent unplugged his phone from the charger and handed it to him, his eyes never leaving the street.

Brenna's phone was in the front pocket of her jeans. She started to go for it when it vibrated. So instead, she opened the envelope in her lap, slipped out Robin Tannenbaum's phone, and passed it over her shoulder.

"Thanks, pretty lady," said the gunman, who called himself Bo. Brenna knew this because he'd already introduced himself. "My name's Bo," he had said, once Trent had gotten to the West Side Highway and headed north, as he'd been told. "And this here's my friend Diddley."

"Bo and Diddley," Brenna had said.

"We can make you sing the blues."

"Good one."

"You think so? Ha! I do, too!" Bo laughed a lot when he talked—like the car he'd just jacked was a cocktail party and he was the life of it, the .38 Smith and Wesson he was pressing against Trent's medulla oblongota no more dangerous than a virgin peach daiquiri. Brenna assumed he was supposed to be the friendly, avuncular one, while Diddley was the quiet one—the one you had to be careful of, crazy beneath the skin. She wondered how long it had taken these two to come up with this act. It was irritating, as all "acts" were—an insult to the intelligence. But really, she only wondered about it because it was easier than wondering about anything else.

Bo said, "And what do you two kids call yourselves?"

You two kids? Brenna thought. *Really?* The phone vibrated again. She cleared her throat to drown it out. "My name's Betty," she told Bo. "And this here's my friend Veronica."

Trent whispered, "Thanks a lot." But Bo laughed,

very loudly—which was what Brenna had been counting on. Much as Trent kept begging her to buy a smart phone (why should she when she had more memory than ten of them?), Brenna was glad she hadn't listened. The average smart phone was husky and very loud. Even on vibrate. Her flip phone, on the other hand, was tiny, and far more discreet—easily drowned out by your average gun-wielding human laugh track.

Bo's laughter, by now, had officially crossed the line between wacky and psychotic. Brenna worried he might burst a blood vessel.

Diddley moved a bit, probably to stare at his partner in disbelief, and the knife budged from Brenna's throat. She slid her hand into her pants pocket and flicked open the phone, tapping the talk button as she shoved it behind her back. All this took about five seconds, but it felt like so much longer, each step hanging in her mind, begging to be noticed . . .

Finally, she wedged the phone between the seat cushions behind her. *Done.* Of course, she had no idea who was on the other end of the line, but beggars couldn't be choosers, could they?

"Where are you taking us?" Brenna said, as Bo's laughter finally died down. She ventured a quick glance at him in the rearview. He had the look of an aging football player—fat on top of muscle on top of more fat, while Diddley—what she'd seen of Diddley anyway—was younger, more wiry. Both had stern faces and military-style crew cuts—Bo's graying, Diddley's bleached blond. And both wore very dark sunglasses, which, intimidating though it was, gave Brenna hope. They cared whether Brenna and Trent saw their faces. They might let them live.

Or maybe they just didn't like the sun in their eyes.

"I said, where are you taking us?"

Diddley leaned forward, put his lips to Brenna's ear. "We're taking you to the bottom of the river," he said quietly, "if you don't tell us where RJ is."

"Who the hell is RJ?" Trent blurted.

"Aw, Veronica. You really don't want to mess with us, trust me." Still the smile in Bo's voice, but he was breathing harder. Brenna heard a click—the safety on the Smith and Wesson.

"Please . . ." Trent whispered. "Please. I'm . . . I'm driving the car."

Brenna took a breath. *Stay calm.* "He isn't messing with you," she said. "We honestly don't know who RJ is."

Diddley's grip tightened around her neck. "Bullshit, Betty."

"I wouldn't lie about that."

Bo said, "RJ's mommy wouldn't give his 'puter to a couple strangers."

Brenna swallowed hard. *Best, RJT.* "RJ is Robin Tannenbaum."

"Bravo, Betty," Bo said. "I'd clap for ya, but as you see my hands are full."

"Please put the safety back on," Trent said.

"Say pretty please."

Trent drew a breath, deep and shaky. "Pretty please."

Bo clicked it back into place, and Brenna allowed herself to exhale.

"So you're gonna stop lying now."

"Listen. We have never met RJ Tannenbaum, and only met Hildy for the first time today."

"Then why did she tell our boss you were RJ's friends?"

"Your boss?"

"Hildy wouldn't lie to him. She knows better than that."

Brenna frowned, her thoughts casting back into the Forest Hills apartment, Hildy rushing for the kitchen to take her call. At the time, Brenna assumed she was simply trying to avoid her questions, but replaying it again, Brenna recalled the spark of fear in her eyes when the phone rang, the quaver in her voice as she spoke. *Oh, hello Mr. Pokrovsky. No, no, I'm fine . . .*

"Mr. Pokrovsky is your boss?"

Bo said, "Yeppers. And he wants his investment back, with the interest incurred. Pronto."

"Robin Tannenbaum borrowed money from him? What for?"

"Pull over, Veronica, and bear left."

At the side of the highway, Brenna saw a row of white Greek columns. "Greek columns. Where are we? Inwood Hill Park?" She thought of the phone wedged into the seat behind her—her only hope and it such a frail, dim one. *Probably a telemarketer, probably long off the line . . .*

"You ask a lot of questions, for someone who don't know how to answer any." It was Diddley talking, the voice quiet, purposefully menacing.

"Mr. Pokrovsky invested in RJ's business venture back in October," Bo said, as Trent made the turn. "Your buddy hasn't paid back a dime. And with interest, he now owes . . . Tell us how much he owes, Diddley."

"Twenty-five thousand dollars."

"That's a lot," Brenna said.

"Bet your sweet, skinny booty, that's a lot," Bo said. "So either you two bring us to him . . . or we're going to have to make ourselves more convincing."

"Oh God," Trent whispered.

"Hang a right, Veronica sweetheart. We're gonna

take that path all the way down to the river." He chuckled a little, then began to sing, very softly. "Take me to the river, drop me in the water . . ."

"Nice," Diddley said.

"We sing the blues, too, don't we, Diddley?"

"Uh-huh."

Brenna glanced in the rearview and saw the Magnum following, at a distance. *Outnumbered.*

"Washing me down, washing me down . . ."

"Look," Brenna cut in, "we're not friends of RJ's. We're private investigators, and we're looking for a woman he may have had contact with, and that's why we have his computer. We never met Hildy Tannenbaum in our lives before today. We're trying to find RJ. Just like you."

"You know what? You are really starting to piss me off."

"Now Diddley, they're just scared is all. You kids oughta quit lying, though, if you don't want to—"

"*We're not freakin' lying!*" Trent yelled.

"Easy there, Veronica."

"The name's not Veronica. It's Trent or TNT if you were a friend instead of a total jank-ass fat loser *which you are.*"

"*Trent,*" Brenna hissed. "*Stop.*"

"No! I've had enough of this crap. If this dickwad wants to shoot me in the head just because I don't know where friggin' *RJ* is, *he can just go ahead and do it! I'm tired of the mind games!*"

Brenna heard a click—the safety releasing again.

Diddley's grip loosened. "Don't shoot him while he's driving," he said, his breath at the back of Brenna's neck, and in seconds she was back into October 2, the stitches fresh in her abdomen, lying in the hospital bed in Columbia-Presbyterian, *and the soft knock on her door as Trent pokes his head in, holds up Brenna's suitcase, smiling at the wall behind her. She knows he's trying not to look at her wounds. And it isn't out of politeness—Trent's hardly ever polite. He doesn't want to look because he doesn't like seeing her hurt.*

"Don't hurt him," Brenna said, back in the car now. "Please." Diddley wasn't being as diligent with the knife and so she shifted around in the seat, looked at Bo. "We don't know where RJ is, but you can take the computer. That's gotta be worth close to the amount he originally borrowed, right? Before interest? Just let us pull over so you can take it."

"Wait—*what?*" Trent said.

"You can take the car, too."

Trent said, "No friggin' *way*!"

"Excuse me?"

Trent made a sudden hard right. The car jumped the curb and careened over the grass, throwing Brenna back into her seat. Bo's gun exploded in a sudden, shattering roar. *No*, Brenna thought, *No, no, no, no . . .* Brenna closed her eyes as the car veered off to the side and began to roll down the hill in slow motion, the thought becoming a prayer, the prayer becoming everything, the gunshot ringing in her ears so she couldn't hear. *No, no, no, no, no, no, no, no . . .*

Brenna felt a thud and the car came to a stop. She opened her eyes and saw the cracked windshield, the trunk of a tree. And then the air bag deployed, socking her in the face. She didn't feel it, though. She was numb, outside herself. *Trent*, she wanted to say, but she couldn't speak, until finally her ears stopped ringing and she struggled to move.

She heard a moaning behind her. Bo. Or Diddley.

She wasn't sure which, didn't care. *Trent, oh God, Trent, I'll kill them, I swear, if they hurt you. Kill them with my bare hands . . .*

Brenna struggled around the air bag. The left side of her face was tender, the whole of it a bruise radiating from the half-closed eye, the vision blurred—a shiner. *Where are you, Trent . . .* She needed the thick bag out of her way, needed to touch him to check his pulse, to see his face, *please let him have a face . . .* "Trent, are you there?" she said.

Nothing.

"Trent . . ."

Brenna heard movement in the backseat, a door opening behind her. Bo or Diddley. Moving. Alive. She hated them both.

Brenna pushed at her own door. She fell out of the car and onto the wet grass, her knees buckling, eye throbbing, but still the hate coursed through her, pressing against her skin until she vibrated with it, making her stronger. *Kill them with my bare hands.*

She stood up, and he flew at her. Diddley—that's who it was. His face full of blood, clumsy from his injuries, his teeth glistening red, knife still clutched in his hand. He was bigger than she, but all that lost blood made them equals. Shiner or not, Brenna was grateful for the air bag, grateful for Diddley pressing that knife to her throat before the car rolled, because no one could have done that while wearing a seat belt, and if he'd been wearing a seat belt she wouldn't have a chance.

An animal sound came out of him—a gurgling howl. He slashed at her left shoulder, but the hate was so strong, she barely felt it. *Trent.* She brought her right hand back, jammed the heel of it into his eye. Diddley screamed, his arm dropping.

She balled the hand into a fist and socked him in the gut. He stumbled back. Her hand hurt. Dots of light swam in front of her eyes. He still had the knife. She stared at it in his hand and a memory tugged at her—*October 2 . . .* but Trent was enough to bring her back. The thought of him in the car, his silence . . .

She heard another car door.

Bo.

Diddley was stumbling toward her with the knife, worse for the wear but still deadly—him and the knife both, the blade dark with Brenna's blood, and now Bo coming. Fat, grinning Bo and his gun, she couldn't see him but she knew.

The car door slammed.

A voice said, "Drop it." But it wasn't Bo's voice. It was Trent's.

Diddley froze, dropped the knife.

Brenna turned to see her assistant, alive, standing next to the wrecked car. His face was pale, blood trickling down the side, staining the collar of his cowboy shirt. He was unsteady on his feet, but the gun made up for his weakness—Bo's gun, held straight in front of him, just the way she'd taught him to hold a gun on *April 5, 2003. You can't shoot, fine. At least let me show you how to look like you can . . .* Brenna bit her lip hard enough to come back from the memory. Trent gave her a tired smile. "Hi."

Diddley said, "Don't shoot, please."

"Blow me."

Relief washed through Brenna. *You're still here. Trent's still here.* "Are you okay?"

Trent looked at her. "You hurt your eye, Bonnie."

Bonnie? Okay, so Trent needed a doctor. But he was alive and he could stand and he could speak . . .

"Check it out." He nodded at the front pocket of his bloody cowboy shirt. "I got the phone back, too."

Brenna saw the rectangular outline. RJ's cell phone.

"Fell on me when the car rolled. How's that for irony? The gun, too. Got me in the head."

Brenna took a breath, but before she could use it to say anything, she heard an engine approaching and remembered the Dodge Magnum. "Trent, listen to me."

"Who else am I going to listen to?"

"Don't let go of that gun, okay? Don't move."

Brenna spun toward the sound, the left whole side of her body aching as she did. The eye, the cheek, the stinging slice at her shoulder. *Get ready . . .*

But it wasn't the Magnum approaching. It was Morasco's Subaru Impreza. It was Morasco screeching to a halt, Morasco jumping out of the car, shouting, "Police!" Morasco rushing up to Brenna, taking her in his arms—Morasco saying, "You're okay." Saying it, again and again, like a prayer.

10

There was a reason that Trent hadn't been able to speak for so long in the car. It was the same reason that he'd called Brenna Bonnie, and it was why, when with the help of one of several uniformed cops who had shown up moments after he did, Morasco had taken the gun, put an arm around him and helped him into a waiting ambulance, Trent had looked at the forty-year-old, childless detective and said, "Dad? What are you doing here?"

He had suffered a concussion, apparently caused by Bo's gun flying out of his hand and hitting him in the back of the head. The paramedics said it was probably a grade two—not very serious, seeing as Trent hadn't been unconscious for more than a few seconds, knew who the president was, and could count to ten without any help. But it wasn't wise to underestimate a head injury, and so they were taking him to the hospital anyway for observation, probably an MRI. Brenna, too.

"Maybe I just happen to look like his dad," Morasco said to Brenna, as they rode in the back of Trent's ambulance to Columbia-Presbyterian.

Brenna held an ice pack to her black eye. Adrenaline

gone, her whole face ached, the ice about as worthwhile as a Band-Aid. But it could have been worse. Everything could have been so much worse. "You don't look like Trent's dad," Brenna said. "Believe me."

"Dude, I'm right here and I love my dad."

"I wasn't being insulting."

"Tell that to your tone of voice," Trent said.

The paramedics shushed him. "You really shouldn't talk or get agitated right now," said one of them—a young, serious-looking woman in delicate, wire-framed glasses.

Trent turned to the paramedic, noticing her for the first time. "Hot librarian alert!"

She actually smiled at him, which only proved how much you can get away with when you're an injured person in an ambulance. Well, an innocent injured person, anyway. Bo and Diddley had been rushed to the hospital as well, but in their case, cops were riding along to arrest them once they were patched up and released.

Amazing, Brenna thought. Because life rarely worked out like this. More often than not, life was random, brutal, unfair. It passed from one moment to the next without rhyme or reason, the good suffering just as much as the evil, usually more so for the shock of discovering that the world is not a safe, just place. Children disappeared, innocent people died, young girls got into blue cars as their sisters watched, and the cars drove away, never to be seen again . . .

That said, Brenna was alive. Trent was alive. And of all the people who could have called her cell phone when she hit send and hoped for the best, it had been Morasco. Not a telemarketer from Idaho or India. Not Brenna's mother or some half-sane potential client or

Kate O'Hanlon wanting another five-thousand-calorie breakfast or anyone else who might have just sat there on the other end of the line, frightened and confused and doing nothing to help. She had hoped for the best, and that's exactly what she had gotten.

"You do realize you saved our lives," Brenna told him.

"Nah."

"No, seriously. Those two idiots got out of a Dodge Magnum to jack our car, but the Magnum kept following us. If you hadn't shown up when you did, whoever was in that car would have finished us off pretty easily."

Morasco said nothing.

"So what I'm saying is, it's a good thing you called."

"No, Brenna."

Trent said, "Jeez, take a compliment, dude."

"No you don't understand," Morasco said. "It wasn't me who called."

"You're right," Brenna said. "I don't understand."

"Maya called your cell phone."

Brenna stared at him. "Maya?"

"She got home from her sleepover and wondered where you were," Morasco said. "She was worried, and so she called you."

"Maya was on the other end of the line."

"She called me from her cell phone while she stayed on with you on the landline. She could barely hear what you were saying—something about Inwood Hill Park. But I called the 34th Precinct and they pinged your cell and got a location."

Brenna swallowed hard. "I was going to call Maya when we got to the hospital. Come up with some excuse so she wouldn't have to know . . ."

"Well, she knows." Morasco stared straight ahead. "Your daughter loves you," he said, "very much."

"Does she know I'm all right?"

"I told her you were," Morasco said. "I don't know if she believed me, though. At the time, I wasn't sure myself."

Brenna tried to sort all this out in her head—her daughter on the other end of the line, her daughter, who shouldn't be exposed to scenes like the one in the Taurus, not ever. Maya, who still kept her copy of *The Very Hungry Caterpillar* and clomped up the stairs in her high-tops, Maya, who loved to draw and was still a child and shouldn't know fear like that. She never should know.

But then they were arriving at the hospital, Trent chatting up the paramedic as she helped him into the stretcher. "You sure you haven't done any modeling?" he was saying now, such a child himself—risking his life, as he had, for RJ Tannenbaum's computer, a high-priced toy. Morasco and another paramedic helped Brenna out of the ambulance, and she realized how much she ached—the bandaged shoulder wound, the swollen eye. "Let me see," Morasco said.

Brenna removed the ice bag. He flinched.

"You need to work on your poker face."

He brushed a lock of hair out of her eye. "I've seen worse," he said. "On you, in fact."

Brenna smiled. It hurt. She flipped open her phone to find a text from Maya: *R U OK???* All caps. Three question marks.

She texted back: *I am fine. At hospital with Trent. Will be home soon.*

"You can't use your phone here, ma'am," said another paramedic, leaning against a wheelchair—a big, olive-skinned guy with glossy black hair and sweet eyes. "Hey, wait. I know you."

"You can't possibly."

Morasco said, "She doesn't forget a face."

"Me neither," he said.

"Yes, but she's infallible."

"You were unconscious," the paramedic told Brenna as he helped her into the chair. "Knife wound, early October."

Brenna looked up into his face, and fell back into October 2, when, so close to figuring out the Neff case, she'd gotten stabbed near Pelham Bay. Again she felt the blade as it socked into her abdomen, the damp pavement against her body, the slicing pain beneath her ribs as the life drained out of her. She felt it all and smelled the brine of the bay in the air, until she was devoured by the memory, fear coursing through her and then that same weird stillness . . . *Breathing is hard, now. Brenna's breath frail like a baby breathing, her body needing more air than she is able to give it. She puts her hand to her pain and feels her shirt—wet, sticking to her. She brings the hand up to her face and sees blood—so much of it, it looks black, like oil on her skin.* I'm dying. *The cell phone. She reaches for it, touches it . . .* Call 911.

Brenna's cell phone vibrated in her hands—just once. A text—and it brought her back to the present. She gasped, the pain fading, the face of the paramedic coming back into focus. "My name is Angel, by the way," he said, which made Brenna smile.

"Of course it is."

She glanced down at the text, from Maya: *WHEW!!!!* All caps. Four exclamation points. Maybe life wasn't completely brutal and random and unfair. Maybe some things did happen for good reason. Not to get too sappy about it, but how could Brenna *not* feel this way when, in just three months, her life had been saved, twice?

Maybe some girls get into blue cars and live.

"Okay, let's get you into the ER," Angel said.

Morasco said, "I'm coming with her."

Brenna gave Angel a pleading look. "Just one more quick text? For my daughter."

He sighed.

"Thank you," Brenna said. She typed up the one-sentence text as fast as she could, hit send, and obediently turned off the phone. As Angel wheeled her into the ER, Brenna imagined Maya reading it, and stifled a grin. She could practically see the eye roll, but also that shy little smile—unchanged since she was a toddler.

The text had read: *You are my hero.*

After their wounds were treated, Trent and Brenna were both given MRIs. Both came out normal—well, free of brain injury, anyway. But predictably, Brenna's made the doctors do a double-take. Because of her hyperthymesia, more than a dozen parts of her brain were larger than usual, some extraordinarily so. She'd been told this three years ago, after participating in the California study that finally put a medical name to what her mother always claimed was God's will. (*Don't you see, Brenna? It's God's will. With that memory, no one will be able to truly leave us again.*)

At any rate, Brenna knew what to expect. What she hadn't planned on was reliving the MRI she'd had on June 23, 2006, as part of the study. It had been the first and only MRI she'd ever had, and the first time Brenna had realized—palpably—that she was a lot more than mildly claustrophobic. No sooner was the MRI tech at Columbia-Presbyterian giving her the earphones than Brenna was back on the table at the City of Hope Medical Center in Duarte, California, in that white room with the vague chemical smell . . . *Her heart pounds as the technician, Doreen, hands her a pair of puffy black earphones.* "Are we gonna listen to some Black Sabbath?" *Brenna tries. Her throat is dry.*

Doreen doesn't smile. "They're to protect your ears. Ever had an MRI?"

"No."

"Well, without these, the sound is even more unbearable than 'War Pigs.'"

"Hey, I like 'War Pigs.'"

Still no smile. "Then maybe you'll enjoy this."

Brenna slides into the tube. A series of shrieking beeps slices into her brain. Test of the Emergency Broadcast System from Hell. Where's "War Pigs" *when you need it,* Brenna thinks. The beeping stops.

Doreen's voice comes through the speakers. "Please stay still, Ms. Spector." *Brenna opens her eyes, but the walls of the tube look closer. The space is getting smaller. She wants to push against the walls. She wants to scream.*

"Four score and seven years ago," started Brenna.

And then the voice of the Columbia-Presbyterian MRI tech boomed through the speakers around her. "Please don't move, Ms. Spector."

. . . *and she was back at the City of Hope again. In her mind, she sees Edward G. Robinson in* Soylent Green *watching peaceful scenes on a movie screen as he is forcibly euthanized. She opens her eyes and the tube is smaller still . . .*

"Will this be over soon?" Brenna said now.

"Yes, ma'am."

Thankfully, it was. After giving lip service to the chief surgeon—who talked about her brain in the same way that Trent talked about particularly well-endowed girls—Brenna met up with Morasco in the waiting room. "Hey, your eye looks better," he said.

Brenna touched her hand to it. It felt better, too. Just a dull throb and nowhere near as swollen. "You think Maya will freak out when she sees me?"

"No way," he said. She couldn't tell whether it was a white lie.

"So . . . Brenna?"

"Yeah?"

"You want to tell me how you got acquainted with . . . Man, I feel like a schmuck even saying their names out loud."

"Bo and Diddley."

"Don't you feel like a schmuck now?"

"Yes," Brenna said. "Yes I do."

"So, how did you wind up with those cretins in your car?"

"Trent doesn't lock his doors."

"Okay. Let's go a little further back than that."

Brenna sighed. "It's a long story," she said. But she gave him the fast-forwarded version, taking Morasco from her breakfast with Kate O'Hanlon to Hildy Tannenbaum's apartment, complete with the call from Mr. Pokrovsky, to her and Trent's wild ride with the two dorkiest named enforcers in the history of organized crime. One of the good things about a perfect memory: So long as you don't get distracted, you can retell a story very well and very quickly, without stumbling to recall facts.

"So, Tannenbaum was in debt to this Pokrovsky guy?" Morasco asked. "What for?"

"That's the sixty-four-thousand-dollar question."

"Incredibly dated reference," he said. "How old are you, anyway?"

Brenna grinned at him. Same thing she'd said to him in Lydia Neff's kitchen on October 1. He'd just quoted her directly. "Way to a woman's heart," she said, "is through her memory."

Morasco looked into her eyes. His smile dissolved and in his eyes she caught a hint of it—that same ache she'd seen there the previous night, as he watched Lula Belle talk about the wounded bird . . . *If Mama were to see me, she'd have been amazed. She thought I was crazy like my daddy. She thought I couldn't take care of nothin' without breakin' it. Mama said that gift for destruction ran through my veins.*

"What's wrong, Nick?" she said quietly.

Someone called out, "Get a room!"

Trent. Brenna turned to see him, getting wheeled through the waiting room by the young bespectacled paramedic, a large white bandage on his forehead.

"Heading home?" Brenna asked.

"Yep. The doctors have officially declared my brain awesome."

"Great," she said. "But I want you to promise me something."

"Sorry, my heart belongs to Claudia here."

The paramedic smiled again.

"You are very tolerant, Claudia." Brenna leveled her eyes at Trent. "I mean it. As soon as you get out of here, I want you to go straight home and rest. Get a good night's sleep tonight. And by getting a good night's sleep, I *don't* mean—"

"Coralling the baloney pony. I know, I know. Trust me. Tonight, the only thing I'll be exploring with my fingertips will be the supple keyboard of Tannenbaum's Mac Pro."

"Okay, now I'm going to throw up."

"That is, unless Claudia—"

"Have fun with the Mac Pro," Claudia said.

"Aw, that's cold, baby." He looked at Brenna. "Seriously, Claudia and I have tons in common. Her brother does computer stuff for the FBI."

"You don't have a brother, Trent."

"No, but see . . ."

"I don't know anything about computers," Claudia said.

Brenna said, "Seems like you have more in common with Claudia's brother. Maybe she should introduce you."

Trent sighed. "Fine, I give up."

Brenna leaned over and gave Trent a quick, tight hug. "Please stay out of trouble."

"Telling the T-Man not to get in trouble is like telling the sun not to shine."

"No it isn't."

Morasco added, "Telling the T-Man not to refer to himself in the third person, on the other hand . . ."

"Or asking the T-Man not to make up stupid nicknames for himself."

"All right, all right," he said. "I promise."

Once Brenna and Morasco were outside the hospital, he put a hand on her shoulder. "So, listen. I want to talk to you about something. You wanna go get a drink?"

"It's barely three o'clock."

"You spent lunchtime in a rolling car, followed by an MRI. That automatically makes the rest of the day happy hour."

She laughed. "Good point," she said. "But I should get home to Maya, and she wouldn't appreciate it if I came in trashed."

"True."

"You want to give me a ride home? My car's in the shop."

"Yeah, I remember that."

"And your car's at a crime scene."

"Remember that, too," he said. "Of course, knowing my luck, it got impounded."

They headed for the curb, and Brenna started to hail a cab to take them to Inwood Hill Park, but Morasco stopped her. "Okay, first of all, you're supposed to let the guy hail the cab."

"Says who?"

"This guy."

"Sexist."

"Secondly . . ."

Brenna's cell phone chimed. "One second." She checked the screen—a number she'd never seen but with Freeman's same area code. She held up a finger to Morasco, put her back to him, and answered, very quietly.

"You're not alone," Freeman said.

"No," Brenna said. "But listen, as long as I have you here, have you ever heard of a Robin Tannenbaum? He also goes by RJ?"

There was a long pause on the other end of the line. "No. Why?"

"He may be with our girl."

"Why do you say that?"

"Well, they know each other and they both disappeared at the same time, and he, for one, seems to be in a whole lot of trouble."

Another long pause. "Okay," he said. "But keep in mind, I'm only paying you to look for her."

Brenna frowned. Her eye hurt. "People don't always disappear alone, Ga—"

"Sssh. Don't use my name."

"Sorry."

"No worries," he said. "Look, I don't want to talk any more if there are people with you. Just remember—if anybody asks you about me—anybody at all . . ."

"I don't know you."

"Right. Talk later."

Click.

Brenna stared at the phone for a few seconds. Good God the guy was paranoid. Did he buy himself a new disposable phone every day?

"Who was that?" Morasco said.

Brenna smiled a little. It was practically as though Freeman had hired him to test her. "Nobody. Just a client." She cleared her throat. "So, what were you going to ask me?"

"You're going to give up this case, right?"

She turned to him, her smile slipping away. His face was more serious than she'd expected. "Of course I'm not giving it up."

"Brenna."

"I can't."

His eyes narrowed. "Why the hell not? One day of it, and you're in trouble with organized crime over this Tannenbaum guy—and he's not even the person you're looking for."

"I can't."

"You almost got killed today," Morasco said. "You scared your daughter half to death. And for what? Some . . . some shadow? Some weird-ass fetish?"

"She's a person."

"So are you. You have people who care about you. You owe them something."

"I owe her, too."

"Who?"

"Lula Belle."

"You *don't*."

Brenna's jaw tightened.

"Why are you doing this?"

"It's important."

"Why?"

"Uh . . . Because I *said* so?"

"I'm not kidding around, Brenna."

"I can see that."

Behind the glasses, his eyes went hard. "Is it because of Ludlow?"

"*What?*"

"You heard me."

She started to remember October 23, 1998, and she shut her eyes tight, she bit it back. "No," she whispered.

"You're remembering Jim, aren't you?" Morasco said.

"No, I . . ."

"You're remembering how he reacted when he found out you'd worked for Ludlow again, even though you'd promised him you wouldn't. "

"Stop."

"You're remembering that night, and you *should* remember that night. You should remember how you made him feel when you put yourself in that kind of danger, just to go work for that asshole—"

"*I said, stop it!*" Brenna's eyes were hot from tears. She turned away from him, tried to catch her breath.

"I'm . . . I'm sorry."

Brenna closed her eyes and thought of the Lord's Prayer, recited it in her head start to finish until the memory was gone. Even then, her eyes were still hot. She felt a tear slipping down her cheek. She swatted it away and breathed very deeply until the feeling passed, and then, finally, she opened her eyes. She turned to Morasco. That much she could do. But still she didn't trust herself to talk, not yet. God, Brenna hated herself sometimes. Hated all her limitations.

"That wasn't fair of me," Morasco said.

She said nothing.

He took a deep breath, let it out slowly. "It's just . . ." His voice trailed off. "This is going to sound stupid."

She didn't help him. Didn't say a word. Just stood there, hands crossed over her chest, watching.

"Your mind is so crowded," he said. "I want in. I wish you would let me in."

"Why? Hell, I don't even like it in there."

Nick's gaze dropped to the sidewalk. "I do," he said quietly.

She stared at him, at his downcast eyes. Much as she wanted him to meet her gaze, he wouldn't and in a way she was glad. She was afraid of what she might see. "You do?"

"Yes. A lot."

Brenna felt herself softening. "You're crazier than I thought."

Nick took a step closer. Then he looked into her eyes. *Nothing to be afraid of. Nothing at all . . .* "I'm not staying on this case because of Ludlow."

"Then why?"

"This." Her hand went into her bag and removed the manila envelope full of Robin Tannenbaum's things. She slipped out the photo of Clea and herself and gave it to him.

"Is that you and your sister?"

Brenna nodded. "That picture was in Robin Tannenbaum's computer. It was sent to him. By Lula Belle."

His eyes widened.

"Half the stories she tells—they're specific stories from my childhood."

"Your childhood," he whispered, his eyes clouding over, filling again with that strange emotion.

Is it pity?

Morasco went back to the picture. Brenna pressed on. "She sent him that photo, Nick. She got him to put at least one of her PO boxes in his name. If I can find Robin Tannenbaum, I think I might be able to find Lula Belle, and if I can find Lula Belle, I might be able to . . ." She cleared her throat. It was harder than she'd thought, putting it into words with him.

"Find your family," he said.

She looked at him. "Yes."

Morasco kept staring at the picture, then lifted his gaze to Brenna's face. "Let's get Tannenbaum," he said.

During the cab ride back to her place, Brenna went through the manila envelope and pulled out Robin Tannenbaum's most recent credit card bill. It was a brand-new Visa with a balance of just five hundred dollars. "He must have done some damage to his other cards," she said. But outside of an Old Navy card and Diner's Club (*who has Diner's Club anymore?*) she couldn't find bills for any others. "He hid his old bills?"

Morasco said, "Maybe he didn't want his mother to see them."

Brenna thought of Hildy Tannenbaum's husband, that stack of *Playboy*s. "Or his mother didn't want anybody else to see them," she said. "She could have just paid them off. Made them go away."

"Too bad she couldn't have done that with whatever he owed Mr. Pokrovsky."

"He owed Pokrovsky twenty-five thousand dollars."
He shook his head. "What a dumbass."

Brenna skimmed the bill. The last charge was on October 9, 2009—sixty dollars at a gas station. In Brenna's mind, Hildy showed her the note:

Mother:

*No need to keep dinner warm. May be gone for
a little while.*

> > > > *Best, RJT*

"That was the day he left," Brenna said. "Check it
out. Filled up his tank. In White Plains—your area."

"I can ask around," Morasco said. "You got a picture of him?"

Brenna handed him one of the photos Hildy had provided.

"Handsome devil."

"He's grown a beard since then."

"To cover up the pock marks?"

"Actually, Trent thinks he did it to look like Spielberg."

Morasco snorted. "Seriously?"

"Yes, seriously. He had a picture of Steven Spielberg taped next to his mirror. Let me find it." Brenna
thumbed through the papers. She didn't see it. "Trent
probably took it—he wanted to do some Photoshopping." She did find another photo of Spielberg—but this
was different, an older, black and white one he'd clipped
from a magazine, probably mixed in with everything
Hildy had removed from Robin's desk. "Hmm. Looks
like he had a collection."

"Go figure. Some guys want to look like Fabio. He chooses a sixty-year-old director . . ."

"Who the hell wants to look like Fabio?" Brenna stared at the bottom of the clipped photo—handwritten words, so tiny she could barely read them:

DEUT 31:6

"He wrote a Bible verse on this picture," she said.

"A Bible-thumping, Spielberg-worshipping porno editor?"

"He's also a big Louise Hay fan," Brenna said.

"Multifaceted."

"You're a good driver, by the way."

"You've driven with me before."

"I know. But I never really appreciated it. Trent drives like he's being chased by a husband with a gun."

They were on the West Side Highway, passing the Chelsea Piers. "I'm still trying to figure out," Morasco said, "what Lula Belle saw in Tannenbaum. I mean . . . you're going to send one person that photo—and this is a long-lost family photo, no matter who Lula Belle turns out to be."

Brenna nodded. *No matter who.*

"You're going to trust that same person enough to let him get you a secret PO box where you receive secret money for your secret job—and let him put it in his name. You're really going to choose the forty-five-year-old porno editor from Queens who lives with his mom and is stupid enough to borrow money from a guy who's connected to Bo and Diddley?"

Brenna turned to him. "Maybe she and Robin go way back," she said. "And maybe he isn't stupid—just hopelessly devoted." She thought about Robin, packing up his winter clothes, taking his beloved film equipment, growing his beard to look like Spielberg . . . *To look like someone else.* "Maybe he borrowed from Pokrovsky because he needed the money in a hurry—to finance their new life."

"Weird," he said quietly. "But I guess it's possible."

"There's only one way to find out for sure."

He looked at her.

"You're going to hate this, but I want to go back and see RJ's mother. Get her to introduce me to Mr. Pokrovsky."

"Us."

"Pardon?"

"I'm going with you. Not up for discussion."

Brenna looked at him. "Since when did you get so friggin' tough?" she said. "Oh yeah, I forgot. You're a cop."

"Actually, I prefer to be referred to as The Fuzz. I'm trying to bring that back."

Brenna grinned.

They'd reached Brenna's apartment a while ago. By now, Morasco had circled the block three times, with no luck finding a space, so he pulled in front and double parked. It was a little after 5 P.M. and already dark out—Christmas decorations twinkling on the streetlight in front of Brenna's house. This time of year, Twelfth Street looked like something out of a nineteenth-century storybook. Brenna rarely had thoughts like this, but she longed for snow, for horse-drawn carriages and hearth light through bay windows. "I'll see you tomorrow morning," she said to Morasco.

"Okay." He gave her a smile. "Take care of yourself."

"You too."

As she got out of the car, a cold wind bit her face, made her black eye throb. She found herself thinking back again to O'Donnell's parking lot. O'Donnell's was in City Island. Brenna and Morasco had gone there after having dinner with Brenna's mother, who had served her usual—chicken piccata with a heaping side of guilt. Evelyn Spector, who remembered things not as they were but exactly as she wanted them to be, with herself as the heroine—degraded, misunderstood. By the time they'd stumbled into the parking lot, Brenna had finished four beers in record time, yet still she couldn't get it out of her system, that frustration . . .

"And you know how my mother said the last time I visited her, Maya was still teething?" Brenna is drunk now, officially. Not tipsy. Drunk. At her height, she should be able to hold her liquor better than this. It's a little embarrassing.

"That's not true, huh?" Nick smiles. Brenna is leaning on him and she can feel his lips moving against her hairline.

"It was three weeks ago!" Her speech is thick and slurry. "If Maya was still friggin' teething three weeks ago, she's gotta be a friggin' shark."

Nick laughs.

"I'm serious. I better call animal control. Or . . . like . . . a top-secret scientific division of the navy. Tell 'em I've got some kind of chemical mutant shark-girl on my hands because my mother said she was teething and my mother is always right."

Nick laughs again. Brenna likes his laugh. She turns to look at his face and feels his fingertips on the back of her neck and around her waist and his lips . . . like that, yes, just like lips should be and she leans into him. It's so easy, like melting . . .

"You want me to wait here till you get your door open?"

Brenna turned to Morasco, put on a smile. "Nah. I'm fine," she said.

He gave her a quick wave and pulled away from the curb and she watched him go, still remembering that parking lot. God, she wished things had happened differently.

Brenna glanced up at her apartment. The lights were on, the shades drawn, shadows moving behind them. *Maya*.

She thought about finding a good movie on TV, ordering in pizza with Maya and eating in front of it. It felt like heaven. She was achy, exhausted. So exhausted, it wasn't until she was heading up the stairs that it hit her: Behind the drawn shades, Brenna had seen not one, but two figures.

She hurried up the stairs, shoved her key in the lock, and opened the door. Maya came running at her. "Mom!" She threw her arms around her and Brenna held her tight. *My baby* . . .

"Is someone else here?"

"I'm sorry," Maya whispered. "I told him what happened to you. I was scared . . ."

Brenna pulled away. She opened her eyes, and that's when she saw him. Leaning against the wall by Brenna's desk, as if he belonged here, as if . . . just like . . . *No, no, no*.

"What happened to your eye, Mom?" Maya said.

Brenna couldn't answer. She couldn't breathe, couldn't look at him, couldn't say anything, except the name of the other person in the room. "Jim."

11

Errol Ludlow did not tolerate lateness. He viewed it as a sign of hostility—the unsaid implication that another person's time is not valuable, and can be wasted at will. And though in Gary Freeman's case he had every right to be hostile, it was definitely not in his best interests to keep Errol waiting. He'd given Freeman a specific deadline. Five P.M. And he'd blown it by seven minutes.

Errol checked his cell phone, made sure the ringer was turned up. *Maybe my phone is broken.* He picked up the hotel phone and called his cell with it. Of course it chimed like St. Patrick's on Easter Sunday.

"What part of 'You have until 5 P.M. EST' don't you understand?" He said it out loud, as if Freeman were here, sitting next to him on the king-sized bed at the MoonGlow Hotel on 108th and Second Avenue. Errol didn't like the tone of his own voice, the pleading in it. He picked up his cell and prepared to call Gary Freeman, talk to him about this man to man . . .

This, by the way, was why Errol Ludlow preferred to hire women. His critics—Brenna Spector being one of far too many—would say that he enjoyed having pretty young girls do his dirty work. But that wasn't the case at all. Young, pretty, or neither, Errol preferred women because they behaved like human beings. Men were dogs—every last one of them, Errol included. Stupid, dirty, jealousy-driven animals who were all too prone to pissing contests.

Freeman was a perfect example. Backed up to a wall, the fate of his marriage in Errol's hands, and what was he doing? Making Errol wait by the phone like a love-struck schoolgirl. How logical was that?

Errol's phone chimed. He glanced at the screen—a number he didn't recognize, but Freeman's same Southern California area code. He crossed his fingers—literally crossed his fingers, on both hands. He hated himself for doing that. "Ludlow."

"Hello, Errol. It's Gary."

Errol exhaled. "You're late."

"I know, and I'm really sorry about that," Freeman's voice was surprisingly friendly, apologetic, even. "I had to get a new disposable phone, and I wasn't . . . uh . . . I wasn't able to safely get away and use it until now."

"I understand," said Errol. Well, he did. Who wouldn't? He cleared his throat. "So, Gary, do we have a deal?"

"Yes, we do."

Errol's heart leaped.

Freeman was saying, "I'm afraid, though, that I won't be able to get you the first payment until Monday. I have to rearrange my accounts in order to make this work . . . you know . . . without it being noticed."

Errol grinned. "Not a problem. I will expect payment on Monday."

"You will?"

"Yes."

"Oh, I'm so relieved. Thank you for being so under-standing."

Was this guy for real? Was he suddenly on medica-tion? Gary Freeman had been so cold during that earlier phone conversation—during all his phone conversa-tions with Errol, come to think of it—and now here he was, bending over backward to accommodate him, complimenting him even, when basically what Errol was doing—not that Freeman didn't deserve it, keeping such secrets from his wife—but it was, after all, a form of blackmail.

For the first time since he'd come up with the idea, Errol felt guilty about it. He'd get over it, of course. But still, something nagged at him . . . Maybe this was how Freeman had become such a successful talent agent— the ability to inspire this feeling in others.

Errol said, "I will do my best to make sure your wife never finds out about Lula Belle."

There was a pause on the other end of the line, a deep breathing, in and out. "Thank you," he said. "I really appreciate that."

"It's only common courtesy."

"Actually, you don't know how *un*common courtesy really is."

Errol smiled at the phone. *A kindred spirit.* "Oh, now that's where you're wrong, Gary. I know. Believe me, I do."

"Errol?"

"Yes?"

"Do you think, under different circumstances, we might have been friends?"

Errol sensed something in Freeman's voice—a type of melancholy. *Strange.* He wondered if Gary Freeman ever felt the way he did—too big for his surroundings. It had nothing to do with Errol's being six-eight, either. Most men—most people, really—could be so petty, so small. He saw it all the time in his job—not just the cheating husbands, but the wives, living and dying to catch them in the act. *He'll be sorry he ever messed with me*, they would say, their eyes so hard and cold it would frighten Errol a little. More than a few of them had even suggested entrapment (*Could you get one of your girls to . . . you know . . . and videotape it?*) Not to sound like a sentimentalist, but weren't these men and women who once pledged to love each other, above all else?

Sometimes, Errol felt as though he'd spent his whole life searching for someone he could see eye to eye with, not physically but cerebrally, emotionally. Not a soul mate—that was a ridiculous concept. Just a fellow human, traveling through this dark, sick world, some-one he could look in the face and say, *Stinks in here, doesn't it?*

"I do think we would be friends, Gary," he said.

"Thank you, Errol."

After he ended the call, Errol stood staring at his reflection in the bedroom mirror. He'd expected to feel elation, but instead he felt rather the opposite—as though Freeman's melancholy were catching. He had an urge to make good on his promise to him—to keep him safe from the wrath of his wife, forever.

A thought crept up on Errol, an ugly thought: What if he hadn't warned Jill off as well as he'd thought? *What if she'd called another number from her hus-band's phone, and what if that person had told her the truth?* No. That couldn't happen. If his wife had found out, she would have gone straight to Gary, wouldn't she? And Errol wouldn't have a deal right now. Gary never would have called.

But what if Jill Freeman is just biding her time?

Just ask. Put your mind at ease. Without another thought, Ludlow called Brenna Spector. She didn't pick up. "Damn it," he whispered. He didn't want to breathe a word of this into her voice mail, and so he ended the call, more melancholy than ever—and now paranoid to boot.

He sighed. Part of it was this crappy hotel room, quite frankly. He'd suggested the Carlisle for the payday celebration, but Diandra had insisted on this fleabag— dark and noisy, with such a creaky old elevator and a lobby that looked like it hadn't been remodeled since Cher had her natural nose. The room smelled of something, too. Errol wasn't sure what—he shuddered to think at what a luminol test could bring out in here . . .

In his early career, Errol had experienced more than his fill of rooms like this one. He didn't even think he could count how many of them he'd holed up in alone after paying off desk clerks, snapping pictures through alleyways or through cracks in adjoining doors. So much depravity and filth and escape . . .

But she'd told him that no-tell motels turned her on, told him over the phone in that purr of hers, hadn't she, his Diandra? And who could say no to a purr like that?

Let's make the celebration dirty, Mr. Ludlow. Just remembering was enough to lift Errol's spirits—in more ways than one. His paranoia started to fade.

He looked at his watch. She was due here in half an hour, his flower of the gods. He had a bottle of Dom Perignon in an ice bucket, a black silk robe to change into, along with that . . . that ring she'd given him. *You slip it on, like this. See? Oh, it's snug.* God, she was adorable.

He had Viagra, because adorable as she was, Errol

was also close to sixty and on prostate meds, so when it came to his own physiology, it was always best to call for backup. He popped one, and smiled. Errol had all these things—plus an extra $20K a month. And soon he would have Diandra. Repeatedly.

There was nothing to be melancholy about. Absolutely nothing at all.

"I'm so glad you're all right," Jim said.

They'd been standing face-to-face for easily a full minute, Brenna and her ex-husband, yet she couldn't bring herself to speak.

"We're both glad, Mom," Maya squeezed Brenna's hand, as though she was trying to anchor her here, in the present. Maya's palm felt sweaty, and, Brenna noticed, she was shaking a little. It had to be so strange—her mother and father, together for the first time since she was in kindergarten. Brenna wanted to tell her, *It's all right, honey*, yet she couldn't get her mouth to open. *Jim*. What was he doing here? If he wanted someone to be with Maya, why not send Faith—and while we were at it, why wasn't Faith here with him?

"Faith is in Pennsylvania for an interview," he said, reading her thoughts. "We had to talk her out of taking the *Sunrise Manhattan* chopper to Inwood Hill Park."

Brenna laughed, because she could actually see it—Faith charming the pilot into going a whole state out of his way, Faith leaning out the open door of a TV helicopter in one of her perfect suits, the wind rippling her blonde hair as she peered out over the Hudson, calling Brenna's name through a megaphone. "I'm very glad," Brenna said, "that Faith is on our side."

Jim started to say something, but it turned into a

sigh. He watched Brenna's face for a while, ran a hand though his hair. "Your eye."

"It's from the air bag."

"You scared Maya."

"I'm sorry."

"I'm fine, Dad."

"You scared *me*."

She started to reply, but the way he was looking at her . . . her voice went to dust. It became August 9, 1994, and she was sitting with Jim in Madison Square Park. She could feel the cool metal bench beneath her legs again, the hot sun on her back. And she could see Jim, young Jim with his buzz cut and his skinnier build and that white oxford shirt with the fraying collar. *She's got his hand in her lap, and she's tracing the lines. She's pretending she knows how to read palms, but really all she wants to do is touch him. She wants to circle her fingers around his thick wrist, to bring the big hand up to her lips, those long, elegant fingers . . . Does he know? Can he read her mind? Jim Rappaport, reporter for the* Science Times. *His hands are amazing, powerful. She envies his keyboard, his steering wheel, the wallet in his pocket . . . any object lucky enough to receive his touch.*

"Now this is your heart line," says Brenna, full of crap. *"It is very strong."* *His skin is so warm.*

Brenna's phone vibrated. It brought her back. She blinked at Jim a few times. "You changed your hair."

"Faith's been taking me to her hairdresser," Jim said. "Stylist. Whatever you're supposed to call the guy. He cuts three hairs and rubs a bunch of gunk in it, and for that you pay seventy bucks."

"I like it," Brenna said. She did. In particular, she liked that it was no longer the buzz cut she'd loved to stroke while he was driving their old Volvo and she was in the passenger's seat, her arm curled around his shoulders. She liked that it probably no longer felt like velvet under your palms, that it laid smooth and flat against his scalp and covered the scar he still had from a seventh grade basketball accident. (*Eight stitches in the left temple. Tripped by that jerk Joey Tablone just as Jim was going for a three-pointer and everybody knew it was on purpose.*) She liked that the new length made the gray in Jim's dark brown hair all the more obvious, that it played up the passage of time and made Jim so different, almost another person from the man Brenna had married, someone she was meeting only just now.

Her phone vibrated again. She plucked it out of her pocket, looked at the number on the screen. *Errol Ludlow.* If that wasn't ironic, Brenna didn't know the definition of the word. She folded it up again, slipped it back into her pocket. Had to be a butt-dial.

"You need to take that?"

"Absolutely not." She took a breath. Maya was still squeezing her hand. Brenna turned to her. "Why don't you go order us a pizza? I'm starving."

"Okay!" Maya rushed into the other room like she'd just been released from a cage.

"I can't stay," Jim said.

Brenna called after Maya: "Order a large! Anchovies on half, please!"

"Gross!"

"Just half, it won't kill you!"

Jim smiled. "You still like anchovies."

"Yep."

"How about that Hostess obsession? Still can't go three days without a Twinkie?"

"Oh no, I've totally branched out."

"Really?"

"Oh yeah. I mix it up with a Yodel every now and then. Sometimes I'll even have a Sno Ball if I'm feeling really adventurous."

He laughed a little. She couldn't look at him laughing.

"I don't change, Jim."

"I know," he said. "I know you don't." Yes, his hair was longer and he was in a suit and tie Brenna had never seen before and there were lines around his eyes and mouth that hadn't been there the last time she'd seen him. But the look that crept into his eyes, the set of the jaw . . . it was the same way he'd looked at her fifteen years ago, when she was holding his hand in her lap, pretending she was able to read the future.

"Maya, can you get them to bring a Caesar salad, too?" she called out. "And an order of mozzarella sticks!"

"Brenna," he said.

"Don't, Jim. Please."

"You could have died today."

"I didn't die."

"Maya was scared, I was—"

"I'm okay."

"I . . . I need to say it. I need to tell you, but it's so hard."

Brenna's phone vibrated again. She couldn't have been gladder for the interruption. She looked at the screen. *Errol Ludlow.* "Seriously?"

Brenna moved over to the window and put her back to Jim and flipped open her phone. "What."

"Brenna, this is Errol Ludlow."

"I know that."

"I cannot speak with you long as I'm expecting company."

"Uh . . . you called *me*."

"Right. Lis-ten." Brenna winced. He actually pronounced the T in "listen." "Have you, by any chance, received a call from Gary Freeman's wife, Jill?"

She frowned. "No."

"Great! All I needed to know. Ta-ta!"

Brenna sighed heavily. *Well, that was interesting.* She turned around, looked at her ex-husband. She tried to focus on the new hair, the new suit, but still a dozen memories flew at her, all at once—June 24, 1997, and April 21, 1993, and February 9, 1994, and her wedding day and the day Maya was born and the night Jim stood over her, in the living room of their Fourteenth Street apartment on October 23, 1998, telling her he could never trust her again.

She clenched her teeth and her fists and hugged her arms to her chest and shut her eyes tight, willing it away, forcing it all out of her mind at once.

"Brenna?" he said.

"I've missed you, Jim. I really have. I've missed instant messaging with you. I've missed our friendship."

"Me too. So much, I—"

"But I can't be in the same room with you ever again."

Jim stared at her for several seconds. And then it was his phone's turn to ring. He picked it up. "Hi, babe . . . Yes, she's fine . . ." He looked up at Brenna. "Faith wants to talk to you." He didn't move any closer—just held the phone out to her at arm's length.

"Thank you," Brenna said to him. "Hi, Faith."

"Brenna!" Faith was outside somewhere, shouting to be heard, yet still she sounded so pleasant. How was she able to do that? Brenna could hear a whirring noise, and she thought of the helicopter and smiled.

"Thank God you're okay," Faith said.

"I'm fine—a good night's sleep, I'll be back to normal."

"Great. Listen, though. I need to talk to you about something."

"Sure?"

"The people who abducted you . . . can you tell me a little about them?"

"Uh, Faith?" Brenna said. "You're not hoping to get a scoop out of this, are you?"

"Heavens, no!" She laughed a little. "Though that would be clever of me."

"Off the record, it was two guys trying to collect money. From our witness. It's kind of a long story."

There was a pause on the other end of the line. "How long have you known the witness?"

"Never met the guy. Never knew who he was until today."

"Oh, thank goodness," Faith said. "Thank goodness."

Brenna frowned. "Why thank goodness?"

"It was nothing personal, right? He's a witness you've never met. He knows nothing about you."

Brenna recalled Robin Tannenbaum's room. The copy of *Extraordinary Children* on his nightstand. The picture on his screen. "What is this about?"

"It's probably nothing."

"What's probably nothing?"

"I never told you about this because I didn't want to scare you . . ."

"That's never a good way to start a sentence."

Maya wandered back into the room. "Are you staying for pizza, Dad?"

Jim shook his head. "Some other time, honey," he said, watching Brenna.

"Faith?"

"Okay," Faith sighed. "Remember when you did my show, back in October?"

Brenna sighed.

"Of course you remember, dumb question. Anyway, we got a whole bunch of calls from the same person— the screener never put 'em through because they sounded a little . . . unbalanced, like a stalker. I think you might be breaking up a little, Brenna. Can you hear me?"

"Yes," Brenna said. "What were the calls about?"

Brenna heard a rush of static on the other end of the line, then Faith's voice came back, " . . . why freak you out needlessly, you know?"

"Faith," Brenna's voice shook. "I lost you there for a few seconds. What were the calls about?"

"Honey," she said. "It didn't have anything to do with what happened to you today. He was asking personal questions."

Brenna's mouth was dry. "Personal questions."

"Yeah, so nothing to worry about."

"Do you have recordings of this caller?"

"No . . ." More static.

"What were the calls about, Faith?"

"I can't hear you! This connection is awful."

"*What were the calls about?*" Brenna was shouting. Maya and Jim both stared at her, then each other.

"Okay, heard you that time," Faith said. She was half drowned by the bad connection, and Brenna strained to hear her, pressed the phone into her ear, but it wasn't working. Her voice was so faint.

"*Say it again! I can't hear you!*"

"*The calls!*" Faith practically screamed it. "*They were about your sister!*"

12

Back in L.A., a casting director had once called Diandra Marie a "super-empath." What he meant was, when she took on a role, she committed so fully to the world of the script that she posed an emotional danger to herself and to those around her. "What if you were to be playing Ophelia?" the casting director had warned her. "Would we find you drowned and floating in the river with flowers in your hair? You must remember what Sir Ian McKellen once said—'My dear. It's called acting.'"

Of course, the L.A. River was about two inches deep, it wasn't McKellen but Sir Laurence Olivier who had said that about acting, and the casting director had delivered those heartfelt words of advice in the show's rehearsal space, after hours, while putting his pants back on.

But while she hadn't gotten the part and couldn't remember the name of the show (or, for that matter, the name of the casting director) he had been right about Diandra—or DeeDee as she'd been known back then. Once she found a role, she wouldn't just dive in, she would drown in it. She'd let the character devour her until she was no longer Diandra Marie, but Ophelia or Juliet or Maggie the Cat or . . . what was this role she was playing now?

Diandra liked losing herself.

She stopped for a moment, checked herself out in the cracked mirror next to the vacant front desk of NYC's "fabulous" (with quote marks around it) Moon-Glow Hotel. Dark sunglasses, black trench. Thigh-high boots. And, unbeknownst to the mirror, nothing else.

She opened her purse, applied bright red lipstick, and then she took off the glasses, stared into her own eyes. Diandra still couldn't get used to the cornflower blue contacts. They made her feel like a Barbie doll. She tried to look past them and into the brown eyes she closed at night, in the quiet of her room. "I would do anything for you," she whispered, not to herself but to Mr. Freeman, knowing in her heart that wherever he was, he could sense it.

Mr. Freeman, her director.

She thought of his voice on the phone today, so helpless, begging her to play this part. *I need you, DeeDee,* he had said, her heart warming with the words, filling with them. Truly, Diandra knew Mr. Freeman better than anyone else did. Who else had heard him helpless like that? Not his wife. Not his kids or his clients or anyone else he hung out with in L.A. No one but her.

We all go through life playing roles. Diandra was surer of that than she was of most anything. *We put on costumes and makeup every day and we walk out into this sound set of a world and we act. Others respond to it. That's what living is, most of the time. Everyone performing for each other.*

When she'd broken up with her last L.A. boyfriend, he'd looked so upset, but none of that was real. *You were just pretending with me*, he had said. *You were pretending all along.* Pretending as he said it—playing his role just like everybody else. Diandra had left for New York and he'd put on a new costume and makeup and started a new scene, pretending his way into yet another dumb romance with yet another pretty actress— this one based on "art," he had claimed, for the new actress "understood" him the way Diandra did not . . . at least until the new girl took off her makeup and went off-script and betrayed him as he should have known she would. *And he wouldn't tell Diandra her real name. Even though he'd promised her, he wouldn't say it, even as his credits rolled.*

But Mr. Freeman and Diandra. They were different. He took off his makeup with her, let her see his true self—his tears, his mistakes, all those things that kept him up at night. He showed her his soul. And he saw hers, too, as no one else had, ever. He cared enough to see it, and so she would play any part for him.

She would do anything.

"What's your name, beautiful?"

Diandra turned to see the desk clerk ogling her. He was old and pasty-faced, with black hairs poking out of his nose, but Diandra gave him her best smile—the Marilyn one with her eyes half closed behind the sunglasses and the contacts and her shoulders drawn up, as though she were shivering from the very thrill of meeting him. She looked at the clerk as if he were Mr. Freeman himself—her director—and then she gave him the name she held tight in her soul.

"Pretty name," the clerk replied, as she headed for

the elevator. She felt his gaze on her ass and imagined the sound of applause.

"She doesn't look like a high school student," Maya said, gesturing at the TV. "She looks like a forty-year-old lawyer."

"Gabrielle Carteris is an old soul," Brenna said.

"I was talking more about her glasses frames."

Jim had left an hour ago. "Good-bye, Brenna," he had said after giving Maya a long hug and telling her he'd see her on Christmas. "It was good seeing you."

"It was good seeing you, too, Jim. I mean it." Brenna stares at the floorboards. She can't look into his eyes. I can never see you again, *she thinks.* I can never look at you again.

After he'd left, Brenna had feared some kind of drawn-out discussion with Maya over the implications of that good-bye, whether it meant Dad could come by on certain occasions, that they could maybe do things other separated-but-amicable families did—celebrate birthdays together, holidays . . .

But that hadn't happened, either. Maya had said nothing and Brenna was glad for it. For someone who'd been through as much therapy as she had—and who demanded such deeply personal information from clients and witnesses—Brenna was pretty indirect about her own feelings. Her whole life, she'd been perfectly happy *not* talking things out, lest the conversation prove hurtful and wind up stuck in her mind forever. But memory issues aside, evading painful truths seemed to be a family trait, passed down to Brenna by her photograph-destroying mother and now down to Maya, who'd spoken more about the cast of the original *Beverly Hills 90210* tonight than about her own father.

Of course, *90210* was as worthy a topic as any, wasn't it?

"Jeez, that guy wears more hair gel than Trent!" Maya said.

They were eating the pizza Maya had ordered in front of the one of the earliest episodes, in which Midwestern twins Brenda and Brandon were still trying to get used to life in sunny, glamorous Beverly Hills and their parents had actual storylines. Brenna owned the first eight seasons on DVD, but she never could get her daughter to watch any of it with her. Tonight, though, Maya had suggested it, her attention now pretty much equally divided between the show, her slice of pizza, and the giant sketch pad in her lap.

Brenna appreciated the gesture. She had a deep affection for old *90210* episodes much the same way she did for her Hostess products—they were fun, palatable, and comforting in their familiarity. (Plus she'd watched them so many times that each viewing blended into the next in her mind; no memories were triggered.) But she certainly didn't expect the same feelings from her daughter, who'd been born two years post–Shannen Doherty, and was barely four years old when David and Donna tied the knot on the two-hour-long series finale.

Usually, Maya had about as much interest in watching *90210* as she did in eating a pizza half-piled with anchovies. (*The smell seeps into the entire pie, Mom. It's like an alien invasion.*) So the fact that she was now doing both at once was a true show of love, divided attentions or not.

Of course, Brenna's were divided, too—with Faith's

phone call, and the jumble of thoughts it inspired, winning out over both the TV and the pizza.

October 6. I'm on Sunrise Manhattan *and a man calls, asking about my sister. Same date, Robin Tannenbaum checks* Extraordinary Children *out of the library, reads about how Clea went missing. The next day, October 7, he downloads a childhood picture of Clea and me (sent to him by Lula Belle). And Lula Belle, in turn, e-mails Gary Freeman, directing him to send money to a PO box in our hometown—which happens to be owned by Robin Tannenbaum.*

Tannenbaum then borrows a significant amount of money from his neighbor, Mr. Pokrovsky. And on October 9, he writes his mother a note, takes his winter clothes and his camera equipment, fills up his tank in White Plains, and disappears.

Lula Belle, did you run off with Robin Tannenbaum?

Lula Belle, are you my sister?

Would Brenna ever know the answer to these questions, or would they run through her mind like this always? Earlier tonight, just after Jim left, Brenna had gone onto her computer, looked up the Web site for Happy Endings, and after getting flashed by so many inappropriate pop-ups she'd thrown a paper towel over the screen in case Maya walked in, she had finally found the tiny "contact us" button and e-mailed the "Company Head" (pun intended?) , begging for any bit of information he could provide on his former employee Robin Tannenbaum, the whole process no doubt choking her computer with spyware, when the odds of Brenna's getting a reply from the Head were about as good as Trent's chances of going on a week-long Caribbean cruise with Claudia the paramedic.

Lula Belle, please let me find you.

Maya was saying, " . . . and if Donna is so insecure about the way she looks, why is she wearing those mom jeans?"

Brenna smiled. "Everybody wore jeans like that back then."

"Seriously? The waist comes up to her boobs. It makes her look horrible!" She sighed, went back to her sketch pad.

Brenna watched her for a while. "What are you drawing?"

"A decent outfit for Donna."

"Seriously?"

"No."

Maya held up her pad, and Brenna saw a perfect likeness of herself—her lips pursed, her eyes gazing up and into the distance, focused on something very far away.

"It's me," she said.

Maya nodded. "Lost in thought. I have to wait till you space out again so I can get the eyes right. Shouldn't take too long."

Brenna sighed.

"I'm not mad."

"Yes, you are. And I don't blame you. Here you went through so much today, and I should be just . . . holding you. And instead I'm . . . I'm just . . . I'm trying to figure something out."

Maya said, "Okay, number one, you're the one who went through so much today—all I did was sit around this apartment. Number two, holding me would be . . . it would be kinda weird."

"Point well taken. Is there a number three?"

Maya nodded. "You can't just tell me you're trying to figure something out, and not expect me to ask what that thing is. I mean, it's not like saying you've got brown hair or your tooth hurts or something. You say, 'I'm trying to figure something out,' it begs an explanation."

Brenna smiled. "It's complicated, honey."

"I'm not simple." Maya set her sketch pad against the wall, and Brenna stared at her own face on it—the pursed mouth, the distant eyes, the shadows beneath the cheekbones, and so many other details, so painstakingly rendered—the way her hair curled against her collarbones, the arch of her eyebrows, the tension around the mouth, the tiny oval birthmark, just above Brenna's jaw. She couldn't help but picture Maya, her artist, Maya watching her while she was unaware, taking her whole face in. Maya capturing Brenna on paper so carefully, so expertly, as if, by way of the outside, she could get to what was inside. Maybe Maya wasn't as indirect as Brenna thought. Maybe she kept quiet about things, not for her own sake, but for that of her emotionally evasive mom.

"Okay, you win," Brenna said.

"Really?"

"Under one condition."

"Yes."

"You will let me keep that drawing."

Maya's face brightened. "Sure." She put the TV on pause.

And Brenna told her everything.

After she was done, Maya stared at her for a good half minute, at least. "So," she said, finally. "You think this Robin guy saw you on TV and realized Lula Belle was Clea and . . . like . . . asked her about it and she sent him that picture of you guys and then they ran away together?"

"Maybe," Brenna said.

Maya swallowed hard.

"Well," said Brenna. "What do *you* think?"

"You're not going to like what I think."

Brenna exhaled. "Try me."

"I'm thinking maybe something bad happened to Robin," Maya said, very slowly. "And if that woman who does that thing with the bottle really is Clea . . . then maybe she had something to do with it."

Brenna closed her eyes. "You think . . . you think your aunt Clea . . . you think she killed Robin Tannenbaum?"

Maya shrugged. "I don't know her, Mom. And neither do you."

"She's my sister."

"Look." She sighed. "I know I'm an only child and all, so I might not fully get it. But if Clea is still alive, it means she left you guys twenty-five years ago and hasn't tried to get in touch with you once. I mean—even after all that stuff about you in the news? Not even a letter or an e-mail? What kind of a sister is that?"

Brenna looked down at her hands. "Her father's daughter," she said, very quietly.

Maya got up from her chair, settled in next to Brenna on the couch. "She's got a gift for destruction that runs through her veins," she said.

Brenna stared at her. Her pulse sped up, and in an instant, she was back into the previous night, Morasco moving closer to the computer screen as Lula Belle spoke, the light from the screen on his eyes and that emotion in them. Was it pity? . . . *She thought I was crazy like my daddy. She thought I couldn't take care of nothin' without breakin' it. Mama said that gift for destruction ran through my veins.*

"Where did you hear that?"

"Huh?"

"Have you been watching those downloads?"

Maya's eyes were wide. "What downloads?" she asked, her voice quavering, and it was only then that Brenna realized how harshly she'd spat out that question.

She took a deep breath. *Calm.* "Maya, I'm not mad at you," she said.

"I don't know what you're talking about. I never should have said anything."

"Don't be like that. I just can't have you looking at them. They're very inappropriate, and besides, what if you accidentally damaged one of them?"

"*What downloads?*"

Brenna frowned.

"Lula Belle."

Maya stared at her. "I haven't looked at those."

"Where did you get that, then?"

"Get *what*?"

"That expression—destruction running through her veins."

"Come on," she said. "You've never heard her say that?"

"Who?"

Maya bit her lip.

Brenna put a hand on her shoulder, looked deep into her eyes. "Who, Maya," she said softly. "Who says that expression?"

Maya stared at her. "Grandma," she said. "She says that about Clea, all the time."

Kevin Wiggins, Desk Clerk to the Stars, called out, "Good-bye!" as that pretty girl left the MoonGlow.

She didn't reply. They never did.

Stupid as it sounded, Kevin was a little disappointed—not over the lack of reply, but in the girl herself. Kevin had figured (hoped, actually) that she was a movie star staying at the MoonGlow to evade the paparazzi. She really could have been, too, what with those big dark glasses, those red lips, and her shining blonde hair swept up into a bun, like Grace Kelly in a Hitchcock movie—only with much bigger boobs.

But no, she was just another paid date—a big cut above the ones that usually came in here, but paid nonetheless. Kevin had clocked her: one hour. *Figures*.

Kevin sighed heavily. He'd been working here at the MoonGlow for going on twenty years, and when he'd first taken the job, he'd imagined things so differently. *A hotel in New York* . . . It sounded so glamorous.

Keep in mind, Kevin had just moved here himself from Cicero, Illinois, and he'd never even seen the ocean before. He figured a hotel in New York would be full of romance and intrigue—even a divey one like this with smoke-dulled mirrors and suspiciously sticky floors and stains on the walls. It was the type of place you could call seedy and mean it literally. But Kevin didn't care. His first week of working here, he expected Gene Kelly and Frank Sinatra to come bopping into the lobby in their sailor uniforms singing about all the gals they were gonna meet on the town tonight. But as it turned out, life wasn't a Technicolor movie—and the only thing that came bopping in here was hopped up on meth, and had a switchblade stashed up someplace you didn't even want to think about too hard.

Kevin always hoped that some big developer like Donald Trump or Roger Wright might buy the Moon-Glow, maybe turn it into a place he'd be proud to work at. But no. Management never changed and the Moon-

Glow never changed—it just kept decaying around him.

Kevin Wiggins, Desk Clerk to the Doomed.

Oh well. Kevin had his little TV in the back room, and on slow nights, he could bring in DVDs of all his favorite films—the classics. He could watch them start to finish, sing along with Gene and Frank and Dino and Debbie at the top of his lungs—nobody cared. He had his imagination, too—and sometimes, pretty girls to fuel it. Boy, paid date or not, she was a nice one.

Somewhere in this building, some lucky bastard was sleeping like a baby.

13

The road was bumpy and Brenna was small. The handlebars curved around the tops of her legs, her sister's strong arms pressing against her sides as she steered. Clea was pedaling fast, she thought. But Clea knew where she was going and so Brenna felt safe.

"Smile for Daddy," Clea said.

Brenna looked up from the road and smiled . . . But she couldn't see a camera. She couldn't see her father. Thick trees swarmed before them, the road getting narrower, darker. Brenna looked down again. The road was pitted with big, slimy rocks.

"Smile for Daddy," Clea said again. But there was no Daddy and then there was no Clea, Brenna riding the handlebars of the blue bike alone, the blue bike from the photograph and Brenna grown up but still small and a cliff looming ahead, the bike flipping and Brenna flying, falling into the dark.

" . . . Mom."

Brenna gasped herself awake, and saw Clea standing over her, the sun backlighting her long blonde hair, Clea, a silhouette.

"Don't tell Mom. I'll call in a few days—promise."

"No you won't," Brenna murmured. "You won't. You lie. You will never call me."

"Mom?"

Brenna felt a hand on her shoulder. Clea shifting into focus, into . . .

"Mom."

"Maya."

She stepped back. "Uh . . . You told me to wake you up at eight."

"Right," Brenna said, the day's schedule arranging itself in her mind: Morasco coming at nine. Visiting Hildy Tannenbaum and hopefully talking to Pokrovsky, checking in on Trent, maybe taking Maya out to lunch and then heading over to that gas station in White Plains where Tannenbaum had filled up his tank back in October . . . *And meanwhile, where the hell is Lula Belle?* Brenna sighed. She struggled up in bed and focused on Maya. "Was I talking in my sleep?"

"Yeah, a little."

"Sorry. Weird dream."

"About Clea?"

"Good guess." Brenna ran a hand over her eyes.

"Hey, listen, Mom?"

"Yeah?

Maya sat down on the edge of the bed. She picked at a fingernail. "What happens if you do find her?" she said.

"Lula Belle?"

She turned to Brenna. "Clea."

Brenna moved next to her daughter, smoothed her hair. "That's a good question," she said. "I'd want to find out if she's okay, first."

"Sure. But then what?"

She shrugged. "Talk to her, I guess."

"What if Grandma is right about Clea, though? What if she's crazy and destructive and stuff?"

Brenna put a hand on her shoulder. "Maya," she said. "Grandma says a lot of things to make herself feel better."

"How would it make her feel better to say her own daughter is a nut job?"

"Maybe it helps her to stop wondering why Clea ran away and never called."

"Okay, I get that . . . But Mom? If you do find Clea . . ."

"Yeah?"

"Do I have to talk to her?"

Brenna searched Maya's face—so much like Clea's, it sometimes made her breath catch. "Honey," she said. "You don't have to do anything you don't want to do."

She stood up from the bed, her eyes grave. "Thanks," she said.

"I am an old man. Why are you troubling me like this?"

"Mr. Pokrovsky," Brenna said. "All we did was ask you a question. If the question troubles you, just answer it and we'll leave."

And not a moment too soon, either. Brenna and Morasco had been in Pokrovsky's apartment for a little more than five minutes, and already the smell was getting to her. Mothballs and stale coffee, mingled with something dark and medicinal and sad. Neither Pokrovsky nor his apartment were anything like what Brenna had imagined they would be when Morasco had told her, on the ride over, that he was a multimillionaire with Russian mob connections who had done twenty years in Ray Brook for racketeering. "I'm sure he moved his money around—they always do," Morasco had said, after he'd shown Brenna the old mug shot—a lean, chiseled man with thin lips and angry green eyes that burned straight through the lens.

Yes, he did live in the same ivy-choked townhouse as Hildy Tannenbaum, but still Brenna had assumed Pokrovsky's apartment would be far more expensively furnished—either sleek and minimalist or *Real Housewives*-baroque. She'd also expected servants, burly "advisers," maybe a young, pneumatic trophy wife. But no. The apartment was a dust trap with drawn shades and creaky old furniture—and Pokrovsky was in it all alone.

He also seemed to have aged exponentially in the thirty years since the mug shot had been taken. The olive skin now had the texture of balled-up parchment and he moved so slowly, Brenna had to fight the urge to physically assist him. But the eyes had stayed the same—bright and hard and eerily vacant. Hildy had brought them upstairs, and he'd opened the door quickly for her. But after she'd made the introductions and left and Morasco had shown him his badge, Pokrovsky had stared at him with those eyes for a good minute, and Brenna had half thought he might strike like a cobra, take them both down before she could even get a word in. Bo and Diddley aside, she could see why Robin had not only disappeared but covered his tracks, growing a beard, laying off the credit card, leaving his traceable cell phone behind.

"You want to know why Robin Tannenbaum borrowed money from me," Pokrovsky was saying now.

"Yes," Morasco said.

"And you call that a simple question."

"It is," Brenna said. "It's a ridiculously simple question."

"You are trying to trap me into saying that Robin Tannenbaum owed me money." His gaze darted from Brenna's face to Morasco's and back again. "I do not know those two men who were in your car. I have never seen them in my life, and how they knew my name, I have no idea. But my lawyer can prove that I had absolutely no knowledge of—"

"Look," Brenna said. "We're not trying to trap you. I don't care about those two, and the carjacking isn't even Nick's case—he's just helping me out."

Pokrovsky stared into her eyes. Brenna stared back. *Misplaced eyes*, she thought. Two shards of glass sticking out of such a weak, sad face.

"I don't know how I can put it any plainer, Mr. Pokrovsky," Brenna said. "How about this? I couldn't care less about you."

His eyebrows went up.

"I mean it," she said. "You could have fifteen bodies stashed under that window seat over there, it wouldn't matter to me."

He glanced at Morasco. "It would matter to him."

"Yep," Morasco said. "It would."

"Then we won't look under the window seat." Pokrovsky took a breath, his shoulders slumping with it. "Why are you so interested in Robin?" His gaze rested on Brenna. "Or what is it he calls himself now? RJ?"

"I'm looking for him."

"I gathered that. Why?"

Brenna thought about Lula Belle. Dare she tell Pokrovsky? Would he understand it if Brenna told him who Lula Belle might be? "His mother misses him," she said.

Pokrovsky sighed. A slight smile crossed his face, and for a moment, the glass-shard eyes warmed with it. "Hildy hired you."

"Yes."

He shook his head slowly. "I don't know why she couldn't have just told me that. Why did she say you were friends of her son?"

Brenna shrugged her shoulders. "She isn't a very direct person."

"True," he said. "Very true." He exhaled slowly, and it was as though the anger, the distrust, was seeping out of him, just at the thought of his downstairs neighbor.

"Hildy is worried about her son," Brenna said.

He ran a hand over his eyes. And when he looked at her again, they, too, looked duller, tired. "I'd like to sit down," he said.

Brenna and Morasco looked at each other. There was a stack of metal chairs against the wall next to the window seat. Pokrovsky took the window seat, and Brenna and Morasco opened up two of the chairs and moved them across from him. Then they all sat there for several seconds, Pokrovsky catching his breath while Brenna and Morasco watched, as if this were the world's most uncomfortable group therapy session.

"You should have seen Hildy Tannenbaum thirty years ago," Pokrovsky said.

Brenna said, "You've known her that long?" The seat was cold against her back. She could feel it through her thin sweater.

"Oh yes. I knew her and her husband Walter and that boy of theirs for . . . well, it was at least ten years before I went away on my extended, government-paid vacation." He smirked at Morasco.

"What was she like back then?" he asked.

"Very different."

"How so?"

"Oh she was a firecracker."

"Really?" said Brenna. Other than perhaps "Amazonian," "firecracker" was the last word in the English language she would have used to describe Hildy.

"Walter was such a stick-in-the-mud, but Hildy, she had this sparkle in her eyes. We didn't speak much back then, but I could tell. I would watch her, the way she'd sing to herself as she brought a load of laundry down to the washer in the basement—always with the Elvis songs, the Tom Jones . . . She would swing her hips as she walked down the stairs. And she always wore a nice dress. That Walter. I still have no idea what he ever did to deserve her."

Brenna thought of Hildy today—the frail, hunched little body in the same faded robe she'd worn yesterday, the quavering voice, the scared, buglike eyes, wig slumping on her forehead. Brenna heard herself say, "What happened to her?" Which of course was the world's stupidest question. What had happened to Hildy was the same thing that had happened to Yuri Pokrovsky, with his chiseled features and his thick blond hair and that death stare of his, so much bigger than his own mug shot. Time had happened. Disappointment and regret and grief and betrayal and guilt and shame and illness and fear and all those other lovely facts of life and time that sap the strength out of you, little by little, until it's all gone and you're so much weaker than you were when you first started out, too weak to live at all.

"You want to know what happened to Hildy?" Pokrovsky said.

Brenna looked at him, and jumped a little. He was staring straight into her, the anger back full-force, the glass-green eyes burning.

"Yes," Brenna said. Her mouth was dry. Instinctively, she slid her chair back, made some space between that anger and herself.

"It was that boy of hers," he said. "Robin Tannenbaum. That's what happened to Hildy."

Pokrovsky had never liked Robin Tannenbaum, not even when he was a child. "He was lazy," he explained after Brenna asked. "He would stay all day long in his bedroom. Hildy would call to him to go outside, enjoy the day. He would say nothing in return. He never mowed the lawn, never took out the garbage. Never said 'please' or 'thank you.' Hildy was forever washing towels for him. That boy would use five separate towels a day. Why does a boy need five towels? He wasn't even that clean!"

At the time, Pokrovsky was going back and forth between the Forest Hills apartment and homes in South Hampton, Princeton, and Sanibel Island. But on those occasions when he was staying here, the Tannenbaum boy tried his patience. "It was all I could do not to hit him," Pokrovsky said. "And I know you aren't supposed to say these things in this day and age. But the way that boy treated his mother, he deserved a lot worse than a *pach* on the *tuchus*."

"He was just fifteen when you went off to Ray Brook," Morasco said.

"Yes." Pokrovsky pulled the shade back a little and squinted out the window, the daylight weakening his features still more. "When I got out, this was the only property I had left. Walter had died, and I assumed Hildy would still be here. Not Robin, though."

"He'd never left home?" Brenna asked.

"No, he was in and out, here and there." He looked at Brenna. "Three years ago, he went to film school out in California. A forty-two-year-old man, can you imagine? Film school is impractical enough if you are twenty!"

She nodded.

"And here again, his poor mother is footing the bill."

"Did he graduate?"

Pokrovsky laughed at that one. "He lasted all of three months."

"Oh."

"I know I have not always made the wisest decisions in my life." Pokrovsky said this to Morasco. "I'm sure that if I had it to do over again, I would have done certain things differently, more responsibly, less on impulse . . . But I have been supporting myself and my family since I was thirteen years old and I would sooner die than treat my mother the way he treated Hildy. Like a slave."

"He didn't last long in California, did he?" Brenna said.

He shook his head. "Just a few years. Managed to get himself arrested, I believe, for something idiotic. Breaking and entering."

"Hildy bailed him out?"

"I don't know, but I'm sure that's what happened," he said. "She flew out to California. Came back with that bad penny of a boy."

She shook her head.

"That young man has had one decent paying job his whole life—editing adult movies. And I'm the one who got it for him."

Brenna raised an eyebrow at him.

"The fellow who runs the company owed me a few favors."

"That was nice of you."

"I did it for his mother, not him. Some people are born with a work ethic. Others need one shoved down their throats." He gazed out the window again, then shook his head. "You want to know why I lent him that money?" He looked at Brenna.

"I'm guessing it wasn't because you considered him a good investment."

He snorted. "No, Miss Spector. You are funny."

Brenna waited.

"That money, he wanted for some ridiculous camera. He told me he was working on a project which would *change the world*—which, believe me, I put as much stock in as that film education."

"Did you think he'd be able to pay you back, at least?"

"No."

Morasco said, "Then why?"

Pokrovsky grinned, and for a moment, Brenna caught a flash of it—the face she'd seen in the mug shot, sharp and hard and merciless. "I lent it to him," he said, "because I knew he *wouldn't* be able to pay me back."

"And you were looking forward to the punishment," said Brenna.

"You said it," he said. "I didn't."

As they were heading downstairs to Hildy's apartment, Brenna turned to Morasco. "What kind of person borrows money from *that* guy?" she whispered.

"Same type of person whose mom does his laundry when he's forty-five."

"We don't know that she does his laundry anymore."

"Fair enough," Morasco said. "How about the same type of person who drops out of film school at forty-two and gets arrested for breaking and entering and runs up a twenty-five-thousand-dollar bill with *that guy* because he thinks he needs some fancy camera to videotape a naked shadow . . ."

"All right, all right," Brenna turned to him. "By the way, I don't know if you learned this at John Jay, but hundred-year-old mobsters aren't always credible witnesses."

Morasco shrugged. "I believed him."

By now, they were at Hildy's door. When Brenna knocked, Hildy opened it so fast, she almost fell in.

"Did he hurt Robbie?" Hildy said. "Is he the reason why Robbie disappeared?"

"It's all right, Mrs. Tannenbaum," Morasco said.

"It isn't," she said. "You don't know Mr. Pokrovsky. He's . . . He means well, but he'd just as soon . . . What did he say to you?"

Brenna put a hand on her shoulder. "Nothing that would make me think he has any idea where your son is."

"Are you sure?"

"Yes," Brenna said. Though she wasn't. At this point, Brenna wasn't fully sure of anything. "Hildy?"

"Yes?"

"Why didn't you tell me that Robbie has an arrest record?"

"A . . . a what?"

"Mr. Pokrovsky says he was arrested in California. You bailed him out."

Hildy stared up at Morasco. "What is she talking about?"

"A minor charge. Breaking and entering?"

Hildy's shoulders relaxed. "Oh, *that*." She looked at Brenna. "That was years ago, and it was nothing."

Brenna looked at her. "It was an arrest."

"It was a prank."

"A prank?" said Morasco.

"The homeowner didn't even press charges. It was a teacher at the film school. Robbie didn't steal anything. It was more of a dare than anything else. And anyway, it wasn't Robbie's fault. It was his friend's."

"His friend?"

"One of his classmates." Her eyes narrowed. "A bad influence."

"Did you ever meet this friend?"

"Only once," she said. "I flew out to California, maybe a month after Robbie went off to film school. I wanted to see how he was doing. When I showed up at his apartment, his friend was there." She picked at a fingernail.

"Was the friend a woman?"

She shook her head.

"What was he like?"

"Do you believe in first impressions?"

Brenna didn't. As someone who remembered each and every first impression she'd ever had as an adult, she knew for a fact that they were meaningless.

"I do," said Morasco, which made Brenna remember her first impression of him: October 16, 1998. Brenna, calling him about the disappearance of a little girl, a girl so much younger than Clea had been, but still . . . Morasco a voice on the phone—all business . . .

"This is Detective Morasco. What can I do for you?"

"I . . . I heard something on the news about a blue car."

"Who is this?"

"My name is Brenna Spector. I'm a former private investigator."

"Okay, well listen. That never should have been leaked to the press."

"No, I'm glad it was leaked because—"

"It was a bad lead."

"A bad lead?"

"It was false."

"So . . . you're saying that she didn't get into a blue car."

"We aren't looking for a blue car. Thank you for calling." Click.

That was cold, *Brenna thinks. What an asshole . . .*

Brenna heard Morasco saying her name, which roped her back into the room, to both of them looking at her. "Sorry," she said. "I didn't catch that?"

"We were saying we both trusted you immediately," Morasco said.

Brenna smiled at him. *Not immediately. Eleven years later. You just don't remember.* She looked at Hildy. "But I'm taking it, it wasn't that way with Robbie's friend."

She shook her head again. "I got this awful feeling from him. I wanted to grab Robbie and take him out of there and never let him talk to this boy, ever."

"This was before the arrest."

"Yes," she said. "That happened two months later. I knew Robbie's friend was to blame. I knew he'd put him up to it. Robbie broke into that house because he told him to do it. And then, when Robbie needed him, that . . . that boy acted as though he'd never even met my son. He told the professor that Robbie was lying about the dare, which broke his heart. Made him flunk out of school. When Robbie came home, he was . . . he was so . . . Oh, I wished he'd never laid eyes on that awful kid."

Brenna couldn't look at Morasco, couldn't let herself think about the many questions running through her mind—questions she dare not ask Hildy for fear of alienating this poor misguided woman and never getting the one answer she really needed. *He had a friend.* Robin Tannenbaum, photographed with no one save his mother and his dead father, alone in his own prom picture, communicating over the Internet with a shadow . . . Three years ago, he'd had a real, flesh-and-blood friend.

"Hildy," Brenna said. "What is Robbie's friend's name?"

A look of disgust crept into Hildy's big eyes. "Robbie doesn't speak to him anymore," she said. "Even if that boy tried to call—which he hasn't—Robbie wouldn't ever . . ."

"All the same."

She looked up at Brenna, her jaw set, breathing as though to steel herself against the sound of the name. "Shane Smith," she said.

Outside the apartment, Brenna texted Trent Shane Smith's name, plus the name of the film school Hildy said her son had attended for three months, three years ago—the School of the Moving Image in Los Angeles. *Tannenbaum's friend from film school*, she typed. *Find me anything you can about him/the 2 of them.* The bright sun made Brenna's bad eye sting. She slipped on her sunglasses as a text from Trent arrived: *On it.*

If he had found anything of note on Tannenbaum's computer, Trent would have texted, called, and e-mailed already, but Brenna asked him anyway.

Just awesome porn. Trying to hack into his e-mail tho.

Good. As she was slipping the cell phone back into her pocket, she felt herself falling back into yesterday afternoon, panic barreling through her as Trent spun the wheel and then the slow-motion roll of the car, coming to a stop, *and the air bag socks her in the face. She's still breathing. Brenna hears a moaning behind her, Bo or Diddley, she doesn't know, care which, and then she thinks of Trent* . . . Trent, oh God, Trent, I'll kill them, I swear, if they hurt you. Kill them with my bare hands . . .

A car whizzed by, yanking Brenna back into the present. She slipped her phone back out of her pocket, texted Trent again: *Take care of yourself.*

He replied: *That's what the porn's for.*

Brenna grimaced. "Way too much information," she whispered.

"How's Trent doing?" said Morasco.

"Back to his old self."

"A blessing and a curse."

"Exactly."

Morasco opened the door to his car. "I can look into that arrest report for you," he said.

"You think it's still around?"

He shrugged his shoulders. "I doubt Tannenbaum would get it expunged for the sake of his porn editing job." He started up the car.

Brenna got another text and glanced at her phone. *Finally.* "The auto shop." She turned to Morasco. "You mind dropping me off there? My car's all ready . . ." The look on his face made her lose the rest of the sentence—the same, pained, pitying look that had crossed his face so many times within the past few days, *the Lula Belle look* . . .

She remembered in front of her computer screen two nights ago, watching Lula Belle say the same words Maya had said last night, and the words came out. Lula

Belle's words. Maya's words. Brenna's mother's words. She couldn't stop them. "She's got a gift for destruction that runs through her veins."

Morasco closed his eyes for a moment, opened them again. "You know," he said.

"Maya told me last night."

"Maya has heard that?"

"She told me that my mother says it all the time."

"Man."

"My mother said it to you, didn't she? November 9."

"November . . ."

"When we went to dinner at her house. Before . . ." She turned her gaze to the car window. "Before O'Donnell's. The parking lot."

"Yes. She said it then."

Brenna took a deep breath, let it out slowly. "Why didn't you tell me, Nick? When you were first watching that download, why didn't you . . ."

"I didn't want to hurt you."

"What?"

"You don't have the ability to block something out of your mind. If I tell you something, it's going to stay there whether you want it or not. And your mother telling me that . . ." He cleared his throat. "I didn't want you to have to keep it."

Morasco turned the ignition, pulled away from the curb. Brenna watched him for a while, the eyes targeting the windshield. The mouth, closed in such a way, it was as though he'd never said a word and never would say one again. *Talk about evasive*. "I'm not made of glass, you know," she said finally.

"Obviously."

"What I mean is, if you had told me my mother said that to you, I could have handled it."

Morasco kept his eyes on the road. "Your mom told me your dad was crazy."

Brenna rolled her eyes. "He'd have to be, wouldn't he? To leave all of us?"

"I don't know that she meant it that way."

"She's mad at him. She's been mad at him for thirty-two years. Who knows how she means anything?"

He exhaled, hard. "She said it to Maya, too. That's . . . that's awful."

Brenna shrugged. "Maya never knew my dad. Hell, I barely remember him." An image passed through her mind—her father, crying against the steering wheel. A fragment of a dream. Or was it a memory?

Morasco said, "I'm not talking about your dad."

"Maya never knew Clea, either," Brenna said. "And believe me, when I was her age, I'd hear stuff in school about Clea that was way worse than her inheriting a 'gift for destruction.'"

Morasco looked at her. "Your mom said that to Maya about Clea."

"Yeah." Brenna frowned. "Didn't she say the same thing to you?"

He turned back to the road.

"Wasn't that what you were trying to protect me from?" said Brenna, but as she said it, she understood—the facts unfolding with a deliberate speed, like stop-action photography of a blooming flower. The distance between them over the past few weeks, the sad way he'd look at her when he didn't think she noticed . . .

"My mother said that to you about me."

"Yes."

"She told you that I'm crazy, that I inherited it from my dad. She said that I'm the one with a gift for destruction. Not Clea."

"Yes." His voice was barely a whisper.

Brenna closed her eyes, and again it was November 9, the four beers swimming through her system and Morasco's chest against the back of her coat as she leaned on him, finding O'Donnell's parking lot. She could feel the cold night air on her face again and his lips against her temple again, the rush of her blood, and again she was talking about Maya, mutant shark girl, teething at age thirteen, her words slurring and bumping into each other. She could hear Nick's laugh, and she could feel herself turning to look at him, could feel the heat his body emitted on that night, his scratchy sweater . . . And how she'd thought she had known exactly what was on his mind . . .

She turns to look at his face and feels his fingertips on the back of her neck and around her waist and his lips . . . like that, yes, just like lips should be and she leans into him. It's so easy, like melting . . .

He kisses her, and his lips are so soft and she brings her hands up to his face and feels the bones beneath his warm skin, the stubble on his cheeks. Her body gives way and for one moment, she's here . . . here and now, and it's perfect . . . and then it was June 25, 1994, on the roof of her apartment building with the sun on her back and the taste of champagne on Jim's lips and Jim kissing her, so deeply, she felt as though she was losing her breath and she could've died in his arms and that would've been fine . . .

Brenna feels Jim pulling away, but it isn't Jim, it's Nick Morasco, and she's in the parking lot of O'Donnell's and it is November 9, 2009. Her stomach sinks. She tries, "What's wrong?"

An emotion pulls at his features—a sadness. An ache. "We'd better get you home," he says.

He knows I was remembering Jim, *she thinks*. He felt me go away . . .

"You okay, Brenna?" Morasco said now, as she was seeing his face in November.

She opened her eyes. Already they were on their way back into the city, the auto shop just a few minutes away. She didn't want to say what was on her mind, but she needed to. "Nick?"

"Yeah?"

"When we were in the parking lot of O'Donnell's, and you pulled away from me . . . Did you do it because you were thinking about what my mother had said?"

He stared at the window. "Yes."

She exhaled. "So funny. This whole time, I was blaming myself."

"Why would you blame yourself?"

Brenna's phone vibrated against her hip. She ignored it. Let the call go to voice mail. "No reason."

"I'm sorry," Nick said. "I shouldn't have let it ruin the moment."

Brenna said, "Try and have a little sympathy for my mother. Poor thing's the only sane person in her family."

He gave her a half smile.

"Plus, her granddaughter's still teething at thirteen."

"Huh? Teething?"

She winced. "Nothing," she said. "Just this crazy thing my Mom said during dinner that I was joking about that night . . . You were . . . uh . . . you were laughing . . ." For some reason, Brenna felt very lonely. She looked out the window. "You're going to want to get off at the next exit. The auto place is on 125th and First."

He nodded, and for a while both of them said nothing. Nick got off the FDR and headed up on 125th, and sure enough there was the auto shop, up ahead and on the right side of the street. He pulled up to it and parked the car. "I'll make sure and get you Tannenbaum's arrest record," he said. "And I'll check the blotter for October 6—see if there were any incidents involving some John Doe with a pricey camera."

"Thanks."

"Hey," Morasco said. "You sure you're okay?"

"I'm fine." She got out of the car and turned to him, watching her so closely through the opened window. "I'll see you."

He swallowed. His throat moved with it. "Take care of yourself."

She watched him drive away, watched the car disappear around the corner before she remembered her vibrating phone and yanked it out of her pocket. One voice mail message, from a number she'd never seen. Brenna was about to check it when another call came in—from the same number. "Yes?"

A male voice: young, all-business. "Miss Spector?"

"Uh-huh?"

"Detective Tim Waxman from the Twenty-fifth Precinct. I'm wondering if I could speak to you in person."

"Concerning . . ."

"An acquaintance of yours."

One of the mechanics was approaching, but she held up a hand. "An acquaintance?"

"He made a phone call to your house last night at around 5 P.M. from his cell phone." Brenna felt herself in her apartment, the phone pressed to her ear, her ex-husband's gaze on her back . . .

"Ludlow." She sighed into the phone. "What the hell has he done now?"

The detective didn't speak right away, and Brenna became aware of background noise—the hum of voices, a crackling police radio, a siren, wailing in the distance . . .

"Can you please come to the MoonGlow Hotel, Miss Spector?" Waxman said, rattling off the address. "I've got some questions for you."

14

As soon as Brenna arrived at the MoonGlow, she saw the coroner's van parked outside. *Oh God, Errol,* she thought. *What have you done?* She hurried into the lobby, pushing past a group of uniform cops and joining five crime scene techs as they jammed into a waiting elevator. The whole while, she was scanning the group for a six-foot-eight-inch man in handcuffs—Errol wasn't someone who was easy to miss—but she didn't see him. One of the crime scene techs hit floor four—a heavy girl with butter-blonde hair and a sweet face. "I'm here for Errol Ludlow," Brenna said to her, trying to sound official.

The girl scrunched up her forehead. "Yeah," she said. "Us too."

The doors opened. Down the dingy hallway, Brenna saw police tape covering one of the rooms, medical examiners hustling in with a gurney. She headed down the hall, where a very young guy in a cheap blue suit was talking to another lab tech, just outside the door to the room.

Brenna heard, "Unusual, considering the age and overall health."

She started to talk to them, but Cheap Blue Suit looked up first. "Miss Spector?" he said.

She blinked at him.

"Sorry," he said. "I recognized you from TV." He smiled—a goofy, guileless smile. "Detective Tim Waxman. We talked on the phone."

"Oh, right."

Detective Tim Waxman looked young enough to use Clearasil on a regular basis. If Maya brought him to the eighth grade mixer, Brenna wouldn't have batted an eye, and yet here he was, in his best bad suit with the sleeves too short and the shirt cuffs frayed, standing in this dismal purgatory of a sticky-sheet motel, cleaning up some awful mess made by Errol Ludlow . . . She felt like covering his eyes. "So, you were familiar with Mr. Ludlow," Tim said.

"Yes, I used to work for him years ago . . . Wait."

"Yes?"

"Did you just say 'were'?"

He cleared his throat. "Yes, ma'am."

"Not '*Are* you familiar.' *Were* you familiar."

He looked at the floor. "Yes."

"Is that significant?"

"I don't know what you mean."

"Did . . . That ME was saying . . . Whose age? Whose overall health?"

"I just need to ask you a few simple questions, ma'am."

"Is Errol dead?"

"Did Mr. Ludlow say anything odd during your phone conversation yesterday?"

"*Answer my question.*"

"Did he complain of shortness of breath?"

"Oh my God. How did he die?"

"Did he say he felt funny in any way?"

Brenna stared at him.

"Miss Spector?"

"No," she said quietly. "He . . . he didn't say he felt funny."

"Did he have any unhealthy habits?"

The past tense. "He didn't smoke. He drank occasionally." She looked at him. "How did he die?"

"We don't know," he said. "But it . . . it was peaceful . . ."

The door to the room opened, room 419, a group of uniforms moving aside to make room for the gurney. "Oh my God," Brenna whispered.

"I'm sorry, Miss Spector."

She stared straight ahead of her. "Not your fault."

"Was he a good friend?"

"No."

And then Brenna caught sight of the body bag on the gurney, the very length of it. *Errol.* The big feet angled out, the shoulders too broad for the platform, the outline of the wide forehead, the pointy nose. She remembered his voice on the phone the previous night, the life in it (*Ta-ta!*) and then she again saw that dark thick plastic, resting on the body, Errol's body. How still it was.

Errol Ludlow in the past tense.

Brenna felt a cold blast at the back of her neck, as though it were June 23, 1991, as though she were sitting in Errol Ludlow's over-air-conditioned office for the first time, staring at this enormous, odd-looking man during her job interview, Errol smirking at her, staring into her face with those dull, black-olive eyes of his . . .

"*What type of drugs are you on?*" he says. *Not* Have

you ever tried drugs? *Or even,* Are you on drugs? *No,
he's too certain for that, this guy. He wants to know
what type.*

*He folds his catcher's-mitt hands on the desk in
front of him and smiles—a slow, dry smile, like granite
cracking.*

*The air-conditioner is cold on the back of Brenna's
neck.* Why does he keep it so cold in here? *But still her
palms sweat. Her jaw tenses. Errol Ludlow is enormous. He dwarfs the desk, the room. If he were to
inhale deeply, Brenna figures, he'd suck all the air out
of it. But she can't think like this. She can't hate this
guy. She needs him.*

Help me find Clea, Errol Ludlow, *Brenna thinks.*
Teach me how to find people . . .

"Miss Spector?"

"I'm . . . I'm not on drugs."

He shakes his head. "You fit the profile of a drug
abuser."

"Excuse me?"

"Raised by a sin-gle mother. A sin-gle art-ist at
that." *Ludlow overenunciates, Brenna notices now.
He spits out syllables one at a time, like seeds. It's very
annoying. She suspects he does it on purpose.*

"So? Lots of people are raised by . . . single artists."

"I'm not through yet." *He leans forward. His big
arms strain against his dark green sport coat, making
it shine. He launches the words at her—each syllable
flying out of his mouth and crashing.* "Sin-gle art-ist
moth-er, run-a-way sis-ter with a slut-ty rep-u-ta-tion
you worked so very hard to avoid that you became a bit
re-clu-sive, didn't you?"

Brenna swallows hard.

"Only a few close friends in high school, didn't date

much, kept to your-self. Your teachers said you always seemed to be in another world . . ."

"You talked to my high school teachers?"

"Just twenty-one years old, yet you've seen three different psy-chi-a-trists. Ivy League college, yes. But as I'm sure we both know, Ivy League colleges are about as full of drugs as Diego Maradona on a Saturday night in Amsterdam."

"Who?"

"And then, the icing on the cake . . . you drop out of Columbia after just two years." He takes a breath. "Now what would you think of that profile?"

Brenna's face feels hot. Her hands clench into fists. "I would think," Brenna says, "that you are the biggest asshat I've ever met."

The flat, dark eyes widen, then crinkle up at the corners. A smile crosses the granite face. He starts to laugh. "I think I like you, Brenna Spector!"

"I know it's hard to lose a friend," Tim Waxman said, bringing Brenna back into the hallway, into the crime scene techs loading Errol's bagged body into the elevator.

Brenna blinked. There were tears in her eyes. "I'm sorry." She took a breath. "Were you saying something, Detective?"

"Just wondering if he might have had a history of recreational drug use."

"Errol?" she said. "Actually he was very antidrug. Why?"

"Was he on blood pressure meds?"

She shrugged. "He drank a lot of green tea," she said, which made her throat clench up again. Crying over Errol. The loss of Errol . . . What was wrong with her? *Must be the shock.*

"I just ask because we found Viagra in his Dopp kit. And the crime scene guys said that Viagra mixed with nitrate-based drugs can bring on a heart attack."

She looked at him. "He brought Viagra."

"Yep. Also a bottle of really nice champagne—empty, though."

"So he wasn't alone," Brenna said.

"Well, he was this morning, when the desk clerk found him."

"Yeah, but champagne and Viagra are usually group activity–type things," she said slowly. She looked at the detective. "I assumed he was working."

"Working?"

"Meeting one of his girls before or after a stakeout."

"His girls?"

"He was a private investigator, specializing in cheating spouses," she said. "Far as I knew, Errol never came to hotels like this for . . . uh . . . personal reasons."

A voice behind Brenna said, "You aren't his wife, are you?"

She turned around to see a man with greasy gunmetal hair, wearing khaki pants, a gray sport coat that looked petroleum-based. She swatted at her eyes. "God no," Brenna said. "I'm a former business assoc— Wait. Who are you?"

"Kevin Wiggins." He showed her a row of yellow teeth. "Desk Clerk to the Stars."

"You found him, huh?"

"Yup." He peered at her face. "Say, anybody ever tell you, you look a little like Barbara Stanwyck?"

"Only my mom."

"What happened to your eye?"

"Air bag."

He nodded, as if that were the most normal response in the world. "Listen," Kevin said. "I'm sorry about your friend, but if it helps at all, I can tell you without a coroner's report that he died with a smile on his face."

"Is that right?"

He nodded. "I've seen my share of 'em in here. Happy heart attacks. I don't need to paint you a vivid picture, do I?"

"Please don't."

"For what it's worth, I'm pretty sure I saw the lady who visited him, and there isn't a man on the planet who could think of a better way to go."

"Did you know her?" Brenna asked. Weird question. She wasn't sure why she'd asked it, or why she continued to care, but she did. Closure, maybe. *The last person to see Errol Ludlow alive.*

"I didn't know her, but she was a looker," he said.

Tim Waxman looked at him. "Did you happen to get her name?"

"Just a first name."

"Let me guess," Brenna said. "Chastity?"

Kevin gave her a sly look, as if this were some Hollywood movie and they were exchanging the wittiest of banter. "You talk like Stanwyck, too," he said. "Delightfully acerbic."

"Thanks."

"Mr. Wiggins," Tim said. "Can I please get the name of the woman you saw last night?"

"Oh." He chuckled, still looking at Brenna. "You gotta understand, it's so rare I get to exchange this many intelligent words with anyone . . . You're probably married, aren't you?"

"Mr. Wiggins," Tim said.

"Sorry," he said. "What was the question?"

"The name, sir." Tim sighed. "What was the name given to you by Mr. Ludlow's last visitor?"

"Right." He kept grinning at Brenna, even as he answered. "The lady's name was Clea."

Brenna stared at him, her heart beating up into her neck, her face, her eyes . . .

Gary shuddered in his sleep—a movement that wracked his whole body and jolted Jill out of a dream about Yasmine, her yoga instructor, performing surgery on a cat. *Wonder what Freud would have to say about that one*, she thought, still half asleep. And then Gary shuddered again. "Are you all right, honey?" Jill said.

He put his arms around her and pulled her close.

Jill smiled. She and Gary had made love last night and she still felt warm from it. It had been wonderful as usual, but also different—more intense. Gary had kissed Jill so deeply, pulled her so close, as though he were trying to become a part of her, climb under her skin, stay with her always. She'd always felt *wanted* by Gary when they had sex—there was never any question about that. But last night, Jill had felt *needed*. Gary had made love to her as though she were saving his life, and in a way, she was.

In a way, they were saving each other.

Part of it was that the two-week dry spell was finally ending—*two weeks*—but more powerful still, Jill thought, was Gary's confession.

"I need to tell you something," he had said, without her asking. Without her having to ask. "I know I've been distant these past few weeks."

And she had stood there, in their bedroom with the door closed behind her, holding her breath, watching his mouth move as though she were standing at the edge of a cliff . . . Only to hear him say the last thing on earth she had ever expected.

"It's because I didn't trust you, Jill. I'm so sorry. I was wrong . . ."

"Wait. You didn't trust me?"

"I thought you were having an affair."

Her jaw had gone slack. "Why would you think that?" Jill had said, but as she said it, she knew the answer. She'd been distant, too—just as distant as Gary had been, come to think of it, though having an affair had been the last thing on her mind.

Wise Up was having its annual fund-raiser on January 7, which was just around the corner, and the publicity firm they'd worked with for the past eight years had demanded double the money. There was no way the charity could afford that without her supplementing. Jill didn't even want to think about that now, but yeah, she'd been spending a lot of time at her office looking for new PR, a lot of time on the phone, her head spinning, her thoughts miles and weeks away. She hadn't talked to Gary about it because he had enough on his mind, why burden him with her headaches? Plus, their plate was so full at home with the three girls and their schedules, feeding them and helping them with homework and making sure they practiced their piano and their cheers and their French and Spanish and that they read for half an hour every night. Worse still, Hannah was in a needy phase so by the time she finally got to sleep, after her third glass of water and her second bedtime story, well, it was all Jill could do to collapse on the couch and stare at HBO for half an hour. This had been going on long before the dry spell, she'd realized last night. Long before she'd started to get suspicious of Gary.

He'd felt suspicious first.

"Why didn't you just talk to me about it?" Jill had said. *Jill the hypocrite, sneaking into her husband's office, copying down numbers from his disposable phone . . .*

"I was scared of the answer," he had said, "I even went so far as to talk to private detectives. I had a phone I was using . . . I threw it out. I'm so sorry."

And Jill had gone to him and put her arms around him, her heart crumbling . . . *You were suspicious of me.*

But that was gone now, the bad times were behind them. After they'd made love and Gary was sound asleep to the point of snoring, Jill had snuck out of bed. She'd taken the piece of paper with the three phone numbers out of her purse and she'd put it through the trash compactor. "Never again," she had whispered.

Gary clutched at her in his sleep now. She kissed the top of his head and shut her eyes tight. Tears seeped out the corners. She loved him. After all these years, now more than ever. She loved him so much it hurt.

Gary murmured something in his sleep. It sounded like "Sorry."

It's okay. Everything is going to be okay, my love, my great love . . .

Jill closed her eyes. She took a deep breath—a cleansing breath. She and Gary had taken a *pranayana* class together just a few weeks ago, and that's where she'd learned it. She'd liked the *pranayana* teacher, Lily. Not quite as much as Yasmine, with all her wonderful medical terminology, but definitely more than that Bikram girl, who was forever missing class to audition for commercials and soap operas . . .

Jill heard a noise. At first she thought it was in her imagination, part of her sleep drifting. But when she opened her eyes, she heard it again. And then again.

A vibrating phone.

The sound was coming from Gary's side of the bed—but strangely, not from his cell phone, lying dormant on his nightstand. No—it was coming from the chair behind the nightstand, piled with Gary's clothes. Jill moved toward it.

Strange, the things you think of when your life is about to change forever . . . Here Jill was, moving toward a vibrating cell phone at 6 A.M. on a Sunday morning—a phone her own husband had kept hidden from her—yet she wasn't thinking about that at all. She was thinking about the January 7 Wise Up fund-raiser, how she was going to hire back that publicist and buy herself a new dress for it, too. She was going to buy that five-thousand-dollar St. John sheath she'd seen in Barneys last week; while she was at it, she'd buy the girls new dresses, too, because they deserved new dresses and even if it was just someone calling the wrong number at six in the morning on a Sunday, the fact remained that Gary still owned a secret phone, different from the one she'd found in his desk, a different brand—a Nokia, she saw now, as she plucked it out of his shirt pocket. Everyone in their family had Motorolas. They shared a Sprint plan, but she supposed this Nokia's plan was different.

A different plan, indeed.

She checked the blinking screen and saw not a number, but a name. *DeeDee.*

Jill hit talk. She didn't say hello. She said nothing, just breathed into the mouthpiece.

The voice on the other end of the phone was a girl's voice, small and fragile, full of breath.

"It's done," the girl said. *DeeDee* said. Then she hung up.

"He will never bother you again." Diandra said this to the walls of her apartment, but in her head she was saying it to Mr. Freeman. She often had long conversations with Mr. Freeman, Diandra did, as if he were in the room with her. She'd tell him stories from her life, and in her mind he'd give her advice. He'd talk to her about everything, but mostly, about her craft . . . "You have it all inside of you, DeeDee. You have the capacity to be a heroine or a villain, a goddess or a tramp. It's all there—every quality of every single character ever written, buried beneath that beautiful skin. All you need to do is bring it up, DeeDee. Show the world. There's no part you can't play. There is nothing you can't do."

This was something he'd told her for real. Or at least she thought he had. The real and imagined conversations overlapped in her mind—especially the ones from long ago. One thing she did know was that he needed her. He needed her like water, for his very survival, and she knew that because he'd told her, over the phone yesterday when he'd asked for her help with Errol Ludlow. *I need you DeeDee. I hope you know that.*

"I do know it," she whispered, now. "I do."

This was what she loved most about Mr. Freeman—his need for her. And so she'd done what he had asked her to do, which was to stop Errol Ludlow. Put him out of his own misery and Mr. Freeman's, too. *He will throw me and my family out on the streets, DeeDee. He doesn't care about us. Stop him. Now.*

He hadn't said *how* he wanted Errol stopped, but Diandra knew. She knew Mr. Freeman, better than he knew himself. The proof: By the time he had called her, she was already prepared.

Ecstasy and Viagra was known on the streets as "trail mix," and it was awfully dangerous—"Russian roulette," Saffron had told Diandra two nights ago. Saffron was a large black man with a shaved head and diamond studs in his ears. He wore a tight white T-shirt and had very white teeth. To Diandra, he had looked otherworldly, glowing. "Want to go to heaven, sugar?" he had said to her upon approach, and it had felt as though she were talking to an angel.

Saffron hadn't been the first man to speak to her at the Rose Room that night but he had been the right one, and so she'd gone back with him to the VIP lounge, which was not quite heaven but as close as one could get on a cold Friday night in Dumbo. Afterward, she glowed, as if she'd absorbed some of his shine. He'd shown her the bag of pills in his pocket, and that's when the idea had come to her—she wasn't quite sure how or why. "Can I have three or four for a friend of mine?" she had said, testing out the idea, watching for emotion in the gleaming black eyes. "He likes to take them with his Viagra."

Saffron had looked alarmed—something Diandra hadn't quite thought possible. "Tell your friend he could have a heart attack," he had said, such a beautiful, helpful man.

And here, she had no idea that the next day, Mr. Freeman would call and beg for her help—no conscious idea, anyway. But when he did, *of course he did*, scared and shaky-voiced and needing her like water, Diandra was able to help him, without hesitation.

If that wasn't a soul-connection, she didn't know what was.

Diandra had convinced Errol Ludlow to take three of them, even though he'd wanted nothing to do with pills at first. "You'll be amazed at your performance," she'd whispered in his ear, easing her fingertips down the length of his chest, slipping them under the black silk robe he'd put on, exploring . . . *"Oooh, you wore the ring."*

"I'll take the pills," he had said, his voice thick from desire. And then she'd given him the pills with a glass of champagne and followed the same trail with her tongue. The entire time, Mr. Freeman's voice was in her head, urging her on.

And he had moaned, Errol Ludlow. He had run his hands through her hair and called her incredible and he had told her . . .

Had he said, "I love you"?

I love you, my sweet . . .

He couldn't have said that. Not Errol Ludlow, who loved no one. Hadn't he told Diandra as much during her job interview? Hadn't he bragged, *Here at Ludlow Investigations, we make good money proving time and time again that true love is a lie?*

"You never loved me," she said now. "You loved who you made me into."

That was the way most men were. *They look at a pretty face, they fill in the blanks, and that's who they love—the girl their minds make you into.* Diandra's stepmonster had said that once while putting on her lipstick—and she did have a point. Why, Diandra's own adult life had been a succession of men, each one filling in her blanks so reverently, ascribing to her such goodness—or for that matter, *bad*ness—she barely had to lift a finger to win their love. *The ancient Greeks called Beauty a virtue. They put it right up there with Truth.* The Monster had said that, too. And if she was right, it was easy to see how the Romans had kicked their asses.

I love you, my sweet . . .

Diandra shut her eyes tight. She didn't like this feeling, this niggling guilt. What would have helped was if Mr. Freeman had said something, anything to her over the phone this morning. He was a busy man and never alone and probably half asleep when she'd called. But still, she'd hoped, at the very least, for a "Thank you."

Diandra wouldn't stay mad at him for long, though, she knew. She could never stay mad at Mr. Freeman— who had listened to her when she was DeeDee Walsh, a mousy brown butterball with zits and food-clogged metal braces and just thirteen years old.

When her stepmonster had first brought her into his office for her audition, DeeDee had been so embarrassed she couldn't even say hello. She'd expected The Monster to carry the conversation the way she always did—with her peekaboo hairdo and her keyhole blouse and her perfect Marilyn smile . . . But Mr. Freeman had barely looked at her. He'd been so kind, asking DeeDee questions, such as "Where do you see yourself in ten years?" and "What are your career goals?" And when she answered, he'd looked her in the eye—as though it mattered what she said. DeeDee had caught sight of one of the pictures on his desk—his two tiny blonde daughters—and thought, *I'd do anything to trade places with one of them.*

Mr. Freeman had believed in DeeDee the way no one else ever had. He couldn't get her many parts, but she knew he was trying. She knew that there were times of the day when he thought of her, and her alone. *You have every character inside of you, DeeDee, beneath that beautiful skin*, he would tell her. *There is no part you can't play. There is nothing you can't do.* And even when she grew too old to be a client and dropped out of his life for years, he kept her in his thoughts—the same way she'd kept him in hers.

Diandra's phone chimed once. Her heart leaped, but just a little bit. One chime meant a text, and Mr. Freeman never texted her, but she looked at it fast anyway, allowing herself that taste of hope.

The text was from Trent LaSalle. It read: *Sup?*

She sighed. Articulate as ever. Timely, too. She'd texted him five hours ago, and coming from a geek like Trent LaSalle who announced his every move on Twitter and Foursquare, a five-hour text delay was unacceptable.

She typed: *Where U been?*

Long story. Later! ☺

Diandra's eyes narrowed. She stared at the words on her screen. The smiley face. *Are you kidding me?* "He's blowing me off."

What would Mr. Freeman say? Diandra had been told to keep an eye on Trent LaSalle—and on his boss, Brenna Spector. *They need to get close to the truth*, he had said, *but we can't let them get too close. Do you know what I'm saying, DeeDee? We need to watch them more carefully than they're watching Lula Belle.*

Of course she knew what he was saying. She always knew what he was saying.

And now Trent was blowing her off. He was wrecking her plans, just like her last L.A. boyfriend had done with his *You were pretending with me*, and his *I'll get you back for hurting me. I'll get you good, you and him.* Just like Shane.

This can't happen.

Diandra took a deep breath. *Calm, calm . . .* She needed a face-to-face, that was all. He'd never be able to blow her off in person. He wasn't strong enough for that. How long had their first encounter lasted? Thirty, forty seconds? He'd done better the second time, but still. Trent was not one for self-restraint.

And besides, she needed to see him, for Mr. Freeman's sake. She needed to see Trent one more time.

Diandra flipped open her computer, checked Trent's Twitter feed. Thank God for Foursquare, and the idiots who used it. Right now, it was telling her—along with his thirty-five hundred other followers—that he was at a Starbucks, just a few blocks from where he lived. Along with a tweet: *The chairs here hurt my ass.* Seriously— was this guy allergic to privacy, or what?

In twenty seconds, another tweet popped up: *Headin' home.*

If there's one thing life had taught Diandra Marie about men, it was that there was much to be gained— *much*—from their stupidity.

Diandra checked herself in the mirror. The jeans worked, but she definitely needed to change her top. She stripped off the tired old "I heart NY" sweatshirt she was wearing, and chose something shinier—a low-cut, hot pink angora sweater that always got her line-cuts at the movies. It worked with the white lace push-up, so she changed into that, too. She applied matching hot pink lipstick, brushed through her pale blonde hair, slipped into matching Steve Madden heels and checked herself again . . .

"Fill in the blanks," she whispered. Diandra threw on her coat, grabbed her bag, and headed out into the brisk Christmasy morning, preparing for her role.

15

The Tarry Ridge station was as empty as you'd expect a suburban police station to be on a Sunday morning—just Sally the desk sergeant and a skeleton crew of uniforms. Nick Morasco was glad of it. Cliché as it sounded, he needed to be alone with his thoughts.

"Catching up on things?" Sally asked him when he walked in. She was riveted to her computer screen—online Scrabble, it looked like. The question was more a clearing of the throat than anything else, and so Morasco cleared his throat right back at her.

"Yep."

He headed for his desk, passing a couple of new uniforms, who stood up a little straighter when they saw him. The Neff case had given Nick a type of luster that he still wasn't comfortable with. Throughout his career, he'd been told time and time again he didn't look like a cop—that he'd fit in much better in a room full of philosophy professors, which he never knew whether to take as a compliment. (He was guessing no.) But still, he was used to it. He wore his dad's old tweed coats out of sentimentality and laziness and went too long between

shaves and haircuts, and for that, he got mocked sometimes. He didn't care. The eye rolls he could handle, as
opposed to salutes. And these two new uniforms had
just, if he wasn't mistaken, saluted him.

"Hello, Detective," said the taller one—a chubby,
carrot-haired kid with pinkish skin and beads of sweat
on his forehead and upper lip. "Is there anything I can
help you with?"

"No thanks."

"Let me know if you change your mind, sir."

Morasco sighed. *Sir.* Yeah, he definitely preferred the
eye rolls.

He booted up his computer. *Take care of the easy
stuff first.* He went onto the national law enforcement
database to see if there was a CCH for Robin "RJ"
Tannenbaum. A CCH, or Computerized Criminal History, was really just a fancy name for a rap sheet, and
he could have made Carrot-Top's day by asking him to
look this one up. But Nick was selfish with the chores
today. The thing was, he liked to be useful while fore-
stalling the inevitable. Plus, he felt like helping Brenna
for a change. Personally doing something to help her—
rather than keeping things from her.

The Tannenbaum info came up quickly, with just
one arrest. Three years ago. Breaking and entering.
Dismissed. At the time of his arrest, RJ had been forty-
two—arrested over something you'd ground a sixteen-
year-old for. Not a robbery, but a B&E. He was caught
in the master bedroom. Just standing there. Alone. *A
prank. A dare.* Morasco sighed, thinking about poor,
withered Hildy Tannenbaum, how she'd blamed the
break-in on peer pressure.

Were all mothers of grown losers completely deluded?

He wondered how much money Hildy had wired Robin over the years, which made him think of his own mother, continually making up excuses for his older brother, who was never where he should be. Couldn't even be bothered to visit Dad when he was dying in the hospital, and yes that was twenty years ago, but Nick hadn't forgiven him. There wasn't a statute of limitations on being that much of an asshole.

How much had Mom invested in Seth, financially and emotionally, to get nothing in return?

When it came to people like that, Nick was with Pokrovsky. He didn't care how many dead bodies the guy had stuffed in his window seat, he'd love to stick his older brother in a steel cage for one hour with Yuri Pokrovsky in his prime—maybe throw in old RJ for good measure. Morasco had a feeling that everyone in that cage would get exactly what he deserved.

He e-mailed the California officers who had filed the CCH, asked them if they could send him back a copy of the whole report, along with any other information they might have on the break-in. Then he sat back in his chair, thinking of ungrateful children. And then, just children.

If he had lived, Morasco's son, Matthew, would be close to thirteen years old right now—the same age as Maya, edging toward the verge of adulthood. He tried not to wonder what Matthew would be like as a child or as a teen, or what his own life would be like with his boy a part of it. But if he had known those things . . . If he could feel what it was like to be a parent to someone old enough to screw things up, then he might be able to understand his mother or, for that matter, Hildy Tannenbaum. Far as Nick could tell, Pokrovsky was childless, too.

He looked at the clock. Noon already. He slid open his desk drawer, took out the letter. He'd read it many times since it arrived here at the station two days ago. Yet still, he felt compelled to read it again, as if maybe the typewritten words had rearranged themselves in his absence to mean something different.

Dear Det. Morasco:

I phoned you a month ago with no response. Perhaps you didn't get the message. At any rate, I am dictating this letter to my niece, who has been instructed not to tell anyone. I'm dying. That isn't the secret here. It is, however, my reason for wanting to get in touch with you, urgently. It is my reason for needing to relay to you this piece of information which I've kept secret for many years. It concerns Brenna Spector. I am aware, through the news, that you are friends. You can tell her, or not tell her. Use your judgment. I do, however, want to give you the option.

I must tell you in person. I don't want this information to get into any other hands but yours . . .

Morasco skimmed to the bottom of the letter—to the shaky signature.

Detective Grady Carlson.

Morasco knew the name. He'd heard Brenna say it, repeatedly. In 1981, Grady Carlson had been with the Pelham Bay Precinct, the head investigator in Clea's disappearance. He'd come up with nothing. He'd been rude to Brenna, to her mother. *Grady Carlson was the most unhelpful cop I've ever met in my life,* Brenna had told Nick. *And no offense, Nick, present company excluded and all, but for me, that is really saying something.*

"Are you sure I can't help you with anything, Detective?" Carrot-Top asked, looming over him like an unpleasant thought.

Morasco exhaled. He wasn't being fair. "Actually, you can," he said. In his coat pocket, he was still carrying the picture of Robin Tannenbaum that Brenna had given him. He plucked it out, handed it to the kid, along with the address of the gas station in White Plains where he'd filled up on October 9. "This guy was last seen at this gas station in early October. Can you call the White Plains station, e-mail them the photo, find out if anyone has seen him?"

Carrot-Top looked as though he'd just won the lottery. "Of course!" He practically shouted it.

"Thanks . . . what's your name?"

"Danny Cavanaugh."

Morasco looked at him. "You related to Wayne Cavanaugh—detective from Mount Temple?"

He grinned. "That's my grandpa," he said. He looked about three years old.

"Small world, Westchester County."

"Yeah. I'll get right on this, then."

Morasco nodded. "Thanks, Officer . . ."

"Danny." He cleared his throat. "Dan."

"Oh, and also, he may have a beard now. And he's got a very expensive camera. The kind a professional moviemaker would have."

"Got it!" Dan leaped over to his desk to make the calls. Literally leaped. That enthusiasm, Morasco thought. That feeling that the world was yours for the taking if you just worked hard enough—why was that a feeling only young cops had?

The thing was, this work beat you down quickly. That was a cliché, too, Nick supposed. But clichés are clichés because they're widely known truths, which, again, is another cliché.

You go into police work thinking you can save lives, and more often than not, you come out of it like Grady Carlson, dictating letters from some hospital room, trying to make up for all the damage you've done. Maybe it wasn't just police work that beat the enthusiasm out of you. Maybe it was life.

Just yesterday, Brenna had said, *If I can find Lula Belle, I might be able to find my family.* The hope in her voice was so contagious that, for a moment, Nick had forgotten about the phone call, the letter . . . Was that hope keeping Brenna going, or was it holding her back even more than her memory? And either way, why did it have to be Nick's job to crush it?

You should know that Brenna and her sister are both pathological, Evelyn Spector had told him, once she was full of wine and Brenna out of earshot. *Those girls have a gift for destruction that runs through their veins. Brenna will destroy you if you give her a chance. It's not her fault. It is genetic.*

Not true, Evelyn, Nick had thought, even then—just a few hours after he'd gotten that first phone message from Grady Carlson. *It's you and the world that want to destroy your daughter. Not the other way around.*

Morasco glanced at the clock on his computer again, then called Roosevelt Hospital, asked for Grady Carlson's room. "He's moving out to hospice later today," the nurse said. "But if you get here within the hour, you can visit with him." Morasco grabbed his coat and headed out the door, uncertainty tugging at him. He needed to know what Carlson's secret was—that was a given. But maybe he wouldn't tell Brenna about it. No one was forcing him to tell.

"Incense, Trent? Really?" Brenna had just been let into Trent's apartment after a five-minute delay at his front door. At the time she thought maybe she'd interrupted a nap. But looking around the place—so much neater than it had been during her last visit on April 24, and with the lights dimmed and a half-empty glass of wine on the kitchen counter next to Trent's boob-shaped coffee cup, not to mention the telltale stick of jasmine incense burning at the center of the stove—she was sure it was a lot more than a nap she interrupted. "I thought I told you to get some rest."

"I don't know what you're talking about." Trent stared at the floor. "I lit that incense because it smelled like ass in here."

Brenna sighed. She picked up the glass of wine, examined the rim. "And you were wearing pink lipstick because . . ."

"I had a visitor, okay? No biggie. Just . . . just a friend."

Brenna gave Trent a long look. She took in the mussed hair, the pink lipstick stains on the bandage on his head and his white mesh tank top that clashed with the lip-print tattoo on his pec but matched the stain on the glass, the distracted look in his eye, the smile he kept trying to stifle . . . She decided not to mention any of it. "Just take it easy, okay? Do me that favor?"

He nodded. "So listen, speaking of ass, I've had myself a little Shane Smith film retrospective."

"Really?"

"They've got a whole bunch of his shorts on the Web site for the School of the Moving Image. I guess he's won awards at that place, which proves this new philosophical theory that I'm working on."

"Which is?"

"Film sucks."

"Okay . . ."

"Don't believe me?"

She sighed at him. "I think *Casablanca* was pretty good. *The Godfather. Bad Santa . . .*"

"Those are *movies*. I'm talking about *film*. Cinema. Whatever. Just check this out and tell me that it doesn't get boned by goats on a regular basis." Trent grabbed a laptop off of the edge of the counter, opened it up, and hit play on the film that filled the screen. A title popped up: *Soul Window. A Shane Smith Film.*

What followed was a black and white close-up of a woman's eye. "Oh," Brenna said. "As in, 'The eyes are the window to the soul'?"

"As in, 'This chomps butt.'"

After around thirty seconds, the eye blinked, and the film was over. Brenna looked at Trent.

"That won that school's prize for best short film of 2006," he said. "I kid you not."

The credits rolled down the screen: *Written and Directed by Shane Smith.*

"Written?" Brenna said.

"I know, right?" said Trent. "How about directed? What'd he do, yell, 'Blink now, please!'"

The Eye: Mallory Chastain
Lighting Designer: Cameron Keys
Editor: RJ Tannenbaum

"So they really were friends," Brenna said.

"You ask me, RJ made a big step up with the porn."

"You find any contact info for Shane?"

He shook his head. "There's a weirdly large amount of Shane Smiths in So Cal."

"No pictures of him accepting his awards?"

"Nope," he said. "Only thing I could find was a group shot of his graduating class. It's pretty blurry, but it isn't that big a group, so I'm working on singling him out, blowing it up, making it clearer. I can try some different looks on him, too—thinner, fatter, beard, shaved head . . ."

"You think you can do all that, just from a group photo?"

"You should know by now I'm a god," he said. "I'll give him the full Persephone treatment." His eyes went a little sad at the sound of the cat's name. "Plus let's not forget RJ's computer in my bedroom. I've been recovering erased search histories, trying to see if he went looking for his boy."

"Listen, Trent," Brenna said. "There's something I have to tell you."

He looked at her. "Is it something bad?" His voice cracked, and again, Brenna couldn't help but see him as a six-year-old beauty pageant contestant. "I feel like you're going to say something bad."

Brenna stole a quick glance at the lipstick stain on the wineglass rim. *Be nice to him, whoever you are.* She put a hand on his shoulder. "Errol Ludlow is dead."

"*What?*"

"He died last night. Probable heart attack."

"He . . . he wasn't even that old."

"I know," Brenna said. "If it's any consolation, it apparently happened during sex."

"How did you find out?"

"The police," she said. "And also, the motel desk

clerk." She swallowed hard. *Keep it together. She's not the only one in the world with that name* . . .

"You okay?"

"Yeah . . . just . . . The clerk told me that . . . uh . . . He said that Errol's date's name was Clea."

Trent shook his head. "Asshole."

"Huh?"

"Obviously he recognized you from TV. He was messing with your head."

Brenna exhaled. "I didn't even think of that." She thought back to the clerk's face. The way he'd looked at her when she'd turned to him. *Kevin Wiggins. Desk Clerk to the Stars.* Not a hint of recognition in that smile, and he'd stared so closely at her face. *Anybody ever tell you, you look a little like Barbara Stanwyck?* "He didn't seem like he was lying," Brenna said.

But then again, there was the way he'd grinned at her when he'd told Tim Waxman, *The lady's name was Clea.* Was it the grin of a lonely man, trying a little too hard to flirt with a stranger—or had he been watching for Brenna's response to the name?

"Listen, Brenna. I screen your work e-mail, right?" Trent said. "You wouldn't believe some of the stuff I never show you."

"Such as . . ."

"Clea sightings."

"Really?"

He nodded "Each one more full of crap than the next. Just last week, some dipshit claimed he knows for a fact that Clea's a one-eyed Wal-Mart greeter in Erie, Pennsylvania. Another freak swore up and down that Clea is his wife's divorce lawyer—and oh, by the way, her name is Alfred now. She's a *dude*."

She shook her head, Kevin Wiggins's grin still in her

mind. "I never should have let Faith talk about Lieberman's book."

His bathroom door opened. A very curvy blonde slipped out.

Brenna looked at Trent.

"Uh . . . That's . . . um . . ."

"Your friend. Who was visiting."

"Yeah, she's . . ."

"I'm Jenny," the girl called out. She wore a pink angora sweater and jeans, both of which she was poured into to the point of overflow, sky-high spike-heeled pumps—your basic Trent LaSalle wet dream. Though there was something a little off about the look, Brenna thought. She couldn't quite put her finger on it, but it had to do with the way her stilettos so perfectly matched the sweater, the deliberate way she tossed her hair and rolled her hips as she moved toward the door. It was almost as if she were in costume, playing a role.

"Sorry to interrupt you guys," Brenna said.

"It's okay," said Jenny. "I was just leaving." She had a high, velvety voice.

"Are you sure?" Brenna asked.

Jenny turned to her, for just a few seconds. "I have something I need to be at," she said. And for the first time, Brenna got a good look at her face . . .

Jenny was saying something to Trent—some hasty, polite, nice-talking-to-you type of comment, her hair flipping into her eyes as she spun back around, heading for the door, shouting good-bye to Trent, Trent making that tired "call me" gesture with his thumb and pinkie, mouthing the words "call me," at the back of her blonde head, just in case she found that gesture too cryptic.

But Brenna wasn't paying attention to any of it. In her mind, she was on the *Maid of the Mist* on October 30, Maya sitting next to her . . . *She feels the chill wind at her back, wet hail hitting her face, so cold it burns. The boat is docking now, everyone stumbling to get off. Brenna watches the others as they pass—the elderly women, the little boy crying against his mother's side, the shell-shocked young girl, her mascara dripping . . . Brenna stares at this poor, pretty mess of a girl, then at her boyfriend standing behind her, his hand on her shoulder, the fingertips white from the tightness of the clutch. She looks at the girl's face, at the mascara streaks on her cheeks, so awful for the wear—* worse than Maya and me put together—*and then, into the eyes . . . such fathomless sadness as she meets Brenna's gaze, her boyfriend oblivious, smiling a little. She doesn't want to be here. None of us do, but . . .*

The girl taps her lip three times like a Morse signal.

Brenna heard Trent's door close and she came back, that thought scrolling through her mind again . . .

She wants to die . . .

Trent was staring at the closed door as if he was about to propose to it. "I like her," he said.

"Your friend. Jenny."

"Yeah."

"You might be a rebound, you know."

"Huh?"

"She had a boyfriend on October 30."

"Cut it out."

"I'm serious."

"You saw her?"

"She was on the *Maid of the Mist* with Maya and me. Some guy had his arm around her. Maybe it was just a date."

"Wait. Are we talking the same boat ride where you saw the lip tapper?"

Brenna looked at him. "She *was* the lip tapper."

Trent's eyes went huge.

"Small world, I guess. Huh?"

"You're telling me that the same girl you saw on that boat—the one who made the exact same gesture as Lula Belle does on the download . . . That was *her*?"

"Yeah, what's the big deal?"

"You're definitely sure? What am I talking about? You're *always* sure. Oh my God."

"Trent, you're overreacting. You don't know because you don't remember faces the way I do, but coincidences like this happen all the time. The world's a lot smaller than you think it is. You'd be surprised at how often I see the same people in different places. Sometimes it's years apart."

"You don't understand." Trent said.

"I do," she said. "Jenny had the same dumb idea I did to go on the *Maid of the Mist* in sub-zero weather. It's not that big a deal."

"I'm serious. You don't understand. Her name's not Jenny."

"Huh?"

"It's Diandra."

"*What?*"

"That was Diandra. I told her to lie about her name because I knew you'd be pissed."

"The Errol's Angel? What the hell was she doing here?"

"I sent her a text today, Brenna, I swear. I told her we were through. Well, what I said was, 'later,' which means the same thing."

Brenna looked at him. "Wow. You broke up with her by text."

"I'm crappy at dumping girls. You're probably going to find this surprising, but I don't have a lot of practice."

"Uh-huh . . ."

"But see, after I sent the text, she wouldn't take no for an answer. I was all ready to take a nap. But then she shows up at my door with those . . . with that sweater." He cleared his throat. "So I un-dumped her."

Brenna stared at him.

"Come on, Brenna. I'm a *guy*," he said.

"Whatever."

"Anyway, I figured I could still hang with her, as long as I didn't mention any cases . . . Hell, she's out of work now anyway, right? Ludlow . . ."

Brenna shrugged. "I'm surprised he hired her."

"Why?"

"She's so eye-catching. Errol's Angels tend to be a little subtler—hard to fade into the background and spy on a guy when you look like that."

Trent swallowed hard. "This is weird, Brenna."

"Well I'm sure she doesn't wear that sweater to stake-outs."

"Not that," he said. "I'm talking about Diandra in general. She'd just started working for Errol when I went to see him for that pitch meeting. Before that, she was on the *Maid of the Mist* with you."

"The *Maid of the Mist* couldn't have been planned, Trent. How would she have even known I was in Niagara Falls?"

Trent picked at a nail. "I'm . . . uh . . . I'm pretty sure I told somebody you were going up there."

"You did? Who?"

"Page Six."

"Oh for God's sake."

"Plus, I mean . . . I know I'm irresistible and all, but she has been on me like you wouldn't believe. I mean, come on. A girl like that?"

"Good point," Brenna said. "You think she's following us?"

"I think she's following the Lula Belle case."

Brenna nodded, very slowly.

"And she taps her lip in the same way Lula Belle does in a lot of those videos."

"Eighteen," Brenna said quietly.

"Huh?"

"She taps her lip in eighteen of the videos."

"Brenna?"

"Yeah?"

What if Diandra is *her*?"

"Her?"

"Lula Belle," Trent said. "What if she knows we're trying to find her and wants to make sure that we don't and so she's trying to distract me . . ."

"So she's sticking around and getting close to all the people looking for her, when she could far more easily leave town?"

"Hiding in plain sight," Trent said. "Oldest trick in the book."

"No it isn't."

"Looks-wise, she could be Lula Belle."

"Lula Belle is a silhouette."

"Yeah, but she's got the body. She's got the flexibility, too, trust me on that."

"It doesn't make sense."

"Why not?"

"Because."

"Because why?"

Brenna was breathing hard, now. Her jaw was tight. "Because she's *just a kid*."

Trent opened his mouth to say something, then closed it.

"How would she know all that stuff about my family?" Brenna said. "How would a twenty-year-old girl like that . . . How would she . . ."

"You don't think Diandra is Lula Belle," Trent said, "because Diandra can't be Clea."

Brenna didn't say anything.

"Listen, whether or not she's Lula Belle," he said, "she's got a sick interest in this case."

Brenna stared at her hands.

"Brenna?"

She couldn't answer. It was the way Trent had said her sister's name—the same way Maya had said it this morning, the same shiver in the tone . . . *What if Grandma is right about Clea, though? What if she's crazy and destructive and stuff?* She thought of Kevin the desk clerk again. The way he'd said the name of the woman who saw Errol, just before he died. *The lady's name was Clea.* Said, not to Brenna, but to Officer Tim Waxman. Would a meek old guy like that really lie to a police officer, just to mess with Brenna's head? Maybe.

But maybe not. Maybe Diandra wasn't the only person with a sick interest in the Lula Belle case. Maybe the real Lula Belle really *was* hiding in plain sight. And maybe, when he'd asked, she'd decided to give Kevin the desk clerk her real name . . .

"Bren, are you okay?" Trent said.

"I'm not sure."

Brenna's phone tapped Morse code. She glanced at

the screen, and saw a text from Maya. *Chanukah tonight*, it read. *You coming home soon?*

Clea, were you at the MoonGlow last night?

Brenna looked at Trent. "I need to see her."

"Who?"

"The woman who was with Errol."

He frowned. "How the hell are you gonna manage that?"

"I've got an idea," she said. "It's a weird one . . ."

He waited.

"I'll tell you later," Brenna said as she texted Maya back and hurried out the door. "In the meantime, keep looking for Shane."

16

"You so owe me," said Maya—a surprisingly deadpan reaction, seeing as five minutes ago, a drunken woman had thrown up on her shoes.

When it happened, Brenna and Maya had just gotten out of the cab on 108th and Second, Maya clutching her giant sketch pad in a way that made Brenna remember her at five years old—March 23, 2002, walking through the living room of Brenna's then-just-moved-into apartment at 7 A.M. holding her Bob the Builder doll to her chest. *Prince Harry and I want breakfast, Mommy.*

Coming out of the memory, Brenna had thought, *God I'm a terrible mother to take her here.* And then a sinewy bald woman in a strapless red minidress had stumbled up and puked on Maya's high-tops, putting exclamation points on Brenna's thought process.

Worst! Mother! Ever!

"I hate to see what this area is like after 5 P.M." Brenna was trying to sound cheerful as she went at Maya's shoes with seltzer water and a wad of paper towels, both of which she'd bought at the bodega next to the hotel. They were in the lobby of the MoonGlow—Errol's body long gone, and the police presence along with it.

It was 3 P.M. now, a bright, crisp winter day on this dismal block, Christmas decorations wilting on the streetlights outside lobby windows so grimy, it looked as though they were under water.

Brenna hadn't paid much attention to the decor in here earlier, but if she were to classify it, it would be mid-twentieth-century-what-the-hell-were-they-thinking. Mauve and tan floor tiles, mirrored walls, a chandelier that looked as though it were made of melted plastic. A big faux Ming vase next to the front desk, filled with the dirtiest fake flowers Brenna had ever seen, and an odor pervaded the space—cheap pine air freshener, tinged with sulfur and cheese. "You're right," she said to Maya. "I do owe you. Big time."

"Mom, I can clean my own shoes. This is embarrassing."

"I don't want you touching them," Brenna said. "And who are you embarrassed in front of? I guarantee you, you're not going to run into any of your friends here."

"Oh my God! There's my history teacher coming out of the elevator. Hi Mr. Stewart! Is that your wife?"

Brenna's head shot up.

"Kidding," Maya said, but when Brenna looked at her daughter, she could see the fear flickering in her eyes. *God, she's still a child. What am I thinking?*

Brenna said, "Do you want to leave, Maya?"

"Mom, stop. I'm *fine*."

"Something I can help you with?" said a voice behind them, which Brenna immediately recognized. "Kevin Wiggins." She sprang to her feet and turned around, stuck out her hand. "Do you remember me, from earlier today?"

He smiled. "Barbara Stanwyck."

Maya said, "Who?"

"This is my daughter, Maya."

Kevin squinted at her. "Uh . . . we aren't really what you'd call a family hotel."

"No, no," Brenna said. "Maya is just helping me out."

Maya, who clammed up with most strangers—let alone an old, greasy-haired desk clerk with enormous pores and hairs poking out of every visible orifice—said absolutely nothing. But to Brenna, there was something comforting in his presence—the reminder of why she was here, what was at stake . . .

"Before we start," Brenna said, "I just want to make sure of something."

"Yes?"

"When you told me about the woman with Mr. Ludlow . . . you weren't pulling my leg, were you?"

He screwed up his face to such a degree, Brenna was worried he might get a cramp. "Of course not," he said.

Brenna was glad she asked—she was ninety-five percent sure he was telling the truth. She looked at Maya. "You okay with this?"

She rolled her eyes. "Yes, Mother. I'm okay."

Brenna sighed. "Maya here is a composite artist."

"She looks awfully young to have a job like that."

"No, no. What I mean is, she's going to be acting as one now. For me—that is, if you don't mind describing the woman you saw."

His eyebrows lifted. "Seriously?"

"I know it sounds strange," Brenna said. "But Mr. Ludlow was a private investigator, and I was working on a case with him, and I'm thinking that this woman you saw may have had something to do with it."

"With what? The case?"

"Yes."

He let out a guffaw.

"I'm serious."

Kevin stepped closer. He smelled of ointment. "Okay, listen," he said. "I don't want to talk about this in front of your daughter, but I'm sure those two didn't even know each other. I mean, outside of in the biblical sense. Wink, wink."

Maya grimaced.

Brenna put an arm around her. "Why do you say that?"

"She was here for one hour. I'm talking to the minute," he said. "Personal friends don't punch clocks."

"Even so. I'd love to know what she looked like."

He frowned at her. "What's your name again?" he said. "And what is this case that you're working on?"

Brenna started to try and explain, but then her gaze drifted over his shoulder, to the open door of the office behind the front desk. An old movie poster on the wall. Something starring Jimmy Cagney . . .

Brenna closed her mouth, leveled her eyes at him, gave him her best Barbara Stanwyck half smile. "'What do you want, Joe, my life history? Here it is in four words: big ideas, small results.'"

Maya stared at her as if she'd just gone insane.

Kevin broke into a huge grin. "*Clash by Night*," he said.

"Yep," Brenna said. "I've probably seen it twenty times. I'm a big fan." It was half true . . . Okay, maybe a quarter true. She did like Barbara Stanwyck. But Brenna had seen *Clash by Night* only once—on March 30, 2000, when she was laid up with the flu and they played it on Turner Classic Movies. She'd sneezed and shivered throughout most of it and fell asleep three quarters of the way through. But she had liked that line.

Kevin was beaming at her. "You've got good taste in movies."

"They really don't make 'em like that anymore." Brenna sighed, the fever from nine years ago still rippling in her cheeks. "You know what I miss? Those big, gorgeous movie palaces. The revival houses, where you could see a classic noir, or maybe a fifties Technicolor movie on a big screen . . ."

"I love early Technicolor."

"Yep," she said. "Now it's all this CGI crap. Movies don't have heart anymore."

His eyes widened. "Yes, exactly," he said. "Say, do you like classic TV?"

"Well yeah, of course," Brenna said. "But I can't stand it when people talk about classic TV as coming from the seventies or eighties. Sid Caesar. Now *that* was classic TV."

"I own the *Your Show of Shows* box set!"

"Oh my God. Me too!"

She could feel Maya gaping at her, no doubt this close to mentioning that the only DVD sets Brenna owned were the first eight seasons of *90210* and *A History of Glitter Rock*. Brenna gave her a quick, sharp look. "Something wrong, honey?" She locked eyes with Maya, then cast a deliberate glance at the movie poster in the office.

Maya's gaze followed hers. "Uh . . ."

"It's nice to meet a young person with such great taste in entertainment," Kevin said, Maya gaping even wider at the description of her mother as young.

Brenna said, "That's funny. I was about to say the same thing about you."

"Unbelievable," Maya whispered.

Kevin grinned—a wide, giddy grin that split his face in two. "I'll describe the young woman for you," he said. Just like that. He didn't even mention the fact that, even though he'd asked her for it, Brenna had never given him her name. *A kindred spirit.* If you were lonely enough, there wasn't anything you wouldn't do for just a few minutes with one. Brenna knew this, because she so often felt lonely.

"Oh thank you so much!"

"We can talk in the office," he said. "Let me just straighten it up a little."

He headed back behind the desk, and Brenna and Maya followed.

As they walked, Brenna turned to her daughter, now looking at her with something that seemed close to admiration.

God, Brenna needed to work on her parenting skills.

Twenty minutes later, Kevin was directing Maya as she busily sketched. "Make the lips a little fuller. Great . . . Okay, and the neck is longer than that. Maybe you could add a shadow, under the chin?"

Brenna couldn't look. She could barely listen. It struck her that Clea, her Clea, would be forty-five years old now. Not a smiling teenager in a class picture or a coltish ten-year-old, clutching the handlebars of a bike. A forty-five-year-old woman with a *gift for destruction.* What did that look like? Brenna's sister. Brenna's living, aging sister . . .

Maya's pencil flitted across the pad, and for several moments, there was nothing in the room but the sound of her daughter, drawing . . . *Clea at forty-five* . . .

"How's this?" Maya said, tilting the sketch pad so Kevin could see.

Kevin said, "A . . . very impressive likeness."

Brenna held her breath. Maya held up the pad.

Brenna's eyes went big. It wasn't Clea on the sketch pad. It wasn't a forty-five-year-old. "Diandra."

Kevin said, "Huh?"

Brenna rubbed her eyes. "Sorry. It's been a long day."

"You're an incredible artist, young lady," Kevin was saying to Maya. "Do you mind if I make a copy of this? The Xerox is right over there."

"Uh . . . Sure." Maya actually looked pleased with herself.

Brenna smiled, a vague dread creeping through her. She tried swatting it away. *So Diandra slept with Errol. That isn't a crime. He could have died hours later.* "I have to make a quick call," Brenna said.

Maya gave her a puzzled look. "Okay . . ."

Kevin said, "Maya. That's your name, right?"

"Uh-huh."

"All right, well, listen. I've got these charcoal sketches of Joan Crawford I did for this extension course. I'm wondering if you could give them a quick look and tell me if they're any good."

"Sure, I guess."

Brenna stepped into the doorjamb as Kevin removed a sheath of sketches from his desk. "Now what do you think of this one?" he was saying. "Did I get the eyebrows right?"

Brenna put her back to Maya and Kevin and closed her eyes, hoping she could do what she needed to do, even with distractions.

What Brenna had said to Trent back at his apartment hadn't just been lip service. It was true. It was amazing what a small world it was, but you could only really see it—and use it—if you had a perfect memory.

Kevin was telling Maya how he tried to capture Joan's quiet strength in *Johnny Guitar.* Brenna took a deep breath and pushed the colliding thoughts out of her head—thoughts of Diandra and Trent and Errol. And Clea. *Why had she told Kevin that her name was Clea?* Brenna pushed away the phone call she'd received last night from Errol, his last phone call in life. She pushed away his cheery voice (*Ta-ta!*) asking her if she'd heard from Gary Freeman's wife. *Why would I have heard from Gary's wife?* She pushed away panicky Diandra, stumbling out of Trent's apartment on her pink high heels, tossing her hair into her eyes when she caught sight of Brenna. *Hiding her face from me. Why?*

She pushed all that into the back of her mind along with Kevin's droning voice and threw her focus onto June 10, 2006, the day she'd been lurking around the edges of a crime scene—a murdered co-ed turned prostitute who called herself Marjorie Morningstar, but whose real name had been Kara Wheeler. Hired by Kara's parents, Brenna was unwanted at the crime scene and didn't stay long. But of course she remembered everything about it. The heat in the Lower East Side walk-up where Kara's strangled body had been found, the walloping death smell as she entered the tiny studio apartment, the lumpy crime scene tech, pushing her out of the way, *his phone dropping to the hallway floor and clattering down the stairs as he hurries in, Brenna thinking,* Would it kill you to watch where you're going?

Brenna picks up the phone. I shouldn't even give this back to him, *she thinks, the smell choking her, making her eyes water . . . She starts to head back in and the phone vibrates in her hand. The theme from* Weird Science *explodes out of it. Brenna rolls her eyes.* Cheesiest lab tech ringtone ever.

She opens the phone, hits send. "Uh, hello?"

A woman's voice, "Hello. Who is this?"

"I just picked up this phone, I . . ."

"I need to talk to Mark."

"We're at a crime scene, ma'am."

"Listen. I need you to tell Mark that Nora called. You got that? Please tell him I can't pick Gracie up at school today. Mark Jr.'s soccer practice was canceled, and I have to get him, So he's gotta get Gracie. Do you understand me? You're breaking up. Service sucks around here . . ." *And she's gone.*

Brenna closes the phone. She starts to call out Mark's name, but stops herself. First, she hits the button next to the screen, and the phone's number appears on it. She stares at the number for several seconds, taking it in. You never know when you might need these things . . .

"Four score and seven years ago," Brenna whispered. The crime scene smell dissipated, replaced by the slightly (but only slightly) subtler pine-and-sulfur odor of the MoonGlow's lobby.

"I don't know," Maya was saying. "It seems like you could . . . like . . . soften these angles a little bit, so she doesn't look so two-dimensional?"

Brenna tapped Mark the lab tech's phone number into her own phone and hit send, thinking, *Please have the same cell phone number.* This was going to be a little tricky, but as long as her voice sounded confident . . .

He answered fast. "Yeah?"

"Hey Mark." She said it in a low, officey voice. "How's it going?"

"Uh . . ."

"How's Nora? I just ran into her and Gracie the other day at Gristedes. Did they tell you they saw me?"

"Uh . . . yeah. Yeah, they did . . . How are you?"

"Good. The knee still sucks, but I'm getting surgery on it next Friday. Hey, how's Mark Jr.? Still playing soccer?"

"Yeah." His voice brightened a little. "They won state championship."

"Fantastic," Brenna said. "Man, I don't get to see you guys enough. I was just telling Ed we need to do something."

"Ummm . . ."

"Sorry to bother you on a Sunday and all."

"Yeah." He cleared his throat. "I'm actually at work."

Yes! She forced a sigh. "Me too. Sucks, right? Listen . . . I could really use your help right now."

"How can I help you," he asked.

His voice was laced with confusion. Clearly, he had no idea who she was but was too polite to ask. Brenna stifled a smile. "Well . . . I'm trying to fill out some paperwork for a recent death, but my computer went down."

"Bummer."

"I know. It's like a conspiracy. So, can you do me a favor and look up Errol Ludlow for me? Died last night. Body found this morning at the MoonGlow on 108th and Second Ave."

Brenna waited.

Maya said, "That really isn't the best way to draw knees."

"It isn't?" Kevin said

"Well, see, I like to shadow this part."

Brenna crossed her fingers, hoping Mark couldn't hear . . .

Mark said, "Sure, one sec."

Yes!

"How do you spell the last name?"

Brenna spelled it. He asked her to hold, and came back on quickly. "Found it. What do you need?"

"Status of the body, estimated time of death . . . The usual."

"Okay," he said. "Looks like he died of a heart attack, but a toxicology report was ordered."

Brenna kept her voice neutral, bored. "And why is that?"

"The deceased was fifty-nine, no history of heart disease, and the examiner noticed a bluish tinge to the skin, indicating possible reaction to drugs."

Brenna closed her eyes. Maybe Diandra didn't know he'd died. Maybe they'd partied a little. (It didn't sound like Errol, but whatever. Midlife crisis happens.) But maybe he was fine when she left the room. Diandra had only been in there with him for an hour, after all. "You have estimated time of death?"

"Between six-thirty and seven-thirty."

"I wish I had my charcoals," Kevin said.

"You can just use a pencil," Maya said. "Like this. See?"

"Thanks so much, Mark," Brenna said. "That's all I need."

"No problem."

"Say hi to Nora for me!"

"Will do."

Click.

"Ms. Stanwyck, your daughter is a genius."

"Tell me something I don't know."

Maya rolled her eyes. "Mom."

"Kevin," said Brenna, "can I ask you a question?"

"Sure."

"You mentioned that Diand— the girl who visited Mr. Ludlow . . ." She swallowed hard. "You said she stayed here at the hotel for exactly one hour, down to the minute."

"Well, maybe not to the minute. But close enough."

"How do you know this?"

"Because I looked at a clock," he said. "I always do that when a girl comes in—look at the clock before and after, guess in my head how much the guy paid . . . Helps pass the time."

"Okay," Brenna said. "So when you looked at the clock and she was leaving . . ."

"Yeah?"

"What time did it say?"

"Seven forty five."

Brenna's mouth felt dry. "You sure?"

"It's a digital clock. Never wrong. Why?"

Errol died between six-thirty and seven-thirty. Diandra was with him when he died. He had a bluish tint to his skin. Drugs. Errol hated drugs . . .

"Anything else?" Kevin asked.

"No," Brenna cleared her throat. "I'm good."

Brenna put her arm around Maya, started walking her toward the door. "Thank you, Kevin," she said.

"Come back again sometime!" he called out after her as she hurried out into the twilight.

"What's wrong?" Maya asked, as soon as they got outside.

"Nothing, honey." Brenna hailed a cab with one hand, called Trent with the other. A cab pulled up quickly. After a few rings, the call went to voice mail. "Trent, listen to me," she said into his phone. "You cannot see Diandra anymore. I don't want to discuss this on a recording, but she is dangerous. Please call me as soon as you get this message," she said, as they got into the cab.

She hit end, told the cabdriver to take them to Twelfth and Sixth.

The cab jolted away from the curb.

Maya said, "Did Trent do something stupid?"

"It wouldn't be the first time," Brenna said, "but I hope not." She glanced at her daughter, staring down at the faint stains on her shoes. *Talk about doing something stupid* . . . "Maya, can you do me a favor, please?"

"What?"

"Please don't tell your dad I took you here."

Maya nodded. "Sure."

On the seat between them, Maya's sketchbook sprawled open. Brenna stared at Diandra's face—the wide, unlined eyes, the full cheeks. Such a kid, beneath all that artifice. She couldn't have been ten years older than Maya. Why had she bothered herself with Errol in the first place? Why was she so fascinated with Lula Belle?

Is Trent right? Are you Lula Belle?

Brenna closed her eyes, remembering the shadow on her computer screen, the sugary whisper of a voice wafting out of the speakers as she and Morasco watched . . . *She thought I was crazy like my daddy. She thought I couldn't take care of nothin' without breakin' it. Mama said that gift for destruction ran through my veins.*

The cab sped up the next block, then jolted to a stop at the red light. "Don't be stupid, Trent," Brenna murmured, as ninety blocks down and five blocks west, Trent was standing in his living room, his senses filled with pink angora and perfume and Diandra's lush body against his, knowing full well how stupid he was being.

17

Trent blamed the cat. He knew that probably sounded dumb, but ever since he found out Persephone wasn't real, he'd felt so angry—self-destructive, even. He would have gone on a drinking binge, but Trent wasn't really that good a drinker. Plus, he only liked sweet drinks with lots of carbs in them—rum and Cokes, mango mojitos, strawberry daiquiris—so a drinking binge would've not only given him the mother of all hangovers, it would have totally decimated his abs.

Hotties, on the other hand . . .

Yes, there was something going on with Diandra and Lula Belle, and yes, Brenna was suspicious and Trent was suspicious and if Diandra had looked like, say, Hulk Hogan, Trent would have been changing the locks on his doors and running a background check on her faster than you could say, "One-way ticket to Ward's Island."

But Trent was a guy. And there was Diandra's breathy voice on the intercom, Diandra saying, "I canceled my plans. I couldn't stay away." There was Diandra at Trent's front door, that damn sweater tugged down to reveal a flash of white lace that he actually felt jealous of. Here was Diandra, throwing her arms around Trent's waist, her teeth grazing his neck and her hands on his ass and her breath hot in his ear, Diandra whispering, "Take me, Trent. Take me, please . . ."

Now come on. What would *you* do?

Diandra was in the bathroom now. She'd left Trent on the kitchen floor in a state of extreme arousal, whispering, "Don't move." As if he could.

"You about done in there?" he called out.

"Yes," said Diandra.

He looked up. She was standing on the other side of the counter, holding the glass she'd left behind, the sweater gone, along with the white lace. "Whoa," Trent tried to say.

"I'm going to pour myself some more wine. Is that okay with you?"

Diandra moved around the counter and to the refrigerator. She opened the door and removed the bottle. "Brrr," she said. She was wearing nothing, save for the pink pumps.

Across the room, Trent thought he heard his cell phone vibrating again, but that could have just been the thrumming in his brain.

Diandra disappeared back around the counter for a few moments, returning into his line of vision with a full glass of wine. She took a sip, then moved toward him. She smelled of flowers and vanilla and she knelt down next to him, brought the glass to his lips. Trent gulped down a huge swallow. Diandra licked the rim of the glass and smiled. "What do you want to do first?" she said, and Trent felt desirous to the point of being overwhelmed, helpless. *Okay, dude. Get it together . . .* He took another gulp from the glass, emptying it. "Anything," he breathed.

"How about this?" Diandra straddled him. He reached out to touch her, but he felt only air.

"Missed." She giggled. She leaned over and kissed him. Girls always wanted to kiss. And though he was more of a cut-to-the-chase kind of guy, Trent could, if called upon, lock lips with the best of them. He kissed her hard and got his hands on her and pulled her even closer . . . but something was happening to him, something strange. The last time he'd been with Diandra, it had been strange, too—but in a rock-your-world kind of way. This was different. It was almost as though she were sucking the energy out of him. He felt sleepy. And funny, too, like his tongue was too big for his mouth.

Trent pulled away. "Something's wrong," he said.

"I'm sorry," said Diandra. And she did sound sorry, genuinely so. She stroked his cheek.

Trent's vision was blurry. He tried to focus on her face, but instead his gaze settled on the floor. On the empty wineglass. He made himself look at her. "What did you do?"

Her face swam in his vision, so soft, as though they were both under water. Trent found himself remembering a book he used to read with his mom when he was a kid—a big picture book. *The Little Mermaid.*

That's not a boy's book, his dad used to complain. *First the beauty pageants and now this? What are you trying to do, Karen, make him into a sissy?*

And Trent would pore over the pages, pretending not to hear, too embarrassed to tell his dad that what he really liked about the book was the Little Mermaid's boobs.

Diandra was talking to him in a soft voice. ". . . going to be okay," she was saying. " . . . just let yourself let go and sleep and everything will be fine."

His lids were getting heavy.

"Saffron said this was really good stuff. Just relax . . ."

I'm just wild about Saffron, Trent thought. It was his mom's favorite song.

"Everything will be okay, honey. I promise. Don't try to fight it."

Trent felt floaty now, outside of himself, the air thick around him like a blanket. He couldn't move. Or was it just that he didn't want to? *What is happening?*

He could feel Diandra easing off him, slipping away. *Where are you going?*

She was standing over him. He wanted to look at her naked body—*couldn't he at least have that?*—but his eyes wouldn't stay open. His stupid, sleepy eyes.

"I really like you, Trent," she said.

I like you, too.

"I'm so sorry."

She left the room, and he began to drift away. He imagined himself under the ocean, surrounded by shells and fish and so many mermaids, gorgeous ones with flowing hair and flashing tails and huge boobs, but the water got very murky, and soon it was too black to see anything.

Trent was so tired.

"Good night, my little prince."

Trent's mom used to say that to him every night, just after she put him to bed and sang him that Saffron song and gave him his three kisses on the forehead. And he could have sworn that when his eyelids fluttered open for the last time to see Diandra slipping by him and out the door, fully dressed . . . he could have sworn she said that to him, too, just before she softly closed the door behind her. *Good night, Trent. Good night, my little prince.*

He also could have sworn she was carrying RJ Tannenbaum's computer.

As soon as she and Maya got home, Brenna checked her e-mail, and the first one she saw was from Trent. Titled "Suckage," it had been sent at 2:55 P.M. She opened it up. It contained an attachment—another Shane Smith film, *Wreckage*, along with a brief note:

B—

Thought you might like to see some more "film." And by film I mean poo. (SPOILER ALERT: This one is two full minutes of a bicycle tire, lying in the middle of a road.) Anyway, I hacked RJ's phone and un-deleted his call log. Piece o' cake. Nothing interesting, but am sending it to you from the phone in a separate e-mail. Lemme know if you don't receive it. Also did some more work on Shane Smith's face, but I'm tired. Think I'm gonna take a nap for real.

TNT

Brenna breathed a sigh of relief. *Taking a nap.* That's why he hadn't picked up the phone. Of course it was—Trent wasn't that much of an idiot.

There were a series of PS's at the bottom:

PS Also attached is a pic of what RJ probably looks like if he's patterning himself after Spielberg. (I look way better as Diesel, BTW.)
PPS I've gone all the way through his computer. The one interesting thing I found (other than

*the porn) is that RJ uninstalled a cloud storage
gateway. You probably have no idea what that
means. I'll explain later.*

Trent was right. Brenna had no idea what that meant.
She downloaded the picture of RJ Tannenbaum and
looked at it—the carefully trimmed beard, the leather
bomber jacket, and the L.A. Dodgers cap. On a guy
from Queens. To Brenna, the photo seemed a case study
of someone trying too hard—a dumpy guy in director-
drag, who actually looked a lot more like Michael
Moore than Spielberg. And judging from what little she
knew of RJ, it was probably as accurate a photo of him
as had ever existed.

She forwarded it to Morasco, along with a note:

*If you want to show this around . . . RJT's new
look, courtesy of Trent.*

—B

Brenna went back into Trent's e-mail and read the
third PS (Trent lived for PSs): *Can you give me a wake-
up call at 4:30? My alarm's been unreliable and if I nap
too long, I get cranky.*

Maya shouted at her from the other room. "Mom,
it's past sunset!"

Time to light the candles. It was the last night of
Chanukah— well, for Brenna and Maya anyway. The
last night for the rest of the world had been Friday, but
as was their tradition for the past two years, they mutu-
ally decided on a "last night" date that did not fall on
a work day or a transfer day and gave Brenna enough
time to prepare (i.e. buy a great gift).

The gift this year was a no-brainer. Maya had been asking for an iPod Touch ever since the previous Chanukah, Brenna resisting every entreaty (Maya already had a laptop. Why did she need to be able to access the Internet via some cute little device? The screen was too small—it was probably bad for her eyes. And what did she need all those apps for?) That is, until the Neff case—and the realization that there are worse things in the world than spoiling one's child every once in a while. Maya's brand-new iPod Touch waited in Brenna's bedroom closet, wrapped and ready to go. "I'll be right there!"

Brenna started toward her bedroom, but when she glanced at her watch, she froze. It was 5 P.M.

Brenna *had* given Trent a four-thirty wake-up call—back in the cab, when she'd warned him to stay away from Diandra. She hadn't checked the time back then, but if it was five right now, it had to be . . .

"Mom?" Maya called out.

"Just a second!" *If he'd expected a wake-up call, he would've turned his ringer volume up and put the phone right next to his bed.*

But Trent hadn't picked up. And even though Brenna had told him to call back as soon as he got the message . . . She went back to her e-mails. No additionals from Trent. Nothing from Tannenbaum's phone.

I haven't heard from Trent since before three.

Brenna called Trent's number, listened to the phone ring five times before finally going to voice mail. "I'm getting worried," she said. "Call me."

She called again. Voice mail. She hung up. Called again. Same thing.

"You okay?" said Maya, now standing in the room.

But in her mind, Brenna was coming home from the MoonGlow again, Maya's sketchpad between the two of them in the backseat of the cab, Trent's voice mail in her ears for the first time that day . . .

"Did Trent do something stupid?" Maya says.

"I hope not."

"You hope not what?" Maya said now.

Brenna grabbed her bag, the dread growing, pulsing through her. "We're gonna have to postpone Chanukah for a little while," she said. "Stay here. Keep the doors locked. I'll call you when I can." On her way out, Brenna stopped at her desk. With her back to her daughter, she quickly pocketed her pearl-handled letter opener—the only thing she owned of her father's. It was sharp enough to kill, if used the right way.

On the street hailing a cab, Brenna glanced over her shoulder to see Maya standing in the window, watching her. "I'm sorry," she whispered.

But she had no time to explain right now—not if she was right about what had happened to Trent. And though she hoped she was wrong, hoped it with her whole body, recent memories kept insisting otherwise . . . *Trent is staring at the door that Jenny just closed behind her, He looks as though he's about to propose to it. "I like her." His voice is like a child's—so much need in it.*

She recalled Trent's excuse for taking Diandra back, despite so many misgivings. *Come on, Brenna. I'm a guy,* he had said.

Errol Ludlow was a guy, too.

Brenna saw a cab with its lights on and ran into the street to flag it down, narrowly missing a town car. "Ninth Street and Second," she said as she threw open the door and slid into the backseat.

The cab driver said, "I'm off duty."

"It's an emergency."

"I don't care."

"Why wouldn't you care about an emergency?"

"You didn't see the light? I. Am. Off. Duty."

Brenna gritted her teeth. *I'll show you off duty.* She shoved her hand into her bag, felt the cool handle of the letter opener, and pictured herself pulling it out, holding it to his throat, scaring that smug tone out of him for a good long while . . . *Deep breath.*

She grabbed two twenties instead, held them up in the rearview so he could see. Forty dollars for a five-minute ride. Nowhere near as satisfying as the letter opener would have been, but definitely less complicated. The driver took off like a 757, got her to Trent's walk-up in less than two minutes. She handed him the bills and pushed out of the cab without saying another word.

Trent's front door was propped open.

Brenna grabbed the letter opener and flew up the stairs. She didn't think about why the door was open, didn't think about anything, save for getting to the third floor and Trent's apartment, fast as she could, feet slamming on the stairs, barely breathing until she saw the closed apartment door in front of her. *Trent's door.* She knocked.

No answer. No answer still when she pounded on the door with the side of her fist. For the hell of it, she tried the knob. The door drifted open. *Unlocked* . . . For a few moments, she couldn't breathe.

Brenna stepped inside the apartment, her whole body shaking, except the right arm—held straight, fingers clutching the pearl handle of the letter opener. "Trent?"

The apartment was perfectly still. She headed for the bedroom, opened the door . . . Empty. She glanced at the Bowflex machine, the neatly made bed (had he ever taken his nap?) the framed ad on the wall behind it—a girl in a white bikini, caressing a huge flat-screen monitor. There was a caption (*Limitless Hard Drive*). But what caught Brenna's eye was the computer in the photo. It brought Trent's voice into her head, his voice of a few hours ago. *Let's not forget RJ's computer in my bedroom.*

RJ's computer was not in Trent's bedroom.

Brenna rushed into the kitchen area, noticing for the first time the empty bottle of wine on the counter and how the coffee table had been pushed off to the side, as if to make room for . . . what?

A bracelet glittered on the floor beneath the coffee table. Brenna picked it up. Alternating diamonds and emeralds, a sapphire at the clasp . . .

It is June 14, and a muggy day. Brenna's hair clings to the back of her sweaty neck. She sits at the white metal table in the courtyard of the new client's Great Barrington estate, cicadas buzzing all around them, ringing in her ears. "Can you find him?" The client's eyes are clear blue and her hair is silky, despite the humidity all around them, the air a solid, squishy thing . . . The woman doesn't seem to know how to sweat. Brenna looks at the photo of her husband—a bear of a man in a madras sport shirt. He has a lantern jaw, bulging eyes, oily skin. Like he was born sweating. Larry Shelby. His wife's polar opposite. "I know he's alive," the wife tells Brenna. Her name is Annette, and she looks as though she was drawn with pastels. Brenna's gaze drops to the tennis bracelet she's wearing— alternating diamonds and emeralds, a sapphire at the clasp.

"I pledge allegiance to the flag . . ." Brenna turned

the bracelet in her hands, caught sight of the engraving on the underside of the sapphire: *Love Always, Larry.* "Okay . . ."

Annette Shelby's bracelet in Trent's apartment.

In Brenna's mind, she traveled back again to that first meeting, Annette slipping her business card out of her shirt pocket, writing her number on the back, sliding it across the metal table. *I can be reached here, any time . . .*

Brenna bumped her palm against the tip of the letter opener's blade, bringing herself into the room. Then she pulled her cell phone out of her pocket and tapped in the remembered number.

Annette answered after one ring. "Brenna?"

"Annette. I know this is going to sound weird, but are you with Trent?"

"Yes."

"What? Why? Is he all right?"

"No."

Her breath caught. "Did you just say—"

"No."

"Please tell me what's going on."

"I would have called you. I was just scared you'd get mad."

"At you?"

"At Trent."

"*Why?*"

"Keep in mind he's still young." Her voice was flat, the words like a mantra. "He's still young. We all do crazy things when we're young."

"What the hell is going on?"

"I took Trent to the hospital," Annette said.

"Why?"

"You promise you won't be mad."

"*Annette, please.*"

"I . . . I went to his apartment because I wanted to talk. When I got there, he was unconscious."

"Oh my God."

"He'll be okay. I know he'll be okay. It wouldn't be fair if he wasn't and life is fair. Life has to be—"

"Was he injured?"

"Brenna." Annette said her name very slowly, as though she were attempting to soothe her with the sound of it. "Trent . . . that sweet boy . . . He OD'd."

18

It was a good thing that Trent hadn't replied to the text Annette Shelby had sent him when he and Brenna were driving home from Hildy Tannenbaum's house. And it was better still that he hadn't responded to any of the twenty subsequent texts she'd sent, or to the dozen or so messages she'd left on his voice mail after his disastrous visit to her apartment on fish market night. Because, while Brenna had always told him not to be rude to people, his rudeness had, in this case, saved his own life.

At least, Brenna hoped it had.

Trent had been in the emergency room of St. Vincent's Hospital for over an hour when she got there. From what Annette and one of the nurses told her, doctors were pumping his stomach and administering a charcoal treatment in an attempt to rid his body of the six-to-eight benzodiazepines he'd apparently consumed with a large glass of wine. That's all the nurse could tell them so far. She didn't know whether he'd regained consciousness, or if he'd suffered any brain damage. She didn't know anything, so she couldn't say anything. Not anything Brenna needed to hear.

"The doctors are working their hardest," she said now—this slender girl with baby fine hair and a child's face. How could you believe a face like that? This was the type of face that you shield from the truth. How could Brenna expect the doctors to give it straight to this girl, who looked as though the slightest bit of bad news could scatter her, like a seeded dandelion?

"Thank you," Brenna said, hoping she'd just go away. Go home. It was past her bedtime anyway.

The girl granted Brenna her wish. Well, she went away anyway, leaving Brenna and Annette to return to their seats—the only two they'd been able to find together in the crowded waiting room.

"I just wanted to apologize in person, but he wasn't opening his door," Annette said. She'd said it before, but Brenna let her say it again. Clearly, she was a nervous talker—someone soothed by the sound of her own voice. Why should Brenna take that away?

Brenna said, "How did you know he was even home?"

"I checked his Twitter feed."

She looked at Annette. That was new information. "You can tell where Trent is from his Twitter feed?"

"He uses that Foursquare app, didn't you know that? Tells you where he is at all times."

"Great." *What the hell is wrong with you, Trent?*

"Anyway, I'm thinking his not answering me is a little over the top, even if I did hurt him. I'm sure you heard the story . . ."

Brenna nodded.

"Anyway, I grab his super and we open the door. There he is, passed out . . ." She cleared her throat. "His pants were around his ankles."

Brenna winced.

"He looked so pale and still," Annette said. "Trent

never looks either of those things. I couldn't even tell if he was breathing."

"Did you hold a mirror to his nose?"

"I didn't think of that."

Brenna closed her eyes. She wasn't a doctor, but she knew a few things about the brain. She knew that it needed oxygen, and that if Trent had spent any significant amount of time not breathing, he could have experienced serious damage, or worse. *No, please no.*

Annette sighed. "I just . . . I never knew Trent was into that type of thing."

Brenna looked at her. "What type of thing?"

"You know. Prescription drugs," she tucked a lock of glossy hair behind an ear, fiddled with the tennis bracelet Brenna had returned to her. "I mean, I've been to a lot of bars with him, and it seems like he can't even stomach a drink that doesn't have an umbrella in it."

Brenna said, "Trent wasn't into drugs."

She turned to her. "Honey, I know you've been his boss for a long time, but bosses don't know their employees as well as they think."

"He wasn't."

"Not to be disrespectful, but you didn't even know about his Foursquare account."

"You have to believe me. I know Trent very well. The Foursquare account makes sense in terms of his general personality, but a benzo overdose doesn't. Trent was high on one thing, Annette. And that thing was called Trent."

"Brenna."

"Yeah?"

"Please don't talk about him in the past tense."

Brenna swallowed hard, all of it rushing at her . . . First Errol, then Trent. Trent on his own kitchen floor,

full of drugs, half dressed . . . Brenna didn't need a
diagram drawn for her. She didn't need to have seen the
lipstick stain on that wineglass or smelled that head-
achy perfume or seen that blonde hair flipping to know
that it had been Diandra. Diandra had put those drugs
into Trent, just as she'd done to Errol. Diandra, that
bitch who had called herself Clea, who was worming
her way into Brenna's life, destroying it from the edges
on in . . .

Brenna recalled September 30, driving to Tarry
Ridge with Trent on the line, his voice in her plastic
earpiece, half drowned in club noise, . . .

*"This blonde . . . she's kinda got a Jessica Alba thing
going on."*

"Jessica Alba isn't blonde."

*"I'm talking from the neck down. And she is mas-
sively checking me out . . . Hey baby, how about I buy
you another one of those cosmos—with a chaser of
Trent."*

Brenna winces. *"That couldn't possibly have worked."*

*"What's your name, gorgeous? Diandra. That is a
name that's made to be moaned in ecstasy. Know what
I'm saying, sweet thang?"*

Brenna hears nothing but ambient noise, thudding
bass. *"Let me guess,"* she says to Trent. *"Diandra's
throwing up."*

"Wrong, Miss Wiseass. She's giving me her digits."

"You've got to be kidding."

*"What? No, baby, no I wasn't calling you wiseass. I
was . . . Yeah, I'm on the phone with my . . . but . . . No,
I'm telling you, this is my boss. I swear, I . . . Wait. Oh
now don't be like that . . . Damn. Completely carpet-
bombing my game."*

Brenna bit her lip hard, and she was back to three

months later, Trent fighting for his life in an emergency room because of her. Because of Diandra, who had ditched him like a bad accessory when he was just another loser hitting on her in a club, but who'd gone home with him so readily once she knew who he was, who'd laid in wait till she could get him alone and begged her way back in, who'd fed him pills and wine, this sweet dumb guy, and all for what . . . for RJ Tannenbaum's computer?

. . . Across the room, a teenage girl sat holding her baby, both of them staring at Brenna with velvet-black eyes. Just as Diandra had stared at her on the *Maid of the Mist*. She'd gazed directly into Brenna's eyes, Brenna thinking nothing of it at the time—a shared moment, that's all . . . How long had she been following Brenna? How long had she been reading up on her in Page 6 and tracking Trent via that ridiculous Foursquare app of his?

Please be okay, Trent. Please live and be okay and come back to us with all your brain cells, Trent you idiot. Please . . .

"Are you praying?" Annette said.

And only at that moment did Brenna realize she'd been mouthing those words, muttering them aloud like a crazy person. No wonder they were all staring . . .

She's got a gift for destruction that runs through her veins . . .

Brenna stood up, took a deep breath. "I'm going to take a little walk around the room," she said, as if that were something that cried out to be announced. She walked by the girl and her baby, nodding as she passed. They looked confused and sad. Who knew what was running through their minds? Who knew what was running through anyone's mind in the waiting room of an ER? She pulled out her phone, snuck a text to Maya:

All is okay, but I won't be home till late. At the hospital with Trent. She stared at the letters on the screen. She could practically hear Maya's response. *You can't just tell me you're at the hospital with Trent, and not expect me to ask why . . . You say, "I'm in the hospital with Trent," it begs an explanation.*

What could Brenna say, though? How could she explain this to her daughter? She typed: *He ate some bad fish,* and hit send. That would have to do.

All she could think of was Trent's face of a few hours ago, still scratched and bruised from the car crash, his chest smeared with Diandra's pink lipstick—but his eyes so wide and guileless, the eyes of a six-year-old . . . *Is it something bad? I feel like you're going to say something bad.*

Brenna came across a bank of empty chairs, a tired-looking love seat, a large wide coffee table heaped with old magazines, and a few books, including a Bible. She picked it up, remembering the small print at the bottom of RJ Tannenbaum's black and white Spielberg picture.

DEUT 31:6

Brenna thumbed through the Bible until she found Deuteronomy, then looked up the passage, Robin Tannenbaum's passage.

Be strong and courageous. Do not be afraid or terrified because of them . . .

"Amen," Brenna whispered. "Don't be afraid."

Brenna was riding the handlebars of an enormous bicycle. She was trying to get back into the seat and put her feet on the pedals, to get some control over this awful hurtling thing, but the bike was too big and it was going too fast and, for some reason, Brenna knew deep in her heart that if she moved, she would die.

A cliff loomed before her, dropping off to the end of the world. She wanted to scream, but her mouth wouldn't open, and the bicycle was reaching the hill, bumping on the rocky concrete. It kept going faster.

"Hold on tight," a voice behind her said. A kind voice. *Clea?*

Brenna felt strong slender arms on either side of her. She saw feet in the pedals, sandaled and bronzed. She saw delicate hands pulling on the breaks, the bike slowing down, stopping . . .

Clea.

She turned to the blonde hair, the long blonde hair so much like Maya's, Clea back in her life, saving her after all these years . . . *I don't care that you never called or wrote. I forgive you. I love you.* "I'm so glad you're here," Brenna said.

A gust of wind blew the hair back, and Brenna saw not Clea's face but Diandra's. The face of Diandra, pulling into a smile, the mouth opening, revealing rows and rows of shark's teeth . . .

"No!" Brenna gasped.

"Ma'am?"

Brenna's eyelids flew open. It took several moments for it to sink in that she was still in the waiting room at St. Vincent's.

"Ma'am?" It was the young nurse—the one with the too-innocent face.

Brenna ran a hand over her eyes. "I fell asleep," she said, as if the girl couldn't even figure out that obvious fact.

"Yes," she said. "I'm sorry to wake you, but your friend, Annette?"

"Yeah?"

"She wanted me to let you know that she had to go home. She said to call if you hear anything."

"And you woke me up for that?" Brenna said.

"I'm sorry," the nurse said.

"No, I'm sorry. That was rude."

"No," the nurse said, "I'm sorry."

"I'm too tired for this," Brenna said. She started to close her eyes again.

The nurse put a hand up. "I'm sorry," she said, "because I put the cart before the horse. Or I buried the lead. Or whatever." She yawned. "I didn't wake you up to tell you about your friend. I woke you up to tell you that Mr. LaSalle is going to be all right."

Brenna sat up fast. "What? Wait—he *is*?"

"Yes," the nurse said. "He's still pretty tired. We're going to let him rest for the night, give him fluids. He's very dehydrated. But he's fine. No brain damage."

"Are you sure?"

"Well . . . He did ask me if he was really in the hospital, or if this was a naughty nurse dream."

Brenna jumped to her feet and threw her arms around the nurse.

"So that's normal for him, huh?"

"Yes." Brenna laughed. "Yes it is." Once she pulled away, she peered at the nurse's name tag. "Thank you, Bernadette."

"Your first name is Brenna, right?"

"Yes."

"Mr. LaSalle asked to see you."

"He did? Can I? I mean, is he able to . . ."

Bernadette nodded. "But just for a couple of minutes, okay? Then we're going to move him into a regular room for the rest of the night."

Brenna followed her through a set of swinging

doors, past a nurses' station and down a long hallway
to a series of beds separated by curtains. They passed
an elderly man attached to oxygen tanks, a little girl
screaming as doctors drew fluid out of her knee . . . next
came a couple of empty beds, and then, finally, Trent.

"Hey, B. Spec," he said.

Brenna didn't even bother to comment on the nick-
name, she just rushed up to him and hugged him, gently,
so as not to disturb the IVs. She could hear the little girl
screaming three beds over.

"They could do something about the atmosphere in
here, huh?" Trent said.

His voice sounded very weak. Brenna pulled away
and took him in—the gaunt cheeks, the hair lying flat
on his forehead, the pallor of his skin—as though the
spray tan had been vacuumed right off him. He looked
like a different person. A frail, sad, scholarly young
thing. With a stupid lip print tattoo on his pec. She
could see it through the hospital gown.

"I look like crap, huh?"

"What happened, Trent?"

"I . . . I can't even say her name."

"Diandra."

He cringed. "I have this like . . . Pavlovian response
to the name," he croaked. "But instead of drooling, it
makes me want to blow chunks."

"What possessed you?"

"Brenna, I—"

"I know you're a guy, but come on. What the hell
were you thinking? And if you say anything that in-
cludes the phrase 'the wrong head,' I cannot be held
responsible for my actions."

"She took Tannenbaum's computer."

Brenna closed her eyes. "I figured that out."

"It's okay." He shifted in the bed. "I'm telling you . . . there's nothing on there but porn . . . and the cloud storage gateway, which he uninstalled. I bet she won't even find it."

"I'm just glad you're alive. You are so damn lucky." She looked at him. "We both are."

He smiled a little. His lips were very chapped.

Brenna said, "So what the hell is a cloud storage gateway?"

"It's a way in to a cloud."

"Oh. Thanks, that clears it all up."

Trent sighed. "A cloud is kind of like a virtual safety deposit box. You can access it from anywhere, even if your computer crashes. So, like, if you have important papers, or some video you don't want to lose, or whatever . . ."

"Why not just e-mail the papers to yourself? That's what I do."

"Cloud storage is a lot more secure." He looked at her. "It's easy to hack into e-mails. Jeez, you should know that. I do that for us all the time."

Brenna nodded.

"But Tannenbaum not only got himself a cloud, he uninstalled the gateway. Know what I'm saying? It's like hiding stuff on an island, and then blowing up the bridge."

She looked at him. "Must have been some very important papers . . ."

He shrugged. "Or some seriously nasty porn that he didn't want his mom to see. Either way, I want in."

"Can you get us there?"

"If we can figure out his password, I can do it through the provider's Web site . . . once I . . . Damn . . . I can't remember the provider's name. Hey, sit down, would you, please? You're making me nervous, standing over me like that. It's giving me flashbacks."

"Flashbacks?"

He shut his eyes.

"Diandra?"

"Oh joy, here comes the insta-nausea."

"Sorry."

"She stood over me like that and . . ." He squeezed his eyes tighter. "Saffron."

"Huh?"

"She said something about saffron."

"The spice?"

"I don't know . . ." He opened his eyes again. "It's gone. I don't remember what the hell she was talking about."

Brenna nodded. She sat down very carefully on the edge of Trent's bed. For a few moments she flashed on October 2, when Trent visited her at Columbia-Presbyterian and their positions were reversed—*poking his head through the door, his eyes widening when he catches his first sight of her, the worry in them . . .* "Trent," she said quietly.

He looked at her, weak.

"I'm ninety-nine percent sure," she said, "that *she* killed Errol."

"Oh . . . Wow." He opened his eyes. They looked much bigger and darker than usual. "Figures."

Brenna took Trent's hand in hers. The two of them sat in silence for what felt like a very long time.

Trent said, "Please don't tell my parents about this. They're mad enough about what happened to my car in Inwood."

"I won't tell them," Brenna said. "I'm glad I don't have to."

Trent smiled—the smile of a kid. It made Brenna's jaw tighten. *Feeding him pills. Leaving him for dead. You left him in the middle of his kitchen floor when he invited you in. You left him there barely breathing. You closed the door behind you. You assumed he would die and you didn't care* . . . Anger bubbled beneath her skin. Her face was hot with it. "You've never been to her place—don't know where she lives."

He shook his head.

"And I take it she's not on that ridiculous Foursquare thing."

"No way."

"You don't know her last name."

"I probably don't even know her *first* name."

She swallowed hard, took a deep breath. "And Errol paid his girls under the table, so there'd be no record there, either," she said. "I guess we've lost her."

"Uh-huh."

"It's for the best."

Trent frowned. "Why?"

"Because if we did have a way of finding her. If we had any way at all . . ." Brenna gave him a meaningful look. "I would *find* her."

Trent stared back at her, and something passed between them. In the six years he'd been working for her, Brenna was sure, she'd never seen Trent's face quite so still. His eyes clouded. He squeezed her hand. "You're not hitting on me, are you? 'Cause I am really wiped out."

Brenna sighed. "Shut up, Trent."

Little Bernadette stuck her head around the curtain and came in, two burly orderlies following. "Sorry, ma'am, but it's time to say good-bye. We've gotta move Mr. LaSalle."

"Mr. LaSalle is my dad, baby. You can call me T-Man."

Bernadette looked at Brenna. "Normal?"

"Yep." She put a hand on Trent's shoulder. "Good-bye, buddy. See you tomorrow."

"Oh, wait, I wanted to ask you something."

"Yeah?"

"Who was it who . . . uh . . . found me?"

She looked at him. "Annette Shelby."

He sighed. "Yeah, that's what the doctor said. I thought he was joking. Of course, that would have been a weird joke since he doesn't know either one of us."

"True."

He picked at a fingernail. "Guess that kinda makes up for what she did, huh?"

"She means well, Trent," Brenna said. "I think she always meant well. She wanted . . . company so badly that it clouded her judgment."

Trent said, "I know that feeling."

"Exactly."

"I'm going to send her flowers. Or maybe I should get her a new cat."

"You don't have to do that," Brenna said. "Just . . . I don't know . . . have a cup of coffee with her or something."

Bernadette adjusted Trent's bed, so that it became a gurney, the orderlies taking positions on either side of it. "Okay," he said. "I'll call her and set something up. But not now when I look like hyena crap. I gotta look hot for Mrs. Shelby. She's got expectations."

Brenna thought about the way he'd looked when Annette had found him—a definite blow to the old expectations—but she kept that to herself. "You're always hot."

"Whoa." He grinned at her. "Can I please get you saying that on video?"

"No." She gave Trent a quick hug good-bye, then moved out of the way as the orderlies pushed him out. It was then, only then, that she realized the little girl three beds down was no longer crying.

Brenna headed down the hallway, something tugging at her, a sadness. She didn't want to, but she found herself thinking again about Diandra. Diandra, who had stolen RJ's computer, who had called herself Clea, who had killed Errol, drugged Trent, and run off, taking this whole case with her. Taking Lula Belle with her.

Cement mixer/Turn on a dime/Make my day 'cause it's cement time . . .

From across the hallway, Trent was yelling something at her. "What?"

"Lockbox!" he yelled again, as the orderlies wheeled him into a waiting elevator. "It's the name of Tannenbaum's cloud storage gateway! Remember it in case I don't."

Brenna watched one of the big orderlies easing him back down, the other hitting the button to close the elevator doors.

At least I've still got Trent, she thought.

It was well past midnight when Brenna got back to her apartment. Their honorary last night of Chanukah was officially over and she'd never lit the candles with Maya. As she opened the door, guilt pulled at her. *No gifts, no latkes . . .* The apartment was quiet. Of course it was. It was close to 1 A.M. and Maya wasn't a night owl like both her biological parents. At slumber parties, she was always the first one down.

Brenna moved through the office space and kitchen, a million voices running through her head—Lula Belle's whispery accent and Diandra's velvety hello and Trent asking Brenna, *What if Diandra is* her? Gary Freeman over the phone: *I'm afraid something may have happened to her. I mean . . . God . . . If she ever existed to begin with.*

And then other voices, far back in her memory, muffled as though she were under rising water . . .

Scooch up a little, weirdo, you're making me lose my balance.

Come on girls, smile for Daddy's camera . . . Do you guys like it? Your brand-new bike . . .

A ten-year-old girl, smiling for her long-gone father. A faded face from a high school photo. A haloed vision in Brenna's dreams. A name given to a lonely desk clerk by a psychotic Barbie doll with no real name of her own . . .

Clea, are you real? Will you ever be?

Brenna was at the end of the hallway now, outside her daughter's open bedroom door. She listened for Maya's sleep-breathing—the one sound that never failed to calm her. She heard nothing.

She stepped into the room. Moonlight streamed through the window, casting a glow on Maya's bed. Maya's empty, neatly made bed. Brenna's throat clenched up. She flashed on seven hours ago—Trent's apartment, still smelling of incense, her heart pounding, the letter opener clasped in her hand *and Trent's bed, empty* . . . Brenna dug her nails into her palms and she was back in Maya's room, flipping the light on to see the note left on the pillow, her daughter's rounded handwriting noticeable even from where she was standing. Brenna moved over to the bed, picked up the note with her hands — shaking.

Mom,

I've gone to Dad and Faith's. Your Chanukah present is on your bed. Open it any time.

Maya

Brenna exhaled hard. *She's okay. Thank you.* On the floor next to the bed was Maya's phone. Must have dropped it in her hurry to write the note and get out of the empty apartment.

Brenna picked it up, checked the screen. Maya hadn't read her text, but would it have mattered? When your mother ditches you on a night you've been looking forward to for weeks, is it any consolation to know it was because her assistant had "eaten some bad fish"?

Maya's okay. But she's definitely pissed, and who could blame her?

Brenna left the room and headed into her office area, too exhausted to sleep. Trent still hadn't taken down the Persephone pictures on his bulletin board, and it made Brenna feel nostalgic to look at them—a glimpse back into that time, two days ago, when she didn't feel so torn up inside.

She slipped into her desk chair, checked her e-mail. There was one new one, from Nick Morasco.

Brenna,

Thanks for the doctored pic of RJ. I've attached his police file for the B&E.
   Also, I need to talk to you about something personal. I think I should tell you face-to-face. Are you free tomorrow?

Nick

Brenna's stomach clenched up. "What do we need to talk about?" she said out loud. "What exactly do we need to talk about face-to-face *tomorrow*?" She thought of the way he'd been looking at her lately—the pity in his eyes—and she got up from the computer, walking away from it fast and biting her lip to keep from reliving one of those moments.

Before she knew it, Brenna was in her bedroom, the Chanukah present glaring up at her from her bed, a Post-it attached:

I'm sorry it isn't wrapped—I couldn't find the paper.

It was Maya's sketch of Brenna. Framed.

"Thank you," she whispered. And then, after a long while, "I'm sorry." Not just to Maya, but to Trent and Errol and Jim and Nick Morasco and Gary Freeman and anyone else who'd ever gotten involved in Brenna's haunted, screwed-up life expecting anything good to come out of it.

Brenna stared at the portrait—into the penciled eyes, focused on some distant point, a point in the past . . . *Thinking about Lula Belle*, she knew. *That's what I was thinking about. Lula Belle.*

Tears sprang into Brenna's eyes. She picked up the phone, called Morasco.

He picked up after one ring.

Brenna took a deep breath. "Did I wake you?" Stupid question. People who are woken up don't answer after one ring.

Nick said, "No. How are you, Brenna?" God, she did not like that tone of voice. He sounded like a concerned psychotherapist.

"Don't you mean, 'How do we feel today?' "

"Huh?"

"Nothing," she said. "Listen, thanks for sending Tannenbaum's police file along."

"No problem." He cleared his throat. "How's the case going?"

She closed her eyes. She couldn't do this, couldn't do the small talk. "I don't like the way you've been looking at me."

"What?"

"Like you feel sorry for me."

"I don't mean to—"

"And I don't want to talk about anything personal with you, Nick. Not face-to-face tomorrow or over the phone right now. Not ever."

"I'm . . . I'm sorry if my e-mail upset you."

Her jaw clenched up. She wanted to hang up on him, to never talk to him or see him again, lest she remember this conversation, this feeling . . . But instead she kept talking. "Errol Ludlow is dead."

"*What?*"

"Heart attack. Drugs might have been involved."

"*Ludlow?*"

"And Trent was fed an overdose of benzos. He got to the hospital in time, but the woman who gave him the drugs was the same one who killed Ludlow, and I don't know her last name or where she lives or anything about her, other than she was an Errol's Angel, she's in her early twenties, and she dresses like a cartoon on a cocktail napkin," Brenna drew a breath, long and ragged. "And she might be Lula Belle."

"Oh my God, Brenna."

"She told a desk clerk her name is Clea."

"Oh . . . man . . ."

"And . . . and now she's gone . . ." Brenna's vision blurred. Her voice felt choked. "Someone is messing with my mind, Nick. Someone out there knows all these stories about my family and they're making performance art out of it and this . . . this . . . this freak of a girl is somehow involved but I don't have any idea how to track her down so whatever it is you have to tell me that's so damn important . . ."

"It can wait." His voice was soft, kind.

"Forever?"

"Yes."

Brenna heard a car whiz by on the street beneath her window, the thudding bass of the stereo within, and she wanted so badly to escape—not from her apartment but from her own mind. A few tears spilled down her cheeks.

Morasco said, "How do we feel today?"

More tears. Brenna swatted them away. "I don't know."

"Tell me," he said. "I'm here."

"Lost," she said. "Confused, scared, unsafe." She drew another long, shaking breath. "Lonely."

For several seconds, Morasco said nothing. Neither did Brenna. They just stayed where they were, both of them breathing into their phones.

"Brenna?"

"Yes."

"Do you want me to come over?"

"Yes."

He hung up before she could change her mind.

19

They didn't talk things through, didn't speak at all. There was no discussion about what this meant or how they were feeling about this or where they were going with this or what was on their minds regarding this or even what they would say to each other once this was over.

There was just this.

Brenna opened the door for Nick and fell into him, her lips on his, on his neck, his chest, inhaling his soap smell and yanking open his shirt, his hands in her hair, on her body . . .

She went for his belt buckle.

"Wait," he said. "Maya."

"She's not here." But still, she was pulling him down the hall, leading him by both hands into her bedroom. She was closing the door behind them and she was locking it. She didn't want to be out in the open.

Brenna pulled him to her. His glasses were fogging up, and when she took them off, there was a look in his eyes she'd never seen there before. No softness, no sadness, no pity . . . The opposite of pity, actually. Her pulse raced.

"My walls are thin. We have to stay quiet," she whispered. More to herself than to him.

And then he was pushing her up against the wall, both of them tearing at each other's clothes. There were buttons flying and zippers ripping open, there were hands and lips and tongues searching and so much breath, breathing together, and such exquisite closeness in that breathing . . .

Nick's hands gripped Brenna's wrists, forcing her back, her legs wrapped around him. She broke free, but just for a few moments, just long enough to guide him in with one hand, both of them breathing, still breathing like that, breathing and moving together and then . . . this. Just this. Just now.

"Thanks, I needed that," Brenna told Nick as they lay in bed, drifting to sleep after round two. It was probably the first time either of them had said a coherent word to each other in the two hours he'd been there.

He leaned in and kissed her gently. "It was the least I could do."

Brenna grinned. "The least? Really?"

"Brenna. I think—"

"Sssh." She put a finger to his lips. "Let's not talk. Please."

"I was just going to say that I think my arm fell asleep."

"Oh."

"I don't want to talk, either," he said. "Just so you know."

Brenna pulled him closer, smiled. *You may be the nicest person I've ever met.* She fell asleep. She didn't dream.

Nick left early to go to work. He could have snuck out without Brenna even knowing—that's how soundly she'd been sleeping—but instead he stopped by the bed, kissed her awake. "Bye," he said.

She smiled. "Bye."

"Look, I know we're not talking. But can I just ask you one thing?"

She sighed.

"Last night."

"Uh-huh?"

"You didn't . . . You didn't seem to go anywhere."

She looked at him. "I didn't."

"Not once? Really? You didn't have one single memory?"

"Not one." She smiled, realizing it herself. She and Nick had made love twice—and as fast and urgent as the first time had been, the second had been quite lengthy. It was probably the longest she'd ever been awake in the past few years without lapsing into at least a brief memory—and that included times she'd been with other men. "You're like an anti-nootropic," she said.

"Awesome." He put a hand on her cheek, and for a moment, she saw a hint of it—that sorry, sad feeling . . . But then he pulled away and grinned at her. "I always wanted an FDA classification."

She kissed the palm of his hand and closed her eyes again, falling asleep as he left.

Brenna woke up two hours later, at seven-thirty. She slipped out of bed, tugged on the oversized Columbia T-shirt she usually slept in, and headed toward the kitchen. But when she passed Maya's room, she stopped. The door was closed. She cracked it open and saw her daughter asleep in her bed, the room sweet with the sound of her breathing.

She came back.

Brenna watched her for a while, hoping her return had happened after Morasco had left. She wasn't ready to have that conversation yet. For one thing, she had no idea what to say that wouldn't gross Maya out. (*Turns out Detective Morasco is great in the sack, honey. But we've made a pact not to talk about it . . .*)

"Mom?" Maya's eyelids fluttered open. She sat up in bed, rubbing her eyes.

"I'm sorry about last night," Brenna said.

"Is Trent okay?"

"Yes," Brenna said. "He's fine."

Maya stared at her for several seconds, her face so flat, it was impossible to tell what she was thinking. "Must have been some really bad fish," she said finally.

God, what a dumb excuse. "You got my text."

"This morning." She lay back down and turned over, onto her stomach. It was as though she was rolling her eyes with her entire body.

Brenna looked at her. "Let me guess," she said. "You didn't want to come back, but Faith convinced you to let her drop you off here on her way to the show. She told you I mean well and that you need to cut me some slack. I have an affliction. But you're sick and tired of cutting me slack—not to mention my affliction—and who the hell cares if I mean well? I left you alone on the last night of Chanukah. That sucks, no matter how you look at it. And while we're at it . . . Bad fish? That's seriously the best I could come up with?"

Maya was sitting up now, watching Brenna.

"Am I right?"

"Pretty much."

Brenna sat down on the edge of the bed. "Look," she said. "I'm not even going to try and make excuses for myself, other than to say that Trent's life really was in danger. And if I told you what actually happened to him, you'd beg me to replace it with a story about bad fish."

"Is he okay now?"

"Yes."

"Good."

Brenna put her hand on Maya's. "I loved your drawing, Maya," she said. "I swear to God, you're so talented, it takes my breath away."

She smiled a little. "I'm glad."

"And I don't blame you for being mad at me. But can you just do me one favor?"

Maya frowned at her. "What?"

"Can you let me give you your Chanukah present?"

Maya sighed. "A present isn't going to make everything better, Mom."

"I know."

"You need to think about who's a real part of your life and who's a memory," she said. "I'm tired of losing out to your job all the time. I'm tired of losing out to Clea."

Brenna looked at her. "You're right."

Maya hugged her knees to her chest, brushed her hair out of her eyes. "Okay," she said.

"Okay what?"

"Okay," Maya said. "I'll take the present."

Brenna hurried into her bedroom, and returned with the wrapped iPod box.

Maya's eyes lit up at the shape of it. Her voice pitched up an octave. "Oh my God. Is this . . . is this what I think it is?" She shut her eyes tight, took a few breaths. "Oh my God, oh my God, oh my God."

Brenna's face twitched into a smile. *Who said a present couldn't make everything better?* Maya jumped out of bed and flew at her, throwing her arms around Brenna's neck. "Thank you so much, Mom," she said, and Brenna was glad for her memory. She could hang on to this moment, keep it with her always. She could take it out on a bad day like a favorite sweater or a framed photo and relive it—these few seconds of pure joy . . .

"How do you know what it is?" Brenna said.

"Oh Mom, it's so obvious!" Maya ripped at the wrapping paper—same way she had done at four years old, tearing into her Polly Pocket Hangout House Playset on the last night of Chanukah 2000 . . . *"Yay, Mommy, yay!"*

"Thank you!" Maya screamed, the unwrapped iPod in her hands. "Thank you, thank you, thank you!" Brenna went back to 2000 again, Maya hopping from foot to foot and hugging Brenna's leg with all her might, *such a tiny bundle of happiness. So much love.* "I love you, Mom," she said, both then and now.

Brenna made breakfast for Maya as she played with her iPod, making sure not to even think about work until 11:30 A.M., when her daughter was dressed and out of the apartment and on her way to lunch and the nearby IMAX theater with her friend Ruby, as per the plans she made with her via one of her brand-new apps.

At that point, she went into the kitchen and brewed another pot of coffee and drank a cup in front of her computer, accompanied by two of the Twinkies she kept stashed at the back of the pantry. Yes, she'd had eggs and tea with Maya, but thanks to Nick Morasco she was still starving. She devoured the first Twinkie in two bites, her hunger only starting to fall into place with the second.

She checked her e-mail. "Whoa," she whispered. She'd actually gotten a reply from CompanyHead@ HappyEndings.com. Brenna opened it up:

> *If you want to talk about RJ, come by the offices today (12/21) at 1 P.M. We won't be open before then.*
>
>   *Sincerely, Charlie Frankel*
>
> *PS Pokrovsky speaks very highly of you.*

Brenna smiled. Now she *really* didn't care how many bodies were in Pokrovsky's window box.

What do you wear to an interview with a porn mogul? This was a pressing and important question, but Brenna had time to ponder it. It was more important right now to download Tannenbaum's police report, and so she did.

It wasn't a large file at all. She opened it and started to read, skimming the description of RJ and the location of the break-in, then skipping straight to the testimony of the homeowner.

"We felt that it was just some kind of film school campus dare," the homeowner told arresting officers in the report of the forty-two-year-old suspect. "Nothing of any note was missing from the house. I'm not a full professor, but I've taught courses at the school, and I'm also a graduate. I'm sure that, in a way, RJ believed he knew me."

Brenna sighed. *Maybe it's Spielberg*, she thought.

But when she skipped down to the homeowner's name—which was typed out in all caps directly beneath the testimony, over the line that read *Case Dismissed*—Brenna's eyes went big. "Well how about that," she whispered.

The homeowner was Gary Freeman.

Gary stared at the note in his lap. He'd read it so many times since this morning, but he couldn't stop himself from reading again—as though if he looked at those words enough times, the letters would rearrange themselves and the note would say something different, something better.

Gary:

DeeDee called. She says. "It's done."

Jill

He'd found the note on his nightstand this morning. This, after a night of great sex with Jill and Gary waking up with an honest-to-God smile on his face, feeling for the first time in months—or even years—that all his troubles were behind him. His money problems would ease. The recession would let up, his client base would build back. Life would get better, and if it wound up being a life without Lula Belle, then so be it. He had his memories. Maybe the past was finally through with him. Maybe he was allowed to move on.

That's what he'd been thinking. What a joke. He'd even had that Bob Marley song running through his head, *Everything gonna be all right . . .*

But then he'd reached out to touch Jill's soft skin and felt only the pillow. He'd checked the time: ten-thirty already—*Why didn't anybody wake me up?* And that's when he had seen the note. Jill had folded it into quarters, as though it were some kind of gift, as though it would be a pleasant surprise for Gary, the unwrapping of it . . . DeeDee's name in his wife's handwriting. What a punch to the stomach.

That'd teach him to wake up smiling.

Now Bob Marley was long gone, and Gary had a different song in his head—it had been stuck in there on continuous loop, ever since he'd seen the note. "Oliver's Army" by Elvis Costello—oh the cruel deejay that was Gary's brain.

"Oliver's Army" had been her favorite song. She'd named Route 666 in Utah after a line in it. The Murder Mile, she'd called it, because she was scared of the numbers. But that was silly, and Gary had told her so. Numbers were nothing to be afraid of. People were.

"We could drive all night," the boy said, *just him and me. "We could beat the murder mile and watch the sunrise in the rearview . . ."*

Gary shut his eyes tight. *You close that door and you lock it. You throw away the key.* He folded up the note again. He put it back into his wallet, but that didn't make it disappear, did it? It had happened. The note had been written. And just like the proverbial writing on the wall, there was no taking it back.

Oh DeeDee, why, why, why? How could you do that? Why would you call my wife?

Jill was gone, and the girls were gone. Gary's life, as he knew it, was over. Would he ever be able to convince his wife that DeeDee had been nothing? One bad mistake, never to be made again? *If I could just find her, if I could find The Shadow,* he thought, *I could make things right.*

But did he really believe that?

Well, he had to believe it, didn't he? If he didn't—if he honestly thought that he could lose it all that easily—and lose it for good—then what had the point ever been? Why had he worked so hard to build a life and a career and a family if it could be destroyed forever by one strong wind?

There had been many strong winds, though. RJ Tannenbaum and Shane Smith and Errol Ludlow. All those names he tried so hard to forget. And DeeDee. *Poor, misguided destructive DeeDee* . . .

The "fasten seat belts" light pinged on as that last name entered his mind, the name he never dared say, even in his thoughts. The Shadow's name. Her *real* name. The strongest wind of all.

"Ladies and gentlemen," the flight attendant announced. "We are making our initial decent into New York's LaGuardia Airport . . ."

It had taken Gary hours on the phone to secure a reasonably priced seat at the last possible minute, to call all his clients with whom he had scheduled meetings or auditions over the next few days and tell them that he wouldn't be there—family emergency, couldn't be helped, but not to worry. Gary would be back soon.

If he could do all that in such a short amount of time, then he could fix this, couldn't he? *I can,* Gary thought, *I will fix this,* as the plane completed its descent, touching ground in New York. Gary's birthplace. His home.

On his way out of the plane, the little girl in front of him dropped her baby doll on the tarmac. Gary jogged to retrieve it, chased the little girl down, and handed it to her, once they were all in the terminal.

"What a nice man you are," said the child's mother. She had bright blue eyes that reminded him of Jill's.

"Thank you," said Gary, who really *was* a nice man, deep down. A nice man who'd made mistakes. As the other passengers rushed to catch cabs or to claim their baggage, Gary hung back. There was an airport bar next to the gate. Thank God for airport bars—open at all hours. It was 10:30 A.M. here in New York, but who knew when someone would be flying in from Singapore. Gary smiled. What Jimmy Buffet said was absolutely true. *It's five o'clock somewhere.* He slipped into the bar and ordered a Scotch rocks—his first drink in three years.

And the first of many.

Standing in front of the toaster oven, waiting for the bagels to be ready, Brenna remembered standing outside Columbia-Presbyterian with Morasco two days ago, and getting the call from Gary Freeman's newest disposable phone. Then she picked up the kitchen phone and punched in Gary's number. She'd been waiting to do this for hours, figuring Gary wouldn't appreciate a call from anyone at 4 A.M. his time, even if it was potential breaking news.

She was very anxious to call Gary, though—mainly because she wanted to hear his reaction. She kept replaying their earlier phone conversation in her head—the long pause on the other end of the line when she'd asked him if he'd heard of RJ, and then, "No. Why?" the "no" so certain, as though this were the first time he'd ever heard the name that he himself had said in the police report.

Sure, maybe Gary had forgotten. But seriously, who forgets the name of some film student who broke into your house just three years ago?

The call went straight through to Gary's voice mail. "I

need you to call me regarding RJ Tannenbaum," Brenna said. Then she ended the call. That was it. No further explanation. The toaster oven dinged, and she slipped back inside the kitchen. *Why pretend you don't know RJ Tannenbaum?* Could have been the porn, or the Russian mob connection . . . or something else it wouldn't befit an upstanding children's talent agent to be connected with. Or it could have been for different reasons entirely. Whatever it was, Brenna needed to know.

Diandra was trying to find clues on RJ Tannenbaum's big flat-screen computer when she heard a noise—a generic ringtone. *Weird.* She lived at the end of a long hall, with no neighboring apartments, so for her to hear a ringtone, it would have to be right outside her door.

"Hello?" she called out.

No answer.

She found herself flashing on Trent, who had two ringtones: Ludacris for phone calls, Justin Timberlake for texts. At Bacon last week, Trent had told her he was going to download a special one, just for her calls and texts—David Guetta's "Sexy Chick." He wasn't kidding, either—he'd done it, right there and then. Diandra felt a catch in her throat. She swallowed hard to smooth it out. *Trent.* Some things couldn't be helped. Some things were best not to think about.

She didn't hear the ringtone anymore. *Probably just somebody taking the stairs*, Diandra thought.

She went back to the computer. Opened another Final Cut Pro file, saw still more porn. Had she not known it was RJ Tannenbaum's computer—the name printed right there on the control panel Trent had open on his screen when she'd come to see him yesterday morning—and if Trent hadn't closed it up as soon as he saw her looking, bragging that he was "busy cracking the mother of all cases," she would have thought that this was some kind of elaborate joke he was playing on her. *Whatever you do, please, oh please don't steal this computer that's got nothing on it but bad porn* . . . But Trent wasn't like that. He was too guileless to play that type of joke. He was more of a hit-you-over-the-head type of guy.

Her emotions tugged at her again. *Stop it.* Why hadn't Mr. Freeman called her? All the hell she'd gone through. Things she couldn't imagine doing, even in her worst nightmares, she'd done them just for him, only for him, and he couldn't even be bothered to thank her?

Diandra moved away from the computer, and that's when she heard the knocking on her front door. It started out soft, but it was getting louder now, an insistent pounding, as though someone was punching it. "Hello?"

Her first thought was Saffron. He'd given her all those pills. Maybe he'd expected reimbursement in actual money . . .

Uh-oh . . .

Slowly, Diandra crept up to her door, put her eye to the peephole. Her heart swelled as though to burst. "Oh my God," she whispered. "Oh my God!" She threw open the door and there was Mr. Freeman, standing in her doorway, Mr. Freeman, for the first time in three years, face-to-face, breathing the same air as Diandra, looking into her eyes . . .

Saying nothing.

He didn't smile, didn't even seem glad to see her at all, but that didn't matter, nothing mattered. He'd had a long flight from California and was tired, was all. He was here. *Mr. Freeman is here.*

Diandra threw her arms around his neck. He smelled

of Scotch, which to her felt like the most wonderful type of déjà vu . . . "Mr. Freeman, have you been drinking?" she whispered in his ear.

He grabbed her by the shoulders, pushed her hard to the floor.

What? Tears burned in her eyes. She'd whacked her knees good, but that wasn't it, that wasn't what hurt so much . . . "What's . . . what's wrong?"

He knelt down and punched her in the stomach.

The wind shot out of her. White flecks danced in front of her eyes. "What's wrong," she said again, her voice dry and weak, tears spilling down her face, snot streaming out of her nose, but too shocked to feel any of it, too hurt.

And still he said nothing.

Diandra hugged her knees to her chest, crying, bracing herself against the only man who knew her soul.

"Why," she whispered. "What did I do? All I want is to help you."

He was still kneeling next to her, moving closer. "Look at me."

She couldn't.

He took her chin in his hand, made her look. His words slurred together, Scotch-stink curling out of his mouth. "You called my wife."

"What? No, I didn't. I swear I didn't call her. I . . ." He drew his hand back. Diandra cringed, but as it turned out, he was just going for his wallet. He opened it, plucked out a folded-up piece of paper, and threw it in Diandra's face. "What's that supposed to mean, then?" he said, as Diandra grabbed the paper, read the words . . .

DeeDee called. She says, "It's done . . ."

"Oh God," she whispered.

"DeeDee called," he said flatly. "She says, 'It's done.' "

"I didn't call her. I swear, I didn't call . . ."

"So Jill was lying?"

"No," Diandra said. "No. Listen . . . I didn't call her. I called *our phone*. She didn't say anything when she answered. I thought I was talking to you."

Mr. Freeman leaned back. He sighed heavily, the anger draining out of his face along with the air. "You called our phone."

"Yes."

Two tears rolled down his cheeks, and then two more, until soon, Mr. Freeman was sobbing. Diandra wove her arms around him, cradled his head in her lap like a child. "I'm sorry," he said. "I'm sorry."

"It's okay."

"No it isn't. I hurt you. I shouldn't have hurt you."

In all the years she'd known him, Diandra had never seen Mr. Freeman shed a tear and here he was, his whole face wet with them, making a wet stain on her skirt. It embarrassed her. "Mr. Freeman," she said.

But still he kept sobbing, until Diandra grabbed both of his shoulders and forced him to look into her face. "*Mr. Freeman*."

"Yes . . ."

"What can I do?"

"DeeDee . . ."

"I mean it. I'll do anything. Anything you want." *Anything to make you stop crying . . .*

"Anything I want?"

"Yes."

"But DeeDee," he said softly. "You don't even know me."

"I know you better than anybody," she said. "I've

known you since I was a kid, and I know you are good and kind and—"

"I'm not." He drew a deep, shuddering breath. She stroked his hair. "You do things for me, DeeDee. You protect me. And you don't even know why."

"Errol Ludlow was blackmailing you. He deserved it."

"DeeDee . . ."

"You hired him to find Lula Belle. You hired Brenna Spector, too, and you asked me to keep an eye on them, keep one step ahead of them, just like I did with RJ Tannenbaum."

"But you don't know why."

She took her hand from him.

He sat up, looked at her. "You don't know why I want to find Lula Belle."

"Well, you were secretly managing her Web site."

"Yes, I was. But that isn't the reason."

He wrapped his arms around her waist, rested his head in her lap again. Again, she stroked his hair. She could have said more, because she knew a little more than that. But that would ruin this moment, wouldn't it? Make her less trustworthy . . . She said, "Do you want to tell me the reason?"

"I do," he said. And then, he told.

Three years ago, when Diandra was still waiting tables at Barney's Beanery, she'd seen Mr. Freeman come in. He hadn't recognized her as his former client—not until she walked up and introduced herself—which spoke volumes as to how successfully she'd grown out of her awkward phase. Mr. Freeman was sad about his finances, and he couldn't tell his wife, who happened to be out of town with his three daughters. And so, that night, he wound up doing two things he hadn't done in twenty years—drinking being the first. The second happened after Diandra had driven him home and taken off his shoes and unbuttoned his collar.

In the middle, he had called her Clea. She wished that was her name.

It had been the most meaningful experience of Diandra's life—Mr. Freeman giving himself to her like that, Mr. Freeman, whom she respected and adored and who had never before been unfaithful and never since. But this—this telling. This meant even more. "You're the only person I've ever told," he kept saying. "You're the only one who knows."

And Diandra held him and listened and loved him anyway. "I will do anything for you," she said. She meant it.

20

"I can't believe you're going to Happy Endings without me," Trent said to Brenna over the phone as she walked up Twenty-fifth Street, looking for the right address. "It's like you're going to a Justin Bieber concert at Disney World without taking Maya."

"Trent? You're recovering from a drug overdose."

"Big deal. So are half the people at Happy Endings, probably."

"And anyway, Maya's over Bieber."

"His new stuff is pretty good."

Brenna peered at the numbers across the street until she found the address 140 West Twenty-fifth . . .

"So, are we there yet?"

"Uh . . . I think so." If this was the right building, if Charlie Frankel hadn't somehow given her the wrong address in his e-mail, then Happy Endings was the biggest architectural closet case Brenna had ever seen. The building was dull and dingy and completely unremarkable—the type of place that may have been a parking garage at one point, before the most minimal amount of work was done on it to make it hospitable to human life. "Okay, so just so you know there are no hard feelings, I ran a credit check on Robin Tannenbaum."

Brenna stopped. "How were you able to do that?"

"Hello? Mrs. Tannenbaum gave us his social."

Brenna sighed. "I didn't mean how do you run a credit check," she said. "I meant, how did you do it in the hospital?"

"Ohhh . . . Annette brought me my laptop."

No more Mrs. Shelby, huh? Brenna thought. But she didn't mention it. She had enough trouble trying to figure out her own personal life these days, let alone Trent's. "So, what did the report turn up?"

"He's in debt up to his nose hairs."

"Well, we figured on that."

"Yeah, but here's the kind of interesting thing. I have a contact at the card where he did most of his spending, and so I found out what he was spending on . . ."

"Yes?"

"Film equipment."

"Why is that strange? He went to film school."

"For three months. He never had a job in film production—just the porn stuff. That Mac Pro was loaded with everything he needed to be a top-notch editor, and guess what? It was registered to Happy Endings. Nice perk."

"I'm still not following."

"The only film equipment he needed for his job was bought and paid for. But for some reason, RJ went nuts buying lights, microphones, one of those Steadicams . . . he spent forty thousand dollars on film stuff in just three months."

"So by the time he wanted to buy that fancy camera," Brenna said. "He was so much in debt he had to borrow from Pokrovsky—and risk incurring a crazy amount of interest on a $3,000 camera." She crossed the street fast.

"Yep. And before three months ago, he hardly ever touched that credit card."

For a moment, she recalled the medicinal smell of Pokrovsky's apartment, again feeling the cold metal chair through her sweater, the hardness in Pokrovsky's eyes . . .

"That money, he wanted for some ridiculous camera. He told me he was working on a project which would change the world—which, believe me, I put as much stock in as that film education."

"Must have been some project," she said into the phone.

"Huh?"

"Trent, did you get any closer to finding out what happened to Shane Smith?"

"No, dude. Smith is a common freakin' name, so it's really hard without a social." Trent sighed. "The so-called filmmaking narrows it down, but there's no Shane Smith in the Directors Guild." He snorted. "Why am I not surprised?"

"I'd really like to find him."

"Why?"

She saw a break in traffic, hurried across the street. "Because Pokrovsky told me that RJ was working on a film project when he disappeared," she said when she got there. "And one guy can't work all that equipment alone."

"Every director needs a crew."

"Yes," Brenna said. But that wasn't all of it. Brenna recalled the Bible passage RJ had printed out so neatly, so as not to ruin the picture of his favorite director.

*Be strong and courageous. Do not be afraid or terri-
fied because of them . . .*

"Everyone who's frightened," she said, "needs at
least one person they can trust."

"Tell it, sister."

"RJ's call log."

"Yeah?"

"You sure there were no calls on there that could
have been made to Shane?"

"I thought I sent you the numbers."

"Never got the e-mail."

Trent sighed. "Do me."

"Pardon?"

"When what's-her-ass came over, RJ's phone was
cued to send it to you," he said.

"Diandra?"

"Oh man, *nausea tsunami . . .*"

"Sorry."

He took a few deep breaths. "Anyway, I forgot to tell
you, but when she swiped RJ's computer, the phone was
right next to it . . ."

"Great. She took that, too."

"It's not that big a deal," Trent said. "The log wasn't
that long. I tried every number, and except for a few
work calls, they were all take-out places. Chinese, pizza,
Thai . . . Dude clearly didn't like his mom's cooking."

"Nothing out of state?"

"Well," he said. "There were like four calls to the
same number in California back in September. Got me
all excited because he hadn't called the number before
or since."

"And?"

"Nada. A talent agency. I asked if there was a Shane

Smith who worked there and they said they never heard of him. Then I asked what RJ had called about and they hung up on me. I hate L.A."

Brenna stood in the middle of the sidewalk, unable to speak.

"Don't get me wrong. There's tons of hot girls out there, and you can get an awesome tan and Disneyland rocks out loud."

She still couldn't say a word.

"Brenna?" he said.

And finally she got the sentence out. "RJ called a talent agency."

"Yep," Trent said. "I'm thinking he probably wanted them for this film project of his and they blew him off."

"Do you remember the number?"

"Uh, no. I'm not you."

"How about the name?"

"Wait a sec . . ." Trent paused for a few moments, thinking. "It . . . um . . . It started with an F . . ."

Brenna closed her eyes. "Freeman Talent International."

"*Yes*," Trent said. "Hey, what did you ask me for if you already knew the answer?"

Brenna stared up at the building, a chill spreading up her back. "We'll talk about it later," she said. "I gotta think about porn right now."

Behind Charlie Frankel's desk hung a series of framed promotional posters for Happy Endings videos. Ushered into his empty office and told, "He'll be right with you" by the receptionist—a heavy, middle-aged woman who looked as though she'd be more at home leading a Jane Austen book club—Brenna couldn't stop staring at them. *Buttman Returns*, *The Bangover*, *28 Inches*

Later . . . all accompanied by movie stills that sold the product in ways artistic renderings couldn't approach. She loved them all, mainly because you couldn't look at them and think of anything else: RJ's calls to Gary Freeman in September, for instance. Or the fact that three years ago, RJ had broken into Gary's house. Or the memory of Gary's curt voice over the phone two days ago, telling Brenna that he'd never heard of anyone named RJ Tannenbaum . . . She glanced down at her phone. The voice mail was empty. Gary still hadn't called Brenna back.

Back to the posters. Brenna's favorite was from the gay collection—*The Wizard of Ahhhs*, featuring Ray Bulger. The artwork brought new meaning to *packaging*, and she was compelled to get up for a closer look. "Whoa," Brenna whispered.

"That's one of our biggest sellers," said a voice behind her. "No pun intended."

Brenna spun around to see an older man in shirt-sleeves and a plain blue tie, with horn-rimmed glasses, benign-looking features, and a neatly trimmed, mostly bald pate. *Company Head, huh?* He also looked as though he'd be happier in the Jane Austen club. "Mr. Frankel?"

"That's me," he said, shaking her hand. "You already met Gloria."

"The receptionist?"

"My wife," he said. "Can't fire her."

"A very interesting family business." Brenna smiled.

He didn't. If Charlie Frankel was capable of changing his facial expression, he'd yet to show it. "Have a seat."

She took a spartan, hard-backed chair across from his small desk. Save for the framed stills, everything in both Charlie Frankel's office and in the reception area defined bare bones, the whole place clearly designed with the idea of as little overhead as possible. Brenna imagined that Charlie and Gloria were very, very rich people who owned about three outfits apiece, had a drawer full of coupons, and wouldn't pay full price for anything if world peace depended on it. Of course, she did hope that the Frankels didn't skimp on Ray Bulger's salary—he deserved a massive paycheck, pardon the pun.

"So you're looking for RJ, huh?" he said.

Brenna tore her gaze away from the poster. "Yes, I am."

"Have you checked with Lula Belle?"

Her knees went weak. "*What?*"

"That was a joke."

"Can you explain the basis of the humor?"

He sighed. "Do you know who Lula Belle is?"

"Uh . . . yes."

"I ask because a lot of regular people don't. But she's pretty legendary in our little community. I introduced RJ to her work about a year ago and he became quite a fan."

Brenna looked at him. "Why is she legendary?"

He pointed at the wall behind him. "See those?" he said. "Our biggest sellers, and she's probably made more money off that Web site of hers than all of 'em combined."

"Really?"

He nodded. "Plus, she does it at no cost at all. No costars, no locations, no production values at all, really. No sex—hence no money shot. Which significantly cuts your need for an editor . . . No offense to RJ but we could've done a lot with the money we paid him."

"Sure."

"Plus she's not even technically porn. She calls herself performance art so there's a lot less guilt attached to watching her, even though probably 99.9 percent of her fans wouldn't know performance art if it slapped 'em on the ass and called 'em sweetie."

Brenna looked at him. "Sounds like you're a fan, too."

"Only of her business model," he said. "Call me old-fashioned, but I like sex in my porn."

"RJ didn't?"

Charlie exhaled heavily. "RJ," he said, "was one of the .01 percent."

"He saw her as an artist."

"Best actress he'd ever seen on screen." He snorted. "Yeah, she's a regular Meryl Streep up there, deep-throating a Coke bottle."

Brenna smiled. "Art is subjective."

"You can say that again. You know what Gloria loves? Avant-garde jazz. I swear to God if I have to listen to Ornette Coleman when I'm balling her one more time . . ."

"Charlie?"

"Yeah?"

"Was RJ in touch with Lula Belle?"

He sighed. "I know you talked to Yuri Pokrovsky."

"Yes."

"So you know he doesn't think too much of RJ's work ethic."

Brenna squinted at him. *Where are you going with this?*

"But the thing was, he was wrong. He didn't know him. If RJ loved something, he was devoted to it. And there was nothing he loved more than film. I was the only one he talked to about it. I guess he saw me as a fellow cineaste."

"Okay, that's interesting, but—"

"He wanted to be a filmmaker. An auteur. He had a project he was working on, and I guess he thought Lula Belle was the only actress who could do it, and so he joined Lula Belle's fan site and he wrote her a letter where it says 'contact me.' Like hundreds of other guys have done, probably." He took a breath and leaned in, his face as still and deadpan as ever, but with a slight intensity to the voice. "He told me she wrote back. From her personal e-mail. They were corresponding. About what, I don't know."

"Who sent Robin that picture, Trent?"

"A Hotmail address."

"Sweetpea81?"

Brenna said, "Did he ever meet with her . . . in person?"

"Not while he worked here," he said. "But."

"But?"

Charlie opened his desk drawer, removed something, and placed it on the table between them. A manila folder. "His letter of resignation," he said. "I printed it out for you."

Brenna read:

October 8, 2009

Dear Charlie:

It has been a real learning experience working for you these past three years, and I consider you to be the best film teacher I've ever had. I'm sure you'll understand, though, when I tell you that the Dream—The Big One—is about to come true.

She's agreed, Charlie.

It is with much gratitude and hope for the future that I tender my resignation from HAPPY ENDINGS VIDEO. No need to forward me my last check, as I'm unable to give you two weeks' notice: My new job begins immediately.

See you in the moving pictures.

All best,
RJT

Brenna looked up at him. " 'She' is Lula Belle."

"She has to be," he said. "Right?"

"And his project—this film he was making . . ."

"I don't know anything about it, other than he needed Lula Belle to complete it. I told him, why not use one of our actresses? Or if he needs someone legit, put an ad in *Casting Call*. He wasn't having any of it. 'You don't understand,' he said. 'I can't do this without her.' And apparently, he didn't need to."

"She agreed to the project."

"Yes."

"And it's been two and a half months, and you've heard nothing from him."

"No."

"And no one in your . . . your little community has heard a thing about Lula Belle."

"MIA. Both of them," he said.

"Maybe they hit a roadblock," Brenna said. "And so he's hiding from his investor."

"Pokrovsky? Maybe," he said. "Or," he said, very slowly, "maybe he never had the chance to get that lens cap off."

"What do you think happened?"

Charlie shrugged at her, a sad look in his eyes. "Pokrovsky's sweet on RJ's mom. And RJ knows it. He's never been afraid of Yuri Pokrovsky."

He didn't say anything more. He didn't need to. "You think he had to run from someone other than Pokrovsky."

"I can't figure out any other explaination."

"Charlie," Brenna said. "Did RJ ever mention the name Gary Freeman?"

"He's not in pornos, is he?"

"Hardly," Brenna said "He's a kids' talent agent from L.A."

Charlie shook his head. "Never heard him mention anybody by that name. Actually I can only remember him only talking about one guy from L.A."

Brenna looked at him. "Who?"

"Some character by the name of Shane Smith."

Brenna swallowed hard. "He talked to you about Shane."

"Yeah, but none of it made much sense," Charlie said. "RJ hated that guy so much, I think he got a little delusional."

"What do you mean?"

Charlie sighed. "Shane Smith, despite having the very marketable name of Shane Smith, is not in the porn business."

"And . . . RJ thought he was?"

"Well, yes and no. You have to keep in mind, RJ always maintained that Lula Belle isn't in the porn business. But I consider her a card-carrying member. No pun intended, but you understand—"

"Wait," Brenna said. "You're saying that RJ thought Shane was in business with . . ."

"Lula Belle. Yes."

Brenna stared at him, the color draining out of her face.

He chuckled a little. "Lula Belle and his buddy Shane," he said. "RJ was convinced they were business partners and lovers. 'I'm breaking them up,' he told me. 'She's gonna leave Shane to help me.'"

That cliché about great sex making you look different? Morasco had never believed it before today. After all, he'd had some pretty damn good sex in his life, and no one had ever remarked on his appearance afterward. But when he showed up at the Tarry Ridge station and asked Sally for his messages, she'd glanced up at him, then looked again in such a way, he half expected a spit-take. "You look different, Detective." She hadn't said anything more than that, of course, but the smile had spoken volumes.

"I shaved," he had offered. But that just made the smile widen, as if "shaved" was some kind of euphemism. Morasco had headed for his desk, fast, only to have Baus—who sat next to him and in truth was not the most perceptive of his fellow detectives—grin at him in the exact same way Sally had. "Brenna finally paid out, huh?"

"Hey, there's this new trend I just read about. It's called getting a life," Morasco said. "You should try it sometime."

"Knew I was right."

"Minding your own business? That's a fun one, too."

"Morasco finally got some!" Baus shouted, drawing applause from neighboring desks.

"Your mom was worth the wait," Morasco said.

Baus hooted. "So I've been told."

Morasco sighed. Mother jokes were no fun if the other person didn't get offended. He turned away from Baus, booted up his computer. As he did, though, he glanced down at the lower drawer in his desk. He knew what was in there—the papers Detective Grady Carlson had given him. Yep, that did the trick. Idiot grin officially gone, along with the good mood . . . *Not talking is great, Brenna. But we can't do that forever, can we? I have papers that were given to me by the lead investigator on your sister's disappearance. Am I never supposed to tell you that?*

He put the thought out of his head. Checked his e-mail for today's itinerary from the chief. It was a light one, as usual. Biggest crime: a break-in at Wax Attax. A bunch of candles stolen. Tarry Ridge was back to its affluent calm following the Neff case fallout, and since Chief Driscol wasn't a gale-force windbag like his predecessor Hutchins, there was no need to provide him with bogus material for his daily press conference.

Morasco much preferred it this way, of course. But he'd have been lying if he said he didn't miss the excitement of working in the city. For a few seconds, he allowed himself the fantasy of selling the house he'd lived in for the past fifteen years—the little cottage on Chestnut that he'd shared with Holly, and then Matthew and Holly, and then just Holly, and then Matthew's ghost.

In his fantasy he was the type of person who could let go of things easily, who could leave this job and Tarry Ridge and move into the city again to work homicide, who could live in a ghost-free place and sleep with Brenna every night without ever mentioning—or even thinking about—the papers in his desk.

Why can't I be like that? Morasco thought about things too much. That was his problem.

Behind him, someone cleared his throat in an overly dramatic way. Morasco exhaled. *Come on, dude. Just say, "Excuse me."*

But when he turned around and saw him, of course it made more sense. Carrot-Top. The one person in this station who found him genuinely intimidating. It took Morasco several agonizing seconds to come up with the kid's real name. "Hey . . . Danny Cavanaugh! How's it going?"

Again with the salute.

Morasco sighed. "You really don't have to . . . never mind. What's up?"

"Well, sir, I've been looking into this missing film-maker . . ."

"Missing wannabe filmmaker," Morasco corrected. "He's never made an actual film."

"Right . . . Well . . . this is kinda weird. But I've been running into brick walls with everything else, so . . . uh . . ."

"Spit it out, big guy."

He cleared his throat again. "Okay, so last night I was talking to my grandpa . . . um . . . Detective Cava-naugh from Mount Temple."

"Yes?"

"I was telling him about this guy, and he said . . . Oh boy, now I think this is probably going to sound stupid."

"Some of the best leads would get buried if we edited out all the stupid," said Morasco, who had once heard Brenna say something very similar. Truthfully, he wasn't sure he believed that. Most of the time, stupid was just, well, stupid. But why say that to this nervous kid, who also happened to be a sweaty one? Already, the beads were forming over his eyebrows. "Go on, Danny," he said. "I want to hear."

"My grandpa said they arrested this guy about a month ago on Columbus. Some crazy homeless guy, who was waving a gun around."

"Okay . . ."

"I guess some teenagers were bugging him and he went all Dirty Harry on them, and when the officers showed up and asked him where he'd gotten the gun, he said . . . Boy this is dumb."

"Danny, I'm not going to say it again."

"Sorry. The homeless guy told the Mount Temple officers that he'd gotten the gun from Steven Spielberg."

Morasco stared at him. "Are you serious?"

"I knew I shouldn't have said anything."

"No, Danny. What you said . . . That's a seriously great lead." He looked into the kid's eyes long enough so Danny could see he wasn't being sarcastic.

Danny beamed. "Thanks!" he said. "Really?"

"Where is he now?"

"Jail. He's still awaiting trial on the illegal firearm charge."

"Beautiful." He gave Danny a high five. Then he picked up the phone and called Brenna.

Gary still hadn't called Brenna back, and now her head was swimming with questions—the first of which was, *Why the hell hasn't Gary called back?*

To be honest, she feared the answer. Every other case she'd ever taken, Brenna had first run a thorough check on her client—not just to make sure that the client could pay, but to truly know who she was dealing with. There were few jobs that required trust as much as locating the missing. If someone had disappeared for good reason, the last thing you wanted to do was drag them back to whatever hell they'd escaped. And so you had to trust in the searchers—you had to believe that their motives were basically good.

You had to know them.

But Brenna didn't know Gary Freeman. She'd never breathed the same air as him and had done no background check on him outside of the world's simplest Google search. He was a successful agent with an attractive family and a kind face to her, but only because that's the way he presented himself online. In reality, Brenna had no idea who or what he was.

Worst of all, Gary had come to Brenna via Errol Ludlow, who, rest in peace, had been less trustworthy than most of the cheating husbands he went after—and for whom a background check had usually meant getting a girl's measurements.

But she'd taken him on—this blank slate called Gary Freeman who had definitely lied about how well he knew RJ Tannenbaum, this unknown entity who'd come to her on the recommendation of the biggest snake she'd ever known and could have lied to her about anything, about everything he'd told her.

She'd liked him based on—what, the sound of his voice? And so she'd let him swear her to secrecy, keeping quiet about him even as so many other blank slates crept into her life—Diandra, RJ, Shane Smith . . . And all this because of some *shadow*, some *weird-ass fetish* who happened to know stories about Brenna's family.

What's wrong with me?

Was Brenna's obsession with her sister that strong, that unhealthy? Would she risk her life—and those of her loved ones—just for the possibility that Clea might be out there on the internet with a fake Southern accent, naked and doing yoga and relentlessly fucking with Brenna's mind?

"You okay?" Trent said.

She was in his hospital room with him, arranging a bouquet of flowers she'd bought at the gift shop—a paltry little thing next to the two dozen sterling roses that Annette Shelby had sent over. And still she couldn't bring herself to break Gary's confidence. "I'm okay," she told Trent. "Why?"

"Well see, for one thing, you'd never know you just got back from the happiest place on earth."

"Happy Endings."

"See? It's even got happy in the title, but judging from the way you look, I'd guess you'd been to . . . hmmmm . . . maybe a puppy funeral where they only play Tori Amos."

"I like Tori Amos," Brenna said.

Trent sighed. "Why so sad? I'm the tragic OD here, after all."

"I'm not sad," Brenna said. "I'm just . . . frustrated."

"Talk to me."

"It's this case. Lula Belle," she said. "I feel like every time we shed a little light on any part of it, the rest of it goes further into the dark."

Trent gave her a smile. He looked a lot healthier today, the color back in his face, the cuts from the car accident barely noticeable. *The resilience of the young.* "What do you want?" he said. "We're looking for a shadow."

"I know," Brenna said. "I guess my question is *why.*"

"Well, I've been working on it and—"

"Not you, Trent," she said. "I'm asking myself. Why did I get us involved in this thing?"

"Actually . . . it was kinda me that got us involved in this thing."

She looked at him.

"Come on. I'm the one who met with Errol. I'm the one who got all into Lula Belle, and I'm the one who repeatedly jumped the bones of . . . uh . . . she whose name we dare not speak . . ."

"True, but you're young and naïve. I'm supposed to protect you."

He sighed heavily. "Falling down on the job," he said. "Oh . . . Speaking of job."

"Yeah?"

"I made a nice, clear rendering from Shane Smith's class picture."

"You did?"

He nodded. "Looks like a real person now instead of a blur with hair. Maybe we can do something with this." He gestured at the laptop on his nightstand. Brenna handed it to him fast, and Trent flipped it open, tapping at the keyboard. "Here it is," he said, finally. He turned the laptop toward Brenna.

Her mouth went dry.

"I've made a few other versions, too," Trent said. "I've got a bald one, a beard, bleached blond . . ."

Brenna could barely get the words out. "Show me the beard."

Even before Trent called it up and showed it to Brenna, and she felt the chill wind aboard the *Maid of the Mist* October 23, *the sting of the hail and wet bench beneath her as the couple passes, the girl looking right at her, mascara streaming down her face* . . .

She wants to die . . .

"Uh . . . Brenna?"

She shifted her focus from the screen to Trent's face. "It's him."

"Who?"

"Dia— she whose name we dare not speak's boyfriend. From the *Maid of the Mist*."

"No way."

She swallowed hard, traveling in her mind back to Charlie Frankel's office . . .

Lula Belle and his buddy Shane. RJ was convinced they were business partners and lovers.

Brenna's phone vibrated. "Yeah," she answered, though she was barely able to move her lips. *Lula Belle, are you Diandra?*

"Where have you been?" Morasco said. "I've been trying to get you all morning."

"Working," she said. "I never heard the phone—"

"Okay, look. It's not important. I think I've got you a lead."

"To Shane Smith?"

"What? No. Better. Tannenbaum."

Her eyebrows went up. "You do?"

"He doesn't want to talk to me, though. He says he's through trying to explain himself to cops. But I think if you were nice to him . . ."

"Yes, fine," she said quickly. "Where am I supposed to meet this guy?"

"Westchester County Jail."

"Seriously?"

"Yes."

"I'm there." After she ended the conversation, she looked at Trent.

"You've gotta go," he said. A statement, not a question.

Brenna hugged him good-bye and texted Maya that

there was no need for her to hurry home. Then she took a cab to the garage and got the Sienna out and pulled onto the West Side Highway and within an hour and a half, she was with Morasco in the lobby of Westchester County Jail, getting processed for her visit with someone named Orion Nichols who still swore, up and down, that on a chilly afternoon back in early October, he'd met Steven Spielberg on Columbus Boulevard in Mount Temple.

21

"Who the hell are you?" said Orion Nichols, his face less than an inch away from the thick glass, nostrils flaring, his voice booming into Brenna's ear through the plastic receiver.

Brenna shivered—not because of Orion himself. (Morasco had warned her he was a "little off.") But because it was ridiculously cold in here. She wondered if prison officials kept the temperature in the visiting room so low to save money, or to ensure that visitors had no inclination to linger after the allotted hours. Brenna and Orion were alone—aside, of course, from the forty or so other visitors, including the woman to her left with the very shrill voice who kept saying, "What am I supposed to *do* about this?" over and over and over to the point where you wanted to scream at the prisoner on the other side of her glass to *just tell her already*. Morasco was waiting in the lobby. Brenna had insisted. Meeting with a cop in front of his fellow inmates wasn't going to do Orion a shred of good—Morasco knew that as well as anybody.

"I'm Brenna Spector." Her teeth were actually chattering. "Is it this cold in the rest of the prison?"

"Like a psychiatric nurse's tit," he said. "What's a Brenna Spector?"

"I've been trying to figure that out for thirty-nine years."

He broke into a smile that was not so much a smile as a baring of yellowed, broken teeth. Orion's lips were very chapped. His dark skin looked raw at the cheeks and nose, as though someone had gone at it with a Brillo pad. *What are they doing to you in there, Orion?* What was he doing to *himself*? Jail is a bad place for those who are a "little off." Brenna imagined that as a homeless person, Orion had been a lot dirtier and nowhere near as angry.

"And what am I supposed to do about *them*?" shrilled the woman to Brenna's left.

"It smells in here," Brenna said. "Like cough medicine."

"Yep."

"Tell me about Steven Spielberg."

Orion moved his face up to the glass again. His eyes were dark and round and opaque, like eight balls. "You making fun of me?"

"No."

"Yes you are."

Brenna exhaled into the receiver. The woman to Brenna's left was sobbing now. "I can't do this alone," she wailed. "I can't, I can't . . ." The medicinal smell was giving Brenna a headache, and at this point she felt chilled to the bone, her fingertips aching from it. "Orion," she said slowly, "do you honestly think I would give up Christmas shopping in the city with my daughter, just to come here and make fun of you?

He bit down on his crusty lower lip and glared at her. "Why do you care, then?"

"Huh?"

"Why does that cop care? I saw Spielberg go into that damn building three months ago, nobody believes me. Nobody believes me about the gun. They think I stole it from somebody. Now, all of a sudden, he comes here. They make me talk to him in an interrogation room. Then you come here and you want to know about Spielberg and the gun like we're old friends. Like you heard it from somebody other than a cop. What am I supposed to think, other than you're making fun of me?" He picked a scab on the back of his hand.

"I'm here because I need your help."

"Bullshit. I don't want to do this anymore." He started to put the phone down.

Brenna said, "*Please help me find my sister.*" It came out cracked, choked, and Brenna realized that it was the first time she'd ever put it that way, the first time she'd ever said it out loud. *My sister.*

He stopped, looked at her.

Brenna mouthed the word at him. *Please.*

Slowly, he put the receiver back to his ear, and then she said it again, into the mouthpiece. "Please."

"You're telling the truth."

It was more statement than a question, so Brenna didn't answer. She just looked at him, her own words throbbing in her head.

"I thought you were a psychiatrist or a lady cop," he said. "Or a psychiatric nurse."

"I'm not," she said. "I'm not any of those things."

"Well, I can see that now." He took a breath. "You got emotions."

Brenna swallowed hard. "Yep."

He nodded at her. The anger was gone from his eyes,

and he looked different. Almost sane. "So how the hell does Steven Spielberg know your sister?"

Brenna closed her eyes. "Rob— Spielberg disappeared a couple of months ago. I think he was with a woman who . . ." Her voice trailed off.

"Who what?"

"She knows stories from my childhood," Brenna said. "If she's not my sister, then maybe she can at least tell me what happened to her." She looked at him, waiting.

"Your sister an actress?"

Brenna said, "I don't know what she is," she said. "All I know is she's gone. She's been gone since I was a kid, and I want her back."

"She left you," he said. "Or did somebody take her?"

"Both."

"Why do you want her back?"

She gave him a long look, the over-air-conditioned visiting room shifting and changing in her mind until it became September 7, 1981, in the living room of her house on City Island, late summer sea air pressing through the window screens, warm and wet and thick like breath. Her mother's voice in her ears, Clea gone and her mother hating her for it . . .

"Get out of my house."

"Clea told me not to tell you, Mom. That's why. Because Clea made me prom—"

"Two weeks ago, Brenna. Your sister could be dead right now."

"I'm sorry."

"If she is dead, it is your fault. It's your fault she's gone. Get out of my house."

Brenna dug her fingernails into her palms. The

woman next to her was screaming, "Selfish pig!" at the prisoner she was visiting, and only then did Brenna realize how much that shrill voice sounded like that of her mother, twenty-eight years ago.

"I want my sister back," Brenna said, "because it's my fault she disappeared."

"She doesn't look like you," Orion said. "But what do I know? I didn't even know Spielberg was chunky."

Brenna's eyes widened. "Who?"

"Huh?"

"Who doesn't look like me? Who are you talking about?"

"Your sister. The chick who was with Spielberg. She's blonde, for one thing, and she's built like a brick shithouse."

Brenna stared at him. *Diandra?*

He held up a hand. "No offense. I'm just saying."

"You saw her."

"Yeah. When he was filming at the building."

"You saw a blonde go into a building with Steven Spielberg."

He shook his head. "They showed up first. He met them there. With his camera."

Brenna gripped the receiver. "What kind of a camera?"

"Movie camera. Very fancy."

"The stacked blonde," Brenna said. "Was she a lot younger than me?"

"I don't know from ages," he said. "Spielberg looked younger than I thought he was, but that could have been all that extra chunk. Or the hat."

"Hat?"

The woman next to Brenna was yelling, "Fine! Go ahead and dump me! You got some bitch in there, or what? Your bitch sweeter to you than I am?"

Brenna put a hand up to the side of her face, as if that would be effective in drowning her out. "What kind of hat?" she said.

"Baseball cap," he said. "L.A. Dodgers. They wouldn't let me keep it in here."

Tannenbaum. "You took his cap?"

"No, he gave it to me."

"Before he went in the building, or after he left?"

He blinked at her. "Huh?"

"I hate you!" the woman yelled.

Brenna squeezed her eyes shut, opened them again. She kept her voice measured, said the words as calmly as she possibly could. "Did Steven Spielberg give you the hat before he went in the building or—"

"No." Orion shook his head vigorously.

"No?" Brenna was starting to wish she *was* a psychiatrist—she might get further with him that way. "I sort of gave you a multiple-choice question there, Orion. Before or after . . ."

"He didn't give it to me before or after."

"You stole the hat? Without his knowing?"

"*No!*"

"*I'm outta here!*" the woman screamed.

Brenna said, "Would you *please* help me out here?"

"He wasn't the one who gave it to me. The film crew guy did, when he left with the blonde. Why can't anybody hear me?"

She looked at him. "They left the building separately."

"No."

The headache was much worse now. It pressed against the backs of her eyes. "Spielberg left the building on his own. The film crew guy left with the stacked blonde."

"*No!*"

"*What the hell, Orion?*"

"*Spielberg never left the building!*"

Brenna froze. She could actually feel the hairs, standing up one by one, on the back of her neck. "The crew guy," she said slowly. "What did he look like?"

"Beard," he said. "Light brown hair. Great teeth. Man, I wish I had teeth like that. Looked like a real winner."

Shane Smith.

"'You keep yourself safe,' he said to me. And he handed me that gun and the hat. And I kept waiting for Spielberg to show up and take that hat back, but he never did." His gaze drifted off. "Never came out of there."

"You sure you didn't miss him?"

"That was where I lived. Right across the street from that building," he said. "I'm a light sleeper and I didn't move from there, ever. I would have seen a world-famous director if he left that building."

A voice came over the PA system, announcing visiting time was over. Brenna thanked Orion. On her way out, she put fifty dollars into his account at the canteen.

Then she found Morasco in the lobby. He started to ask her how it went, but she cut him off. "Did you find out from Danny exactly where Orion was arrested?"

"Vacant lot next to a parking area. Middle of Columbus Boulevard," he said. "Why?"

"Because I think Robin Tannenbaum was shot to death by Shane Smith. And if we go into the building across the street, we'll find his body."

Morasco called both Danny Cavanaugh and his grandfather Wayne and arranged for them both to meet him—along with Wayne's partner, Danny's partner, and a team of squad cars from the Mount Temple station—at the parking lot on Columbus Boulevard where Orion Nichols had been arrested. "Got a tip on a possible murder in the building across the street," he said to Wayne, who followed up with his office, no questions asked. That's the type of clout Morasco had now. Brenna *and* Morasco, actually, thanks to the Neff case. When Morasco let Danny Cavanaugh know, over the phone, that private investigator Brenna Spector was coming, he told her that the young officer had "squealed. Literally. I kid you not."

Flattering as it was to know that she'd made a cop squeal, the best part of all this was that Brenna no longer had to sneak onto crime scenes—at least not in Westchester County. She hoped it would last.

She was in her Sienna, following Morasco's car to Mount Temple, when her cell phone chimed. She looked at the screen, recognized the number of Gary Freeman's new disposable phone. Finally, he was returning her call of this morning. *About time*. She hit send, activating the Bluetooth in her ear.

"Yes, I'm alone," she said, before he could ask. She really couldn't stomach that question one more time.

Gary Freeman said, "You found something out about RJ Tannenbaum?" His voice sounded strange. Slurry. From what she'd read about him online, Gary Freeman didn't drink. Plus, even if he did, it was before noon in California. Maybe it was just the connection . . .

"Yes. I found out two things," Brenna said. "The first is that three years ago, RJ Tannenbaum broke into your house."

He breathed thickly into the phone, not saying anything for close to a minute. Brenna followed Morasco onto the ramp for 287. They'd already passed the Katonah exit by the time he finally spoke.

"What's the second thing?"

"Mr. Freeman," Brenna said.

"*Please don't call me that.*"

"Uh . . . Okay, Gary. You can't just change subjects on me."

"That's still the same subject. You told me the first thing. Now I'm asking you for the second."

He pronounced it *shecernd*. Definitely drunk. "Is something wrong?" she said.

"I don't give a shit about RJ Tannenbaum. I don't know who he is. I hired you to find Lula Belle."

There was something so strange about him—and it wasn't the fact that he was clearly lying about knowing Tannenbaum, or even that he was early morning drunk-calling her after posting an essay on the Wise Up Foundation's blog November 25 called "Why I Always Say No to Drugs and Alcohol."

No, it went beyond that. Gary Freeman of the warm character actor's voice, Gary Freeman, whom Brenna had decided she liked, without really knowing why— that Gary Freeman seemed to have disappeared.

"I explained to you," she said, as patiently as she could. "RJ Tannenbaum was, in all probability, with Lula Belle when she disappeared."

"*I don't care about him! He's a fucking nobody!*"

His voice roared in Brenna's ears. She gritted her teeth. "He went to your alma mater."

"Only for three months."

Brenna's eyebrows went up. "You do know him."

"No."

"He called your agency four times in late September," she said. "What did you talk about?"

"I never spoke to him." *Schpoke.*

"Do you know Shane Smith, Gary?"

"No!"

"How about Diandra? I don't have a last name on her, but that's an unusual enough first name, I'd think you'd—"

"*You're fired.*"

"What?"

"*You're fired, you mental freak!*"

Click.

Should have run a background check. Brenna kept driving. "I'm finding her anyway," she whispered. "I'm finding Lula Belle." She clutched the steering wheel and stared out through the windshield. "But first," she said, "I'm finding RJ."

DeeDee's view was spectacular. Of course it was. Gary paid the rent and it was astronomical. Three years ago, when she'd left L.A. on his suggestion and found this place, Gary had considered it a small price to pay for her continued silence about the evening they'd spent together—an evening he remembered very little of, to be honest, blacked out as he'd been from Scotch. He never drank.

A year later, when, after buying the Bat Phone just for emergencies, he'd found himself calling this girl and confiding in her on a regular basis—about his money problems, his career troubles, his hopes and fears and finally, his past—Gary had thought of the rent as therapy money. And once DeeDee had begun telling him, "I'll do anything for you," and *proving* it . . . (He wasn't exactly sure how she was proving it, mind you, but he sure as hell hadn't heard from RJ Tannenbaum again, which said something.) Well, Gary kept depositing the checks. Enough said.

But now . . .

Now as Gary stood on DeeDee's balcony, the wind biting his face as he watched puffy Christmas clouds swirling over the East River, Gary could only think of the havoc DeeDee Walsh had wreaked on his life, financially, emotionally, spiritually.

She loved him, for all his flaws. Supported him through every bad thing he did, knew his darkest secrets and still hung on, hung on to him tight, even when he knocked her to the ground. She hung on to him and kept him afloat when it would have been so much better if she'd just let him sink, so much better for them both.

DeeDee. His girl. His poor, misguided girl. *Did you give away our secrets, DeeDee? Did you find a confidant of your own?*

Shane Smith. Good-looking kid. Took a seminar on working with child actors Gary had taught as a guest lecturer. He'd asked lots of questions. *To be young again*, Gary had thought. Gary, who had once been very much like Shane. Same swagger, same grin. Ready to take over the world . . . *We can beat that Murder Mile, baby. We can beat it straight to death.*

Once, Shane had stayed after class as Gary collected his things, waiting with that smile on his face, like they had a shared secret. "My girlfriend used to be a client of yours as a kid," Shane had told him. "DeeDee Walsh. Do you remember her?"

Gary, who hadn't remembered her at all, had said, "Sure. DeeDee. Of course."

"She talks about you all the time."

"She does?"

"Says you are the most gifted man she's ever met."

"No kidding."

"Uh-huh. To tell you the truth, I'm a little jealous."

"What's she doing now? Still acting?"

"Trying. She's gorgeous. All she needs is a break. For now, she's waiting tables at Barney's Beanery."

And who could blame a man for going out to dinner on his own, just once? Who could blame him, if his wife and kids were out of town and he couldn't cook worth a damn, to grab a burger at Barney's Beanery, where he hadn't eaten since . . . man . . . since back when he was Shane's age . . .

It had been three years since that one night out, but it may as well have been thirty. Gary felt so old, so tired. The walls in the apartment were lined with black and white head shots of DeeDee—or Diandra Marie, as she was now known. In one, she was wearing glasses and a high-buttoned shirt. In another, she had wet lips and hair, her shoulders bare . . . What kind of road was it that brought him here to this overpriced actress pad, this grown-up playhouse, when less than forty-eight hours ago he was sitting in his kitchen in Pasadena, Hannah complaining to him about the Tooth Fairy?

DeeDee was at her regular job right now—waiting tables at a place called Harry's Hamburger in the theater district, which wasn't really all that different a name from Barney's Beanery when you thought about it. *You get some rest*, she had told Gary in that practiced, breathy voice of hers as she headed out the door. *I'll be home before you know it.*

For the life of him, he still couldn't remember her as a client. Of course he had no desire to try.

DeeDee had been working that Harry's Hamburger job since she moved here, taking a brief hiatus to become one of Errol's Angels and spy on Ludlow. Gary wondered what DeeDee's coworkers at Harry's thought of this showplace their fellow waitress lived in. *Sugar daddy*. They had to think that, right? He wondered if DeeDee had told *them* about him, too.

She'd told Shane about him, after all. *Shane Smith*— Spector had named him, over the phone. And if ever a name could knock a man down . . .

The Bat Phone was in his jacket pocket. He grabbed it, called DeeDee's cell. She answered after the first ring. "Hello?" Gary heard restaurant noise in the background—the hum of voices, pop music, a baby crying . . . which made him think of Hannah.

His brain was thick and foggy, headache settling in. Scotch and hangover fighting it out in his skull. *A battle royal, to be sure.* "What's going on between you and Shane Smith?" he said.

He thought he might have heard a gasp. "Uh . . . let me take this outside."

"Take it wherever you want," he said. "But you'd better tell me the truth."

As she hurried to find a quiet place, Gary could hear DeeDee panting into the receiver. He could almost feel her trembling. She was such a kid, really, and for a moment, he felt sorry for her. His half-full glass of Scotch was on the living room table. He took another swig, felt the strength of the burn, the softness in his chest dissipating.

"What are you talking about?" DeeDee said now.

"Brenna Spector was asking me about you, RJ Tannenbaum, and Shane Smith," he said. "What does Shane Smith have to do with anything?"

"How should I know?"

"*Don't take that tone with me.*"

"I'm sorry," she stammered. "I . . . I used to date him back in L.A. But he means nothing to me."

"I don't give a damn what he means to you, DeeDee," he said. "I want to know what he *knows*. I want to know what you told him."

"Nothing."

"Nothing? Well, why did Brenna Spector—"

"Maybe RJ told him something, before . . . you know. They were friends back in film school for a while."

"Have you been in touch with Shane since you've been in New York?"

She gulped air. "You don't have to worry about him. I swear that on my life."

"DeeDee?"

"Yes . . ."

"Do you know anything about Lula Belle that you're not telling me?"

"No."

"Does Shane know about Lula Belle?"

"*No,*" she said. "If he did, I would have found her for you."

"*So you have been in touch with him, liar!*"

She was crying now. At work, which wasn't a good thing. Gary couldn't risk another scene. He needed to lay off the alcohol, stop feeling sorry for himself, get his head back together . . . He thought of the way he'd spoken to Brenna Spector over the phone. He heard his own voice in his head—like those drunk Mel Gibson tapes people were making ringtones out of. He cringed.

That wasn't him. Talking like that. To her *sister*. That wasn't Gary Freeman, whom everyone liked. And now he'd gone and done it. Raised red flags in Brenna

Spector's mind, and she's an investigator. With perfect memory. She'd remember that rant always—his anger over RJ Tannenbaum. *The way he'd exploded at her when she'd asked about the phone calls—but he couldn't help it. He'd remembered those calls, RJ saying her name—The Shadow's real name—saying it to Gary over and over again, RJ flinging open that door in Gary's mind with his questions, breaking the lock, destroying Gary's life. . . . Four phone calls, each one more unbearable than the last. He had to be stopped. But would Brenna understand that? No. She would never understand.*

And soon she'd find out what Tannenbaum was working on and then what happened to him and she would put two and two together . . .

Her sister.

God. If she found out . . . If Brenna found out, Gary would never get his life back again. The door would fly off its hinges, shattering everything. He would lose his clients, his reputation. His family—whom he loved more than anything—he would never be able to get them back.

He would be alone forever. Alone with his own, ugly past.

Why had Gary ever contacted Ludlow? Why had he thought that involving Brenna Spector would be a good idea?

Gary thought about calling Brenna back, apologizing. But what could he say? The horse had been let out of the barn, as they say. The damage had been done, and the only damage control he could hope for in the world was on the phone with him right now. Crying.

Calm, calm, he told himself.

DeeDee gasped, "I don't know what you want me to do."

Gary took a deep, cleansing breath. His lungs puffed full of air, and then drained themselves—slowly, fully, until he truly felt clean. He heard himself say, "You're as special a woman as I've ever met."

She stopped. "I am?"

He took a cleansing breath. "I love you, DeeDee," he said. "More than anyone."

"Oh, me too, Mr. Freeman. I love you so much."

"Can you help me, DeeDee?" he said. "Can you help me one more time?"

"Yes," she said. Just like that. No questions asked, pure and unconditional, which was the very nature of love, wasn't it? Without another word, she listened as Gary spoke to her about Brenna Spector, relaying their conversation, voicing his concerns.

22

"Found something!" Danny Cavanaugh called out. Brenna and Nick looked at each other. They'd been on every floor of this decrepit building, working their way from the ground floor up, until this one, floor seven. It seemed as though someone had started to knock the place down, but had given up on it, leaving the rare visitor to navigate around piles of bricks and debris, on floors that were falling apart to begin with. In certain spots, you could see straight through to the support beams. Treacherous. Brenna couldn't believe the elevators still worked.

The ventilation system, on the other hand . . . As cold as it was in here, the whole building had a smell to it that seeped into your pores. No wonder Orion preferred to take his chances outside. This wasn't a place to squat in, even if you were desperate.

"You think Danny really did find something this time?" Brenna said.

Morasco shrugged. "He is a little quick to cry wolf."

An understatement. On the sixth floor, Danny had called everyone into a rank little room, right next to the staircase—only to find, behind a crumbling wall, what turned out to be a dead coyote. On the third floor, it had been a couple of dead crows. On the first, a good-sized pile of animal waste. *What now*, Brenna thought, as everyone hurried down to the end of the floor, to a room with no door on it, Danny standing there, perfectly still in his regulation blue coat and his protective mask, pointing at a tarp in the corner of the room as though it were Scrooge's grave, he the Ghost of Christmas Future.

For a split second, Brenna thought it was another false alarm. But then the smell came barreling at her, and one of the uniforms pulled back part of the tarp and she saw it. A leg, in jeans. A blue Nike with a white stripe—the exact same kind of shoe Spielberg had been wearing in the picture next to RJ's mirror. The uniforms yanked off the rest of the tarp, revealing what was beneath. The body. Brenna saw dark blue skin. She saw black, caked blood, a shattered face. She had to turn away, not because the sight nauseated her, but because of Hildy—Hildy's big sad eyes in her head, Hildy's frail voice . . .

Robbie's hurt me plenty, but I don't want to make him disappear. He's my boy. I want him back.

Her only son. Her only child. "I'm so sorry," Brenna whispered, remembering Hildy in her apartment, her curled, hard little back beneath her hands as she hugged her. So frail and brittle Hildy was, and this would destroy her, Brenna knew. Brenna had one child, too, and so she knew. This would turn her to dust.

She could hear Wayne Cavanaugh, calling the medical examiner's office, and then she heard her own name. She turned to see Morasco, standing near the body, beckoning to her.

"I can't. Not yet."

"No," he said. "Look at this."

She moved over to where he was standing—just a foot away from the body. He removed surgical gloves from his pocket, put one on, and picked it up off the ground—a glittering chain. "What did you say her name was, again? The girl who drugged Trent and Ludlow? The one who dresses like a cartoon on a cocktail napkin?"

"I never told you her name," Brenna said. "It's actually Diandra."

"We should probably find a last name for her," Morasco said.

"Why?" Brenna moved closer, as he held the chain up and she saw the pendant at the end. It was a tiny silver D.

Hildy agreed to come to the Westchester County morgue and identify her son's body. Brenna waited in the lobby for her with Morasco, that pendant filling her thoughts. "I've got to find her," she said.

"Diandra."

"Yes."

"You think she killed RJ Tannenbaum, as well as Ludlow," Morasco said.

She shook her head. "Diandra killed Ludlow and tried to kill Trent," she said. "But I don't think she killed RJ. I think Shane Smith shot him in the head while she looked on approvingly."

"Why?"

"Shooting isn't her MO," she said. "If she was the one who'd killed RJ, his pants would have been around his ankles and his face would have been in one piece—probably still smiling."

"No," Morasco said. "I mean, why do you think RJ was killed?"

"I'm not sure," Brenna said. "But I bet Diandra could tell me."

"Hello, Brenna." It was Hildy Tannenbaum, standing over her, Pokrovsky looming behind her.

"Hildy." Brenna stood up and hugged her, flashing back as she did to two days ago, just two days ago in Hildy's apartment, hugging her good-bye, this tiny woman with the curled turtle shell back, this woman with a missing child—distant and cold as he was, behind his locked bedroom door with his typed, formal note good-bye, he was still her child. *"I want to help you," Brenna says, Hildy's wig stiff beneath her chin. And she does, so very much. She wants to help them both . . .*

Brenna came back to the present, hugging Hildy again over her son, her dead son, dead two days ago and two months ago, without anyone knowing. Rotting under a tarp in that broken-down building, no better off than that coyote or those crows.

"It's good to see you," Hildy said.

Brenna was gripping her too hard, she knew. She glanced up at Pokrovsky and pulled away. "I'm so sorry, Hildy," she said.

She looked into Hildy's eyes. They were dry, but as she saw now, stricken. Pokrovsky took Hildy's tiny hand in his big, gnarled one and stood holding it, saying nothing. Brenna wondered if it was the first time this had ever happened, Hildy allowing Pokrovsky to hold her hand. She gazed up into his face, the glass shard eyes warm and sad. She decided it was. "You don't need to stay," Hildy said. "Yuri will come in with me and help me identify."

"Are you sure?" Morasco said.

She nodded and closed her eyes, getting herself ready. "I suppose it was a mistake," she said quietly.

Brenna looked at her. "What was?"

"Robbie going into professional filmmaking."

"He was a grown man, Hildy. You couldn't tell him what to do with his life."

She smiled, or tried to—a grimace of a smile that didn't involve the rest of her face. "When he was in high school, his father bought him a Super 8 camera. 'Maybe that will get him out of the house,' Walter said. But to Robbie, it was as though we'd given him a pair of eyes. He fell in love with that camera. He filmed everything. He was obsessed. He'd film birds outside. He'd film me, ironing."

Pokrovsky said, "You are beautiful, ironing."

She didn't look at him. "It gave him a social life, that camera. Began making little films with the other kids in the neighborhood. He joined the audiovisual club at school. He had friends . . ."

"I don't remember this at all."

"It was when you were away," Hildy said. "Life doesn't stop when you go away."

"I know," he said softly, and something passed between them. A moment Brenna didn't understand. She looked at Morasco. He shrugged.

"Nothing made Robbie happier than the movies, and then the movies killed him," she said. "Was the camera with him? Or did someone take it?"

"It was gone," Morasco said.

"You see, Yuri? That camera he bought. With your money . . ."

Brenna said, "I don't know that the camera was the main reason."

"The Southern woman. Was she the reason?"

"I don't think so," She stayed quiet about Shane. Let the Mount Temple cops bring up that name with Hildy. Brenna didn't want to see her face crumble, not now, not right before she had to go in and identify her son's remains. A young uniformed officer walked into the lobby—a dark-skinned girl with cornrowed hair and a regal bearing. "Mr. and Mrs. Tannenbaum?"

No one bothered correcting her.

"If you could just come this way."

"One moment," Hildy said. She opened her purse. "I found this in Robbie's nightstand drawer." She plucked out a small key and placed it in Brenna's hand. "It's for that PO box," she said. "Since it's what brought us together, I was thinking you should have it."

Brenna took the key, giving her hand a squeeze as she did. Hildy really did have the smallest hands, like a child. "Thank you."

"I wish we could pray together," Hildy said.

"We can if you like."

She shook her head. "It would be disrespectful," she said. "Robbie was an atheist."

Brenna watched Pokrovsky and Hildy follow the officer out of the room. Before they walked through the morgue door, Hildy said, "Thank you, Brenna."

"What was she thanking me for?" she asked Morasco, once they were gone.

"An answer," he said quietly—that look, once again, seeping into his eyes, the look Brenna didn't like. "She lived with a question for two and a half months," he said. "You gave her an answer."

Morasco started out of the building. Brenna followed. It was four-thirty and close to pitch black. Brenna hated that about the winter.

Morasco turned to her. "I should head home," he said, that look still all over his face—the Thing We Need to Talk About. "Nick?" she said.

"Yeah?"

"Not everyone needs answers, you know."

He nodded. "I know." He touched her face, and then he kissed her, very gently, as though she were some fragile, breakable thing. She didn't like it.

"I'll see you tomorrow," he said.

"Okay . . ." Brenna headed for her car, the feel of it lingering. The saddest kiss ever. Yes, she understood the need for answers. Of course she did—she'd quit college and gone to work for Errol Ludlow and wrecked her marriage, all because of that need. But why did she have to get them from Nick? Why couldn't they just shut up and screw every night, without ever discussing anything deeper than who gets what side of the bed, and can I get you anything from the kitchen?

Of course, there was one answer Brenna did want, and the question had nothing to do with Nick Morasco. She thought of that question as she opened the door to her car and slipped inside:

If RJ Tannenbaum was an atheist, why did he write "DEUT 31:6" on the bottom of a picture of his favorite director?

Brenna's cell phone chimed. She checked the screen, saw Trent's name, and hit talk. "Yeah?"

"I've got good news, good news, and weird news. What do you want to hear first?"

"The good news."

"Okay. I'm out of the hospital."

"That's great!"

"Yep, I'm a first-rate physical specimen," he said. "What do you want to hear next?"

"What would you like me to hear next?"

"The good news."

"Shoot."

"I found Shane Smith."

"You *did*?" Brenna's eyes went huge. "He killed RJ, Trent. I'm almost positive."

"RJ's dead?"

"Yes. We need to get the police in on this. Bring Shane Smith in now. Where is he?"

"Okay, that's the weird news."

"Tell me."

Trent took a breath. "Shane is in Niagara Falls."

Brenna frowned at the phone. "He stayed?"

"He didn't have much choice."

"Excuse me?"

"Brenna," Trent said. "Shane Smith has been dead for two months."

According to a news article Trent showed Brenna back at his apartment, Shane Smith's body had been found on December 2 by rescuers looking for a Japanese tourist who had jumped the guardrail and tumbled into the falls. Shane had drowned weeks before, but because the body had spent all that time in freezing water, it was unusually well preserved. They were able to identify him not just by dental records, but by his many tattoos. As far as they could tell, Shane had drowned during the last week in October, which made it probable that he had died the day Brenna had seen him—October 30—on the *Maid of the Mist*.

She wants to die . . .

"Do you think Diandra pushed him?" Trent said.

"Yes."

"No question in your mind, huh?"

"Nope. She had this look on her face when I saw her on the boat . . . It's hard to explain," Brenna said. "I think she was . . . steeling herself to do it."

"Why were they on that boat with you?"

"That is one of the many things I'd like to ask Diandra when I see her next." Brenna flashed on her, rushing out of Trent's bathroom in her pink angora sweater, calling herself Jenny in that high, little girl's voice . . .

"Whoa," said Trent, staring at her. "You totally want to kick her ass."

"That obvious, huh?"

He cocked an eyebrow. "It's kinda hot."

"I mean, I want to kick her ass in a non-*Grindhouse* kind of way. I want to genuinely hurt her. Trust me, it's very unsexy."

He stared at the newspaper article on his computer screen, at Shane Smith's smiling young face. "She got him to kill RJ and then she killed him. Maybe so he wouldn't tell," he said, very quietly. "Maybe he was feeling guilty about it."

"Maybe."

"And you know what, Brenna?"

"What?"

"If I saw her again and she hit on me? I don't know that I'd turn her down."

"God, you're an idiot."

"I know." He didn't smile. "I know I am." He stared at his hands for a while. "Hey!" he said. "I just thought of something."

"Yeah?"

"What if she's committed a crime?"

"Yes?"

"I didn't tell you this, but I can tap into NCIC now."

"The FBI database?"

"Yeah. Remember Claudia?"

"The paramedic."

"Duh. Of course you remember her."

Brenna looked at him. "Her brother does computer stuff for the FBI."

"Right. And . . . she kinda worked a deal with me," he said. "She gave me an NCIC password, straight from her bro."

Trent called up NCIC on his computer. When he got to the page with the password prompt, he pulled his wallet out of his pocket. Removed a business card. At the bottom he'd written out a long combination of numbers, letters, and punctuation marks, which he proceeded to type into the computer. Brenna stared at him, her gaze moving from the card, to Trent, and back again.

"What was your end of the deal?" Brenna asked, wheels turning in her mind.

Trent mumbled something.

"Huh?"

He repeated himself. "I . . . uh . . . I had to stop hitting on her."

Brenna smiled. "Makes sense," she said, the wheels turning more furiously—*printed words at the bottom of a card. Everyone printed out their passwords somewhere, and what better place for a filmmaker than at the bottom of a picture of a favorite director* . . .

"See, we don't have a last name for her, but if we type 'Diandra' into this field here . . . Hmmm . . . No luck. I guess maybe she hasn't been arrested or Diandra's not her real name or . . . Why are you looking at me like that?"

"The cloud," Brenna said.

"Tannenbaum's?"

She nodded. "Did you really mean it when you said that all you needed was the Lockbox account password?"

"Yep," he said. "Do you have it?"

"I think I might." *Why would an atheist write a Bible passage on a picture of his favorite director?* "Try Deut 31:6."

Trent went onto Lockbox, typed in the user name he had for RJ and then, in the password field, Deut 31:6.

Incorrect password.

Trent looked at Brenna.

"How many letters can you have in one of these passwords?"

"In Lockbox? A lot."

"Try Bestrongandcourageous."

Trent typed.

"Oh my God," he whispered. "We're in." The screen opened up to show several smaller screens with play buttons. "Video footage."

Brenna looked at him. "I thought you said cloud storage was as secure as they come."

"Unbelievable."

"Never write out passwords, Trent."

"That's easy for you to say. You don't need to."

"Hit play," Brenna said.

Trent did, on the first screen. The first screen of footage on RJ Tannenbaum's cloud. *RJ's project. The Dream. The Big One.*

The little screen went blue, and a title appeared: SEARCHING FOR LULA BELLE.

The next image was the picture: Brenna and Clea on the bicycle. Brenna's breath caught.

"There's sound," Trent said.

"Turn it up," she whispered.

Up came a voice, a man's voice, nasal and sad. *Lula Belle. I have loved her, ever since I laid eyes on her. Ever since I first heard her voice. Yesterday she e-mailed me this picture. She said it belonged to her. But our journey starts earlier.*

The image on screen slowly faded to live action—a little, dark-haired girl, riding a bicycle through the woods. It was a haunting image—a sadness you felt in the pit of your stomach, without really knowing why.

"He's a hell of a lot better than Shane Smith," Trent said.

Brenna nodded. She couldn't speak.

The voiceover began again. *Our story begins three years ago, when on a dare from a film school friend, I broke into a man's house.*

The image of the little girl faded into a shot of Gary Freeman, standing amid Wise Up balloons with his wife and daughters.

This man. Gary Freeman.

Trent said, "That's the cornflakes guy."

Brenna looked at him. "Our real employer."

"He *is*?"

"*Was*. He fired me."

I was dared to break into his house, take this diary, and put it under the floorboards of his bedroom closet.

The image shifted to murky footage—a slightly younger, unbearded RJ Tannenbaum standing in front of a king-sized sleigh bed. Holding up a blue book.

I filmed myself putting it back. The person who dared me to put it back didn't know.

On screen, RJ removed something from the blue book. He walked right up to the stationary camera. Held it up to the lens.

"Oh my God," Trent said.

Brenna couldn't speak.

It was the picture of her and Clea on the bicycle. Same day, same swimsuits. The same picture Lula Belle had sent RJ.

Brenna flashed back to RJ's room, two days ago . . . *The picture from the computer screen—Brenna and Clea on that bike, Clea's bike—was that in Clea's room? Has she seen her sister looking at it? Placing that very picture in a blue book and slamming it shut as Brenna walks in . . .*

"How does he have that?" Trent was saying. "This is freaking me out, Bren. I don't understand—"

Brenna held a hand up. "Sssh," she said. The voiceover started again. *I thought I was sneaking some random journal into a professor's house. But as it turned out, I was replacing it. The person who dared me—Shane Smith—had stolen it and wanted it returned before the professor found out. I now believe that he made a copy.*

A picture of Shane posing next to a movie camera lens appeared on the screen. *Shane Smith, director of the Lula Belle films.*

An image of Lula Belle straddling her chair.

Art, he said. *Performance art. Created from the lost diary of a missing teenage girl.*

The picture of Brenna and Clea that had been on RJ's computer screen. *This missing girl.*

The footage ended. "There's more," Trent said softly. He was touching the screen—an additional box marked "audio." He clicked on it. The timer read :25. He hit play:

"Mr. Freeman, this is RJ Tannenbaum."

Next came Gary's voice over a speakerphone: *"I told you before, I have nothing to say to you."*

"*You must have something to say, sir. I saw Clea's diary. I know about Lula Belle.*"

"*You don't know anything.*"

"*Mr. Freeman, I'm going to keep calling you until I get an answer.*"

"*You don't know a goddamn thing.*"

Click.

Brenna and Trent stared at each other, Brenna imagining this entire case bursting into flame, everything about it a lie, from Freeman's first phone call on: *You did one interview, I guess? You mentioned a sister?*

"Gary Freeman had my sister's diary," Brenna said. "Gary Freeman knew my sister."

"And Diandra," Trent said. "She's helping him cover that up."

23

Diandra got off her shift early. It was a busy night, but her boss had no problem with that. He never had any problem with anything Diandra did. "I can work an extra shift later on this week," she'd said, smiling at him, her eyes full of promise.

"Sure," he'd said. "Anything." He hadn't noticed that snippy new waitress, Claire, standing behind him and rolling her eyes at Luis the busboy. But Diandra had. Dollars to donuts Claire thought Diandra had a date of some sort, or maybe she couldn't wait to go to a club and party. *Oh, if you only knew, Claire,* she thought. *You wouldn't be so snippy.*

Diandra didn't bother getting changed. After all, the waitress uniform gave her a certain approachability. It made her look even younger than her twenty-two years, its lacy high collar providing a degree of innocence, along with the regulation ponytail. *Sweet, young, bouncy.* She doubted Brenna would buy it for long—she'd seen the way Brenna had stared at her at Trent's place—as if she knew her, and with that memory, she might very well. Diandra threw on her heavy black coat. It was so dark outside now, and cold, too, the cold biting at her face, piercing her eyes. The weather, beating her up, just like the world . . .

For a moment, she let herself remember lying on the floor, Mr. Freeman's fist connecting with her stomach. Even as it happened, she'd vowed to forget it, that feeling of being hated so absolutely. But Diandra couldn't help it, and as she did, she stopped in her tracks, tears forming in her eyes, hating Mr. Freeman, hating herself for what she was about to do . . .

And then it was over, the memory gone, almost before it began, almost as if it had never happened. And in a way, it hadn't—had it? There had only been the two of them there for it, and Mr. Freeman had been so drunk, he probably wouldn't remember, either.

She headed around the corner onto Greenwich Avenue. She could see him from here, lingering in front of Fiddlesticks as if he were debating whether to go in and grab a beer. Ebony skin, white camel hair coat. Diamond studs glittering in his ears. Saffron.

Diandra hurried up to him, her heels clicking on the pavement. "Do you have it?"

"Sssh. Take a chill pill, okay? There's people watching."

"Oh," she said. With another guy, she might have sweetly told him where he could stick that chill pill if he didn't show her more respect, but with Saffron, it was different. He was like Mr. Freeman in that way. "Sorry."

Saffron stared into her eyes. With his index finger, he lightly traced the outline of her mouth. Without dropping her gaze, she swirled her tongue around the tip of the finger, grazed it with her lips. *It's all a role. It's all playing a role. It's what we do in the theater, the movies. It's what we actors do and it is life . . .*

"Nice," he whispered. He took her hand. At first, she thought he might place it somewhere, but instead he placed something in the hand, something cool and sharp and so scary-efficient, it raised your heart rate, just holding it. Something that felt like danger.

"Milano stiletto switchblade," he said. She wrapped her fingers around the hilt, and it made her think of this anime show that Shane used to love, about a boy and his sword, only the sword was, at heart, a beautiful girl and could change at will. The sword had chosen the boy and in every episode, she wound up saving his life. It was very romantic.

"Thank you, Saffron," she said, playing her role, staying in character. It was just 8 P.M., and she could walk there in five minutes. She could do what she needed to do, then come home to Mr. Freeman. The two of them could celebrate till dawn, celebrate their love, like that boy and his sword. They could hold each other, and share their secret, and he would need her, always.

You're as special a woman as I've ever met.

She placed the metal blade in her pocket and hurried to the address, half walking, half skipping. Soon she was all-out running, almost there . . .

Diandra was winded by the time she got to Brenna's building on Twelfth Street. She took the time to catch her breath, grasping her knees and then slowly standing up straight. She did some face stretches. "Mee Maaa Mooo," she said.

She shook her hands out and touched her toes and then, finally, she buzzed Brenna's apartment.

She heard a muffled "Yeah?"

"Brenna?"

"No, this is her daughter. She's . . . um . . . un-

available right now." *A girl's voice. A very young girl.*
Diandra's heart sank. She'd hoped this wouldn't have
to involve children. She found herself thinking back to
her own life at that age, those awkward years of hers,
when her dad would go out of town on business and
The Monster would take her out to hotel bars. *Beats
paying for a babysitter,* she'd tell the men who hit on
her, all of them laughing and laughing, as though
DeeDee wasn't even in the room. "Oh what our mothers put us through," Diandra whispered. Then she
slapped a smile on her face and introduced herself to
that poor, poor girl.

"We're going to Bacon," Brenna said.

Trent looked at her. "Seriously?"

"Yes. Let me text Maya first. Let her know I'll be a
little late."

"Bren, just because Diandra got her hootchie on
with me at that place, it doesn't mean she lives there."

Brenna blinked at him a few times. "Got her
hootchie on?"

"Whatever," said Trent. "You can't go to Bacon
dressed like that. You've got way too much fabric there.
What do you have in the back of your closet? Tube top?
Maybe a bustier from your Madonna phase?"

"I never had a Madonna phase."

"Come on. Work with me. What's the sluttiest thing
you own?"

Brenna's phone vibrated SOS. "I got a text," she said.

"Oh sure," he said. "Avoid the topic when I'm only
trying to help."

The text was from Maya. A picture. Brenna downloaded it. Her phone was old and slow, and so it
took a little while for the picture to take shape on

her screen . . . until she saw it and she screamed, the
phone clattering to the ground.

And then Brenna was grabbing her coat, picking up
the phone. "I'm leaving." She felt as though she were
outside her body, propelling it forward.

"Where are we going?"

"You can't come with me, Trent. No one can come
with me."

"Why?"

Brenna showed Trent the photo: Diandra grinning
at the camera, holding a stiletto knife to Maya's throat.
Maya crying, Maya's face a mask of fear and pain . . .
And the caption: *Be here alone. Or else.*

"Let her go," Brenna said. She hadn't been in her apartment that long, maybe around twenty seconds. But
she felt suspended in time, as if the air around them
were a thick gel, slowing everything to stop. There
was Diandra, wearing some stupid waitress uniform.
Diandra, sitting in Brenna's living room, on Brenna's
couch, having tied one of Brenna's dishtowels around
the mouth of Brenna's daughter, holding a sharp, angry
knife to her throat. Brenna's gaze fell upon the half-full
glass of milk on the coffee table, the open bag of Dori-
tos, the TV screen frozen on Jack Black, caught mid-
grimace. She thought about her daughter's evening—a
Jack Black movie and a snack, her iPod Touch close at
hand—a kid's calm, safe night alone, interrupted by
this freak. *How dare you.*

Maya made a noise, a whimper. Tears spilled down
her cheeks, and Brenna saw now that her arms had been
tied behind her back. "Take me, Diandra. I'm who you
came for."

Diandra cast her gaze from Brenna to Maya and

back, considering. "I'm probably going to have to get rid of you both," she said. "It's just one of those situations that can't be helped. Your daughter is a lovely girl. You should be proud."

Brenna squeezed her eyes shut. "I used to work for Gary Freeman, you know. Just like you. He wouldn't let me tell a soul about him or his involvement with Lula Belle and so I didn't. Right up until today I was keeping his secrets. Look where it got me."

"What are you saying?"

"I'm saying," Brenna said, "that he isn't a very loyal person, Diandra."

"I . . . I don't know what you're talking about. I don't even know who Gary Freeman is."

"Bullshit."

Diandra grabbed Maya tighter. Maya whimpered into the gag.

Brenna gritted her teeth. She wanted to hurt Diandra, badly, but she couldn't. Not yet. She breathed in and out. *Calm, calm . . .* She stared at the knife at Maya's throat, and she felt herself lapsing into a memory, back to October 2, Pelham Bay . . .

"Four score and seven years ago, our forefathers brought forth—"

"What?" said Diandra.

Brenna pulled her gaze from the blade. She looked into Diandra's eyes, ignored the blue contacts and tried to see into them, through them. "Gary Freeman has a daughter the same age as Maya."

Her eyes softened. "I've seen his daughters."

Brenna closed her eyes for a moment. *I knew it, I knew it . . .* "Listen to me," Brenna said. "I need Maya, just like Gary Freeman needs his daughters. I need her to grow up. I need her to live."

Diandra loosened her grip a little, her eyebrows knotting. Maya edged away.

Brenna tried, "I'm sure your mother feels the same way about you."

Diandra rolled her eyes like a teenager. "My mother died when I was six. *Please.*"

Brenna couldn't angle with her anymore. She couldn't wheedle information out of her, couldn't play games. All she could do was stare at her only daughter, her heart crumbling. "I need Maya."

A tear slipped down Maya's cheek.

"Kill me," Brenna said. "Let Maya live."

Maya screamed into the gag—a garbled "No!"

Diandra jumped back. "Shut up, shut up, shut up!"

In one motion, Brenna grabbed the glass of milk off the coffee table and slammed it into the side of Diandra's face. It shattered, shards flying, a spray of milk and blood. Diandra screamed, dropped the knife. "Run!" Brenna shouted, and Maya was up, stumbling toward the kitchen, Brenna grabbing the iPod, throwing it in after her as Diandra moaned. *Use that iPod. Contact someone with it . . .*

Diandra lurched toward Brenna, but Brenna was faster. She didn't have much practice fighting, did she? After all, this was nothing like drugging a helpless man . . . Brenna socked her in the stomach, and Diandra gaped at her—her face a mask of pain, with something else mixed in.

Is it shame?

"Mr. Freeman," she sputtered her eyes closed. "Please don't."

And Brenna was on top of her, her hands wrapped around Diandra's throat, the words chorusing in her head: *I knew, it, I knew it, I knew it . . .* "What is Gary Freeman hiding?" she said.

"I can't tell you."

"Why does he have my sister's diary in his home?"

"I won't."

"You had better tell me. Or I will kill you and there will be no one around to protect him and he will go to jail for the rest of his life."

A stretch, Brenna knew—she wasn't sure whether Gary had done anything capable of landing him in jail, but Diandra didn't protest. She gazed up at her, her eyes dazed, her pink cheeks spattered with her own blood, mascara running down her face—and then Brenna was back on the *Maid of the Mist* on October 30, Maya sitting next to her, plastic raincoat wet and heavy on their backs as they watched the other passengers leave . . .

She looks into the girl's eyes with the chill wind biting their faces and icy water everywhere, so cold it burns. Brenna stares at her—poor, pretty mess of a girl. Then at her boyfriend standing behind her, his hand on her shoulder, the fingertips white from the tightness of the clutch.

"Mr. Freeman can't go to jail," Diandra said, bringing Brenna back. "He'd die there."

"Why did you kill Shane Smith?"

"I don't know what you're talking about."

She looks back at the girl's face, at the mascara streaks on her cheeks, looking so awful for the wear—worse than Maya and me put together—and then, into the eyes . . . such fathomless sadness as she meets Brenna's gaze, her boyfriend oblivious, smiling a little.

"You didn't want to kill him," Brenna said. "It hurt you so much, especially after all he'd done for you. For you and Mr. Freeman."

"Stop it." Diandra struggled against Brenna, but Brenna jammed her knee into the girl's stomach.

Diandra cried out.

"What did Shane know? What did RJ know? What am I getting close to knowing?"

"I won't tell."

"What did Gary Freeman do to my sister?"

"Mr. Freeman loves me more than anyone."

"He doesn't love you. He loves the role you play. He wants her, not you."

"Her?"

"If you care so much about him, why did you stop playing the role?"

And then Diandra had her hands around Brenna's neck—suddenly strong, Brenna's breath going, and she was on top of Brenna, flecks of light dancing in front of her eyes, the bloody face in and out of focus. The runny mascara and the eyes—those sad, fake blue eyes.

The girl taps her lip three times like a Morse signal. She wants to die.

"What role?" Diandra was saying, her grip loosening, Brenna's breath coming back. "What role does he love? What role did he tell you he loved?"

"Lula Belle," Brenna coughed.

Diandra's eyes narrowed, her bloody lips went tight. "What?"

"He told me he's obsessed with Lula Belle. That her voice is in his head all the time." Brenna was wheezing, sore inside and out. "He said he couldn't get her off his mind. He needed her. Why did you stop playing the role? Did RJ's documentary scare you off? Did Shane want a new actress?"

"I'm not Lula Belle."

Brenna stared at her, the rest of her breath coming back . . . "You're not?"

Then who is?

Diandra said, "He needed her?" Her voice was like a child's, so sad and small.

Brenna heard sirens outside her building, the rush of feet up her stairs as the officers opened the door. It must have taken longer, but it felt like moments, time moving the same way time moves in dreams: the officers pulling Diandra off of Brenna, dragging her across the room, Brenna's eyes seeking out Maya, then finding her, hands untied, gag off, rushing toward her, hugging her. She couldn't hug her hard enough, Maya whispering into her hair, "Im sorry Mom. I know I'm not supposed to let anybody in, but she sounded so friendly and she said she was—"

"It's okay, honey."

"She said she was Clea."

Brenna pulled away. She stared across the room at Diandra, pushed against the coffee table as a female officer secured handcuffs and a male read her her rights. Her jaw tightened. *She said she was Clea.*

Brenna put her arms around her daughter again and held her close. "You did good," she whispered. "You did good, honey."

Three cops started to lead Diandra toward the door. Brenna approached her, the girl, this poor, dumb, misguided girl watching Brenna through those angry red scratches, her eyes hard and bitter. *She's not Lula Belle.* "Is Trent okay?" she said.

"Yes."

"I'm glad."

Brenna nodded, waiting.

"I spent the night with Gary once," Diandra said. "He was drunk. He didn't know I was awake and I guess he felt guilty, and I saw him. He was reading that diary and crying. I saw him put it back, and when he was asleep I stole it. And I took it home. I just wanted to understand him better."

The officers stopped moving and watched her, one plucking tentatively at a notepad and pen.

"I read that diary to my boyfriend Shane," Diandra said softly. "I acted it out for him. 'Do a Southern accent,' he said, and I did, and he said it was the best performance he'd ever seen. He said, 'Let's make this into art.' Our art. But I said no. I made him put it back. I was dumb. He found someone else." She gave Brenna a sad smile. "They say the best art is fueled by passion," she said. "Shane hated Mr. Freeman for stealing me from him. So he found another girl and made his art with her, and boy, did the two of them ever fuck with Gary's mind."

"Who was the girl?"

"I have no idea," she said. "That's why Shane and I were in Niagara Falls. We heard she'd gone up there and we knew you were up there too and we thought maybe she wanted to tell you . . . Shane wouldn't give me her name." She closed her eyes. A tear seeped down her cheek. "He said he wouldn't let me hurt her."

"Diandra," Brenna said, as the cops started to guide her out the door. "Why did Gary Freeman have my sister's diary?"

"Ask him," she said "He's at Sixty-sixth and Second Ave. Apartment 2518. Ask him about the Murder Mile."

"The Murder Mile?"

"It's from some old song," she said. "It's what your sister called Route 666."

Brenna's jaw went lax.

"Ask him how your sister spent her eighteenth birthday."

Trent had been waiting outside Brenna's apartment with more cops, and when she and Maya finally got through being questioned, she asked him to bring Maya back to Faith's. "Do me a favor, Trent," she said. "Don't tell her and Jim about this."

"No, right, please don't," Maya said. "They'll freak."

Brenna knelt down next to her daughter. Looked into her eyes. "Are you okay?" she said.

"Mom," Maya said. "You saved my life."

Brenna looked at her face, and remembered it at six months old, *Dora the Explorer on the TV behind her, singing with the map. Brenna spoons strained carrots into her mouth. "Yummy," Brenna says, and Maya starts to laugh. She spits out a mouth full of carrots and her laugh sounds like bells. It's the most beautiful sound Brenna has ever heard.* October 8, 1996, thirteen years almost to the day from when Hildy Tannenbaum lost her only child. She brushed a lock of hair out of Maya's eyes and kissed her on the forehead, just as she used to do, every night, when she was a baby. *"A kiss on the forehead keeps the bad dreams away."* "Do me a favor," Brenna said. "Don't ever ever let anyone into the apartment that you don't know again—no matter who they say they are. Or I will ground you until high school graduation."

Maya laughed a little.

"I'm not kidding."

"Okay," she said. "Okay."

Trent started to lead her away.

"Remember!" Brenna called out. "I'm meeting with a client, and that's why you're bringing her!"

But they were already engaged in another conversation, Trent saying, "So what's this I hear about you not liking Bieber anymore?"

Brenna headed back up to her apartment. She waited until she was sure Trent and Maya were far enough away not to see her leaving it again, checking the window, just to make sure.

Then she went to her desk, removed her pearl-handled letter opener, and headed outside to grab a cab uptown.

"DeeDee?" Gary Freeman said when Brenna knocked. He opened the door a crack, and Brenna fell in on him, catching him off guard, knocking him to the ground and holding the letter opener to his neck.

He looked into her eyes. "Oh . . ."

"You thought she killed me."

"No," he said. "I knew she couldn't."

"She killed all those others."

"They were men, Brenna . . ." His eyes were calm, the pupils slightly dilated. "Men get stupid around her." Beads of sweat formed on his upper lip, and he didn't look like his pictures. He looked drugged and hollow and lost. "My God," he said. "Your eyes are just like your sister's."

Brenna held the knife closer, anger barreling through her. "What did you do to her?"

"She was beautiful," he whispered, Brenna thinking, *The past tense. Oh my God, he used the past tense . . .*

"I could kill you." She said it very quietly. "I could do it easily. I know the police and I'm kind of a hero in this city after the Neff case. So if I told some cops I slit your throat in self-defense, even if it was in an apartment that's not my own . . . even if it was right here"—

she moved closer to him bringing the blade up, under his chin—"they'd believe me."

"Do it," he said. "Please."

She closed her eyes, her stomach churning. Such sadness crossed his face. It grabbed at her. It felt familiar. *Keep it together. Stay here.*

He said, "Is DeeDee dead?"

"Who?"

"Diandra."

"No. She's with the police."

His face fell. "She'll tell everyone. My wife . . . God, my wife and kids will be humiliated. I've let so many people down."

She stared at him, Diandra's voice in her ears. Poor Diandra, who had thrown out her whole life for this shell of a man. "*Mr. Freeman loves me more than anyone.*"

"Gary," Brenna said. "I need to know about the Murder Mile."

"Oh God."

She inhaled sharply. "You said it yourself. Everyone is going to know. Why not tell the one person it means something to."

"I closed that door."

"Look into my eyes, Gary."

"God."

"I have a daughter who looks just like her. Will she ever see Clea face-to-face?"

"Stop."

"Look at my eyes," she said. "She used to call me weirdo. She tried making pancakes for breakfast one time when she was ten and burned them and set off the smoke alarm. The first time she kissed a boy, she told me it was like sucking the inside of an overripe tomato."

He averted his eyes. "You loved her."

"I still do," she said. "Did you kill her, Gary?"

He drew a long, shaking breath. "The Murder Mile was Route 666 in Utah. I'd picked your sister up hitchhiking a week earlier, in Portsmouth, Virginia. She told me she'd been on the road, alone for a month. She'd ditched the guy she'd been traveling with. She said she didn't like him anymore."

I've been with him for three weeks and I don't like him anymore. He keeps looking at my neck like he wants to bite it, and sometimes I could swear he's got fangs. . . .

Brenna looked at him. "You went to Louisville, Kentucky next."

"Yes. And then Nashville and then Cleveland and then Pine City, Utah."

"Lula Belle's PO boxes."

"Yes. I remember them all. They went in reverse of our trip—Clea's trip. I didn't . . . I didn't tell you Utah because I didn't want to remember Utah."

"It's where your trip ended."

"Yes."

"Did you kill her?"

"It was an accident."

"Is she dead?"

"I . . . I don't know."

She stared at him, some of the anger returning. "How can you not know?"

"Clea and I were young. We loved to party. One night, I got us a whole bunch of black beauties. Did you ever know what those were?"

"Speed."

"Yes. We were drinking Jack Daniel's and I took about six black beauties. Clea took the same and . . .

well, she was a lot smaller than me. She started . . . she had some kind of seizure."

"Did you call the hospital?"

"No."

"Nothing at all?"

He grabbed the hand that held the knife. His grip was surprisingly strong. "I was starting classes at School of the Moving Image, and I had an internship at William Morris, he said. "I . . . I couldn't . . . l was scared. I was young and selfish and scared."

"Did you do anything? Drop her off somewhere or—"

"I left her in our motel room. I paid in cash. I drove away." He started to sob. "It was her eighteenth birthday." Brenna stared at him, her anger building.

"I only cared about myself. Not her. She was . . . She kept twitching and she went pale and she passed out and . . ."

"You left."

"She wasn't breathing."

"You left her for dead."

"I called the motel from the road. They checked the room. It was empty. I don't know what that means," he said. "I don't know if someone . . . got rid of her or . . . or if she left by herself."

"Is Clea Lula Belle?"

"I kept her diary," he said. "I kept it with me to remind me to be good. To remind me to use that second chance."

"Tell me."

"I married Jill and I was good to her and I never drank, never drank for twenty years. I lived a good life."

"*You left my sister for dead, that isn't a good life!*"

Hate coursed through Brenna's veins, her skin growing rigid with it. Gary's grip grew tighter around her wrist. "No," she said. "Tell me whether Lula Belle was Clea. At least give me that."

Gary stared into her eyes, his grip going lax. "I didn't know who Lula Belle was, but I hoped she was Clea." He said it in his old voice, his kind voice . . . "Man, Brenna. You should have seen my face when I got that first download. It was like . . . like being with an angel."

He smiled, and then his grip tightened. She tried to pull away, but he was stronger, drawing the blade across his own throat. So much blood and there it was, done in an instant, the human body so frail, so fragile. Just as her sister had been.

"You don't deserve this," Brenna shouted. She grabbed her phone, called 911. "Suicide attempt!" she yelled into it, but he was gurgling and twitching, leaving her even as she spoke. By the time she'd given them the address and hung up the phone, he was no longer breathing. She put her hands over the slit throat. She tried CPR. Nothing.

First Clea. Now me. You left us both.

She heard sirens outside. The second set of the evening. Brenna didn't move. She stared down at Gary Freeman. At his eyes, wrenched open. She didn't try to close them.

Epilogue

One week later

"So why didn't you call me?" Morasco said, as he pulled up to the curb on City Island, just in front of the post office.

It was the eighth time he had asked Brenna that in about as many days. She was tired of answering him, but it still made her smile.

"I'm in a knife fight, I don't think, *Hey, I should invite Nick Morasco*," she said. "Anyway, you'd probably show up wearing the entirely wrong thing and embarrass me."

"Not fair."

"Yes, fair. Tweed and stilettos do not mix—and I'm not talking about the heels, though that's pretty much a glamour-don't, too . . ."

"Don't you even know the rules?" He got out of the car, went around to her side, and opened her door before she could get her hand on it.

"Excuse me?"

"The rules, Brenna. You're the lady PI. I'm the cop boyfriend. I'm supposed to save you in the end."

She grinned at him. "You just said you were my boy-friend."

"Okay, okay." He sighed. "This is going nowhere."

They were on their way into the post office for a reason, which—like the manila envelope Morasco had handed her yesterday—was something they'd chosen not to talk about.

"Here's the thing," he had told her, yesterday morn-ing, in bed. "I don't want to keep secrets from you. But I don't want to force them down your throat, either."

"So where does that leave us?"

Morasco had slipped out of the bed, gone into his top dresser drawer, and pulled out the envelope, that ache in his eyes, that pity she'd come to hate . . . "This is from Grady Carlson."

"Oh . . . God . . ."

"He gave this to me a week ago. He died yesterday."

"What is it?"

"A secret." He looked at her. "Your secret. Do what you want with it."

Last night at her apartment, Brenna had cracked open the envelope. She'd seen police papers. She'd seen her father's name. And she'd ended it there, closing the envelope. Slipping it into her desk drawer and moving away from it, like a bad memory. *Some other time*, she had thought. Not now. There was too much going on now. And though she knew—she knew deep down where she'd inherited her gift for destruction, felt it in the awful rush of blood to her skin with every Lula Belle viewing (*She knows. She knows it all . . .*)—she couldn't turn over that rock and look at it. She wasn't ready for the confirmation . . .

"*Daddy took his gun, and he put the barrel of it*

right there at his temple, and he pulled the trigger and his whole head exploded . . ."

Brenna shut her eyes tight. *Not now.*

Morasco raced to the post office door, opened it for her.

"If you don't stop being such a gentleman," Brenna said, "I'm going to stop having sex with you."

He let go of the door, fast.

"That's better."

City Island always triggered memories for Brenna—and it didn't help that it was essentially unchanged in twenty-five years, a sleepy sea community with the same fake fishing net restaurants, the same quaint little homes and narrow streets leading right up to private beaches on the bay, the same maritime museum and the same library and so many of the same people as had been here, living life, when Brenna was growing up here and her sister's disappearance was the talk of the town.

The sight of the elementary school—which went all the way through eighth grade, still—had been enough to set Brenna to remembering that first school assembly with Clea missing, September 7, 1981—and it had only been Morasco, making some joke about the lobster place across the street, that had brought her back.

It was good to have him here, she decided. Because for all his jokes about rescuing "the lady PI," she needed him now, and not for knife fights. She needed him to rescue her from her memory, from her past . . .

The post office brought back memories, too, of course, but for now, the present was more important. Morasco made for the large mailboxes against the wall as she clutched it in her hand—the key Hildy had given her. Morasco had been the one to come up with the idea, based on the final details Diandra had provided this week while confessing to the murder of Shane Smith, which were as follows:

Gary had never known about Shane stealing and copying Clea's journal. But Diandra had. As soon as she learned, via Gary, of the Lula Belle videos, she knew Shane was behind them—and she was livid. She longed for a day when she could get back at her ex-boyfriend for exploiting The Most Gifted Man She Had Ever Known, just because he was jealous she had slept with him.

When Gary had received the phone calls from RJ and begged Diandra to stop him from going public with his knowledge, she saw her opportunity—and readily agreed. Back in contact with Shane, she convinced him to hack Lula Belle's private e-mail, lure RJ into meeting him, and kill him in order to preserve the "great art" he'd been creating with the mystery woman he'd replaced her with. She'd wanted him to kill Lula Belle, too—lest she spill the beans to Brenna —but though they tracked both Lula Belle and Brenna up to Canada in late October, they couldn't find Lula. And Shane chickened out—refusing to give Diandra Lula Belle's real name.

Diandra had let her anger get the best of her. *He didn't deserve to die*, she told officers. Though Hildy Tannenbaum clearly had reason to feel differently.

At any rate, over dinner at his place last night, Morasco had said to Brenna, "If Lula Belle knew her e-mail was compromised," he said, "what's the safest way she could have gotten ahold of RJ?"

Brenna had replied, "His PO box."

And that's why they were here. "Hey," Morasco said. He was standing in front of a mailbox. RJ's mailbox. Number 35.

Brenna made her way over to it, her hands shaking, sweating around the key.

She unlocked the mailbox.

There was a package inside, addressed from Montreal, postmarked October 20. No name on the return address. Brenna's heart pounded.

Lula Belle, are you my sister?

She opened it—pulled out a stack of Xeroxed handwritten pages. She recognized the handwriting. *Clea's handwriting.* "Oh my God," whispered Brenna. She held her breath, hoping.

"There's a note," Morasco said.

He spread it out in front of them, and they both read:

Dear RJ:

I hope this finds you well. I'm sorry we never got a chance to hook up for this interview. I remain disillusioned with Shane and his "art"—and I think your project is worthy and important. But I'm sorry to tell you, I must leave town. It's for happy reasons, actually—I got a role on a soap in Montreal. I don't know if you know this, but I speak fluent French, so the part is perfect for me. Plus, I will get a regular paycheck, I don't have to hide my face, and I no longer have to keep anyone's secrets.

At any rate, good luck with your documentary. I'm sure it will be really great. Again, I'm sorry we never got to meet up in person, but I hope the enclosed is of help.

All best,
Lula Belle . . . aka Mallory Chastain

"Mallory Chastain," Brenna whispered, her heart sinking a little.

"Not Clea."

She shook her head. "I know her."

"How?"

"I saw her in one of Shane Smith's films . . . Well, her eye anyway."

He sighed. "All those people, thinking she'd gone up to Canada to talk to you. But actually, she'd just gotten a soap opera part."

"Irony," Brenna said. But she really wasn't thinking about it. She was too busy reading the first paragraph of her sister's journal:

> I just finished reading the Diary of Anne Frank. My mom thinks diaries are lame. She thinks they reveal too much about you, but I don't think so at all. I think they can keep you company when everyone else lets you down. I think they can hold your memories for you while you're off making new ones. I think they are a way of living forever—which probably explains why Mom hates them so much.
>
> Anyway, Anne named her diary Kitty, and I want a Kitty, too. But since that name is taken, I'm going to call you something else. Something pretty.
>
> I'm going to name you Lula Belle.